THE
IMMENSITY
OF THE
HERE AND NOW

a novel of 9.11

BOOKS BY PAUL WEST

FICTION

Cheops
A Fifth of November
O.K.
The Dry Danube
Life with Swan
Terrestrials
Sporting with Amaryllis
The Tent of Orange Mist
Love's Mansion
The Women of Whitechapel and Jack the Ripper
Lord Byron's Doctor
The Place In Flowers Where Pollen Rests
The Universe, and Other Fictions
Rat Man of Paris
The Very Rich Hours of Count von Stauffenberg
Gala
Colonel Mint
Caliban's Filibuster
Bela Lugosi's White Christmas
I'm Expecting to Live Quite Soon
Alley Jaggers
Tenement of Clay

NONFICTION

Oxford Days
Master Class
New Portable People
The Secret Lives of Words
My Mother's Music
A Stroke of Genius
Sheer Fiction-Volumes I, II, III
Portable People
Out of My Depths: A Swimmer in the Universe
Words for a Deaf Daughter
I, Said the Sparrow
The Wine of Absurdity
The Snow Leopard
The Modern Novel
Byron and the Spoiler's Art
James Ensor

THE
IMMENSITY
OF THE
HERE AND NOW

a novel of 9.11

BY PAUL WEST

Voyant Publishing
Rutherford

Portions of this novel have appeared in considerably different form in the following: *Agni, Conjunctions, and Witness.*

THE IMMENSITY OF THE HERE AND NOW
A NOVEL OF 9.11
Copyright © 2003 by Paul West
Published by Voyant Publishing

Library of Congress Cataloging-in-Publication Data
West, Paul, 1930–
The immensity of the here and now / Paul West.–1st Voyant ed.
p. cm.
ISBN 0-9665998-5-3
[LOC #]

Designed by Gil Y. Roth
First edition

www.voyantpub.com
Printed in the United States of America

Contents

I. The Burial of the Dead

II. The Recovery of the Dead

THE
IMMENSITY
OF THE
HERE AND NOW

... everything could be seen and heard in
simultaneous depth because, turned 'round toward
the immensity which he had once left behind him,
he saw through it into the immensity of the here and now,
looking backward and forward at once. ...

—Hermann Broch, *The Death of Virgil*

I

The Burial of the Dead

Anyone's death always releases something like an aura
of stupefaction, so difficult is it to grasp this
irruption of nothingness and to believe
that it has actually taken place.

—Gustave Flaubert, *Madame Bovary*

1
Shrop

WHEN I AT LAST LOSE CONSCIOUSNESS, IT WILL NOT BE TO regain it. Can it really be me who, with one foot planted firm on the scaffold, wriggles his other in the exposed tripes of the man just beheaded, my big toe tapping the liver, the bearded head having rolled away, wearing a drastic grin? Who cut the belly open for me to disturb his innards in so imperious and sloven a way? I will always hear that squelching sound, even though not always find myself in the seventeenth century, will I? To have been an unwarranted me in so many places is sickening, as if history were making repeated assaults on me, anxious to claim and denounce me century after century whereas, in truth, I am not such a bad lot after all. Whence, then, this whole-hearted guilt? I think I was once a philosopher, who now can remember none of his concepts or precepts. I may, dimly, have been a swimming pool attendant, though I have no dream of drowning anyone, or one of those worthies who leads a parade twirling an enormous baton around his neck, faultless juggler equal to the high throw. Little of either job survives, but more than what I thought in that peculiar habit of philosophers who *think* for a living. I am a haunted man, victim of appalling dreams, both night and day variety. No, it is an optical illusion: I stand behind the headsman's brawny arm as it roams about in the body cavity while the other holds aloft the wretch's heart.

"On."

Ever the obedient blackguard, I do as I am told. I am not here in this room of opaque glass to say nothing, to lapse into silence while, God help his parents, Quentin Montefiore del Patugina ("Quent" or "Tin" I call him, presuming on a long friendship that has repeatedly failed the test of time but passed the test of need.) He hears me out, far out, then dismisses me until next time, even if only to urge me with his callous-seeming "On" or "And then." He has heard it all before, but hopes to find something in the disparities of telling, some incongruous facet I let slip. Better, he once told me, than hovering or dawdling in the downdraft from the chapbook, whatever that meant. He seems at his greatest ease when hearing me. I wonder why. Surely my babbling rocks him and unnerves him, but on he sits, open to anything I say, neither commenting nor clearing his throat. He once swam in a pool I ministered to, stark in yellow trunks of bright yellow sailcloth that rattled and snapped.

Then he would shout, "Come on in, the water's fine."

And I would answer, "So's the air. No fear."

Did he seriously expect me to plunge into all that slop?

It was enough to keep it clean and ogle its blue dialysis. It was always more lucid than I was.

"*On*," he says again, a touch snappier, and I obey, chastened into new babble.

He could be writing a book about me, his tape recorder stashed safely in the bookcase, his literary aspirations couched in my own rattled language, his plot and style wholly in my own hands as I recount my miserable career, his memory become the vacancy mine is, but helping himself three times a week to whatever scenes and opportunities my mind throws up. In truth, I am his ghost writer, over whom he has no control. I pay him to listen. I pay him extra because, he says, there is more than one of me to contend with. All the bills that arrive at my hovel show me his Ph.D., flashing it a bit needlessly I think, whereas my own poor beleaguered name, Shropshire, echoing a certain famous lad, I suppose, though he never an immigrant, always has a look of sapped sunlight. Had I been unluckier at Immigration, I'd have ended up Shropshin or Scrapsir, but no, I was a lucky lad all right, wondering if on the isle of detention I'd run into some congeners such as Hampshire and Herefordshire, all the home counties, but I never did. What, I always wondered, was a Shrop?

"Good morning, Shrop," he'd say, which I never answer, not knowing what a Shrop might have been in the days when I knew things. "Shrop up, and let's get started." We did, he pressing me forward from "On" to "*On, On*."

I had begun, back then, to link my loss of memory with the sudden erosion of what we fancifully called our infrastructure: first the mails, going from hand to hand throughout the republic, then the money and the newspapers, followed logically by the hospitals already teeming full. So, while, amid the fever and fret of making retaliatory war against the assassins for a series of atrocities, as for a more recent series of gentler-seeming biological sorties, we were busily bombing them into their caves so that we could then seal them in with mortar, rocks, and concrete, almost borrowing from the old Christian myth of the entombment to get even. Deep within the belly of the mountains, the assassins could starve, scream, and finally drop dead. The only trouble had been that assassins yet among us, some of them committed to suicide missions, wreaked biological havoc on all our precious ways of life, on the lares and penates, the banks, the public toilets, the very food.

I ask you, then, if a man might not lose his head in such circumstances, deprived of his rational contacts, his toys and tricks, his salaried validation? How hold on when all was lapsing into a lethal menace, with banks and restaurants turned into hospitals or emergency clinics?

"On," he says again, voicing his habitual goad, as if all I was telling him was a novelty, data about another society he was concerned with.

I even heard him chortling when I told him, as often, that I had arrived fresh from the toilet, cleansed by a touch of what was left to us, a Cottonelle of fresh folded wipe that (and here I quoted) "let you feel cleaner and fresher than dry toilet paper alone, anytime, anywhere," alcohol-free, great for the whole family, convenient when traveling, flushable, sewer- and septic-safe. Also available in tubs and resealable travel packs. Visit our web site. Who could want anything more? Indeed, this was one of the things that got us attacked. We had the cleanest rear ends in the solar system, and assassins, doomed to a regimen of leaves and desert sand, envied us our wipes. Hence the hijackings that began it all, just when my memory began to fail.

On, he was murmuring; he had heard it all before. He wanted new pablum. He wants. I oblige. He claims not to have lost one jot of *his* memory, which means my response to events differs from his. We are not alike. He, he claims, can help me, but not I him. That much is clear. I grope for a word, relic of something cerebral from my earlier days, perhaps such a word as "ideal," to which I must have attributed some special force, but the word's associations had fallen away from it like ribbons from a baby's rattle. I made do with "deal." Now, for no good reason, I mentioned Rachmaninoff's *Suite for Two Pianos*, an old favorite, but remembered only the title. It must at some time have been an object of love, like so much else.

Again bidden to resume, I used what little brain I'd salvaged to suggest to him that, since I no longer had any direction, there was no longer any point in my trying to tell things in any kind of rational order. "It is no use even trying to move forward," I tell him. "Panic has wiped out the best of me. Do you not know how stress abolishes memory?"

He does, as his grunt proves. On I go then, explaining how it all began, what I call the vastation, from the very first day of my amnesia, the first thing to go being whatever philosophy I had come up with after thirty years of pondering. My skull felt shrunken. I no longer felt inclined to respond to anyone, never mind what they said. A low-grade shiver invaded my system, followed by pins and needles across my shoulder blades. Headaches, yes. Arthritis where I'd never known it before, yes. Weird fluttering touches along my legs as of invisible ants, yes. I could feel the entire daily structure breaking down: no more three meals a day, faintly evoked in that old expression "three-square meals and found." Or have I got it wrong, as I often do? No matter, I tell Quent. Who cares? Take a bus? No, no schedule. Drive a car? No, anthrax in the gasoline. Only the internet remains unpolluted, and the telephone (which will be a goner any day soon; they leave it for us to bemoan our fate with, not out of kindness).

"The safest way to communicate with anyone in your own household," I am telling him, "is electronically, each with a personal screen. That's the safest, even to tell them what you have noticed about how anxious people walk, when they hardly dare breathe or touch, their shoulders hunched forward as in some forgotten last fling of a discus, their legs rigid from the thigh, their heads half-averted from what they dare not look at: the future. You've no doubt seen those films of prisoners in the camps, as they stagger out of their infested huts to greet the just-arrived Americans and kiss them repeatedly? Well, it's a similar movement, except, being the most adept technological nation there is, we move a little better, more portly, say, and by now—what is it, three years?—chubbier from not getting out so much when you have to stay home to concentrate on the needlepoint, crocheting and quilting. How does an anal retentive walk? Like a Bulgarian. Sorry. On. One way, I suppose, of settling the hash of the assassins among us, once you catch them, is to cram their mouths with wet concrete, as with the caves and tunnels. Stuff them up see, until, next day, they can't breathe or eat. Then they won't be so slick at communicating with each other in all the civilized countries. Have to ferret them out, even if it takes years.

He excuses himself to get a glass of water, without which he would be better off; but Quent is a risk-taker, or he would not be giving me the time of day. If I am not one of the walking wounded, with my heartbroken memory of succinct phrases on clear cold days, I must be one of the stumbling sane.

"Don't you recall," I ask him, "how, of all the music we've heard, you and I, especially when sunbathing in the best days, the noblest feel came from Elgar and Sibelius, the former in love with sweet fat privilege and royal pageantry, the latter raised in a harsher society full of sleet and depression?"

He is looking at me in a very odd way, as if I have just left some bad stench between us by evoking those early years when I was to intellect as he to psyche.

"Or Villa-Lobos," I add, determined to please him. "Just as noble. I would dearly like to devote the rest of my life to exactly pinning down the concept *noble*. What can it mean in a society as shredded as ours, the ancien régime in tatters, kids scared to go to school, technicians afraid to venture out to work the TV stations. No planes, trains, few cars. A glorious inspissated silence has taken over the poisoned land, and I am sometimes glad of it. The amnesiac thrills to the new Blitz. It might be worse, Quent, it really might. What better for the mind washed clean than to start again from scratch? What do you think? I am on edge."

With one hand he motions what I say backward, then like a commissionaire or a traffic cop motions *me* onward again, applying what I sometimes (knowing him and his mannerisms as well as I do, Columbia men both) describe as the poultice of quiet. He is here to hear me out. Then, when I haven't a single idea left, when I have milked my mind, he will come and hug me for holding nothing back. Does he care that much or has he wearied of me and my mental contortions? All I can ever do is try him again, in both senses of that word.

"Are you there?"

"Are you listening, Quent?"

"Hearing me all right?"

I construe his silence as invitation and launch again into the chilly stratosphere. "We were talking about the mind wiped clean and that's being a good time to teach it the old tricks all over again. Have I ever told you before about being in England and studying aeronautics, eventually cooking up a tiny jet engine they attached to the tips of the propeller? If I had been brighter, I'd have seen that, having come up with the jet, I no longer needed the propeller. It's a nightmare, really, wondering why I was so foolish, so unobservant. Too green, I suppose."

2
Quent

I WONDER IF HE IS DOING ANY WORSE THAN THE REST OF US, anxious, shaken, spavined, no longer in the first paroxysm of terror, but adjusted to prodigious uncertainty as one by one our toys and triumphs get turned against us by an enemy who seems always to be there, never quite stamped out. I doubt it. What makes him different is that, whereas most of us have lost our cherished routines (going to the mailbox, putting the garbage out, cloaking the hosepipe sockets for winter), he has lost that entire system of ideas he took such pride in. Key concepts have gone, and he remembers none of the reasoning that took him from place to place. Such is the fate of the oral philosopher, with no more permanence than the balladeer of old. Such papers as he published and can get his hands on show him little, as if the current no longer runs through them. He is a stilt bird walking gingerly from one lily pad to the next, murmuring Did I really think that? It does not help him either that, having to make do in the yard with traps to catch birds, coons and squirrels, now that the canned goods have given out, and then cooking such roadkill, the taste irks him. He thought best when he was responding not at all to the taste of his food; it went down like a baby-paste, a slime to be converted into its approximate equivalent. He has, as we say, lost it, meaning not one thing only, but all of everything. He used to have a grid that made sense of life; now he has nothing of the kind.

Is his the nagging fright of the commando landed on an alien beach, deathly afraid of the bullet that's aimed right at the bridge of his nose, out of nowhere with a fast lisp he does not even hear? If, as at the beginning, there were noise as the topless towers of Ilium bit the dust, but now it is all surreptitious according to a menu of horrors, from discarded diseases to maliciously disguised talcum powder. Is it anything like walking in quicksand, or blindfolded on a cliff's edge? With so much to worry about, even if you elect never to go out, we endure a kind of blind man's bluff as, hidden away in fake identities, they watch us dither and twitch, bit by bit losing the civilization lovingly assembled since the time of the ancient Egyptians. This is no doubt why, after having called him many things during our long friendship (such nicknames as Shrop), I now in my private files have come to refer to him as the Chaos Attractor, special in that he just doesn't put up with the horrors; he finds them coming toward him, fangs bared, the taste of him already familiar. They want him, he whose system was the most meticulous, so much so that in his present disheveled state he cannot remember it, and nobody else needs it. Raw importunity assails him at every corner, and life is a jigsaw puzzle with no interlocking pieces. He takes it all on the chin.

How can it be that the very things we have evolved to soothe us— Bach or Ravel, the overdry Martini, Matisse or Samuel Palmer—no longer speak to us? The things we used to love have become as wormwood, and people are all we have left to cling to. The blind lead the blind just because we have been wounded, chronically disrupted for three years or so, living in a ghastly ruined landscape, or, as I used to say, all from having been geographically raped out of the blue. What's to be done when those who hate life devote themselves to destroying it year after year, never happier than when being swallowed up in the atrocity themselves? I suppose most of us still take some pleasure in atmospheric phenomena: rain, wind, sunsets, whereas the taste for literature seems to have gone out the window. We have no ideas, and the one thing we dread is being singled out for having an interior of some kind. Pavlov's dogs have had more *nous*.

So I say to him, off-duty: "Doodle on a pad just to see if any of the old ideas come." No book from him, which is why he cannot find himself in the reference works, and why, in some perverse fit of self-regimentation, he goes to the encyclopedia and filches from it the volume titles on the spine, from *Freon-Hölderlin* and *Mélange-Ottawa* to *Excretion-Geometry* and *Number-Prague*, carefully avoiding *Reti-Solovets* and *San Francisco-Southern*. No Shr— of course.

3
Shrop

"Nihil," I say to him, "it's all about nihil, isn't it? There's *all this*, meaning Creation with capital C, and the urge to turn it all to dust, even for those who like it, and the related desire of the destroyer to have no life at all. Where did I read—how's it go?—whoever kills one innocent person has killed the whole of humankind?"

"There is the old Emily Brontë position," he says in a welcome moment of recapture. "She says the prospect of death dismays her so much that she wants to die. Well, even with all that on our minds, the most wuthering of heights surely, we somehow manage to hang on as long as we can. And we do not in the least understand the demons who want to lose their lives in taking ours, by whatever means. It's that sort of stuff that has immobilized what I used to know. Damnit, there were times when even I liked having ninety-something channels to surf on, however pointless the yield. Now, all we seem to see is walls and windows collapsing as if some deadly elevator had passed through them. Thousands mauled in an instant or two. And then the preposterous image of an entire nation's police forces looking for someone *who might have mailed a letter!* Maybe we don't deserve to survive after cutting so stupid a figure."

"Oh fui," I say agitatedly.

"Steady now, Shrop," he says. "Are we here to right a public wrong or to get you back on an even keel, spouting at us those vital words of yours, that only you can come up with? I would prefer you to remember them for yourself. Or, rather, their special meaning for you, their pith and skewed tenor. Did you realize that an entire population has suddenly begun making its wills? Here we are, menaced by a tiny regime as small as the Nazi party once was, who permit no kites to be flown and no snowmen built. To eat ice cream, which no doubt has more ice in it than cream, their women have to reach under their veils to let the spoonful pass. We have put men on the Moon, to Borges the most outstanding human event of his time, and we allow a pack of madmen to turn our loveliest inventions against us, with money and newspapers to follow. Oh, you've heard me go on about this already. Sorry. You are the patient, I'm the listener. *On!*"

I provide him with my warmest grin, the rictus of one who walks the tundra incessantly. "The problem is to get the system back, if system it was, and then somehow apply it—the grid that makes sense of things, like the rules of baseball or hockey." From where I lounge, I can see his keys dangling from a drawer, making against the wall the perfect shadow of a perching tsetse fly: a bit of leftover, unannulled civilization. "What is wrong with me," I ask him, "that I can do nothing with phenomena? They just tumble all over me, like grains of sand, I who used to sort them out real fast and bundle them away into groups. What's wrong with me?"

"Part of your mind's become unhinged."

"Say again."

"Overload," he says. "Flooding, a metaphor we steal from grief control. Too bloody much, old friend. Kübler-Ross."

"And one mind, presumably uninjured, can minister to another, less injured?"

"*Ming yi:* brilliance injured," he exclaims. "The *I Ching.*"

"I once read it."

"You will again," he tells me. "But not now."

"What then?"

"Shattered mind."

"It feels more like being numbed," I say. "Spiritual inanition."

"*Accidie* or *akedia,*" he answers, "as with all those heartsick medieval monks."

"Do you think I need to start illuminating letters?"

"Whatever works."

"Tell me, Quent," I ask him, "do the Irish have a word for *mañana?*"

"Yes," he answers, "but it lacks the urgency of the original Spanish, and don't you try out your old gingersnaps on me."

"No more golden oldies," I whisper, alluding to the sprightly give and take of our long friendship. "How sad."

"The trick," he is saying, "is to come up with a better punchline, saying haste or hurry to begin with, and then, maybe, panic or sleepy intonation. See?"

"Too difficult for me."

"Well then, what about fitting little jet engines to the tips of the propeller blades? And not realizing, so long ago, that you had turned your back, as a onetime student of aeronautics, on a great discovery? You walked right past it and went away somewhere to study math."

11

"With Roselli, at Cambridge."

"Good God!"

"What?"

"No, not Roselli. It was an exclamation at the—er, fatuity of it. Straight to math after passing up the jet engine as a complete source of power in its own right, long before Whittle, Heinkel, and the rest."

"Well, we eventually reached the point at which he said he'd taught me all he knew. It was time to move on."

"You always know."

"I have to do it, I suppose."

"You always used to."

"A river vessel attached to the Austrian army."

"You're older than you look."

"I know what would be better, Quent."

"Do say."

"Waiting till my complex or syndrome had come full circle, was full-blown, and then come to see you."

"Ah, so you can grovel to the max."

"No, not come to you half-hatched, so to speak."

"No, I'll take you at any degree of hatch, but the sooner the better, when there aren't as many causes to have effects."

"Well, screw that."

"You're more than halfway gone already, dear friend. May we please get back to the riverboat and the Austrian army? I see that we have already deserted aeronautics and the jet."

"Alas."

"But bully for old Whittle."

"Whoever."

"Captain Steignitz was a bully."

"Kicked you around somewhat, eh?"

"All of us. Captain of vessel, not the rank between lieutenant and major."

With his mouth, somewhere in the side, he makes, almost, the sound of an Austro-Hungarian-German soldier clicking heels.

"A lout, a drunk, a slime."

4
Quent

H E MAKES AS IF TO STAMMER, BUT ASSUMES CONTROL OF THE movement, as one can. Once again he is searching for some pat formula that will impose order on the proceedings: breakfast in New York, lunch in Rome, crow in Istanbul. Like that. Only the design he has in mind is not strong enough to hold things down. He misspeaks, saying contingency for contingent, and the shaking of his face evinces the disruption he always feels, horrified beyond measure by a double dose of the impossible, beginning, as he puts it, with an avalanche of rubble bigger than any mountain has produced. The first precedes the second by a little while. Flying low and fast, a jet swings into the first tower and actually seems to fly through it, slowing of course, slowed by walls and doors, bodies and tables, but matchstick flummery to a missile traveling at over five hundred miles an hour. Inside the tower, it has been sedate and purposeful up to now, but suddenly amid an inferno of noise and fire the disintegrating fish-nose of the fuselage munches toward them in a fairly straight line, idealess and melting, but intact enough to engulf all before it amid inaudible screams, fans of smoke, gusts of flame, arms and legs and faces all of a sudden rendered soft as babydick, and then the mess has moved onward, carving ever lower, heedless of floors and folk.

It is this, and comparable devastations, that dog him incessantly, an incendiarist's abattoir dreamed up by some mild-mannered suicides. He hadn't thought of it, and, even after seeing it he cannot fix it in his mind, next seeing in the downward moraine of wreckage the tailplane gliding along more or less intact, somehow tilted and twisted, riding what it has destroyed, but vanishing as the deluge from above smothers it, smashing it to bits. He will never see it again, but he will never forget the newsreel version. It is as if God has failed an examination in decorum and should instantly be re-examined just to keep people's hopes up. *All fall down,* he whispers for the sake of anything to say, an elderly nebbish recovering childhood cries (a different society from this) such as *Bags I,* verbal part of a shout demanding precedence at a game, or, similarly, "*fog*" and "*sec*" for first and second, the memory of them shaken loose by broken masonry and unseen bodies lapsing into the vast pour. Not unsophisticated by any means, or unread (his time as a poolman and a parade leader having given him ample time for self-improvement), he now knows that Thomas de Quincey, in an earlier century squinting through Lord Rosse's telescope at something too gruesome to endure, also frightened himself to death, not half to death, but wholly, mainly because such a thing just could not be, but also because a human had no means of coping with it except to shriek No and gibber into madness.

Which he does not do, not quite, but the very sight of an amputated tailplane gliding down amid a tide of dust and stone is, to his mind, forbidden. He thinks of how a box of tissues suddenly drops when one is plucked out from above; there is a momentary hang-fire and then the join between folded tissues and the selected one fails, and Mister John Wheeler's gravity takes over, downing the box, which dangles longer only if one or two tissues remain and the box appears to float, the body freed of its bulk and swept into the overall scheme of shadow and poxlight. Now he knows, he confesses, how to throw a Nuremberg egg, his mind having flinched off into the unknown regions for a little allusive privacy.

"Honest, Quent," he gasps. "A lance-corporal salutes the Milky Way." I know how to take him, after a while anyway, having spent years accommodating my rather staid mind to his baroque excesses, before his trauma, about which I am trying to keep calm as I see my friend edging toward yet another abyss, someone having taught him years ago that life made sense, otherwise why have an educational system, school to university, at all?

"The likes of me," he exclaims. "The likes of me!" That is how you have to take him, raw and intractable, if you aim to do him any good. Without the double crash, he would have gone on living a semi-normal life, listening perhaps to Saint-Saëns's piano concerto, *The Egyptian,* composed in Luxor. There used to be a German doll, before Hitler, with three heads for different moods. Perhaps he intends to initiate himself into the literature of pain, shoving his nose into dread and atrocity until he can honestly say he does not mind, convinced he is responsible for everything, like a sailor watching a clear sky. He talks of ancient mummies being burned in modern locomotives and mummy bandages being used for brown wrapping paper. *His* fault. There is going to be no limit to his savvy self-deprecation. "Look, Quent," he says, raising his mug to eye level and squinting at me over it, "I see history as it affects, impresses, me, not as it was. But I am beginning to think they're the same thing, the impact and the as it was. It's like being shipwrecked on Jupiter, if you see. . . ."

Of course I see. I have to. Now, what's actual is the one and only subjective. He claims he's developing a lazy eye that lags behind, rolls and floats, making him virtually monocular, and that (as if pursuing the brace image further), when he wrote to a friend consoling him for having lost a testicle to cancer, he said how sorry he was that the world was the way it was, and there would be the usual ribaldry. The friend never wrote back. Such events persuade him there is no guiding principle in the universe, no charitable reflex, and I am just amazed he got this far thinking otherwise. *Rock on,* I whisper. *On.* Whatever he comes up with will be part of a mirage.

So, in his disheveled way, he begins to tell me about being on the river boat, hearing the unmilitary gurgle of the engine, extolling the times when one boat or another leaned sideways in the silt, giving him exactly the right angle to loll at. I formed the impression that he was not a very energetic or shipshape sailor. Hearing him talk about rivers and riverboats was almost like hearing him talk about Mörbisch am See, the last village on the western shore before the Hungarian border. Whitewashed houses with deflowered porches and outdoor staircases, clumps of maize hanging from the walls. He talks of passports and bicycles, crossing the border into Hungary, a summer festival on a floating stage where Hungarian and Austrian operettas are staged next door to the marshes and reed beds. It is as if a fantasy from a child's storybook has overlaid his raw experience, and they have become interactive. Having heard him several times prate about Mörbisch and especially the lake, *Neuslieder See,* it graces, I formed the impression that, just like the lake itself, evaporating and flooding (dry from 1868 to 1872), the image in his mind waxed and waned according to his emotional needs, some of the time cloudy, shallow, warmish, at other times almost a dry bowl. Hence his addiction to the theme of a boat grounded, awaiting heavy rain or the melting of heavy snows. Even more is his languid evocation of the lake's odd behavior, the water level falling with a strong wind, then resuming its former depth as the wind drops. The only tributary, the Wulka, is similarly capricious, evaporating four times faster than it fills. I sensed in his water memoirs, spoken with irresistible candor, a fluctuating emblem more related to childhood than to military experience, but always valid whenever he wanted to recoup some aquatic image he could relate to pool-skimming, for instance, or time spent in wintrier climes such as Skjolden in Norway. His lake, which I sometimes decipher as his amalgamation of rivers and channels (all his waters scooped up), has a melancholy quality he attributes to Austro-Hungarianism, to the fact that Austrian steppe begins so close to Hungarian puszta. He finds the waters brimming with pain, four fifths Austrian, one fifth Hungarian, shallow as a tearing eye. No doubt it reminds him of the Danube Delta. In one of the observation posts that dot the reedscape, he has watched whinchats, little ringed plovers, blacktailed godwits, purple herons, penduline tits, avocets, and white-spotted bluethroats at their ceaseless tasks, giving himself over to a domain or dimension of birds amid a pandemonium of dwarf irises, king's candle, and luscious salmon asters, to which collusion of taxonomies he brings all his riverboat memories, dilating them to fill a beloved region he tends to call Pannonia. Leisure boats now replace the boats he remembers: those of reedcutters and fishermen and the flat-bottomed craft of wildfowlers. He often ends his rhapsodical reveries with a favorite joke, culled from colder waters and some film he has seen, when a trio of marooned women find themselves paddling about in chilly waters off Sumatra, and one recommends to the two others to "spend a penny" for its temporary warming effect. This he says with childlike gusto, perhaps wondering to what portion of his shattered life he can relate so mild an impropriety.

You can see how his almost feverish insistences pluck one in, most of all those you have heard before, because you sense that in one of the variants you might find the key to him and his lost ideas. I, at any rate, listen to him with cautious zeal, on the qui vive for flubs and slips that might become useful later on, rendered back to him as the keys to the lost kingdom. Besides, I am being paid, even as he skips from river duty to a stint in an artillery workshop and then, a couple of years later, in a howitzer regiment on the Russian front as an artillery spotter, where he was decorated for bravery, quite lost for a time his memory of birds. His martial career, as he likes to call it, was taking off and, if anything, becoming too appetizing for a man so cerebral.

My question to him would be, often is, Is this a natural progression of a gifted youth or merely a clutch of patches? How often do we pretend to ourselves that our onward advance has both method and aim when, in truth, it's more ragged and haphazard than an old holed fishing net? Perhaps, even then, he was a marvel at harmonizing the disparate, melding the discordant; the pattern he showed to the outside world; the higgledy-piggledy he kept to himself like the irritation in the oyster. If only, I used to think, he would admit to being a hodge-podge of aeronautical engineer, poolman, baton twirler, riverman, artillery spotter and lake lover. Maybe one of these was the key to the others, and brought them all into symmetry, converting a Dalmatian into a Tintoretto. You have always to wonder about someone who comes to you early in life for therapy, lacking, oh, an even flow, a coherent career. He really came to me to find out if his own private self-integration was a success, or was he fooling himself? A man apart as distinct from a man of integrity? All I had to do with someone so adroit at self-coordination was demonstrate his virtues to him, agree, and send him on his way. Indeed, it was a pleasure to find him so well meshed, easily the master of whatever outlandish thing he undertook. There seemed to be nothing he could not adapt congruously into his arsenal. He was the opposite of the literary student who hates to be told to go read the dictionary, look up in it any unknown words, thus assigning to literature the thinnest, most anonymous nature. He craved only to be led far afield so as to show off his expertise, readily joining balloonist to Wichita lineman, glass-blower to pediatrician, not that he embarked on all these callings; you just knew he was on their brink, ready to enroll.

How different then his disintegration, his loss of philosophy's vocabulary or of the meanings of its words. I soon began to suspect he was improvising professions, callings, to drop into the gulf where philosophy used to be. Almost a Jack of all trades or a snapper-up of unconsidered trifles like Shakespeare's Autolycus in *The Winter's Tale*, he used to need none of that, only too readily making sense of things and assigning them, hinged into the album of taxonomy by a supreme philatelist. How swiftly the debris of one's daily life fell into shape under his analytical glance, "worried" to death by a cerebral terrier. Teaching here and there, always with grand éclat and affable discipline, he wandered about like an old-time troubadour or trouvère, tidying up the mental landscapes of his spellbound hearers before he moved on. Was he a poet then? Of the explicit, yes. And to cool his soup wherever he stopped off, he filled his mouth and squirted it back into his bowl. "Soupositor" he sometimes called himself and when sighting through a host's telescope often made fun by aiming at the yellow lamp on a neighbor's porch, crying out "I have him, he's beautiful! *Mars!*"

Such this man had been, now flensed by the atrocities of terrorists

17

5
Shrop

THE THEORY IS ALL VERY NICE: I PRESENT MYSELF TO MY OLD friend, Bouvard to Pécuchet or vice versa, and pour out my heart, or at least such of it as remains. From this avalanche he is supposed to figure out what ails me, and how to put me right, meaning what I think I might have forgotten. At least he is not bogus, like the Dr. Marcelle Bergmann, Assistant Professor, University of Akron State, in the newspaper offering a lecture or an ass-wipe on "Creating Communities of Reform Images of Continuous Improvement Planning Teams," whatever any of that means. You have to be careful of which imbecile you traffic with. Has he, I wonder, the variety of experience needed to cope with so scattered a person as I? Is he not too much by nature a mechanic, a tinkerer, than an originating thinker? Most of all, after jets made over into streaking bombs, anthrax contaminating the hands and envelopes of an entire nation, the American way denounced by cave dwellers, he doesn't seem to have lost his way, his backbone, or his professional memory. Indeed, quite simply he might foist upon me another man's career in place of mine, I being none the wiser. He claims I was a philosopher of some kind, but refuses to go into detail; so I might have been a Leibniz whom he replaces with a Hobbes. You see the problem. It could end up a matter of fancy and preference. I would be nobody at all, a changeling, almost a performing fool.

But, *soft* as they used to say in blank verse plays, I came to him to be put right, or merely to rant; he did not come in search of *me,* having heard his old friend was rambling quite out of character. So we must be careful. I clean the pool and try to rub a certain splotch away, but find it is only a mote wafting around in my eye. That kind of thing. Or claiming *Carmen* is an opera to which few men would take their wives and no men their daughters. What kind of clue would such an assertion give him? I miss the keening, weeping music in old movies, the permanent sentimental backdrop to the forlorn elements in the action. A dead giveaway? Or, as he claims in one of his few onslaughts on my manner of presentation, what he calls my jussive vocatives, I hector the listener with too many come-ons, such as, "Will the listener please explain to her that . . .", "This alone explains his subsequent acts," "You, silent-listener," "You are to remember," and so forth: not leaving the auditor to make up his or her own mind. "You overreach," he tells me, "telling the other person what to think before you have told him anything. So, don't."

"I am in too much of a hurry to regain myself," I tell him.

"You are being previous."

"Nowadays, naturally a time of depravity, they say proactive."

"Just so," he scoffs. "Here, we will strive to be correct."

He has my first passport photograph in hand, a face of teeming innocence, so vulnerable and sensitive and high-strung as to make immigration officials blanch and wonder why they should admit so evident a patsy, at Chiasso, Tokyo, New York, and a hundred other places as the tender visage hardened on the rivers, in the aero-engine shops in Manchester, beside the artillery in the Austrian army, up in the Norwegian fjords, in the military jaws of a howitzer regiment, rather than as an artillery officer with several decorations for bravery "AND," I scream at him, "the facial torsion and chronic agony of working day by day at complex problems of logic and philosophy!"

"You were having a life," he says. "A *real life.*"

"In spades."

"Which no longer recurs?"

"Which no longer recurs."

"*Zut!*" Ancient French oath of his.

"Yes, screw it. I want the whole thing back, and, most of all that skein of ideas with which I reduced the world to common sense. How would *you* like it, dear Quent, if *you* had discovered penicillin and then, with no other records, forgotten the whole thing? I discovered the source of the Nile, but cannot find my way back to it."

"And never will."

Again I catch that sly, pawnbroking look of his. He is wondering if I went bonkers before the attacks on the twin towers, heralding the end of a civilization, or if after them. What I consider my tangential allusions he finds superfluous fireworks. If I have genuinely lost something and no longer recognize it, nor can tell what it was from something else of somebody else's, he finds me manageable, but not if I sound off at all angles, gladly recovering and reciting scraps of knowledge from hither and yon. He's a bit puritanical about his patients, does not like them double-barreled. Perhaps I am consulting the wrong man, the wrong one among many wrong ones, but it's friendship that draws me, the desire to hear the awful news from a friendly mouth. Trouble is, though, as I've said, he could equip me with someone else's system. Or, worse, re-equip me with my own without my ever recognizing it. Perhaps a few hints from my own system, proffered by him, would bring the whole thing back to me, as if you were to whisper "thrown" to Heidegger or "monad" to Leibniz. Not necessarily so, but worth a chance. And at once the rest of their system would spring forth, lucid and contained as a map of the London Underground with key names like Bank and Shepherds Bush springing into the light like startled hares. I wish it might be so with me, but Quent's efforts so far have failed.

6
Quent

A S ANY RATIONAL PERSON MIGHT, HE WONDERS WHO ARE THESE people, human antibiotics, who hate the very idea of life and by whatever means undertake to kill it, with smallpox, nerve gas, anthrax, or the suitcase that contains a nuclear bomb. They have always existed, but have never needed to massacre because the dread diseases of human history have done their work for them: the Black Death, the 1918 'flu epidemic, AIDS. Their mandate, however, goes over and above such blights and calls into question, on presumably moral grounds, the right of humans to persist. As they see it, the planet mould be better off without both their human targets and themselves. Kamikazes they may be, but ranged against the entire civilian population simply because it is there. He had heard from varying sources that these nihilistic fundamentalists come in various kinds: paupers who loathe capitalism; sons of plutocrats who ape Mick Jagger and other rockers; religious purists to whom women are filth. He has even heard that Taliban means "students," but he isn't sure of this, and he has a sneaking suspicion that something Quaker thrives in them, and that they have joined up so as to have something to belong to. It is Eliot, he reminds me, who in one of his essays suggests that a human only joins the universe when there is nothing else to join, which leads Shrop to comment that joining the universe is mere vacuous pretension, a nihil gesture, but that all that is not universe isn't worth joining either, not even the US Airways Club or the Red Cross. In other words, his peculiarly sensitive psychology seems to demand only the most meaningless of organizations—Dada, Surrealism, OULIPO. Cleverly testing out shades of meaning, he favors a harmless nihilism over a harmful one. There is within him a touch of the fundamentalist, the purist, as Roselli had noted when he commended Shrop's "intellectual purity to a quite extraordinary degree." All the same, he is nobody's chump; his purity is not a minimalism but only something that is not anything else, like pure lunacy or pure arrogance. And he thinks along these lines only because he has lost his philosophical memory, any vestige of what his philosophy was—so much so that I suspect he no longer recalls what *anybody's* philosophy was. In a word, he has forgotten philosophy and the claptrap, all the verve, that accompanied it. Perhaps it was worth forgetting, as so much bull, and ranked well below such a chore of contemplation as the price of cabbages from the Dark Ages to 1789. All of which has led me to arrive privately at the following conclusion: he was predisposed to damn any fundamentalism other than his own, and it is this that has driven philosophies from his head. He does not want to fell the topless towers of Ilium or anywhere else; he wants to purify the dialect of the tribe. He wants us back to basics: to handwriting, bush telegraph, cooking over an open fire, bow and arrow hunting. A Luddite, yes, but also sharing Lear's version of the bare, forked animal as something to cherish. Only this evacuation of the mind would have made room for his idea of clearing things out, emptying philosophy down the toilet. So he may be said to have connived against himself while, on the other hand, denouncing fundamentalists both pure and murderous. Was this a useful, worthwhile mental transit? Only if you came back from it, or so I thought. If it required slaughter, then no, of course. If not, then to come there was surely a rich harvest of god-given things. Confronted with the plenty or foison of the universe, who would gladly reduce human life to minimums? No one but a madman, which he is not, not yet, not quite.

He comes close, though.

He is beginning to be someone else, without trying, without recognizing the degree of impersonation in all he says.

Perhaps he will get a glimpse later on, even granted the embellishments he contributes to the other life he appears to be taking over. By and large it will be someone else whom he knows or knows about, and whose life he recalls in a peculiar way. Who are you? I ask, but he only says he will soon know. "Plums are quite special," he ends up telling me in his inconsequential fashion, "but they gotta be organic."

7
Shrop

WHENEVER I TAKE STOCK OF HIM, NOT ALWAYS FOR PROFES-sional reasons, I have to remind myself that, fixed as he is, he has more time for reading than others do. An unshrinking soul stationed between two bicycle wheels he never propels by hand, he has seen more of life and death than many of us. Not merely a *mutilé de guerre*, he is an officer of the peace, a justice of it. Spoiled for later life, in a rice paddy while descending from a chopper, he quickly slid in between layers of living, as I suppose a volunteer would. He was much younger then, not given too much hope of achieving a ripe old age, and so has done well in lasting until the new millennium, cheerful and popular, with as few clients as he can manage, and no one feeling sorry for him (all *that* went out with the twentieth century). With his one eye, he has been a Cyclops beacon flashing upon works of literature and psychology he'd previously neglected. He used to tell me stories of grunt life, none of them in any way embellished, and I in my full-memoried way would make erudite comparisons, long before I became a man who could remember only losing his memory confronted by a man who seemed to forget losing his legs and eye. True, certain stark reminders leapt at me from immediate circumstances: how he'd been injured, how hospitalized and cared for, but not much more than that. Every now and then he talks to me of Mozart's nineteenth quartet, the "Dissonant," or the third movement of Beethoven's fifteenth, and I receive this information like a man in a mist, wondering what it happens to be an echo of, ever dogged as I am by the misheard—the phrase "returnal home" instead of "eternal home," in that old hymn, which we sometimes falteringly try to sing together. "Fats Waller," he says, and I think it's an echo of "Fat Swallow," whoever that can have been. He tells, in his bizarre way, of ostensibly free checks that arrive in the mail, come-ons from his credit card bank but with his account number imprinted thereon for all to see, so he tears them up, not owning a shredder, and dismembers the bit bearing his number. The debris he then drops in the toilet bowl and flushes it away, an event he describes lovingly as a group of deer static and at rest, then spinning away as they flee downward. I wish I always remembered his analogies as well as just now, which has cost me some effort. Only rarely can I bring him something novel I remember from reading; only my delight at encountering something unusual. As once, when I tell him, managing to recover something graphic from a sliver of newsprint, "Did you know, Quent, that the SR-71 Blackbird, originally called Archangel, left smoke rings behind it?" A major effort for me. I am ever colloquial. I'm like, "Wow." He goes, "Hot-dog!" It's only a pose of two old salts talking younger than their years, but it does sometimes break the tension that can build up between us, so we relax into a mistaken version of the National Anthem, while he peppers me with questions I can never answer: "Who was Carleton Palmer? Who was Craven Cottage? What was Hitler's art like? Can you quote the Eton Boating Song?"

No use. It used to go on for hours, when we met for play and gossip, but now that I see him professionally he sees no point in posing questions I can never answer, unless, as sometimes when you are reading an eye chart, one letter or even an entire line comes clear, a memory or the engram of it swims into the open and I become all remembrance as on Veterans' Day, or Poppy Day as the English call it.

He watches me float around amid the flotsam of recall. I tie a knot in my handkerchief (obsolete folkway, I know, I know), but cannot remember what it was for. He uptips himself from his wheelchair in a gesture of romantic aversion and invites me to take his place while he lounges on the rug as if coming up from the depths for air, his lower half still at sea. "To jerk your memory loose," he says. I try it without success, then lift him back, noting how he always seems lighter, eternally doing without.

There are so many flubs and blotches in my telling that I am tempted to repeat all this in front of a mirror, so that I can at least see myself in the act of doing it. As it is, I write "he told" or "he tells" with a dizzy awareness that the moment is already gone and therefore not to be remembered; I would be better off writing "he is telling" and then break off before he finishes, or even write "he is telli—" so you can grasp the evanescence of what I'm telling. But then I recognize that to know the words, any words at all, is to give the game away, or rather call the whole enterprise into doubt: "To be the way he is, you'd have to have lost language too, wouldn't you?" So, it's all a compromise, with me suggesting an impossible loss through imperfectly couched sentences, which of course is not what's happening at all. Rather than remember something, I should *dismember* it, trusting in the reader's good heart, getting him/her to say: He remembers as little as he can just to express his loss of memory. Truth told, it is only the shape, paradigm, and language of my contribution to abstract thought that eludes me, as Quent ever the noticer has told me. And no amount of refresher brings it back, even as I somehow recall the life that went along with it. So with regret, I am *Yours:*

* * *

The Fire Sermon

I F SOMEHOW, PERHAPS BLINDFOLDED WITH PLUGS IN YOUR EARS, you can attune to it without recoiling, one inhalation of combined burning rubber, scorched beef and baby caca will last you a lifetime. They call it Ground Zero, though there is nothing zero-like about it except the absence of human life. It is the ground gruesomely fed and fostered, upheaved and manured, with, deep down, blocks of gold odorless amid the debris of plundered bodies. Smoke wafts and spirals from the lower depths as from an inexhaustible supply. What is on fire beneath? You may well ask. It is as if corpses develop into a new fodder they never knew in life. And there are hundreds of them as in some ancient Scandinavian burial zone where bog people reign, and you wonder how in years to come the diggers of the day will construe the jumbled carnage that reposes here, crammed together in an instant as if an instant were some kind of creative maestro, devising in that split moment fresh combinations of human limbs and trunks undreamed of in Japanese sex manuals or the *Kama-sutra*. No voices to be heard among the hisses and creaks. Nothing much to be seen in the rump of sludge that lids the cenotaph around which an increasing circle of sightseers gathers, in the fashion of villagers who grouped around the actual cenotaphs of older wars, envisioning if they could the twigs of humanity buried there in clinical disorder, they presumably having propelled the world to a humaner understanding as their relentless, heroic gift. The war artist, Paul Nash, visiting the trenches of 1914-18, reconjured the fetid scene in a canvas he called *Totes Meer*, Death's Sea, in which the stochastic waves of rippled linseed are the remains of folks, the remains, elongated and contorted tunnels for surfing through. Even the title is German, as if English were too chicken a language for this, and of course you try

Zero Grund or something such, but this masterwork of depravity is the result of Mecca-nization.

The day may come when souvenir hunters turn up with brand-new shovels for the occasion, and Saks bags fresh off the rack to hide the obscene sample in. Museums, galleries, the private underground bunkers of obsessed collectors, willing heirs of Hermann Göring all, will receive the left-overs, perhaps to intimidate the future with, warning against—well, what? Terror, catastrophe, hell on earth? Or will there come a team of white-clad operatives, habituated to clearing the toilet tanks of jumbo jets, ready to suction up the effluvia and purge the site until it lies spic-and-span as an empty swimming pool, whitewashed and sanitized, and most of the remainder goes to an unnamed island where potter's field has become Cain's acreage. Spread bonily thin, with blobs of toe jam in between the ossuaries, a banquet for seagulls, this panic in the year zero oozes and fumes as in some Japanese tea ritual misconstrued as a disaster.

Or it is a garden to be left as such, neither pruned nor primped, all samples forbidden, even if you happen to be one of those old Irish peat-cutters and burners. Unimaginable burning, or it would be so if last century had not been itself. This hell is its own oven, its flowers might have been faces (coleus or rhubarb), its squirrels will be nocturnal rats obliged to forage for themselves among pesky coils of wires and the sour, undernourished taint of brand-new charcoal. Will there be signs telling of 9.11, or will the site be left to self-explain until the distant day when no one remembers anything at all about it? Will it say *Do Not Light Fires or Set Off Fireworks*, as if you were some tyro taking the oath in the Bodleian Library, Oxford, or entering any similarly holy place? Perhaps it will remain a place notorious for Dangerous Air, all witnesses warned of the risk, supplicants in masks and plastics. It will work its way into and out of our minds like the badge of the brute, twice smitten, ever awry.

* * *

There, I sigh, feeling somewhat weak at the knees, I've said it. I've put it better than usual. Odd how certain words you didn't know you remembered come into play once your wheels are warm and you've decided to say something final. Sometimes, when the words themselves start warming up, the numbers follow. If you say to yourself $2 + 2 = 4$, or visualize it, you can somehow sense an increase as you move from the first 2 to the second one, so that it feels like having 2.1 + .2 + or even 2.01 + .02 + .03. The equation implies an increase unexpressed in digits. So 2 + 2 is not only a finite process, it's a fluid movement from 2 to 4, and sometimes our reckoning needs to take that movement and all the intermediate stages into account. Arithmetic isn't as cut and dried as we think it is. Didn't Rosselli tend to go on about this kind of thing? If you spill crumbs, you have to undergo the punishment of picking them up one by one. How I used to love logic and numbers, not this sort of tenderfoot claptrap, but the real thing: God's math, as not (I hope) expressed in Ground Zero, Dead Zero, Dead Sea, or whatever you choose to name it. Whoever brought about that atrocity, if the word didn't have epic or heroic connotations to some, we would call him a prick. I now think of Quent as if he suffered his wounds in that precise place, not so long ago, where it is still smoking. Shot down, he remained intact for two days below the treeline, and was fired on only while reaching up for the extractor hook dangling from the chopper. Ah but for a second or two. So he eventually went back to the career of his mind, seated between his two wheels like Queen Victoria on the old penny coin.

Hovis, a buxom young Polish girl training to be a nurse, is his Girl Friday, shopping for him, to and froing to the library downtown, the post office, the bank, and such. He lives at one or two removes from society, making whole again, if he can, those of us whose minds ride a wheelchair. Monday he makes out his lists for her, hands over his credit card and courtesy cards, then marvels when she returns and, as if to please him, place-kicks toilet rolls and cubic boxes of Kleenex down to the other end of the severely bright hallway, emitting a yell of triumph. It is a house tradition, dating from the first installation of bell-pushes and interfacing mirrors, telescopes and microphones. A program at the local airport offers flight training to the paraplegic; he already knows and disdains the ad when it appears on the Wings channel. What will he do, though, when she qualifies and goes out into the world as an official nurse in a year's time? It's a job she will find hard to resist, so she is looking for an ideal replacement, and the wait agitates him, especially on Mondays. The wounded surgeon plies the steel.

"How about a man, for the lifting?" I ask, but he shrugs, looks away, executing with his remaining body a winsome twist I can only identify as a flounce meaning never mind.

He has little desire to go out, somehow subscribing his inmost mind to a doctrine about shut-ins developing more intellectual power than gadabouts. He is defying the life to come, I believe, and then I decide he's looking to me to succeed her, two half-men making one. Could this be? Surely not, as I am the weaker, frailer member, requiring his hyperfine ministrations, although I sometimes wonder if what he trains me to remember is altogether my own. Am I indulging in variations on a theme of Quentin Montefiore del Patugina's, or what? Surely Quent is not doing variations on any theme of mine. Ephebophilic Father Jerome comes weekly to hear his confession, but it's only an empty routine, Quent being a ragged Catholic, much as I am a ragged pagan. He was wounded in the land of jungle leaves, I in the land of heart's desire. Little to choose between us. You might say his remaining life is well organized, not least because he maintains a satisfactory career as a shrink, though with too few clients, all of whom, I tell him in my rambunctious way, ought to be assistants in training, taught the ropes while he saves their minds.

8
Quent

J UDGING FROM WHAT HE SAYS FORMALLY, IN OPINIONS NO DOUBT meant for publication, and in offhand remarks clearly intended as mere table talk, he perhaps omits from his purview the hundreds of toilers on the anthill, both paid and unpaid, not just firemen and rescue crews, but volunteer ladies dispensing shrimp and burgers free, stockbrokers and doctors who decided their duty lay here and not on the job elsewhere. Supplies keep coming in, but not for the dead, although the various brands of clergy are. He has not compared enough, I think, with destruction in other cities such as London and Coventry, Warsaw, Dresden, Manila, and such a village as Lidice. That is not his way, he who fixes on the caliber and configuration of the scab, attending like so many New Yorkers to the symbolic aspect of the twin towers' destruction, here where precious little has been blasted apart (although more than a short memory might conclude), excepting the well-known American yen for destroying old structures so as to replace them. What, I ask him, about old wheelchairs? I myself have seen them blow up outside suave cafés on Saigon streets.

"No," he answers, "not those. I am thinking of the thousands underground, grossly maimed. What can be done?"

I mention eleven hundred degrees, the heat underground, but he gives the figure the merest nod, intent on the mythic or anthropological angle, actually transforming the mess as he recalls it, guessing at the future status of the site and its relation to recorded history, to art even. But what can you expect from someone who is losing it, doomed to eventual Alzheimer's way beyond his lapses in everyday and specialist memory: he will not know even me, or the meaning of the word philosophy. If he proves unlucky. What is clear, to me at any rate, is that he has found in Ground Zero an image to fix on, something recent he has had no chance to forget although his version of it is highly choosy. In some way, he sees himself as akin to it, butchered and destroyed by some unthinkable outside force, mad mullah or well-heeled student. Is it his own nihilism that drives him? Does he see himself entombed at over a thousand degrees Fahrenheit, all smashed up, or does his skewed vision of it operate from the outside only?

"Are you identifying?"

"How so?" He has this daunting, sour look.

"Have you made it your emblem, in some wacky way?"

"Only to the extent that the hijacked jet has flown right into me. Didn't someone find three seated dead, blasted in?"

"Point proved then. Are you identifying with the dead as well?"

Obviously not; the thought has not occurred to him, and he takes his time before not even answering, like someone who takes a hint or message from history without heeding the ephemeral particulars with which the hint or message was involved. Surely he cannot think this atrocity has given him some validation, although I can cite case histories in which dithering patients, obsessed with some vile happening, have eventually taken the evil upon themselves in a kind of sibling copycat vein. They think that only something catastrophic, outright evil, could have miserably afflicted them, and they settle for it. He blames all horrors for his state, and all I have to do to my old friend is sort him out. We are already beyond the stage of facile similes, say, as when someone scraping a carrot with a knife makes a noise similar to that of a young pig oinking. I can only hope he does not wish to become the Ghost of Ground Zero after the fashion of the Madonna of the Sleeping Cars, that old French pipedream.

"You won't get too far ahead of me, will you?" Asked, he grins miserably, the queasy grin of the resolute suicide, and shakes his head without the least conviction.

"Oh no," he tells me, "I promise you plenty of warning, old pal. Don't I always? Didn't I? Won't I?"

9
Shrop

H E'S A CHARMER ALL RIGHT, WHAT WITH THAT ITALIAN BLOOD on his mother's side. Much hand movement, from palms amply spread to an Indian *namaste* with palms planted close together. Rather than gesturing, he swirls and matches this with an almost groveling obeisance of the face, while what he says, from what I have seen, is silkily ingratiating, speckled with Italian phrases that come naturally to him, though he always gets the Italian right, unlike most people. Thus he wins everyone over, as he did when lecturing, seeming to make an overt, outright appeal to each individual listener: not challenging, but tenderly beseeching—an Ayn Rand in reverse. His boyish glow has never left him, or the mercurial play of his lips and eyes as if the occasion is something romantic rather than philosophical. Charm tips you one way or the other when he speaks, usually with quite superfluous daintiness of manner: his mother in him, of course, little countered by the stiff upper lip of his British father, a soldier. So you can be won over by him, put off your guard while he is deftly summing you up, noticing you don't ripple as much as he or display a pretty smile. Even in the old days, the more you became like him the more he kept you at bay, wanting no imitators.

10
Quent

HOW THEN, YOU MAY WELL ASK, DID YOU TWO TEAM UP, BECOME an item? Was it that the bass-baritone voice lured him, at least in the mornings before food and drink sludged it over, weakening and heightening it? Or the big Joseph Stalin mustache that I used to wax to two points, befitting a fighter pilot? Or did *his* soldier father sing through Shrop's demeanor to the military man I was? Perhaps he fancied my craggy, intrusive, burly face, my huge hands? It was certainly not the legless pantomimic object I have now become, wheeling myself about with my pants legs folded neatly beneath me. He enjoyed my severeness of mien, I guess, the no-give in my eyes, my willingness to listen to his kind of philosophy. After all, how many pilots took him seriously or had heard of him? Or of Hampshire, Merleau-Ponty, Ayer, Jaspers? Each was exotic to the other in the haze of post-existentialism, a philosophy just about designed for a military man. His sense of humor was feline, mine gruff, but we now seem to have swapped roles, he gruff in his loss of memory, I feline after all that reading and a switch in career. Does he simply look on me now as a castrato with no musical future? Do I now regard him as a pitiable amnesiac who once had everything at his fingertips? It's hard to say, as we no longer show each other the candor of old, life having carved into us in different ways, for keeps.

"I have no memory, you have no legs." How dare he sum us up thus? Between us, would we make a whole man?

"Better," I inform him, "that I comment on your memory. That at least."

"And your legs then?"

"One picture tells a thousand stories."

It isn't going well today; perhaps it never will again, as when each rejoiced in the other's laughter, smirked along with his cynicism. I think he blames me for filling up his empty memory with bogus data. I certainly blame him for staring at my leglessness. Yet we press on, somehow determined to do each other good, though perhaps not in obvious ways. we have already decided not to pray together, like Nixon and Kissinger, or eat the same foods, attend the same movies, so all we seem to have left between us is music and planes, not a bad mix really. Plus the act of psychoanalysis, which would go better if only we didn't know each other so well. He has sat in my chair and I have pretended to his lost memory, but that was only so much folderol, a flawed reciprocity. He is older than I by five years, negligible as years and careers go. I tell him how Gilbert of the Gilbert-and-Sullivan duo died at 71, trying to save a woman from drowning in the lake on his private estate, but only giving himself a fatal heart attack instead. By way of response, he tells me that in Japan at Christmas the store windows are full of Santas being crucified, all done in compact, carnal images. "Topsy-turvy," *I* say.

II
Shrop

"IN THIS CITY, IN THESE YEARS," I BEGIN, SOMEWHAT AWED BY the way the phrase scans, "there are advertisers who refuse to run a Presidential speech instead of commercials and even insist that, aboard doomed planes, the passengers with only minutes or seconds to live deserve a last fleeting look at the advertising on their screens, just in case. . . ."

"I see you're switching to burlesque," he says. "Bully for you. There's many a nascent critical gift installed in a contrary attitude. In *attitude,* period."

Sometimes, announcing things in that public way of his, he seems to be ensconced on a throne, I the supplicant or knighthood candidate. He gets loftier week by week.

"Let's get back," he adds, "to what we used to talk about. Your loss of memory, to an extent. You used to put me in the picture, recounting your earlier days. So then what?"

"So then *what?*"

"The next phase," he says witheringly. "After the eastern front, then your transfer to the mountain regiment in Italy."

"I kept writing in various notebooks all through hostilities, and lugged it around on my back. Logic and math much of it, so I soon had a complete manuscript I sent off to Rosselli to see what he could manage to do with it. At that point I was a prisoner of the Italians and had precious few freedoms. From there, through Rosselli, I tried to interest publishers, but also under my own steam. When someone finally accepted the book for publication, it was all Rosselli's doing, and I was mighty pleased because people hailed it as deep and powerful. Imagine such a book, put together with the sound of gunfire in the background, and heavy gunfire at that! Amazing that the salvos didn't deafen me to the rhythms of my own prose. It must have been that I was able to concentrate to an unusual degree. Just a whole series of comments, almost asides, better organized than Cioran's of course, and displaying a mathematical training. What a short book, seventy-five pages only, to stir up such a fuss. All about language, as you know. Death included, as well as good and evil. Yet I have no more intimate acquaintance with that book than with a ghost, as if it has been sucked away from me, amputated, spirited away from me into some filmy zone. It all had to do with language, as some books do, but that's all I can recollect. My brain is always sneezing. My head fills with mucus. Oh to be clear-headed again."

He smiles a tutor's smile at me and says, "It has to do with the notion: How can one say anything? The account of something must exhibit all the details the something has. What we say about anything must be logically derived from it. Honest."

I am dumbfounded. I am founded in dumbness. How forget anything that ragged?

"I was remembering," he says, "something very similar in the realm of music, Shrop. This French composer, also a prisoner of war, had to sleep in an enormous drawer in a chest of drawers, which is how the Germans ran things in those days. He called it *Quartet for the End of Time* and they actually procured the right instruments and performed the piece in the prison camp in 1941. Pretty understanding Germans, hein? It was Olivier Messiaen, of course, better known for helping himself to the calls of birds. The quartet was what issued from the war."

"I wonder if he remembered it."

"Of course he did."

"I should play it for you some time."

"We should play it for *you*."

"As you wish," I say huffily. "I was just adding a memory."

I like that idea of his: sleeping in a big drawer because there weren't enough beds to go around. Amazing what a piano, clarinet, violin and cello can bring into being, once you've found them. But then, *Germans* would. And shoot them all afterward, after recording the music.

Three years ago, and still smoking while my stomach persists in its quiet revolt, something between a gnaw and an ache; food won't settle there among the acid; air bubbles occupy my chest, my throat feels full no doubt from the famous esophageal reflex, and my head aches, daunted by a pain that moves about, sometimes needling, often thumping. Nothing in between then and now, other than memory loss, has afflicted me, and I hazard a guess that the very thought of all those stacked below like bolts of cloth has a double whammy: physical dismay plus loss of memory—almost more than you can bear, if you can bear to bear anything more. The ruins do not go away, and neither does the body's anguish. It is all a glut of excess, hamstringing just about everyone in the city because, distance themselves from it as they may, it comes after them night and day like some blood-soaked, battered golem, asking nothing, offering nothing, but personifying the old ghost of perfection.

"You feeling gloomy again?" Sometimes he seems dense.

"Same old same old," I tell him. "The mess."

"No business as usual."

"What," I ask him, "would that mean to a philosopher, an ex-philosopher?

"It's three years gone," he says. "Another plane crash."

"Three."

"I find the stomach sooner or later recovers. Really."

"Not for me. Three years of pangs, as if some force is gently twisting my innards, and everything bubbles. I do not want to eat, or even throw up, but remain in a state of arrested barf."

"Disgusting."

"But human."

"It'll go."

"Has not gone yet. Nothing is going to put right the groundswell in the pit of my tummy."

"To our moutons, then."

"These *are* the bloody moutons."

"Then let's. Shall we go farther, into—"

"Into you cannot think what you cannot verbalize?"

"Something like that."

"What did you do next, Shrop?"

"Oh, I gave all my money away, such as it was. A mere cannoneer's fee, exchange rate of then. It was the nest-egg I had inherited from my father. Behold the uselessness of money. He had no need of it, I gave it away. If I had friends, I didn't want them to want me for my money, but I was a bit of a fundamentalist too, not fancying luxury or too much ease. I was and remained frugal. Do you think I undernourished my brain?"

"Inhaled too much smoke maybe."

"And not just smoke. The fumes and fug of hell."

"All those." He knows what I mean. We're still tight.

"Blackening my passageways, larding my insides with tar and so on."

"You weren't the only one."

"We're a team of bad breathers, killing the oxygen we need. Yet, you know, there was the constant urge to go and see it, time and again—the madman constantly probing his toothache in his sleep. You've heard of such things."

He has. He has in one way or another heard of nearly everything. Savant extraordinary. Nothing but books after they shot him down. Which is why I go to see him, to test my own loss and experience against his wealth of life, all the experiences I've never had. I always used to think American men had no gift for friendship, being mainly concerned with power; but maybe I was wrong. They need to be maimed first, just to disillusion them about the extent of power.

"And then," he is saying. "You tell me you still wear your gas mask, in rehearsal, and try to do as the government tells you: be commonsensical. You've given up the antibiotics, but you still have a stockpile. Always open your mail in plastic gloves, wearing a nasal mask. My God!"

"That's nothing, Quent. I want to know, and have wanted to know from the very first, exactly what kind of pain the thousands suffered: heat, mutilation, choking. And moment after moment. It's amazing how little they tell us of the final agony. They lump them all together and just say they all died, but never how, although that is no doubt the most important fact of all. Don't ask me why, but I want to experience everything that they did, as if I, although alive, were not going to be forgiven. They could even shows us photographs of the dead, just to calm the bug in us that claims they died happily. Just think of the babies and the children, none of them hardly even born."

"Well," says Quent, "I'd call that vicarious agony, whatever _you_ call it. Not recommended. No point in paddling your fingers in it. You might never sleep again. I learned that much in the military. Leave it alone."

"I can't," I tell him, "it takes over my life. I want to know how you mourn three thousand or whatever the number was without lumping them all together like peas in the pod of pain. If I may take what you reported to me about the remarks in my long-forgotten notebook, the way we talk about such things should in all its details replicate the event in life. Well, 'x thousand dead' doesn't do it, nor even a long alphabetical list of the victims. Between the event and what you say about it there's a gulf. There always was."

Had I rehearsed what to tell him so that, when the day of my appointment arrived, I would be word-perfect, certainly after mumbling most of the way by cab? Don't forget the headaches, I said, the neckaches, the shoulder pains, the abiding sense and smell of soot and burned plastic, the belly-ache with and without food, the constant sense that, when previously I had only ever felt fairly safe, now I felt on the brink of savagery, biological, chemical, aeronautical. Everything around me had been raised to its highest dangerous power, so much so that, after I was allowed back into my blasted domain, I felt afraid either to stay there or to go out again. The so-called sheltering sky did nothing of the kind. I quivered at contrails and shook at the whine of a jet. Even my teeth ached, and I kept having to clear my ears of wax. Of course, much of what I rehearsed en route I never said to him because, into the bargain, I shrank from the session itself, as if I might poison my being all over again just by talking about it. So what he told me did not exactly hearten or fortify me; his presence *qua* human being gave me a boost, the boost of seeing an old friend again, but his professional scrutiny always made me feel worse as if, he not having been near Ground Zero, we were members of different clubs.

"Can you help me?" I told him each time. "I am losing touch with who I used to be. I am the newly vacant man."

So, did he help me? I doubt it. I was lonely and seeing him cheered me up, but it in no way brought back the self I kept losing, even though, ever the gentleman, he continually addressed me as the philosopher I used to be and never as the jittery refugee I had become. I thought I was developing asthma, but he said no. Migraines danced before my eyes and my head was sore to the touch, but he said, "Nothing to do with it." I had developed a droop of the fourth finger on my left hand, or Dupuytren's Syndrome, but he shushed me and indicted rheumatism instead, not trauma. You might think that all this distraction would encourage me, but it seemed not to. Now, years after the event, I was a worrywart, telling myself not to fret, it would never happen again. So, perhaps, what affected me most was the fact of military tribunals around the country, results never known, the constant requirement to produce a current ID, the ghastly Byzantine complexity of making airline bookings, requiring one to produce three years' tax returns, canceled checks, and proof of employment. You also had to be fingerprinted, just in case. Even such trivial things as a chef from Hong Kong flying home with two meat cleavers undetected in his carry-on stirred the morbid side of my imagination. Nothing that happened failed to provoke me, and even if he did not care to brand me "chronic trauma," I did, as if the SS had hauled me in and tattooed me with my blight. In the subway, one young man had exposed a tattoo on his arm. It read

9.11.01
Never Forget

Now that punitive inertia of his begins to lift. He has heard enough to interest him, and I begin to wonder if telling him things in the past or the present works better, concluding that he likes the past because it's congealed and finite whereas the present feels on top of him, always beyond his grasp—an odd response for a former fighter pilot, yet not, I decide, for a paraplegic.

"Earthworms wriggling?"

"Not yet," I tell him.

"Phlegmy throat then?"

"Only as the day wears on and it gets coated with food and post-nasal drip."

"Ah, dripping."

I do not answer him, having said a sufficiency. He sets his head far back and yawns. I wonder if he has been asleep.

"I would like you to escort me there, not all the way, but in and around the site. You never know. Have you tried revisiting?"

"I live close, don't you remember?" No doubt he thinks the atrocity has altered geography. He has been nowhere near it in years, having had not the least desire. And I get to wondering how many former pilots have turned to the mind as a subject for study and a career. A different form of flying?

"I was wondering," he says after an ostentatious pause, "if it was the cataclysm itself that did you in or the steps the government took afterwards. I mean fighter pilots ordered to shoot down any hijacked planes, which is to say that the President's life is worth more than yours plus those of the hundred-odd other passengers. Is this the source of the amnesia? A profound hurt sustained as self-worth goes for naught? What a surprise. I must say I, as a fighter pilot, wouldn't care to explore too closely the implications of that. Should not a president take his, and his home's, chances as just another man among men? I mean, subjected to the lottery of life and terrorism, aren't all suckers equal? Has any man, least of all the murderer, the provocateur of all this hair-splitting, the right to order another man shot down? Isn't this the royalty theory gone over the top?"

It hadn't even occurred to me, but, occurring now, it set the bile roaming my insides. Was I that low on the totem pole? I recalled seeing on TV not long after the disaster a couple of young pilots nervously licking their lips and avowing as how, yes, they would do it if ordered to rather than let the hijacked jet cruise on to its deadly rendezvous with the White House, the Empire State Building, or whatever. Those pilots might never again get a good night's sleep, but surely some fancy medallion courtesy of a saved official. Quent was right.

II

The Recovery of the Dead

And burnt the topless towers of Ilium?

—Christopher Marlowe,
The Tragical History of Doctor Faustus

12
Chain Mail

S O THEIR REGULAR MEETINGS TURN INTO CONFRONTATIONS, SHROP increasingly irate with Quent, who feels flummoxed by a growing hostility that has replaced friendly indulgence, for Quent has always craved indulgence since being mutilated whereas previously, a jock and he-man as well as a show-'em-all pilot, he sought out envy and admiration, had almost a superiority complex. Now, perhaps to salve an ancient ache, he wants to visit Ground Zero in a gust of fellow-feeling, in his wheelchair executing as best he can a kind of swiveling flounce while Shrop shakes his head at the antic, not so much wanting back the friend of before (all the Quents antagonized him, he now decides) as craving somebody new who can at least stand up and argue like a man. If their friendship is not to spoil, they will have to move on into different selves who can spend the rest of their days trying each other out without fear of plumbing the bottom of the barrel. After the deep, another deep yet. "Ha," says Quent, "Kierkegaard! Happy over seventy thousand fathoms." If Shrop recognizes the quotation, he gives no sign, but wishes he had remembered it in time to beat Quent to the punch. Yet who is to say if Kierkegaard was more shrink than philosopher? Was it the tortured soul who said it or the tight-wound philosophe?

"You remember reading him," Quent says tactlessly.

"As a youth. I hardly remember being a youth."

"But the fathoms dwindling down beneath your feet?"

"Fuck fathoms and fuck him, whoever he was." Shrop can feel two parts of his brain, maybe tiny, trying to come together to clinch a memory, but flinching away from each under the pull of identical charges. His head feels full of pumice, light and holey. Shrop is definitely going off, and he has not even been shot down into the jungle.

Now Quent broaches the matter. "You could take me and wheel me to the plywood runway, full of holes already."

"No hope, old boy. They'd shoo us away."

"A war hero wearing his Medal of Honor?"

"Again with the war hero!"

"Don't come it, Shrop. In uniform, half a uniform, the other half a skillfully disguised midden of greasy horrors. I'm not the man I was,

I'm not even the man I never was." He feels some inchoate yearning for devastation, the kind of life force that pulverizes others, making them more like himself. The expert logician, trained as an afterthought, is succumbing to the war-wounded, previously transcended. He feels like a doyley with big holes cut in him, then sewn to be permanent. Fingering the stitches that keep the wounds open, he wants to go up again in his jet, to pull all those G's, the leaden feather, but he never will, he knows. He is lucky to be flying his chair and to keep on saying to his few clients, "the likes of me." They find him more and more strange, his professionalism coming off him like slop, his couchside manner ideal only for the Shrops of this world because (they know none of this) out of care and compassion he has been fitting him out with another man's life, filling the spaces with concrete hints. Shrop is grateful for any illumination proffered; all is grist to him when all else is moving, vanishing into someone else's memory. The day will come when, emptied out, he has to mop up the rejecta membra of just about anyone who has lived a life, just so that he can remember what a hand, a foot, a knee is, no longer even from the distant tutelage of his nervous system he no longer knows how to shake a hand, raise a foot, kneel a knee. Take Quent to Ground Zero? Why not, then? Any bloody destination aims him, gives him purpose, even if the horrors launched by those few seconds haunt him ever after. Hell, he murmurs, they're bound to go away, like everything else. I am the man split open and emptied out like a coconut.

If Shrop had become habituated to stares and gapes at his ruined state, Quent had long ago traveled beyond them into a dimension where symmetry, poise, balance, "normalcy" and shock did not exist. He too had sheets of paper crushed into his groin, or what remained of it. Ash had burned his eye, leaving a perpetual scum white as burned magnesium ribbon. He was also in Dresden and Hiroshima, becoming one of the spavined, as he calls them. The lace handkerchief rammed in his behind while flying burst upward like broken glass, under the impress of he never knew what inflammation of silica. He is not going to be shy about this, just a fellow mutant visiting headquarters.

"Up and over," says Shrop, as ever, powerful as in his days with the Austrian artillery. "In we go." Hoisting came naturally to him now after so many excursions together.

Not far. Doable via limousine, but Quent prefers what he calls the yellow proletariat of taxis, ever hoping for an Afghan driver with horrendous story to tell, almost as gruesome as his own. Intestine flung upward like soapy ribbon. The driver sat, watching Shrop perform with all the rehearsed boldness of a male nurse.

Up and at 'em, they whisper together, breathing hard, Quent relieved to be briefly rid of his chair, now compactly stowed, aghast at the sensations of his rootless buttocks on the horsehair escaping the taxi's seat. He feels a lick of triumph, with the coarse yellow tongue of its wolf lolling between his hams. A distinguished broken pilot is off to greet the war, gone like our youth too soon. He should have gone before this, yet, still, it is one of the great cities of the world, even now, with the Statue of Liberty in coppery green smithereens. Being a wise, holistic shrink, he says to himself, after the famous line of Mick Jagger to McKenzie Phillips, "I've been waiting for this since you were twelve." Now he attends the puberty of the city in its most dusted-up, devastated form; against the bogus concept of gentrification, which always made him snigger, he sets barbarification, a word deserving to be lost and wasted. They are arriving at the police cordon. He fishes out his Presidential *exeat* (let him go out, let him come in) and hands it over for inspection, by as it turns out not only police but firemen and ambulance workers, all of them veterans of asbestos, benzene, dioxin, and PCBs, spitting blood and gritty phlegm from the first, still coming to work because, well, this is now where they come to work, and always will, with a treasure isle by the name of Mesothelioma lolling in their future. "It's where," they counter, "*it's where*." To them, he's a hero, an amputee, one who has gone before. Who can deny him, not so much coated in medals and ribbons as made of them, some of them actually pinned on his sleeves for the sake of *Lebensraum*.

Two officers detach themselves from the crew to escort him. Shrop sits him down, wheels him gently forward at funeral pace, up a slight incline the better to view the pool of sludge big as an airfield in which bronze statues appear to be copulating around it, among intact skyscrapers the demolished ones, almost like blood-soaked bone split and rent but still uppish, their tops fractured into spears and splinters leaning out at an uncouth angle.

"Told you," Shrop tells him. "It's putrid."

Not a body in sight, Quent decides. Boy, have they done some clearing up, and yet it's almost as bad as it was years ago, what with seepage and rain, snow and avalanches. It must be even worse down below. The policemen nod, being of a later generation than those of the day and its aftermath. What is it like on first view then? Moshe Dayan's eye socket after the bullet has squirted through the binoculars and buzzed him with glass fragments. Deteriorating picket fences lurch and sag in the coils of razorwire. There is no way through.

"Told you, Quent," says Shrop. "No wheelchairs allowed. How'd you like to swim in all that?"

Quent is brooding on all the plane crashes he has seen, and on how they relate to this skid-track of mighty Lucifer. Odd, he thinks, how much so-called routine life—napkins being unfolded, cellphones not melting, hankies absorbing phlegm, vased dahlias shedding, poached halibut steaming—are going on right now in adjacent buildings, while . . . yes, well *while*, I can't stand to finish it. Were it not for death, so many would be crowding even my waiting room, beshitten with trauma. Ply the steel, o you wounded, legless wonder, make us well!

He sways where he stands on his stumps on the cushion applied to the wheelchair's seat, as if he has emitted the cry. But no, they will not be besieging him. They have, as he wryly puts it, bitten the dust and chewed it silly, making mud with their leftover spit. Time to leave, Shrop is saying, anxious to erase this foul emblem from his leaking brain, but Quent says, "No, I want to go beneath." And they let him, almost as afflicted by his paucity as by the wisdom-teethed sump.

"Don't," says Shrop. "You'll be sick."

"I've never been sick yet," Quent observes. "I'm an authority on colleagues returned to us in a bag of sundried cowflop. Lead on."

"*Lay* on," Shrop corrects him, for once remembering something. "Dream on, sir."

"Oh, this is different," Quent is gasping through his coughs as he surveys bloodsoaked collisions of dead cars, charging one another into weird forty-five degree encounters culled from Godard's *Weekend*. Gothic arches made of tin. Wheeled to a little flat disc of soil, he now sits in his shorts, whose legs have been sewn up, half-delighted by mess. Unprofessional thoughts are stirring within him, at least those of a headshrinker. He would like to know how badly you have behaved to merit such a travesty as this. He presupposes a world of balanced justice, wondering if his own mutilation matched the napalm he'd laid down or the bombs he'd released. But from equating thousands murdered with this appalling bloodbath, he shrinks, happier to wonder what happens when you stand against a wall, last cigarette uncertainly smoking, blindfold refused, hands bound, feet bound, a hapless pawn erect before the squad, just waiting. Is there a first impact, warning and numbing for the first fraction of a second, or does the first impact in the heart electrify you with a pain instantly quelled, smashed, as the rest of the volley burns its way into your chest? Do you get chance to tell yourself I have been shot already and it will soon be over as the sundered heart fails in its final beat? What does one ever know before, during the massive insult to the body? Is that the kind of thing that squares a debt? Does being shot merely give you a colossal dunt you have no chance to characterize?

Standing as he does, he feels ready for execution, but by whom? His escorts have receded, hanging back in deference yet appalled by his antic on the chair. He sees no corpses (long ago cleared away), but hankers for a glimpse of something human, replaced for his solace. An impulse to speak to the dead cars rises and wanes. They are here forever, maybe even scrubbed, but not polished, gray incinerated ghosts. He would like to address some crowd, but there is only Shrop, lost in a mesmerized glaze, not sure that, to enter here, he has not forfeited something human. He watches Quent, truncated and lowered, trapped between oration and laughter, responding perhaps to communal questions voiced in this place and then dissipated.

"Who's there?" Unuttered.

"Nobody but us ghosts." Unheard among the scuffle of rats, the dribble of water from above, the groan of something or somebody still not at rest. He peers ahead with gloom-habituated eyes and discerns what he cannot believe: an interior room, in which something glints and a shiny surface blooms as if recently deposited by a furniture-moving van. Intact. It cannot be. Nobody warned him. None of the hastily produced guidebooks explained the presence of what he saw: an almost dainty bar with bottles aligned on shelves against the wall. No customers, of course, but a gleaming brass rail unscathed and preposterous in that wen of salvage.

Quent sits to be wheeled, having left his electric wheelchair outside out of respect. Shrop moves him gently from the dim-lit zone to the worse-lit but shiny interior, with the mahogany bar on one side, the subway platform on the right, where trains no longer pass, depositing passengers for a drink and picking them up afterward. It is like a drowning man's last vision of his own nursery, inexplicably saved, there for ever, made over as an ante-chapel, a pearl among the devastation, to be relished, adored, then left. Who would dare drink in it now, or even sip, inhale? The two of them hear their own breath, shocked by sheer survival as they are. Quent thinks of his finest clients, the ones who went back to the world and prospered. This little chamber was like them. Shrop was thunderstruck he had not been here before. Could this be a secret the police and rescue workers were keeping to themselves, angelic crèche or eternal vestry? Surely, to be allowed in, you had to have your palm imprinted. To leave, you had to be rubber-stamped again.

"Eye of the storm," Quent says. "Just look at it."

"I'm wondering who the last drinkers were." Shrop has an insane desire to pour himself a large cognac. He goes inside the bar and clutches a bottle, but it is glued down and (he jests to himself) charged with cyanide so that the black hole might trap an extra victim. Hardly a stopover for the ambulances that came shrieking down from Albany and Latham.

"They want us to go," Shrop says. "Time's up."

"I'd rather stay," Quent answers. "This place is like the fountain of youth, where you can prolong your life. What's its story, I wonder? Hey, lift me up, big boy."

Heads canted back, they stumble out, back into the raw entryway, as puzzled as if they have encountered a phone booth in the garden at Versailles among all those conical trees and fretworked lawns.

"Did we imagine it, out of defiance?" Quent is not sure what he has seen, and now he's certain it was an illusion.

At his most complicated, Shrop, ever frantic for what he is losing, even the stuff that Quent feeds him about life as a philosopher, says he's sure they're in someone else's dream, someone dreaming them to a climax that will send them shuddering back to Quent's place of business, their minds crammed with prosaic questions about riverboats and wheelchairs.

"No," he says. "We were *vouchsafed* it." He feels proud of that verb, much as he did only the other day, telling Quent he no longer needed the verb *to be*.

"Oracular imagination then." Quent is lost.

"And blithe aversion," Shrop answers, taking refuge in sheer vocabulary, as if words were safe havens for time-travelers, amnesiacs, and phoenixes. The next hour, over hot Darjeeling tea, they stare at each other, confounded.

What breaks their spell, overpowering subdued Sibelius on the radio, is the so-called test of the EAS, three sudden barbaric blurts of ill-coordinated noise, too late and intrinsically inexact. The horse has flown. Years ago. Perhaps it was only when the Eiffel Tower was cut in half that the world knew civilization was over and done with and the heart to rebuild had begun to tire. The world was now full of makeshift maneuvers, stopgap features, arranged against the next attack, in a week or a month. There were many more devils than anyone had known; the faster you stamped them out in Indonesia, say, the faster they got to work in China. It was going to take the pair of them some time to assimilate the experience of Ground Zero, long postponed, and better postponed forever, thinks Shrop, pointlessly tapping his foot against the ottoman. One of the strangest things was the way the recycling department stuck to its rituals, even in the midst of carnage, ruin, refusing to pick up a bottle crate that had cans in it, and vice versa, refusing to accept newspapers in bins, boxes not reduced to flatness, and plastic bags of trash left by the roadside but not in garbage cans. Time and again, Shrop had phoned them to request pick-up at the end of pick-up day, arguing the toss with a supervisor until he or some other came, slung the offending garbage into the trunk of his car, and departed at LeMans speed, vowing never to get sucked into supplementary pick-ups again. Neither Shrop nor Quent had ever been able to disentangle the Byzantine rules of trash propriety observed in the middle of chaos, like some holy mysticism of the discarded. But Quent could see their point: where all was moving, shattered, reduced to dust and rubble, almost any firm rigmarole kept them calm, especially after the abandonment of postal service, express companies, parcel service, and the hesitant resurgence of barter. Only e-mail kept them going and talking in this electronic Eden perched in the lap of atrocity.

An old bitch gone in the teeth, Shrop murmured, unable to quote further. Didn't Auden stick a rotten orange on his mantelpiece in Oxford, putrid side outward? Already, he *knew*, even if to come there were men on the moon and robots on planets. The world as they both knew it, and in which the civilities of the psyche demanded and received a sensitive hearing in shrinks' offices planet-wide, had been given over to the louts and the kamikazes, simply because they knew how to work mayhem on a society too clever for its own good. If those who want nothing have even less, that spells the end of an acquisitive polity, does it not? Actually, Shrop's constant visits to Quent assumed for them both an almost liturgical aspect aloof from the disasters of

13
The Great

LOOKING BACK ON YESTERDAY'S EVENT, SHROP CANNOT UNDER-
stand why, in that crematorium of clerks and CEOs, the police
had troubled to frisk them both. Were they going to profane a
holy site? How would they do it? By spilling champagne, performing
lewd acts, playing loud rap? He supposed it merely gave the cops something to do; perhaps as curators and guards they felt like some old
Egyptian pharaoh overlooking the serried *mastabas* of his family and his
workmen, no longer there to do a practical job but to gloss a memory
too brutish to bear. Away from Quent, he felt himself regaining not
poise or serenity, but an evil sense of things, with portions of his former self vanishing through the spaces in a net. Was that what happened
to all visitors at the death pond? Unable to sustain their personalities,
they slid, sapped, into this huge La Brea of the mind? That was it. How
did it go? You visit the atrocity you think you yourself must be guilty
of and at once undergo a sea change along with millions. He had heard
of another sinister folkway that required the fit and well to hate the
aged and infirm, but up to now he had not realized that, confronted
with a horror, you at once assumed culpability for it, no excuses made.
It so much belonged to the race entire, there was no backing down
from it. Hardened criminals declined into lard at the very thought of it
and took the blame without a murmur. We all, he said to himself,
brought this down on us, merely by not being careful, but we also invited it simply because the scrapers we build antagonize the rest of the
world. It is architecture that gets us into trouble: monuments. To tell
him this, he called Quent, but the line was busy, Quent once again at
his computer. In the old days, Shrop told himself, a huge cinema organ
would have suffered the same fate. It was no longer a matter of showing the world the vast aspirations of the American dream. It was a matter of recognizing how low the so-called topless (he smirked mirth-
lessly at the double entendre) towers had been made to sink, as if
beheaded, and certainly not top-less in the sense of infinite altitude.

Hubris, he whispered. "Sheer fucking hubris. Not on the human
scale at all.

"Ours is bigger than yours." That too.

On a sudden whim, he lumbered over to a bookcase shedding volumes horsehair-fashion and tugged out a paperback entitled *Irving Snepp's Guide to Great Movies* and, wincing, murmured the titles he found therein: *The Great Adventure, The Great Adventure, The Great American Broadcast, The Great American Cowboy, The Great American Pastime, The Great Balloon Adventure, Great Balls of Fire, The Great Bank Hoax, The Great Bank Robbery, The Great Battle, The Great British Train Robbery* (aha), *The Great Caruso* (oh well), *Great Catherine* (ugh), *The Great Chase, The Great Dan Patch, Great Day* (English village awaits a wartime visit from Eleanor Roosevelt: guilty or not?), *Great Day in Harlem, Great Day in the Morning, The Great Diamond Robbery, The Great Dictator* (forgiven), *The Great Escape* (not guilty but Americanized), *The Greatest, The Greatest Battle, The Greatest Love, The Greatest Show on Earth, The Greatest Story Ever Told, Great Expectations* (not guilty), *Great Expectations* (vastly superior), *Great Expectations* (songless musical), *Great Expectations* (ho hum, will they never quit?), *The Great Flammarion, The Great Gabbo, The Great Gambini, The Great Garrick* (Americanish), *The Great Gatsby*—here he almost throws up, scorning the next *Gatsby* and some forty-eight others, certain he has found a principle vile in conception and blasted by history, yet reluctant to blame the U.S. for all of it. Oh, it must be more than fifty now. Grandiosity abounding, he says. Is this why? Is it partly Edna Ferber's fault for *So Big* and A.B. Guthrie, Jr.'s for *The Big Sky*? Had they built their scrapers low, would they have been flyable into? No one has yet jetted a pyramid, Egyptian or Mexican. One day soon, he decides, he will be on the right track for discovering why. If America had pursued the humble life? Tiny graves like the proles who built the pyramids. No, there is more to it than that, he thinks; it goes beyond grandiosity and humility into, well, all the different kinds of adjustment Bach wrote about, when the chastened lyric soul alights on the notion of the bow, when one sings *Sleepers Awake, Heart and Spirit, Jesus, Joy of Man's Desiring*, or even *I Stand with One Foot in the Grave.* That sort of self-denial, acceptance, forbearing, unostentatious enough to get him forgotten soon after his death, which is what he was writing about anyway, and his music with him. Soon after he died, a sheaf of his cantatas went for fifty dollars, the engraving plates for *The Art of Fugue* were sold as scrap metal, and old Bach manuscripts got used as wrapping paper by Leipzig butchers.

That kind of I'm Nobody, he whispers in the dark as the winter sun has gone down. "*He knew.*" You have to endure a passage as a nobody first, in which case I will qualify as a man without a memory, whose memory is that of someone else who did not much enjoy being anyone at all. He phones Quent again, but the line remains busy while, out there, not far downtown, the Brea sump, as he now calls that ghastly hecatomb, waits for him to visit it again, not with shovel or drill, but with his shortened friend, the most genial guru the sump has seen.

14
Nurse Tumulty

QUENT'S PIPE DREAMS INCLUDE, SINCE SHE LOOKS GLAMOROUS, Ethne Heinkel, who flies down to Florida in her own plane, complete with two pilots who sleep in an adjoining room, and her two spoiled children. On a whim she is gone, returning a week later with a tan. But it is not she who occupies his mind today, it is Nurse Tumulty, ever presumptuous: "We're not too good today, are we? We're not fair to middling any more, we're a little bit poorly, I can tell." This is the accomplice plural, as he calls it, implying her share in his condition without her feeling an atom of pain. She uses this plural on all occasions, even for defecation: "We're having a bit of trouble getting it out today, aren't we? Have you been up to some hanky-panky now?" He sometimes thinks there are two of *him*, the well him and the sick one, not just the sick one magnified beyond praise. It is her way of interfering with him, this fat we, far from royal. Quent remains convinced he can pluralize himself without any help from her, but she won't listen. Never mind, he counsels himself, it's a habit that will come in useful whenever you feel a bit divided, at odds within. She used to nurse Alzheimer's patients with an extra diagnosis, the violent and coprophilic ones, so she's come up in the world, has Tumulty.

Tumulty, he decides, is beefy enough to clean anyone's clock. A parade of beeves, she is diabetic, but persists in swigging soft sugary drinks as if she were King Farouk, and wolfing cheeseburgers plunged in county mayo. He estimates her weight at two hundred pounds, maybe two fifty, it's hard to tell because he needs to see her simultaneously from all angles. When she has the needle out, she sometimes brandishes it at him, but never delivers the dose, all of a sudden cooking up sympathy for the shrink in the wheelchair.

"Well, bad boy, what did *you* do?"

"Took a little ride with Shropshire," he says lamely.

"Oh, him, the dependent one. I'll soon have the pair of you to look after." Off her comes a whiff of peppermint laced with apricot or tangerine, he can't be sure, and it's an aroma stronger than the one coming off the little rubber-ended sticks she shoves her cuticles back with. Fragrant in a vulgar way, she never comes for duty without a bouquet of something or other wafting off her. Truth told, she haunts the make-up counters for free samples and thus, as she sees herself, makes herself desirable day after day; but Quent's vestigial desires fix on Ethne Heinkel, who one day, he's certain, will whisk him away to Palm Beach for an interminable stay, one among many riding chairs.

Well, what did he see down there? A spoiled vacancy plus a crowd of dancers and gesticulators all in black oilskins, goggles and black rubber boots, their habitual get-up, color of mourning. Indeed, they have daubed themselves with oil, tar, and reddened bandages from a long-forgotten war. It's the kind of outfit that dreads death, then emboldens all to welcome it, lament its passing, laud its reappearance. He is shocked, of course, but perhaps no more than when peering at later Rothko for some object to fix his fighter pilot's vision on. He knows what he likes, and he likes populating voids with figures, so as not to be alone with the massive forces of nature. Hovis Tumulty is massive, yes, but he has taught himself to relish her bulk, the insouciant aroma of greens and sulfur she leaves behind in the toilet as he chugs his way toward that tainted shrine. He has, you might say, the beginnings of an utterly impersonal view of just about everything, which is not to say he does not care. He does, but he has already achieved what he calls indifferent distance. Whatever happens, he notices it and sees right through it, murmuring This is what happens next. It is within this corral of ideas and responses that he finds the answer to Shrop's amnesia: merely the proximate thing, to be savored as much as deplored. He long ago gave up the professionally decorous notion of not responding, not interfering. Shrop is a friend and remains so. He would take offense if his friend and shrink unbefriended him. So he holds forth, gently equipping the bereft philosopher with the facts of another man's life, all ideas: in other words to give him a life back without the pain of having to think about it.

None of this stops Quent's mind from questioning, though, wondering why so many hate the US of A, say for scorching Hiroshima and Nagasaki, for swinging a big stick, for inventing a civilization of advertisement. It could also be, he thinks, a simple and obvious dislike of American speech, clothing, money, much as post-war Italians used to despise Germans with their can of corned beef, their lederhosen and rasping glottal stops. What had the gang of young people been singing down there, under the huge anthracite scab? "Hard times come again no more," which in its paradoxicality expressed, he thought, a hope for

15
Idlewild

LMOST AS A RELIEF FROM HIS PREOCCUPATIONS OF THE DAY, Shrop is juggling names, going back over what he now supposes is his life story, told him by Quent and then read back in tentative certainty, or improvised by Shrop himself on premises invented by Quent. He doesn't quite know, but thinks it better to have, or have had, a life rather than a ghost of one. Ground Zero, Death Sea, La Brea II seem adequate yet not quite right, and WTC no use at all. After reviewing possibilities, he begins to consider that old favorite of his, Idlewild, with its suggestion of weeds running riot, uncared for and in every sense unoccupied. Perhaps Idlewild will do, he thinks, for a hateful blemish, and he resolves to try it out, gradually shifting his mind from an Austrian lake to something much less fertile, though contrary. If that was a no-brainer, this will be a no-breather: after three years, the fumes and smoke go on and, because there was twice the heat required to deprive steel of half its compressive strength, the columns had buckled, stripped of their ceramic fireproofing. Some devil had made us a gift of this.

Nor is this newly named Idlewild the only strange thing that is going on. Where Quent lives, there are bizarre neighbors, not just Ethne Heinkel who has two private pilots and an eight-seat Hawker jet at her disposal, if she can only stomach the one-hour ride to Teterboro airport. Her name prompts him to consider further, picking out Jonelle Bormann, she who works on some local newspaper infamously dubbed the Shite Sheet and, weirdly, goes from door to door tapping and asking for sugar and sunblock cream as if they belonged together in some ritual blessing. Surely she formed a matching set with the gin-sodden Londoner Elspeth Tod, whose many chains jingled and jangled, announcing her imminent arrival as if she were a Swiss heifer. Linked with the gigolo, Ettore Helldorf, and the French baker Claes Barbie, these people seemed cut from the same cloth. Mentally he lined up the names as on a hymnal board in a church and surveyed them severely:

Heinkel
Bormann

Tod
Helldorf
Barbie.

Nazis all, he concluded with miserable glee. Now, what of their first names, carefully calculated to deceive?

Ethne
Jonelle
Elspeth
Ettore
Claes.

Window-dressing, he thought. Then he added the real-estate broker Pensée Fegelein, and Sigourney Speer whom be had not met, and that clinched it. A Nazi cell, not going to any great lengths to conceal itself, and already equipped with a private jet for escape, if necessary, to Argentina. So where did the Rumanian aspirant novelist, Nadia Fortescu, belong? Was she the red herring, the mastermind of the group, she who claimed her dog forwarded her mail from Bucharest? These, he guessed, were infamous descendants of Nazi sadists, eager to hide but unashamed of their names. Did they in some way, right next to the legless war hero cum shrink Quentin Montefiore del Patugina, complement him, as psychopaths reclaimed, or historic seed transplanted? Elsewhere in the building, he knew, well apart from this oddly compatible platoon of neighbors, there was the prolific novelist Saul Poindexter, a man with no time to talk, not even to say hello: a fructophobe, a nightworker, and addicted to French fries. Surely this titan among men could have depicted Quentin's neighbors with his usual flamboyant mordancy, but he had not bothered to, so maybe Quent should have cultivated him more instead of the others. Shrop marveled at the haphazard way things grouped themselves, leaving interpretation to thinkers. Surely, he reasoned, these theoretical siblings would one day do something so atrocious, the world would end, but not before all of them had been hanged from clothes-pegs with piano wire.

For the first time, he had become aware of Quent's clique, of what lived and skulked around them when they were together. He could tell he was on the point of weary distress; usually he took things better than this, certainly not seeing demons where there were none, whatever their names were. The smoky horror he now called Idlewild had demoralized him, but also Quent's response to it. An out-of-the-body experience, he called it, lurking in the pit of the stomach afterwards, exposing its viewers to ruin and nightmare, perhaps only because thousands had perished in a twinkling and for the most part were not going to come back. Millions more had died in other wars, but not as briskly, and he could not rid himself of the notion that he would never recover: terminally sickened, uselessly degraded, perfunctorily ended; he no longer felt he qualified as a man, whoever he was. There was no longer any possible identity for which he qualified. He could not free himself of the supposition that it was all his own fault for—oh, irrelevant reasons, forgetting his philosophy, exploiting his old friend Quent, mocking the war hero cut off at the thigh. He could not quite decide if he had been seeing Quent before the event, or had the event started him off? Perhaps he had already been going to the dogs months earlier, in which case it didn't matter. He was a junkie of some kind, but the new addiction—aching to go back again and again just to prove to himself how ugly it was—had started three years ago, on 9.11 or the twelfth, and he was now suffering from some new type of existential fugue, hoping to outstrip it, but how, seeing it was like sea-sick jet-lag on top of food poisoning. He had been punched in the solar plexus by Jack Dempsey, who bathed his own face in beef brine and chewed pine to toughen his jaw. If a shrink could not help, and over three years he had merely kept Shrop psychological company, as Shrop thought, without striking to anything but amnesia as the cause of it all. That Quent might be playing tricks on him, out of frustration, he did not consider. Anyway, if he could no longer be Shropshire, then he might as well lift the name of that old fogey airport and become Idlewild himself, just to mystify the next retinue of shrinks.

Arriving at his usual time, he told Hovis Tumulty, for no good reason, "I've been denatured, honey. I really need help now. Is he expecting me?"

Actually, Dr. Quent was not, having put himself and his chair into the hands of a cab driver who would take him back to the site for further absorption. Now Shrop saw it: as in Sf movies, the witnesses felt an urge to revisit the touchdown site of the saucer and dared not disobey.

* * *

He went, heedless of arrangements, in a hurry to do what? After him, I start blanking out, able to think only of a bog littered with cranes and ladders, improvised tents of canvas and garbage bags, heaps of assorted rubble, the soft and smeary, the coal-hard, the in-between stuff like congealed plasticine, all waiting to be carted away. What I eventually find is an isolated-looking Quent, erect on the edge, clearly having been refused clearance this time, balanced on his stumps in the mire, so that it looks as if he's a normal human who's been planted. Chest bare, with his medals all confined to two sticks fastened to his chest skin with two safety pins causing him no apparent pain. Military aviator's cap, much maltreated, on his head, and around him a small gaggle of New Yorkers (I presume) all dressed in dun or shiny black plastic. He seems to be raving, but, halted in my tracks, I am not close enough to get his full drift.

"The pain in the belly from nights of worry, the *something something* of tormenting yourself that the whole thing is your fault, yours and mine." He lifts his cap to them, and now I distinguish the pale blue ribbon around his neck. He is giving them what he used to call their money's worth (phrase purloined from therapy). Here's a nice reversal. He's giving them his own stuff, raw and presumably unrehearsed, not the almost de rigueur stanzas from Auden that, skeptical and clinical, have become the event's facile litany. No, this is the Quent of military days, I guess, before he was abbreviated. If they think he's planted himself in the muck, they have another think coming. Did he get all this from a book, or think it up himself? They do not argue with him, not yet anyway, and with this ghost of atrocity past they may not, since he has an antique flavor to him, still retains the military rasp in his voice. Hey, I almost yell, that's my shrink you're messing with. Leave him alone for those who have an appointment.

There is no rhythm to what he says, and I catch only a word here and there: *honor* and *Roosevelt* and *infamy* (of course), *shame* and *rebuilt*. It is the spectacle of him that speaks to them. Now he raises his thigh, what is left of it, and they gasp at the lack of leg, the wobble he has to make to stay erect, and that image of him, cruising his right stump over the mud makes them wonder about the left, either buried or just missing. Long ago I read some German novella about a family who planted their kid in the garden and watched him thrive. This is different, though. He will never thrive; he has no stems.

At last he has seen me hovering, but he merely flashes a perfunctory salute, a senior man's casual response to a junior's flat open palm up by the eye. No time for all that. Now he sings God Bless America, a hearty tone coming from so short a frame, but he carries it off well, unfurling a flag he has had secreted on his person, in his shorts, and sagely wraps himself in it against the chill of October in Manhattan. Raggedly they join in, no more able than he to hit the high notes, but mouthing it like daunted wolves. I add a voice to his and theirs, but it's a feeble chant best abandoned, and all I can think of is, elsewhere or even close by, caviar and champagne, fresh cooked shrimps in a piquant sauce, the habitual nouvelle cuisine poetic dispersal of almost no food at all in thin layers on a costly plate. Life goes on, as we like to say, whatever goes wrong, and I think of Dresden not that long ago, their last supper before Bomber Command arrived over them. Is this *Schadenfreude* I am feeling? Or just the pique of one whose appointment so blatantly has been nuked? Will I now sit in the chair if I can, and will he now spout his misery in fifty-minute blurts? Stop him, Shrop. No, leave him to it, it's an outing of an obscure type. Is this the Italian side of his nature coming out, and should such sentiments as he professes be better made through the grille to his confessor, Father Jerome? And, come to think of it, where are the cryptic Nazis of his retinue (if such) on this day of days?

* * *

He bears Quent back after washing his thighs down with a nearby hose. The walk will clear the air, he thinks, finding Quent oddly silent after his speechmaking debut. For October, it is windily warm, as it would be in Paris, and for the short trip back the only sound that passes between them is an occasional squeak from the wheels. However, once Quent is back home, he becomes voluble, complaining of sadness and melancholy like some physical animal stranded in his abdomen, making him feel inadequate at his work.

"You skipped my appointment," Shrop chides him. "What if I'd needed urgent attention?"

"I canceled them all before going out," Quent tells him. "You'll find the message when you get home."

"Screw that, old friend. Too late to count."

"Then I'm sorry," he hears. "We'll start again. Thank you for escorting me home." Hovis Tumulty has been and gone, leaving the apartment a hive of glitter.

"It's time," Quent tells him, "we got back to your life story, such as it is. You were telling me."

"You up to this? I mean just resuming."

"Of course. Isn't the mind the nimblest creature in the common fields? We underestimate it."

"It can wait," Shrop says. "It's more important to get you back on an even keel, which is what you weren't earlier on."

"You said that you gave away your money because you fancied a simple life. Very impressive."

"I rather fancy," Shrop tells him, "it had to do with my feeling that I was all washed up as a philosopher. I had no knowledge, so I wanted no money. I was emptying myself out, see. So I took to school teaching, oh just tiny villages hither and yon in Lower Austria. I called this my suicidal period, toiling away at something I felt would be good for me, but wasn't. Something to drink?" He fetches wine from the freshly scrubbed kitchen. "But the kids saved me from myself, from all the rows I had with their parents and the other teachers. Are you sure you want all this now?"

"On, on."

"Instead, I took up employment as gardener's assistant at a monastery near Vienna, a sort of Saint Fiacre. That was a good, simplistic time. But you already know all this. It was you who told me about it, wasn't it?"

"No, you had already suggested much of it in exchanges you don't remember. Then you designed a mansion for one of your sisters. I know this, and marvel at the sudden changes you went in for."

For Shrop the scene changes abruptly, their two voices vanishing into aural mime and, instead, out of thin air, as we say, as if a horde of gulls were dive-bombing a fish tied to the head of some poor sailor overboard, as in old Scandinavian myths, the voices shrill and dwindling terminate among the thousands of paper sheets floating to the ground in no great hurry with lots of sideways motion. These were the voices of hundreds plunging from windows in that traditional New York exit, as if saying to themselves dream on, this is not real, you are really on the way home to a woman with skin smooth as piano keys, among you a smattering of undesirables and some politicos of indifferent stamp, all of them in swandive wrenched past the brown bared teeth of the exposed buildings. Note the final cries from high howl to a series of bass grunts, almost a kind of orchestra, less attainable on a morse tapper than on a canvas where everyone is moving in front of buildings also on the move, almost melting. And the watcher forms "dove" in the mind, faintly aware of its being a rebuked past tense, but as well the waddling bird of peace. What *were* those suddenly chopped-off cries, ranging from "God" and "Mother" to "No" and "Help," not quite the agonized repertoire of the soon-to-be-dead pilot, who may have rehearsed this exit more than once, even if only for the Safety Board's transcriptions that eventually show up in the aviation magazines unless asterisked or dashed out. "God," that vast omnivorous appeal should have had a life of prayer and supplication behind it, though none of that would count anyway, apart from evoking an old legal teaser, to wit or viz. If you shoot a jumper who pours past your window, are you a murderer? God bombs, they say. Then there is "Mother," a respectable cri de coeur, except she is exempt from help and at best can only stand below to receive the body, unless there is some magical bail-out clause permitting the umbilical cord to somehow stretch, bungee fashion, and catapult the jumper back home again. Even rehearsed, it somehow loses force, while "No," akin to Quent's jussive "On," appeals to a god of negatives, requiring a halt in the proceedings. Or "No" means let it not happen, it is beyond the bounds of rational possibility, and it is the no that gets smashed at so many feet per second per second, begging its own cancellation. Would anyone cry "Help" (or "Wolf"), on the off chance of intercepting during the crash-dive a free-faller from higher up equipped with twin parachutes who will scoop you up just like an eagle with a trout, the same swinging motion of the claws, striking home in aeronautical splendor? No one yet, at least among the recorded, has let out with "My husband tried to bring a pail of bent nails—which he intended to straighten out on the way down." Soon the studious faces are at rest, their infatuated loathing of this event washed clean away in a slurry of wasted fluids, and there is absolutely no help for them because they were jumping from fire, smoke, gas and volts into fire, smoke, gas and volts, unless there is the possibility that they just aim themselves at the zone where people are, and hope for the best, gravely self-tutored in this final act that there is no bounce at the end of plunge, none of that old snow-drift stuff that saved a few wartime pilots who fell minus their chutes and came to at the bottom of a shaft, stars peeping up on high and a German voice bellowing *Wer da?* Getting out was always a problem. There is none of the semen-soaked brass of Tchaikovsky to herald arrivals from on high, not even a polite question expecting no rejoinder: "Where do you think *I'm* from?"

Then, Shrop wonders as he imagines the jumping hordes briefly alongside their insurance forms, and vainly reaching out to them for support; this can hardly rank as *Fantasia for any Gentleman* composed by a blind Rodrigo. Without the mere thought of music, and how music is, he cannot bear to think, even though, chez Quent, he thinks so well

65

of Hovis Tumulty that he picks up his debris before she arrives to clean. The trick, he finds, is to imagine them all bouncing back up to their windows, now encased in flame. There is no Ellis Island to land at, mercy only for a few tokens grabbed before jumping: a photograph in a redhot frame (what wrecks a burning palm?), a bit of phone melting off its cradle, a glass of water used to douse. The few moments in the incendiary room are worse than the half-gainer into hell below, worse by far than the last few moments in a DC-3 after hooking on and wishing the green light would fail at the end of whoever's dock. Could one soar to one's smash-up while trying to memorize a snatch of Debussy, say, one of the six sonatas for four flutes, viola and harp? Just a few bars to enter the other country with. Shrop cannot think of any more. He knows it all happened, not far away, and wonders if the tilted glacis of either tower might have formed a sled-run down which to slide on one's back, supine akimbo, to an eventual snap of the ankles and knees, but survival at almost any cost, unless you went headfirst. He imagines the human relics contorted in the high octane mud, blood and the milk of human kindness boiling away together.

He is profoundly shaken up, by even this vignette of cataclysm; zealous scholar of himself, certainly of his abstruse philosophy, he worries about the words uttered during the fall and recovers from his punctured memory that old phrase of Western Union: For free repetition of doubtful words, please call. . . . How doubtful can those words have been when they seemed so predictable? Were they what had inspired Quent to impale himself on his own decoration? and stump into the mud? Certainly Shrop thinks, whoever cannot face the memory and enduring image of it belongs in a *Wimpiad* all of his own. Now, should they rebuild it? They have tried but without much hope. Then rebuild it elsewhere, in another country. In Iraq even.

"What do you think?" Quent, stumps swathed in Tumulty bandages, is supping a mug of soup. Shrop asks him again and waits.

"Build the towers again?"

"Not bloody likely," Quent blurts. "If they do, I'll pretend they did no such thing."

"Why?"

"'Sa graveyard, that's what it is." There is hard liquor in the soup. Quent is recovering from anti-climax, and Shrop abandons all hope of returning to their tidy deal.

16
The Hot Gates

WHY WAS HE CLINGING TO OLD FORMULAS SUCH AS LANGUAGE itself and verbalizing screams and howls that remained, for the whole of the distance down, uncouth cries from the heart, too primitive to be dressed up in dictionary stuff and akin to what came out of those singers who performed vocalise from scat to melismatics: a raw shout doing duty for the human soul confronting the unspeakable? Shrop had no idea, but realized he was gussying things up a little to keep his mind from nonstop suffering as the chorus (or indeed choirus) of several hundred doomed hit home with ghastly penultimate wail, all in a few seconds at that, in each tower, the throat shudder of the articulate animal going down to death at gathering speed, yet with obstinate mind functioning full tilt to the very end. Put together, those screams gave back civilization to the jungle, red in tooth and claw, yet with all that verbal detritus of forms and papers fluttering slow motion around, alongside, them, having no intrinsic weight. *Ah, oh, ugh,* degenerating into indecipherable fear, phoneme from the lion's mouth, the wildebeest's rear end. Maybe a Roman noise, raucous below the fiddling, maybe a Jewish one from the dank steps into showers—oh certainly a Jewish noise, yet lost because those who heard it best were those dropping down among it.

Perhaps even worse, the slow-motion spectacle arrives of a solitary human spreadeagled against the grid of the northern tower, having jumped or scrambled outside only to fall as if slowed in egg-white, invited to have a long final meditation on what he has just done, in that dwarfing set of fire and smoke appointed chief meditant of all office workers, his image burned into the concrete, at ease as much as a waterman on the meniscus of a swimming pool.

When will Shrop see worse sights, or have them brought to him fresh and searing by those whose eyeballs have seen too much already? As he peers at this image of the falling cross-shaped human, working his brain for some kind of meaning, he remembers how several floors collapsed into a space of three feet, crushing but themselves crushed. A blare of shredded debris falls from the sky, black in silhouette and twirling in lost sunlight. *Don't look up* had been the order of the day, pounded into megaphones by those who *had* looked up and looked down fast. Erect bottles of beer on the dust-caked bar haunt him, there to taunt and dishearten. It will never go away, but always get bigger, more and more noxious, easily of greater visual heft than parroted reminders that, during a cable TV sale being conducted even as the dust settles and blows up again matching an old lyric about a whiter shade of pale, it will be possible to show a different movie on each screen in the house, even if no one is alive to watch.

This is just how his head feels, full of raucous dissonance and, as his feet falter, stairways from which whole sections of steps have been untimely ripped, so that nothing connects with anything, and that is what has happened to his godforsaken memory. Why then recall so much of what the world calls 9.11 (except Europeans who, speaking bald and coarse Euro, write their date 11.9, which somehow lacks the fatidic ring of the other, seeming more destined, more diabolically contrived). He continues to nibble away mentally at a rough and ready formula he phrases as follows: having lost a piece of his vital memory, he allows Quent to fill the space with a purloined life that is vaguely familiar to him, which he then recycles to Quent as his own—Shrop's—thing, promptly refurbished and embellished by Quent into a fine and happy slice of life. This, he says, animated by horror into a new and suspicious vigilance, is what it is to be Quentinized. As a witness, then, as one who hears the dastardly report from a bearer doomed to execution merely for having carried it from Thermopylae, the *hot gates*, is he still competent or has magically subverted amnesia somehow disqualified him, from remembering or reporting, from the proverbial eyeful to the equally poignant cry from the lungs? He has not enough ballast to respond to these self-inflicted questions, though with enough to formulate them, only to have them answered by a gaping hole in the flank of a once immaculate tower. The main question happens to be the simplest: has disaster ruined him even at a distance, he already beginning to roll downhill under an avalanche of details to be pursued and overtaken by another avalanche of urban debris triggered by a bang?

Could anyone be thus undermined by catastrophe, or would he somehow soldier through, like everyone else, they sapped and stunned as never before, as a tower and a myth have collapsed together? Already he had become used to having Quent officiate over him, bidding him do this or that, fortify such and such a memory, let another one bleed away into the dark hereafter of snubbed ideas. He had actually allowed Quent to dictate his previous life, even to own and dominate it as a condemned playground of his own—Quent's. Now this condition, a usurper's sleight of hand, was worsening: the usurper was become a madman or at least a mutant taking on airs and graces, bucking for five star general on the terminal moraine of disaster. So then, he murmured, what now? Can you see his way through, how he might come back into his own now Quent has failed him? It is the kind of question Lady Murasaki sometimes caches in her dawdling, not exactly demanding a finite answer, especially if you know her ways that well and have some glimmering of high-falutin, soulfully esthetic Japanese courts. Here, though, the intruding question should be smacked on its bum and sent packing, since it invites a participation in excess of readerly compliance. *Que faire?*, as they often remarked at another court already mentioned. What a dither.

What would *you* do?

Have you already spotted Quent's ploy and guessed whose life the bewildered Shrop has been tempted into living?

Clearly he has to do something about Quent, but the pair of them have passed the watershed; supposedly, a one-minute exposure to Ground Zero will change your life irrevocably, thus earning you the contempt of London's blitzed millions and Dresden's dead and Hiroshima's vaporized. The generation that worried itself sick about the bomb has been succeeded by one that dreads white powder and the ultimate knock-out. What we have now is not so much the blind leading the blind as the maimed leading the maimed, the bully pulpit leading the lost. They are not going to hang fire, oh no. They daren't.

17
A Cry Lost

THE ONE CRY HE DID NOT THINK OF IN THIS CONNECTION WAS the looping orgasmic one, not exactly remote from his personal experience, nor in its very nature devoid of a certain delicious pain. People leaping to their deaths are not supposed to rejoice with quite that degree of babbling falsetto or baritone gasp. It is possibly only that those who do have not been recorded; final, appetitive cries have less audience than famous last words, although our literature might just as well be replete with the former as with the latter, *vide* all the talk of bridegrooms' hungry zeal as they enter the bedchamber, and so on. Shrop wishes he could have been there, even if only to hear the roar of ruin blotting out all human cries, even the cries of those who having jumped get brained by falling debris on the way down. As the floors of the building telescope downward one after another, translating the height of each room into the depth of each floor, the building is no place to be, upright, flat or crouched. The concertina principle holds sway, though many felled by it had no idea that such a thing existed. Freedom of choice, he murmurs; who was the pianist who refused to play concerts when it was not snowing and the noise of traffic garbled the tone of the hall? He does not know or care, knowing that the older you get the less you care to know about your own random thoughts, where they come from and whose they once were and who will copycat them from you. Better by far, he thinks, not to have such thoughts at all, when there is no temptation to hunt them down and mount them on your walls.

They roast, they jump, they land with a gravity-thick thud that has no forgiveness in it unless they have launched into snow. Ah, that's where the pianist's snow came from! He wonders if there has yet been a count, a triage dividing jumpers from roasters. The streets, if any remaining, were such a shambles that no one could possibly go through to make a count. And the various cries are gone forever, all of them combining in the last and fatal abstraction (there is nothing else to fall into), but unavailable to the ear that had never thought to garner such things. Like everyone else, he has never before thought of such events and the peculiar privileges attending them: a cry heard, a cry lost, whether of friend or foe, the entire recitation of infuriated incredulity wasted on a world of noise. What, he wonders, would have been his own contribution on 9.11, if not death so quick it was voiceless? Would he have burned or jumped? He thinks he would have burned, raising a colossal squeal until oblivion set in. Now it is all headstones shattered and shredded amid their coating of poisonous white ash.

Somewhere, not from Quent, he has picked up a monstrous piece of media English: "such a size differential between the two of them," meaning one's bigger than the other, and he loathes it, lamenting that no matter how much ruin there has been there hasn't been enough. He envisions all the bad constructions in the world heaped up and shattered, but abandons the pipe dream, instead fixing on such unjokesy double entendres as the surnames *Isay* and *Onslow*, which yield up "I say" and "On slow," and even the complete names such as that of the composer *Deems Taylor*, whose first name is also a verb. Small provender, needed by a desperate man losing things both recent and distant.

"Are you back down to earth then?" He doesn't mean to provoke Quent, but now wonders if he should.

"If I had feet," his shrink answers, "they would be in this basin of water."

"Well," he says, "am I still your patient-client?"

"If you wish, Shropshire."

"How formal of you. Can we rebegin?"

"Whenever you want. First, though, would you oblige me with a kettle of hot water? *Medium* hot."

Off Shrop goes kitchenward, grumbling, doomed to another recital of stuff not his but, if not, then whose?

* * *

Shrop is back in his life as a gardener's assistant, longing for the smell of loam, the sour tang of stale chrysanthemums, the purple autumn splurge of ornamental cabbages, just about shirking the invitation to design and build his sister's house, as if there were no link between gardening and building. How come, however, if this was his life, he knows so little about it? He is much clearer about his musical talents, mainly at the clarinet, but also when whistling; he could whistle long passages of demonstrable difficulty, sometimes even intervening in chamber music being performed for friends and being taken seriously as a theorist and critic by the chamber players themselves. He would not quite whistle at them, but expound his theories with pointed élan, swiftly moving from diffidence to bravura display. He might have been Mahler or Strauss himself. Among the serious questions raised about him was the possible influence of a clever mind on his musical taste, and vice versa (much the unlikelier of the two hypotheses). No composer, he remained a harmonic analyst, and, as some discerning observer put it, did with his voice and mind in impromptu lectures what he might have done with the clarinet had he been called upon during a chamber performance. Often speaking off the cuff, as was his habit, he would pose a series of questions to himself and then spend a good deal of time answering them, apparently without previous pondering. No one believed this of course, but they found themselves lulled by his technique of serendipitous wandering, as if, a true gardener, he were doing a pensive survey of his verbal garden.

A fellow of his college, he nonetheless despised academic life, especially the would-be brilliant repartee at high table, from which he removed himself quite early on, snacking on a pork pie and country bread in his own rooms, and opening a can of sugared fruit, or treating himself to fish and chips with vinegar, which he ate while strolling the back streets of Cambridge. Almost an affectopath during this period, he nonetheless remained difficult to get on with, sometimes chiding friends for intellectual lapses without recognizing the hurt he caused. It could only be said that he was even tougher on himself.

Now, at last, Quent, his stumps somewhat soothed, breaks in with what seems a merely querulous question: "Did you not write a book that was to be published only after your death? If so, where is it?"

Shrop shakes his head, bewildered, unable to think far enough into the future to anticipate his death. No title, as there might have been, and no date, of course. How puzzling.

Deftly shirking an impulse that tells him it is time to become interested again in Quent and his uncanny doings, Shrop shifts instead to the provenance of Idlewild, noting how, around 15,000 B.C. the glacier had stopped along the area now occupied by the Grand Central Parkway, and the melting of its terminal moraine left behind ridges and hills dotted with kettle ponds. Tidal basins formed in what would later become Flushing Meadows. Ten thousand years later, during the Paleo-Indian/Big Game Hunting stage, tools were found in Bayside, the work of Indians who lived in small bands, hunting mammoths and mastodons. His blood warms to this prospect, and the shambles or knacker's yard it truly was. Rushing past the Mattinecock Indians of around 1500 A.D., he envisions the marsh, a blank sump, that eventually became the Idlewild golf course requiring the filling in of acres of marshy tidelands with hydraulic fill. The old Indian name for this place, *Idalwilde,* meaning peaceful and savage, has always taken him by storm; he must have murmured it thousands of times, ever heading back from the golf course and the marshes to his old friend the glacier and its terminal moraine. He needs this wilderness, most of all when disconsolate, weary, indecisive, misanthropic, managing through some sleight of mind-body to adjust to the topography of the time, to a startling miscellany of conditions ranging from 15,000 B.C. to 1948, when Idlewild Airport opened on July 1st.

At first a thousand acres, Idlewild grew to five times that size, and Shrop exults in the way people referred to the place casually, as to something cherished and taken for granted rather than bumped up into what it soon became, to honor JFK's memory: John F. Kennedy International Airport. Perhaps because built on the site of a golf course, haven of peace and quiet, self-centered serenity and patient walking, the place appealed to non-strident emotions much as a vision of tundra or ocean beguiles the human race, making them crave salt of the sea, tang of the turf. The airport, as Shrop saw it, survived even the rededication of 1963, the point of the repeated ritual being to clear the mind of glacier and terminal moraine, priming it with peppy slogans such as "Grab a bite for your flight" and "Do some gift shopping." Those millions who did had no idea they were squelching in the marsh, skidding along on ice. For him, Idlewild has always had a built-in nostalgia despite the constant slithering about of construction workers and kangaroo cranes. Neighborhood diehards refused to call the place anything but Idlewild, surrendering to an atavism they did not know they possessed, but kind of siding with Mayor La Guardia who once, returning from a trip that brought him back to Newark Airport, refused to leave his seat on landing, complaining that his ticket said New York was his final destination. He too looked beyond the airport of his name to the aerodrome at the golf course but without Shrop's veritable land-hunger, his dread of what the future might bring: a third-world airport, ill-succeeding Idlewild's early historic architectural presence. Shrop's constant dream of the place demanded long low piers, DC-7s and Constellations lining up beside them, four piston engines

apiece with, farther back, under roofs like transparent umbrellas, the
rest of the fleet hugely housed, making him half-remember a French
poem about the granary hangars of Port-Aviation, manmade mono-
liths all, vast enough to inspire dreams of a Creator coming into his
own at last without help from Mother Nature.

Of course the romance of the place speaks to him. Is any airport
quite devoid of glamour? La Guardia field stands on the grounds of
Gala Amusement Park, the former Glenn H. Curtis Airport and the
later North Beach Airport, evocative names to Shrop who, however,
finds magic only at Idlewild, starting point of the nightly Sleeper to
Paris, first class only. He might be said to have succumbed to the aerial equivalent of the Madonna of the Wagons-Lit, except *his* madonna
has a thousand Hellenic faces. He responds to even the savvy clinical
cry of the hygienist at the dental office situated right at the end of one
runway, Robert Trager, D.D.S. presiding, there since the opening in
1948, complaining about people from India who chew "the beetle nut"
that makes your teeth completely black. When you fly, he says, and you
have a bad tooth, if it's open you can get airodontalgia (Shrop con-
vulses: is he kidding or on the level?); where the air pressure decreases
the higher you go. The gasses thus expand and you can get a terrible
terrible pain. Something else they do (Shrop still convulsing with drastic joy), he claims, is Forensic Dentistry, when Customs doesn't fancy
your passport photo, they send you to me to X-ray your third molar
and your wristbone, just to settle how old you are. So come on in. "At
the very least, if you have a layover, make sure you've flossed." Ah,
breathes Shrop, I am home again, and that was Wesley Weissberg for
The Savvy Traveler, air courier, from Room 2311, Terminal 4.

Dream on, Shrop tells himself: in 1956, because they were making
a movie there, Marilyn Monroe and Arthur Miller visited Idlewild and
waved at us from the rear window of their limousine. Size: 31½ x 23
and five-eighths inches, thirty dollars; condition: rolled, mint. She has
thin manipulative hands well-oiled, huge arched eyebrows, a gamine
haircut close to the head. What is she going to do to, with, him once
the wave is done? Condition: rolled, mint, as the advertiser says. In
those olden days there were lockers at Idlewild. Customer agents had
Red Coats, a touch of style before the Brooklyn Brew Club, the
Eurasia Coffee House, the Napa Valley Wine bar, and Wok and Roll
expanding its menu to include sushi and bento boxes. Is he quite ready
for a golf-themed restaurant, never mind its hint of better days, Le

Cybercafé, or Big Apple Bagel, ribs of pork chops, "Best sinful snack": a double scoop from Edy's Ice Cream? He is more likely, in a mood of raw spirituality, to visit the altar and stained glass in the interdenominational chapel in Terminal 4, even if only to remember (a slight homage to Ground Zero) that the glass was salvaged from three other chapels. The old terminal, for which he hungers, holds Alexander Calder's *Flight* mobile and a reproduction of the Arshile Gorky ceramic mural done for the old Newark Airport. It isn't here any more, what he looks for, but an expert tracker can locate it, or the four thousand swallows, egrets and laughing gulls that sometimes cruise the runways for food every spring, so there are birth control pills, cannons, and predatory falcons in the marshes. He surrenders his heart to the 44-passenger flying boat *American Clipper* with tailplane growing out of its twin booms, inviting him to Luce, Camoon, Ihlros, Caravellas, Tacha, Pacasmayo, Tumaco, Florianopolis, Arica, Antofagasta, Davio, with direct connections via "S.C.A.D.T.A." to the Interior of Colombia.

Before he knew better, he expected the sound of feet in the terminal to be a clatter, but it's more of a soft swooshing surf, as if coming from afar with individual feet merged together: something surreptitious and hypnotic, easily capable of dispelling forlorn or downhearted feelings that afflict him from time to time, almost smothering the will to action. And what is action anyway? Fraudulent window-dressing. He sometimes catches himself leaning one way or another in public view, against mural or door, surrendering his ghost until another chance confronts him and he comes into his compulsive own, setting his ticket down forcefully, sighing with relief that a headwind will make the ocean journey even longer than usual. He loves the sense of being between worlds, briefly aloof, interrogable by neither, yet knowing the reprieve is short. Wherever he goes, important questions await him, now more than ever because he is a creature of too many worlds, pleased to be mostly adrift high up, absently sketching in his head the invisible curvature of the planet, which he knows you can see if flying plutocratic *Concorde*. The feeling of subtraction delights him and keeps him from pledging lifetime commitment. Not quite the man who lives on a ferry, he nonetheless is the creature who bides his time in between movements of a symphony: the sonata mudskip.

Now, having heard pilot and co-pilot do their terse litany about altimeters and clock, navigation lights, deicers, parking brake, aileron

and rudder boost, landing gear lever ("Down—three in the green,"),
he turns flight engineer, chanting to the co-pilot:
Fuel dump valves.
Closed.
Generators.
On.
Crossfeed valves.
Closed.
Spark control.

Retard, he correctly says, confirms the load of fuel (2,525 gallons), and starts the engines on the pilot's command, confident in his Mittyish way that they are "all set," with 60% flaps, flight controls free, mixture rich, fuel pumps on high, cowl flaps 30%. A truant piece of his mind lifts off, as ever, as the five runways beneath him dwindle into skewed pentagram and the prospect of ten or so transatlantic hours opens up, a delight in its slowness, like an old Remington requiring much elbow work. For some reason, coziness maybe, he loves the way the prop spinners occupy almost all of the open space behind them: radial turbines, so close to being streamlined.

Sometimes mere information, because it seems so recondite, lures him in, transforming the world in which he stands, telling him that each airline has a passenger weight table, in which the weight of an average passenger increases by five pounds from summer to winter: heavier clothing shoes, gloves. Why, they even weigh the magazines they have on board. Some of the actual codes used by airlines give him a delightful complicitous frisson: 4XLY is Tel Aviv, Dhahran in Saudi Arabia is HXDR, and Milan is ITMP, and Shrop maintains his amazement that the code letters do not always seem to derive from the actual place name, which to an outsider suggests a further degree of security. In this fashion, a so-called identifier—a group of letters, not an observer—can be left wondering why MCI is Kansas City when MIA is Miami, and PWM is Portland, Maine, while SYR is Syracuse. He relishes the thought that airline staff, the light militia of the lower air, have to memorize over four hundred of these runes from CAR (Akron/Canton) to YYZ (Toronto): hardly a secret society but secret enough to keep the average Idlewild customer at arm's length, as might the name foisted on the navigator by his crew, "Magellan," and the progress report he must give to the captain: "Howgozit." The naming of planes appears a simpler affair, manageable by any outsider. Shrop lingers on a couple of names he has spotted and retained over the years: *Star of Ceylon* and *Star of Windsor,* knowing that other modes of naming come into play, but he likes the formula and often tries the star game, at times going far afield, from Gander to Goose Bay, from Timbuktu to Sidi Barani. Best of all, as he plies his way by night from Idlewild to Paris, he "repairs" to his first-class berth and drifts off to sleep with an open magazine on his stomach, heedless of St. Elmo's fire outside as the Connie flies through a storm and of Boeing 707s flying to and from Europe at twice Constellation speed (600 miles per hour), an unsoggy omelet to come, plus sugar bun and coffee. Off to Trorp radio range (a horse-racing place), which talks the Connie down through the overcast to its instrument landing. He does not mind at all that they deplane down a staircase to the ramp (no jetway, of course) or that his flight left Idlewild at mid-afternoon so as to arrive close to eight in the morning. He rather fancies the old-fashioned way of doing things, before it got too slick, too easy. Always, with the glacier and the marsh beneath him, he feels aggrandized, a Gulliver stalking mammoth, never sensing that his supply of stuff is meager or skimpily obtained, Shrop's picnic rather than Shrop's banquet. His zone of peace he easily enters, disinclined to share it, and already at work in the intimate stithy of his brain off the most vexatious image of all: dead Idlewild, sacked and savaged, beneath the cranes, fences, middens and smokeholes of Ground Zero. Idlewild, much to his disgust, vanished under a bouquet of fancy bureaucratic names, and those old Indians with it, as did the underground dimension of the WTC—subway, shopping, garage—when the restaurants from up on high fell on top of it. The image will not behave, feels alive to the touch, but he *is* trying to master it, at least fold it in upon itself like a cap badge so that it denotes both depth and width, with time, only seconds in total, to be read by the hopeless imagination.

Sight of the dead ground has driven Quent one way, into a bare-chested medallion show and full voice, plugged in on his stumps, but it pushes Shrop into a pipe-dream of low technology. The question remains of whatever they retain in common after eyeballing the trauma of years ago, from which they had shrunk until now. Can it be that both men, injured in different ways, both losing something, can sustain further trauma?

18
A Talisman

THANK GOODNESS OUR MEMORY OF HIM AND HIS OWN DOINGS is a superior faculty. You see, he remembered enough about swimming pools and baton-twirling, but could not actually position himself thus; the concept free-floated in his mind, an unplayed card until somebody reminded him of how he swabbed the pool bottom, felt the baton slipping from his grasp in the rain. Such stuff as that eludes him. He would tell Quent about vivid scenes remembered: the beach at Coney Island littered with used condoms without any attempt to identify potential humans wasted during the fruition of pleasure, brought home by the rolling tides. It was as if the couples had coupled out in the ocean, leaving their fluids behind them, certain the sea would bring them back again. With a little prompting from someone legally or philosophically inclined, he might have come up with some theory of proximate cause ("why I lost my memory"), but he doesn't, always drawing a blank as he zeroes in on the final stages before a huge dose of death and devastation rasa-ed his tabula. But he knew the American Dream was over: destructible after all, not privileged, not unique, never again the non pareil of the melting pot, as Henry Cowell called it. America now was just another country, its civilians mere cannon-fodder just like the rest of the world. And this creamed him, it blew him apart, blotted out anything approximating rational thought.

"Jew see?" Quent has become laconic and obscure.

"What?"

"Jew see?"

"Did I see?"

"Yes."

"I saw all right. I'm glad they never rebuilt."

Actually Shrop remained unsure if the WTC had been rebuilt or not. He saw it as it was, but also as it had been in its days of imperial glory, atop it *the* place for fancy weddings. If they had rebuilt it he hadn't noticed, but Herodotus never mentions having seen the Sphinx. Shrop had begun living in the past, the present, and the future, mainly to block things off and keep them from ever invading his tidy routines.

"Well," he moans, "we have been and seen and we were conquered. End of story."

Quent, not in the least aghast at his own antics on the sacred site, remembers all he saw in punishing detail: nests of jumbled wires, cars crushed to the depth of a shoe box, children (in photographs) as flat as if a tank had pushed over them. If these were things of the past, they still bossed his present, and there he sat, whispering words to fit: *seared, scorched, graven, branded,* among them.

Was it as if he too had now lost his memory, meaning the part of it that sifted rational from nonsensical? He found himself on the brink of feeling guilt for what others had done, which was clearly not true. There they had been, as in some gross kitchen travesty, mixing several thousand people with steel and concrete in a Cuisinart spun by hijacked jets. This had nothing to do with him, but he felt guilty it had happened at all, which only meant he must have transgressed some unwritten bond saying no one was permitted such horrors. The whole human race was supposed to feel guilty because humans had done it. This made no sense to him on the rational level, so why was he perturbed? Why had he gone and looked and, as it were, gone straight beyond himself, pulling rank and airing his medals and airily speechifying? Now, instead of trying to fathom Shrop and equip him with some kind of memory, even the life of someone else, he felt obliged to probe and assess his own case. Could it be that, to some extent having misled and even defrauded Shrop in the matter of memory and the conduct of recall, he had done something akin to the attack on the towers? Had he pillaged him in the name of, under the aegis of, friendship? Had he destroyed the tower of his lifelong friend who, already ruined, needed a different kind of help? The analogy, if one, did not at once become clear, but he could sense an accurate match in the offing. Was he now going to enlarge on that misstep to assume guilt for everything foul done in the name of humanity? To what extent, he wondered, was he his own fanatic? The terrorist of his friend, not only pitching facts into the void of the man's memory, but repeating them until they seemed substantial to him, a talisman, a comfort, a dream? Did he hate humanity that much, or merely sense its incompetence, to be remedied by one who thought himself, so broken and severed in body, so perfect in mind?

"Deep in thought," says Shrop. "What are you remembering?"

Quent has no answer, almost drowning. It is as if what he has sometimes heard spoken of as the noetic floodgate—when the mind pours out after someone has hit the wrong (or even the right) button—had blurted out everything, the hero-shrink copious and ashamed, when in truth humanity without such saviors of the soul as he pretends to be would have little chance of surviving sane amid a surfeit of horrors and mild little irritants writ large.

"Something bugging me," he finally responds. In the dim light of the apartment, his face grows dark, not merely with shadow but with the hue of a dark cigar, turning shaggy in the gloom while, on a whim, he considers what he has become, in terms of Russian aircraft fobbed off with English nicknames: Flogger, Hogger, Foxhound, Fencer, Flanker, Mainstay. Sick of that, he peers at Shrop, attending as if for the first time to the wavery, undulating mode of his voice, in this very much his own man although losing some of his best-colored marbles.

"Quent! Art thou sleeping there below?"

No answer from the stationary chair, but a well-tuned groan as of a man with a telegram in his fist. "I do declare, Shrop, after all this, your balls are bigger than mine."

"And who's the shrink then?"

"I've been betraying you all along."

Suddenly Shrop feels a cold polar wind invade his being, not the icicle rammed up the rear end of which Quent often spoke when reminiscing at Shrop's expense, but a denuding, subtractive gale of the outer planets. Sore afraid, Shrop murmured.

Hearing nothing, he simply says, "Square One, let's get back to that, Quent. No more games."

Now Quent, without saying anything, decides he has been infected with appalling evil, just for having gone to the zone Shrop had begun to name Idlewild. It was a combination of sick at heart, shame, self-loathing, and, more unusual, the hero's peptic misery, coming together, tearing him apart.

The promised or anticipated session does not begin, however, and Shrop decides to occupy the paid-up time with something else: TV, perhaps, or a close scrutiny of neighbor nameplates entailing a march or two around the hallways. Who *were* these people? Was it better to have Nazis on the premises than terrorists? Instead, presuming to guess where Quent has disappeared to, he finds events well ahead of him in the bathroom where Hovis Tumulty, who must have sidled in half-expecting trouble or novelty, is busy shaving Quent's head, the gray along with the brown, a neat job, less like the forgotten egg of Yul

Brynner than the convicts in the third or fourth *Aliens* movie, called (he thinks) *Resurrection*. No, that is number 4, he decides. What the hell was the third one called?

"Chilly stuff," he chides Quent.

"You would know, of course. Ignore him, honey, just you scrape away."

"The loins as well?" Shrop is feeling distinctly prankish, yet he fears for his friend's equilibrium while quite jocund himself. He knows about shattered mind, but can there be shattered country? Did Quent when he flew have a shaven head too? If so, who shaved his head then? British pilots, he knew, had batmen (servants), but not the doughty warriors of the US, all of them self-helpers to a fault. He offers to take over, but Tumulty swings her razor shoulder up at him and yells something, with more motherfuckings than fuckings in it, a redundant portmanteau insult unprecedented in her previous behavior. Wordlessly he agrees with whatever suggestion she has made and makes himself note mentally that, no matter how vile the situation is, or its aftermath, there will always be room for idle witticism and overuse of the copulative vocative.

By now, Quent's head is clear, and certain dents in his scalp have become evident. Wounds? Surely not; more likely where the midwife sank her horny thumbs to get him out of Mama's belly. He tries *chilly* again but receives no response from either. Now she does Quent's chest and shoulders with the same razor, wiping him off with paper towels and then with hot washrags. Quent, he has to hand it to him, excels at standing on stumps, so maybe the quartered butt end has developed some leathery quality over the years and might be used for almost anything. She leaves thighs and groin alone, not that he is hairy there. Quent has acquired an old man's look or that of the condemned man awaiting the coldwater sponge that goes under the skullcap in the electrocution chamber and helps speed the current through. No, Quent puts on a jaunty baseball cap reading BELLANGA, in tribute to Giuseppe, designer and aviation pioneer. "Wooden planes," says Quent, and that is the end of that.

The small blood-flecked gashes where the medals had been attached seem to give him no pain. At one juncture Tumulty had swept the razor right over them, but Quent did not flinch. Swathed now in a fleecy white robe, he looks an almost holy figure, face stern, eyes puckered, shaven head gleaming under the stark light of the bathroom. Behold Quent *rasus* next to the huge bulk of Tumulty, whose technique for lifting him by his armpits had been perfected over months of beefy trial. It is almost as if she were lifting a figurine or a bust, clearly now more in accordance with her maniacal lust for hygiene. She approves of him, smacking her chops to show how toothsome he has become while he secedes into a private, almost little boy's dream, being dandled by a mama. Imagine the scene as Shrop slouches in the doorway watching and wondering, not exactly hoping for a role in this miracle-play, but feeling more *de trop* than ever, yet sensing already that his knowledge of the goings-on came more from immediate travesty than from anything learned beforehand. He is working, he knows, on instant data, making no comparisons with anything previous, which is to say accepting the present event as a singularity, a one-off in which uniqueness buries surprise.

Has he done this kind of thing before, doting on the present even as it evaporates? Does it feel like the old existentialism, living in the now? Or was it merely a caricature since that philosophy called for much attention to the project of oneself? Good: he remembers something, finally, and need not make a bugbear of himself, going around asking questions of his inferiors. Quent's project of himself seems to have taken wings, though outrageous in furor and severity. He certainly has lost the older man in the never one. As Tumulty reaches into a cupboard beneath the sink, fumbling for a steelware basin, she exclaims, recoils, slamming the basin down on the ledge of the sink. Are they leeches or what? A seething morass of black wormlike creatures makes a brief appearance before she tosses them into the toilet with a fastidious grunt and flushes them away. What, whence, why?

"Were they yours?" Shrop asks helplessly.

"Like personal property?" Quent is shaking his shorn head.

"Did you bring them back with you from—"

"No, they're home grown, whatever they are."

It is too late now for identification, and Tumulty doesn't care, still shuddering with her massive arms.

"Did you ever see the like?" She checks the toilet bowl to make sure they have all flushed away, there to breed and infest. Shrop is wondering what might lurk in the soil at Ground Zero, sumptuously fertilized or drastically killed. No one has reported life forms, but there would surely be some, extras generated by cadavers going bad. Will he take a sample of soil then? No, he will not, it is not the Amazon jungle. Can a new life form have taken root in ideal conditions, or has this particular one been there all the time, squirming in the basements, looking for light? Shrop's twitchy mind leads him astray, setting up the worms: as a special species requiring only transportation to Mars to become a race of super-savants to whom interstellar travel is a snip. Withdrawing from so preposterous a thought, he concentrates on Quent's shaven head, halfwondering nonetheless if this is the first of some extra-terrestrial sequence: 1. miscellaneous terrorism reduces Earth to ashes; 2. black worms take over, capturing human samples for teleportation up the Milky Way; 3. Those left behind congregate at the ground zeroes and surrender to the sludge, deadly as it already is. No, he knows life on his planet will simply dribble away, pounded by various biological agents released by crashing hijacked planes. He is having a poor day, the first of several hundred accursed ones.

19
The West Coast of Ireland

THE HISTORY OF ENTOMBMENT IS A FATEFUL CHORE. THE DEAD, it tells us, are best buried, even if initially dug up. They're best put back, even sometimes in the eyes of those craving what they call closure. It all depends on their finding a souvenir or a body part among the earthbound carnage, which seems to release a calming enzyme. All the same, there is decorum to think about, which does not include hundreds of macerated corpses squashed higgledypiggledy in the ground. Merely to get them out deforms them further, and so rescuers may be obliged to tighten their teeth and accept that what they tread on, seek vainly to penetrate, is a block solid human terrene, a fiendish assortment best left alone. There is no way of putting the mess to rights without fear of miscombining body parts, never mind how noble the impulse behind it.

Shrop has thought about all this and come to a humane conclusion. It would be better, he thinks, to leave Ground Zero as it is, pave it perhaps, or plant permanent meaningful blooms with names culled from one of those books almost universally titled *The Language of Flowers*. It does not occur to him that by thinking "permanent" he may be dreaming of artificial flowers; for the instant, he does believe some are perpetual. In any case, such flowers will have to be replaced on a vigilant basis: a full-time job for someone. The next problem in a different series is: Should those exhumed, if so, be reburied here or elsewhere? Should the contingent, like some lost battalion, remain together? If not, then some arbitrary scheme of sculpture or hydraulics will create a garden of remembrance, or, in the good old Yankee way of knock 'em down, build 'em up, slam two more towers in on the same spot, but higher, even more tempting. Even with Big Ben, the Eiffel Tower, the White House in ruins, the notion appeals to some whose defiance has a military edge. Shrop sees no virtue in rebuilding, either here or elsewhere, being of what he likes to call an Egyptian cast of mind, the dead being honored in commodious apartments; but being so hardly helps him to individualize those in the explosive muddle below Ground Zero. All he can muster to this dilemma is the thought that, out at Idlewild, the glacier underlay the terminal moraine on which the marsh formed, and the golf club sat on that with a certain amount of indignity, yet providing a huge meniscus of green quiet as well. He thinks in layers. The last thing he wants here is a heliport; better a clock-golf site than that. It pleases him somewhat that one airport out there in Queens replaced another, but he thinks that sacred cenotaphs can outdo airports in holy decorum. He wants no more mayhem on the site and is clearly in favor of leaving well alone, a shiny black wall of memory installed with every name chiseled. He is unlikely, he thinks, to have the last word in this, such being the chutzpah of those who cherish a skyline.

Such is his to and fro thinking on the issue, already on the boil for three years amid the continuing series of terrorist attacks: a world-wide corps of assassins and suicide bombers does not dispel itself that easily. In this, he hopes, he joins Quent, who fancies the site as a locus for oratory and dismal chants. Neither believes much in hotels or trade centers; the one is mourning a lost memory, the other a third of his body and a lost career. They somewhat overlap, but have begun to diverge, perhaps unable to talk the matter over without snapping. But talk they will even as Shrop stays steady as much as an amnesiac can, and Quent begins to vary his approach, ever conscious of his wheelchair, almost to him, now, a kind of mobile grave.

Head dry.

Tumulty gone, vowing to return now they have messed up the bathroom.

Shrop is relieved that Quent has quietened down and may return to the recital of Shrop's earlier life, reminding Shrop of it or telling him about what he might have lost.

"If we must, *as* we must," Quent is cryptically saying, "let us get to your behavior in more recent years. You left Cambridge, where you had quite a name, and became a porter at Guy's Hospital in London. Quite a switch, if you don't mind my saying so. I wonder how many porters have become Cambridge dons. Then you worked as a lab assistant at the Royal Victoria Infirmary, about which switch I have roughly the same comment. You hated academe, did you not?"

Shrop remembers no such thing, but finds himself preoccupied with Quent's new appearance; it is like being addressed by a light bulb; blood speckles his shirt from where he'd pinned his medals. Were his stumps bleeding too?

"I remember none of this," he says. "It doesn't matter. I lived on, thinking, thinking."

"You even," Quent informs him, "went and stayed in a cottage somewhere on the west coast of Ireland until bronchitis set in. Your next move only took you to a platelayer's hut at Bletchley. You became the muse of the railroads. And that was the end of it. I can see that your destinations have much in common; you would be unlikely to recall them."

"Oh, I don't know," Shrop tells him. "Given the right monkey gland, I might make amazing progress. I came to see you, whom I already knew. And look where it got me. Don't you think I'm suffering from some kind of trauma, which talking isn't likely to cure me of?" Quent yawns and leans backwards.

20
Nervous

I T IS PERHAPS AT THIS POINT THAT SHROP BEGINS TO LOSE HIS OLD esteem for his friend and analyst, who once seemed to him extraordinary because he combined, however haplessly, the active life with the contemplative one. He had walked the walk and talked the talk, as uneducated people liked to say, and he had played that uncanny game, equipping old Shrop with a life they then explored together, although Shrop always felt there was something fishy about this mnemonic prosthesis. It *sounded* familiar, but it lacked the feel of a warm life normally lived, so maybe it was some heavenly catechism Quent had concocted for the sake of discussion, indeed lest discussion flagged. According to him, Shrop wondered, who have I been? What was my name? Silly me, *this* was my name; it's just the circumstances I find strange, although the shape and texture of longing, certainly as affecting Idlewild and my passion for that glaciated golf club, seemed all right. I shouldn't be too hard on him, even though he appears to have gone afield, never to come back. I once read a novel called *Nervous*—I remember that much—but I remember nothing of it other than a dizzy, fluttery feeling in my stomach. Ever since three years ago, and that appalling attack, I have felt uncertain, breathless, as if something inside me were hovering and askew. Maybe I should take off for the Italian Lakes or Hong Kong, just to ban the shakes from my system. It's as if the ground were sinking all around me, earthquake style. I am not who I was, but I hate to attribute the shift to an attack by jet planes loaded with gas. It should be more internal than that, more of a seachange according to temperament, as found in the Great Romantics at the first sight of Lake Geneva or the Dolomites. Can sordid killers bring such changes about? They seem to have done it to poor old legless Quent, vulnerable to begin with, but who'd have believed it after they heard him picking my daydreams and dismal recall apart? Is this *tension* I feel, or *suspense*? Am I wondering where disaster will strike next or, more precisely, which of our monuments will crash? Are these the same thing, or do you really have to have a ticking bomb for the latter?

I ask him.

But his mind is off in Samarkand, or the old days of dropping napalm, seeding the landscape with those long black eggs, when he boasted to himself of having all that power over what he termed the latefundia. What in hell's— Why, he told me, it's the wide foundation, I used to think it was the milk-drinking population. Imagine that. No shit. Absent Quent, seemingly lost in his chair in a crusading sleep, he tries to work it out for himself.

And so he does, with imperious innocence, asking if the deadly combination coveted by terrorists (ever hunting hypergolic chemicals that explode when combined) happens to be tension followed by the ticking bomb or, worse, the new tension that follows the ticking bomb after it has failed to go off. In other words, generalized anxiety followed by a bomb (or clock) that starts ticking, and then the same anxiety all over again. He thinks of the water torture, but chooses the huge fever that assumes responsibility for an entire city, a whole landscape, knowing they won't blow up Idlewild until it has passed its glacial, moraine, and marsh stages, or even its brief era as a golf club. But the instant it becomes JFK, or something equally commemorative, it's a sitting duck at which some planes blow up while boarding takes place, others while landing or taking off, yet others during cruise-climb, so there are fires everywhere and folk are in a dither, asking airline reps if this is suspense or tension they are feeling, and how can they put an end to it.

"Hide," they hear, and then there comes this ghastly automotive passacaglia as they all scream out of the parking lots, never to fly again: not suspense or tension, but agony.

Maybe, Shrop thinks, this is all much ado about nothing. Beirut, Kosovo, Blitz London were worse; we can still walk our streets without fear of shrapnel or bullets. The day may come, but for the time being we get these long intervals of comparative peace. What do they say about flying, as it was in the old days? A calm life interrupted by moments of stark terror? And now? The other way around. It may sound like wartime, but it isn't wartime through and through, is it? Ask some longtime resident of Warsaw, for example. There, that time, the only safety was in the sewers. Will we ever get that far, which is to say beyond anthrax and smallpox wafting in and out, passenger jets used as missiles, and the mail, the money, the newspapers all contaminated? Can you really get used to almost anything, like the inhabitants of Peking with the Japanese at their throats in 1937? Surely there's an overload amount, past which we neglect to function and no longer care, take no more precautions merely to save ourselves for further torture in some other way. True too that terrorists sometimes get bored with their own tricks, give it a rest just to crank up the anticipation. And then there are those who live heedlessly anyway and go around saying Sufficient unto the day is the carnage thereof. Tomorrow is another day. Do those old saws still have teeth?

He and Quent are going their different ways, having already abandoned the idea of living together, each befouling the other's bathroom and kitchen. End of that brainwave. As Shrop sees it, Quent is plotting some kind of public show, not air show, while he himself recognizes the end of their semiprofessional relationship, throwing him back on his own resources, if they exist at all. It has been a curious, bogus arrangement anyway, not cheap or intimate, but impromptu and imaginary. Shrop wonders how he ever got into such a bind, at once diagnosing his own laziness and his constant preference for the doctor he knows over the doctor he doesn't. Who on earth can replace Quent, whose wheelchair and shaven head seem to be calling out for other components of an emblem? What will Quent do without a following, a claque? Have *I* been his following all along?

Out of perverse interest he forms the habit of taking a cab down to the site, just to see if he coincides with Quent, and soon realizes Quent now mounts a daily performance, not uncouth or slovenly, standing on the seat of his wheelchair at the thin-rimmed American salute, surrounded by a rag, tag and bobtail from the apartment house, with Tumulty, brawn and some brain, standing a ways off urging people to stand in silence in his orbit. A question later and Shrop has identified Ethne Heinkel, Jonelle, Elspeth, Ettore and Claes, now vaguely conscious of a nice little clique of Nazi descendants clustered around the little-boy look of Quent, whose firm demeanor just about qualifies him for the status of palace guard. But what, he wonders in a mesmerized fit based on his miscellaneous reading, is Fraülein von Kulp? Where is Hakagawa, bowing? Could they be involved in all this too? They mill about him, providing animation where he has none, almost as if unaware of the atrocity that happened here and committed to a fresh-air festival honoring Quent, war hero turned shrink. They do not look vicious or, for that matter, repugnantly mild, all middle-aged and sleek. Surely he did not choose them himself; they no doubt venerating him in memory of the old days and other *mutilés de guerre*, espying in the site

89

something comforting and heartening, a type of scene they were accustomed to, though emptied by now of seemly corpses. Could it be that Quent, with his newfound fans, was planning to fly south with Ethne Heinkel in charge, and was just paying his final respects to the image of glory? To some, Shrop reminded himself, this zone of outrageous carnage was a shrine of military skills, like Pearl Harbor to the Japanese. Indeed, it could be taken in both ways by the same observer, both rubble and honor. There was surely nothing like it in the entire country, not even Gettysburg and Antietam coming close for blood shed of civilians.

Had he really identified the Germans by their or their fathers' faces? No, he had merely assumed who they were, en masse, unable to tell a Bormann from a Helldorf. Yet their looks and bearing tipped him off that there was something Teutonic, and perhaps the addition of a Fegelein and a Speer had reinforced the impression. He counted up. Seven. They could at least have dyed their hair. He was dabbling in gross generalities, that was clear, yet he was convinced they were who they were: the clique who had replaced him at the non-existent feet of Quent. No Tumulty in this group, nor, he surmised, Nadia Fortescu either, no doubt home awaiting mail from her dog in Bucharest. Something military in the bearing of the seven reassured him, although, yet again, he was arriving at positive opinions in the absence of evidence. Empires have fallen on the basis of such suspicions, however, and he was willing to commit himself. Why were they present? And what had happened to the rest of them? Tornquist, De Baillache, Fresca, Mrs. Cammel and Mr. Silvero (the two living apart from spouses, clearly), not to mention Verdenal, the dead one whom he nonetheless remembered. His head was in a whirl. Perhaps these missing ones were not Nazi enough, "*Narzi*" as Churchill said it in speech after speech. What was the secret of Quent's historical hold over the others? Had he exercised a similar hold on Shrop himself, masterminding where he should have fostered and guided? In the foreshortened shrink of old acquaintance, was there something hypnotic that egged them on and sucked them dry? Shrop suddenly found himself agonizing about the exact nature of the bond that had endured between the two of them for years. Was this what all relationships came to, given enough yielding in the one and enough domineering in the other? Now, as things began to come clear, at least to the hot head with which Shrop appraised things, he began to wonder at the life substituted for his forgotten ideas, and at the supplementary fact that he had already forgotten what that life was like. He just had this lumpish sense of having been defrauded, and then let go in the shadow of the terrorist atrocity while an old proverb from who knew where haunted and depressed him. How did it go? "Shocking events will produce in their witnesses emotions equally shocking." Was it one of Quent's lamer ones, or had Shrop invented it himself? In the sense that the group with Quent was doing nothing wrong, but merely standing there at attention while Quent perched perilously on his stumps in the braked Rascal, they were doing nothing wrong, and indeed it was a moving, dismaying sight, almost a burial scene, with the shaven head shiny in the sun as if greased, and on the faces of all involved a look of mutinous solicitude. Half-tempted to join them, and thus inject his own brand of aggrieved disrepair into the prevailing mood and stance, Shrop held back, not quite sure of his Nazis, deterred also by a couple of professional-looking photographers, and overtaken by a sense of the ridiculous at so much freak-show next to a real tragedy. Why, they were still selling tawdry-looking medallions made from the sundered steel of three years ago as if memory were not enough and had to be supplemented by tinpot tokens such as one of the shabbiest dictators might have had struck in his own dishonor in Belem or Bucharest.

* * *

Hovis Tumulty arrives to clean house, and this begins to soothe Shrop in the old manner; since childhood, he has always felt subduedly intact in the presence of anyone doing hard physical labor. Something rhythmic and hypnotic sends him off into something between a doze and a coma, perhaps stimulating as music does the subdominant hemisphere of his brain. This is where Ravel, Debussy and Fauré live, where dead princesses cool off, fauns scamper in mid-afternoon, and Melisande plies the spinning wheel. It is not merely the domain of childhood, however, but of what Fauré called *L'Horizon chimérique*: the nightmare horizon. The bray of the vacuum cleaner, the faint whisk of the broom, the nasty scratch of the scrubbing brush, all suffice to sedate and gratify him, so much so that he would have Hovis Tumulty, always pregnant, clean his own quarters just for the noises she made, as if, at last, someone had come up with a plane on which he loved to dawdle, voluptuously captivated and altogether diverted from the affairs of life. This is not just to indicate the depth of dream he cultivated, but the relaxed force with which he lolled his body, surrendering to the sublime banality of maids. As things used to be, it was in this secret trance that he came up with his best ideas (when he had them), mostly not writing them down, alas, and therefore quite often deprived of them, to poignant disadvantage. Now, however, still subject to delicious torpor whenever Hovis hoovered, he had become the tenant of a vacant brain, which made him more passive than ever, so much so that, hanging around after his session with Quent, he preferred her to be working, no longer for stimulus but for (as he jeeringly told her) "relaxation."

Quent had slowly learned the nature of his patient and friend, and knew that, properly calmed, he could be fed ideas galore, which he attributed to nobody at all, but called excelsior: plastic chips to cushion things in boxes. Quite candid about his lifestyle, he would readily admit what he was like: "I walk around in a dream, I often feel someone else is dreaming me, and the pretty tendrils of that experience come creeping into my own dream. It is like being invaded by petals." No doubt Quent had taken advantage of this tendency, possibly becoming the invader, willing even to admit that their two dreams had coupled in his head. As a friend, Shrop without being fey or too exquisite had a delicate hinterland in which outlandish runes were born and never vouchsafed, or even remembered. Quent, who ventured into this strange domain, had long ago decided that Shrop's flagging memory began with inertia of the imagination, knowing almost nothing of Shrop's fascination with Idlewild. If any man was going to survive his discomfort with the appalling mess of the twin towers, it was Shrop, who held on to the glacier-moraine-marsh-golf club-aerodrome image like a drowning fanatic, oblivious or indifferent to all else. Idlewild had seeped into his sleep over the years and remained impregnable, despite all Quent's efforts to rub his nose in Ground Zero. Shrop had reached the stage at which you held tight to something heraldic and ancient, much as some held on to collections of coins or unique foreign stamps. In this way, while conceding the sadistic horror of the attack, Shrop the dreamer sanitized his inmost being against the rude and haggard onset of the world.

In this sense, he was inviolable although empty.

He remembered the outlines of various emotions, but had no idea of the detail within them.

Was he then some kind of dumb ox? Not really, he was more a case of voluntary anesthesia, or the blank as volunteer, as Quent had described him.

Hence the one man's fascination with the other, the realist with the fantasist, although Quent the stunted had a restricted view of dread while Shrop the dreamer was fixed on only one thing. In this, they had something in common, both having shed what was extra, in other words cleaving to the bare bones of their dilemma.

Either man might have predicted the monomania of the other, but the degree of self-saturation they went in for kept them from any such thing. Quent's obsession could not recognize Shrop's, and would not unless, somehow, the one coiling and uncoiling bumped into the other in the stern corridors of nightmare. Indeed, could either even heed the other's gathering craze? One doubts it, having studied them at length, knowing that acts of infamy can stun, stop, stymie people for life, no matter who urges them on, or back, or like Quent with his perpetual "*On*," wants the future to come. Perched at the pinnacle, then, equipped with what life has left them (two legs and a memory missing), they have drifted apart, but may remain together for mechanical reasons. Had Shrop gone to almost any other shrink, he might have been renewed. Had Quent dealt with almost any other patient, he might have made some headway. Instead, like two lion cubs voicing pangs of hunger in their squeaky-wheezy way, they stay together, thinking that is all they have in common. They thus re-enter the world of men merely as generic creatures who have been born and frightened and are therefore worthy of note thus: They lived, they flinched, they were there, and heaven praise them for enduring.

21
Sleeper to Paris

NOW HE IS HOVERING AT THE DOOR OF 18F, NOT KNOCKING or buzzing, but peering at the name card: HONELLE, it says, not HEINKEL. Changed at the last minute? He cannot see why. Did he misread it? Had someone misreported the name to him? So far as he could tell, Honelle had no connotations whatever. Before embarking further on what was to have been a little anti-Nazi crusade, he went on to 17B in search of the person he had identified as Bormann. BURROWES is the name that greets him, and so on throughout the early afternoon: Tod has become TODD and Helldorf HALDANE. 2C has no name at all, no card. He gives up, wondering if someone has committed a prank on him, or if he has become genuinely delusional, as, he surmises with a feeble grin, he often has been of late. So: there is no posse of waiting Nazis, only a claque of devotees with common or garden names such as Burrowes and Haldane, inoffensive and faintly familiar, part of the eternal background come to life. He feels disappointed, but in any case what is he doing roaming around someone else's apartment house, gaping at name cards? Looking for truth? All he can muster by way of extenuation is an old saw, retrieved from who knows where: When you have them by the balls, their hearts and minds will follow. Well, it was not he but Quent who had them by the balls, and their hearts and minds had already followed. Instead of assembling a retinue of notorious names under the presumed aegis of Ethne Heinkel-Honelle, he had better put them all out of his mind as Quent's own, whatever they were: Bible-bashers, Seventh Day Adventists, Jehovah's Witnesses, and not children of the damned. I could use a troupe of them, he thinks, but for what? Having no aim, he counts himself aimless, waiting to be tempted by yet another fantasy while awaiting the next decline in his memory, so bad by now he can't remember the first phase of rot. Bad dreams, he tells himself, that's all it comes down to, worse than ever. Maybe Ethne H. will take me too down to Florida when her jet next flies. There is no point being here. He has already canceled his least favorite magazines, although copies keep on arriving, always a month ahead of themselves, no sense of season. Is there, could there be, some form of habitation available out at Idlewild, or must I take the sleeper to Paris nightly, returning by day upright in my seat? Ground Zero frightens him with its corpses, dismembered all, its lost policemen and firefighters, children and priests, slime-tracks of enormous caterpillars, fencework and bridge-work, all somehow given over to a giant quicksand of the new century. If only—No. He decides to stay factual, to think of the intact bar and the crushed cars, the smashed subway and the layer cake of a score of floors all compressed. In only seconds he has swapped all that for Idlewild, not destroyed but converted. It is no use going there; the there that was has gone, exists only in mind and a few reference books, a few expensive brochures and even more expensive obsolete time-tables. Junk to most, to him manna over which to pore in the long evenings of modernity. He is content to remain an old fogey, a geezer with his DC-7Cs in mind, staffed by matronly girls in conservative gear, the permanent smile out of Colgate by Palmolive. Always prof-fering you a blanket or pillow. How many hours to Paris then? Thir-teen, we hope. His mind tracks the pre-flight checks, does a gratified nod at all's being well. This is the opium dream that saves him, keeps him calm when the brains go out and yet another delusion bites the dust. He will not forgive the Haldanes and Todds for not being who he thought they were, and they will linger in his drifting mind like snakes, to be avoided and reprieved.

Confronting Quent, he waves an imaginary farewell to the Nazis. Tumulty is getting ready to shave Quent's head again. The apartment looks untidy, as if a boisterous game has taken place between the man in the wheelchair and the maid. What if? Shrop is not welcome today: no appointment, and maybe never again. He is on his own with his imagination. This used to be his job anyway, the imagistic side of his metaphysical calling. His forte, for years, carefully inscribed in copper-plate in the pages of an album he embellished with actual stills begged, borrowed, or made at home, the images piled up: errors mainly, but some shots winning on the grounds of sheer fascination. For an entire year, he had scrutinized a restoration of *Lawrence of Arabia*, eventually settling for a six-pack of fizzy drinks on the table in front of Peter O'Toole in Damascus, clearly a moment of thirsty haste, and, in the same movie restored, a near beaver shot of O'Toole's loins goosed by José Ferrer, the thin-mustached, rosebud-lipped sensual Turkish offi-cer. He enjoyed the errors more than the daring shots, but he would not have wanted to be without either. Somehow, the album, which he

95

called *The Well-Tempered Clavier*, helped fortify his failing memory by becoming a metaphor for it, in either role a revelation: something forgotten, something suppressed. It gave him heart, this album, even long after he'd neglected to keep it up to date, watching movies he now neither reviewed nor savored in recension. No doubt of his keen eye, which lasted long, or of his almost voracious sense of things visual. What failed him was, as he sometimes said, what showed up on the walls of Plato's cave and stayed put for everyman but him.

While the real world failed to register for long, the fresh-made engram rotting almost instantly despite his best promises to remember, he kept up with scenes, which he recalled rather better, such as O'Toole arriving with native bearer at the bar in the officers' mess, Cairo, or showing up in the same place in a shabby uniform, the epitome of the socially maladroit—yet promoted each time. Shrop also took a fancy to Claude Rains, *petit maître* of Tunbridge Wells retirement dorm, playing Dryden the civil servant, dapper, terse, and criminally at ease. These were his ikons, for even longer than some of them lasted, the sense of having been fortified by something surviving its appearance.

Shrop, the movie buff and critic, would always order two lemonades for himself and his Arab friend after crossing Sinai together. It was his permanent way. He had even read Walker Percy's *The Moviegoer*, wondering why doctors' books about the arts were so visceral.

And now, for the sake of constantly reprinting the image, he feels a need to go back to ground central to watch Quent speechify while standing on his wheelchair, just to get the entire image as firmly engraved in mind as that of Idlewild. Where all of life is fleeting, what shall he hold on to? He suffers, one can see, from both eidetic and noetic amnesia: both things and ideas.

The temptation, as ever, after being seduced by one glimpse or several, was to bask in the atmosphere of a given movie, enjoying several facets of it. That this seemed to fly in the face of his conclusions about memory loss did not trouble him; he saw it as a bonus, a bit of the recovered main. So, with *Lawrence*, as he dubbed it (no, *named* it, he corrects himself), the matter of the flags interests him all over again, the point being that the war flags of the desert tribes were, as we say of neckties, self-colored: pale-green, light blue, darker green, which comparative lack of emblem he associated with sand and sun, that tended to wipe out embellishments, leaving over the years only a pale shade of blue or green. This reduction of the flag's hue struck him as mysterious, with as it were nothing much said about the bearers, who galloped about (say, the Howitat) with a plainish flag above them, concealing more than it announced. What atrocities a plain fabric suggested, as if it had been washed clean, bleached, then washed clean again. Of blood? Who knew?

It was this kind of overreaching interest in details that kept him alert, possibly missing the vast point of some epic movie, but retaining minutiae to the point of obsession—something for which his reviews had been notorious. He saw much in little, but when he lost that little had nothing to cling to.

He has never, as a member of clan or tribe, galloped under a flag of any kind, but he supposes any US citizen goes about his business under at least an implicit Stars and Stripes, most of all when the country is under attack after spending so long in disrepute. If this happens to be yet another angle on his Idlewild fixation, then so be it; around he canters on the moraine and marsh, pretending to play polo at the golf club, happy with a society that goes nowhere at all. Well, under what Arabian flag did the marauders of 9.11 come? Was their pernicious flag a blank as well, suggestive of all, attributable to none? He feels again the familiar griping emptiness in his gut, a throwing-up that will not come unless he sticks a finger down his throat. It feels as if he has suddenly been deprived of gravity, made motherless in thousands of different ways. And he far enough away from Ground Zero not to be in overt danger. And someone else is missing too.

Perhaps, in some devious way, his groping for Nazi offspring is merely an attempt to make friends, of whatever stamp; someone to talk to who has "been through it." He wonders, absently asking himself why he feels guilty for not having spoken at least a little to the thousands who had perished on that day before their porridge and bacon with eggs had gone down. Loathsome, and who was to say how many more atrocities were planned on top of the five or six already committed? Always that same missing someone.

Back he veers to the blank flags of the desert, thinking they might stand for such Hollywood tropes as The Deep and The Big Sky; when you had all that on your side, who could beat you? In a way he was relieved not to have found true Nazis in the goodly company of Quent, aiding and abetting him, seeing him through, unloading and opening up his wheelchair. All that. These had been Shrop's duties for years, from before Quent became the shrink, and he had never minded. Now, however, with what seemed a rift, caused perhaps by only their different responses to Ground Zero in successive phases, he was glad to have someone filling in for him, but why not Hovis Tumulty, adding one more physical chore to those she undertook around the apartment, whose mice had vanished three years ago? Shrop contemplates loss of friends, recognizing that to lose one big friend alters somewhat the roles of minor friends, prompting you to discover missed virtues and overlooked vices. Was he ready for that kind of upheaval, all just possibly predicated on the aftermath of the assault? Why, even Columbia graduates had been among the slaughtered, kids with new degrees in biology and economics, on the fringe of their first jobs. It makes him sick. What about their friendships, their siblings, their folks? He is closer to being maudlin than ever, with no big consolation to hang on to, and his age-old shrink suffering a sea-change. Missing, missing, always missing, killed in action, presumed dead.

* * *

Showering the brain, the micrometeorites of memory are the theater of the unexpected, making us cringe and forget. Shrop tries to estimate his averages: how much lost against how much arrived, but he cannot really do this, favoring as he does some images over others, certain scraps of conversation, certain tremblings in his limbs. With Quent to guide him, it was easier, even if Quent misled him merely to give him something to bite on, for Quent, never mind how deceitful, retained nonetheless the guidance ethic of his second career. In leading Shrop up or down the garden path, he also held his hand and exclaimed en route at the lewd candid goblet of an amaryllis in full flower, or the silver track like a drowned bridal train of a roaming slug. So, Shrop is used to better, as he knows, and opens his eyes wider, as one can, letting in a good sixth more of the visible world as if it would always conduct him to stark truth, such as the fact that one fourth of all the drugs we need are to be found in the rain forest, although we have studied only two per cent of that region's vegetation.

Hearing about plans to erect a Christmas tree on Ground Zero, as in previous years, Shrop wishes they wouldn't, preferring a mass of flowers even in the snow, preferably cut and dead for the obvious metaphorical impact. A crucified Santa, flown in flash-frozen from Japan, would suit him better, loath as he is to Christianize the horror beneath. No one has asked him, however, and he realizes that Quent, bizarre in his wheelchair, has a little more clout, is more theatrical, and might even ask for something different, such as a roaring fire replenished all season with fresh timber from Norway. Almost in counter, Shrop allows his mind to envision a huge array of some five or six thousand amputated feet set out in the firelight. As he sees it, the sense of outrage must not be allowed to die, like our youth too soon. Sensitive to echoes, he begs pardon for the final phrase but lets it stand among the surviving meteorites.

Then, as if nothing untoward has happened, there is this exchange, in the fresh-cleaned apartment, with Quent, who seems himself to have forgotten his open-air performance after waiting almost three years for the vibes, the dead, the dust to settle down.

"Weren't you in a cottage on the west coast of Ireland, when last heard from?" Retching, phlegm-laden.

"How amusing," Shrop says. "In that other life I died, weary of going on. But I remain alive enough to tell you about it."

"Then the business is concluded. We *can* move on."

"Oh no," Shrop tells him, "there is Idlewild to come, the basis of us all."

22
That Old Protein

AS OFTEN WITH SHROP, THE IMMEDIATE YIELDS TO THE REMOTE, not so much a backing down as an impetuous desire to use reliable fuel, in this case *The Spirit of St. Louis*, seen several times with various cuts on the tube. He recalls the cloth flap over the outdoor telephone fastened to the wall of the airways shack, almost the same shape as the flap used to save the necks of desert soldiers, the French Foreign Legion say, from the sun. Such connections bolster his courage, make him feel more at home in the world that one day will see the word slip from the noun, reducing him to pointing and gesturing. He wonders why the phone, enclosed in a lidless box, needs the flap anyway, but isn't sure; there is after all rain and snow. More vivid are the carefully filed moments when the boss of Ryan Aircraft cooks sand dabs with an oxy-acetylene torch, generously offering them to anyone nearby, but Lindbergh doesn't say how bad they taste until Ryan has built his plane. Ever the diplomat, you'd think. Shrop sees the virtue in thus holding back, not so much for courtesy as for linguistic reasons: holding the word back in the mouth like a greyhound eager to go. Words saved up, he thinks, get said later with greater emphasis, as with the lady from Philadelphia who produces a circular make-up mirror when Lindbergh asks for something round that will reflect his magnetic compass. You came all the way from Philadelphia, he tells her, after allowing her to sit in the pilot's seat. "I had to bring you the mirror," she says with trenchant finality, and Shrop can see him savoring the whole idea of "had to," something inevitable only just revealed, proof no doubt that the Creator works in mysterious ways.

His way of watching a movie is to pick on a scene and let its heft or wit spread out like a drop of ink in water, so much so that he sees the whole movie through those images only, distorting all the rest to fit, or even, as with *The Spirit*, linking the dun brown churns from which they pour gas into gascolators to similar churns he has observed in footage of Iraq, sacred to anthrax or even worse. These links have led him astray several times, setting up a bogus analogy his readers chided him for; but free association in lieu of lost memory is important to him and not to be blamed. He is like those squatters in Cairo who jerry-build apartments on top of apartment houses and go unpunished. Amazing is it not that someone who joins up the world's scattered phenomena so well, in order to remember them, has (so he thinks) a poor sense of them after scrutinizing the details of each, which slip away even as he mates them with something else?

"I have come to the conclusion," Quent tells him, "that what you complain about does not exist, does not matter."

"Well," Shrop retorts, "there are the lost and wasted ideas, once precious to me. Am I to blame if I stick images in their places?"

"You don't need a shrink," Quent says, "you just need an emergency to make you sort yourself out."

"*When something emerges.*" Shrop is musing.

"To wake you up."

"Don't be harsh on a fellow amputee."

"Really!" Quent's voice quivers with disgust.

"It's the same thing. Your loss. Then mine."

They go on with it, but their exchanges are predictable whereas, to Shrop, the world is not, not even when one image minimally echoes another. He has no doubt that Quent and he are in the same kind of situation and hopes to persuade him of this; the analogy is plain as day, but he is no shrink to Quent. If he were, he thinks, he might be able to persuade his old friend after all, and then they could go back to the beginning. Were Quent to grow new legs, were Shrop to regain his ideas, what a marvel that would be, cutting out all this babble.

Only a few days later (Shrop anxious to start again on what he and Quent used to joke about as an even playing field), the situation has veered off into novelty. Both Hovis Tumulty and Quent are nude on the floor, which is alive with roaches and beetles that have climbed out of white plastic soup-tubs, open and mostly empty. Not a word uttered. Quent is on his back, Hovis on her front with her massive hindquarters inviting a challenge or a golf shot. Shrop, inclined to grin, does not, but treads as carefully as he can, his mind recovering death-row cells of all sizes and shapes from B-movies he thought forgotten. "*Hola*," he whispers to the crawlers. "Hola," Tumulty sighs. Is this orgy day? If so, with whom? He has been lingering on something called *Blame It on Rio*, in which the bosomy Michelle Johnson, before coupling with Michael Caine on that famous Brazilian beach, removes (1) her bubble gum, or (2) her mouthpiece, or (3) her upper dental plate. She is only twenty, not a boxer or noticeably chewing, so it must be her dental plate. Shrop is amazed to discover that he responds more fully to Michelle Johnson than to the creepie-crawlies in the apartment. Can this be *nostalgie de la boue* then? Has Quent opted for degradation after all? Up the walls the insects go, out into the bathroom and bedroom, questing and scuttling, a few Palmetto bugs among them, over Shrop's shoes and socks.

"Dywanna stay?" Quent.

No answer.

"Dywanna eat?"

"No, I don't wanna eat. What's all this?"

"Sa kinda prayer, youse guys."

"Shagged out, huh?" Shrop.

"You betcha, buddy." Tumulty seems asleep.

Shrop is not unaware of the reverence with which the Indians of India treat their snakes, letting them pursue a house's rats through corn. Indeed, there are temples in which rats run wild, being continually fed; but surely that sort of ritual is more spiritual than this conversion of an apartment to a roach motel. He tries to envision the ultimate triumph of it all, the naked body smothered in black, the high elitism of the shrink reduced to the humility of the fakir, the ears and nostrils occupied, the body's other gashes turned into staging areas, the eyes already blurred from spiky invasions, the hair all tousled by new applicants, the mouth open and crammed. Does this necessarily demonstrate self-denial, self-humiliation in the face of . . . ? Shrop has no idea, certain that he, if anyone, should be practicing self-abnegation, but naked with pigs, say, or sheep. He now feels he owes the pair of them something, formulaic and ripe, sucked from the spavined marrow of his being: a gesture to death from the half-dead, as he fashionably thinks of himself. He has seen people covered with bees, some of them eager to experience it, some panicked, but has never discerned anything spiritual or transcendent about them. Would it be different if the beetles could inflict a grievous bite? Was danger the catalyst missing here? Was this just the mildest form of the ritual Quent had dreamed up, soon put right by a bath and some heavy Raid? Primary abasement, he decides.

He asks and Quent starts laughing at him, as a shrink would. Preliminary abasement, he then whispers to himself. Nothing too much.

From now on, he fears, arriving at his shrink's was not going to be too pleasant, and it would get worse. Mice, rats and snakes would follow, then the eviction, the humbling transfer to some other unlucky hotel in which the ABZ of self-humiliation would demand sawdust, soot, or snow. Quent has gone beyond him now and may not be bringable back from his gradual descent into myth (the legless man repudiating his rightful inheritance, his military pension, his Arlington grave, his various passes and tickets).

Shrop is wondering which shudder to adopt, his erratic mind wandering back to a heavyweight fight between Merciless Ray Mercer and Don Steele, in which Steele as if to egg Mercer on kept hitting himself in the face and chest. The harder Mercer pounded him, the more Steele struck himself, as if to boast. In the end, Mercer knocked him right out of the ring with a body shot, causing him to somersault through the ropes. Now, Shrop tells himself, should I hit myself like Steele, just to show how much more I can take, more than Quent can ever dish out? What comes next? Snakes? Otters? Mountain lions? It is going to get harder to deal with him, Shrop knows that, now going to sit in the wheelchair like the master of ceremonies, awaiting the next word from Quent, professional or otherwise, flinching at every insect touch on his face, hand or above the top of his sock. How far does one go, he wonders, getting back to nature, to the raw antics of the squashable? At least, as far as he can tell, Quent is not eating the beetles, that old protein trick from the prisoner-of-war camps in North Korea, or collecting them up again. To say his place was overrun would be too gentle an estimate, but neither Quent nor Tumulty seemed to mind, having rigged the range of human response beyond the usual: response not to the weather but to black or brown crawlies.

* * *

Airlines no longer have pursers, but back in the old Idlewild days they did, requiring an age between 23 and 35, height between five feet six inches and five feet eleven, suave personality and a well-groomed head. High school preferred, plus some experience in hotel, bank, or restaurant. Even college graduates were acceptable. On top of all this there was the stiff physical examination. The training equips pursers with conversational French and Spanish. Italian and Portuguese welcome. Shrop still sees himself in the trainee class at Idlewild, constantly being groomed and polished, taking and retaking the course in foreign currency, for when he passes down the aisle with duty-free temptation. He also thrives on another course, that in international timetables, so that, if asked, he can get someone from Karachi to Altoona without looking it up. He also learns until he is letter-perfect the long list of airport identifiers. In his head he fills out manifests (cargo and passengers) and other Customs paperwork. He has to be told about Greenwich and Zulu time (= zero hours, zero minutes) and acquainted with such phrases as Greenwich Mean Time (GMT). He regularly rehearses his flight check, round-trip, after which he becomes available (on call) for overseas flights, complete with flawless knowledge of ditching procedures. Every six months he goes from Idlewild to the Coast Guard Station at Floyd Bennett Field in Brooklyn to check first-aid out in the bay in a rubber dinghy that self-inflates. They all jump from the Coast Guard boat into the water, life jackets inflated, to board the life raft. A plume of orange smoke drifts away from them as one of their number fires a flare. For three hours they practice with desalinization gear, oars, sea anchor, and signal mirror. Shrop always loves to work the portable radio, stern rehearsal for when, in his cap, he sits on his tiny ledge of a seat and fills out his forms, jacket buttoned, necktie immaculately knotted, the huge emergency door of the Connie behind him, with instructions in English and French, on his face a look of amiable obsession, between his equally spaced legs an entire drawer from the filing cabinet. He purses his lips and wonders if left-handed pursers are allowed. He is the steward, or *stig-ward*, who guards the hall or sty and makes sure the passengers are comfortable. Yes, he says, the first crew member they got rid of was the purser, and it was downhill from then on. On his sleeve he wears a special stripe, wider than a hostess's, and a golden stripe on his cap to distinguish him from the hoi polloi. People, he muses, used to know how to address him, always beginning their sentence with "*Purser*," very much in the accosting vocative because they recognized him and knew his function. You could always count on your purser for anything, and the only reason he did not fly the Connies was lack of time. *Oh, Mr. Porter* was the railroad movie; *Oh, Mr. Purser* the aerial one.

Well, Shrop thinks, this must be it: nothing extra to be coped with, just a trot to a small benchmark in progress by huge Hovis and the diminished figure of Quent who, presumably, rides her like a mahout with pointed stick and all. By comparison, Shrop's place is flawless, with elegant tables on which his collection of purses is carefully laid out so as to catch the afternoon sun. The mere sight of him ceremoniously bearing the purse of the day, en route to the movies to do a review, has irked many a moviegoer of limited tolerance. Shrop no longer reviews, but he will (as he says it) bare his purse collection of some hundred for discerning viewers. Asked what it is that takes him about them, he half-mentions coruscating pouches, claiming that the pouch is one of the salient icons in human exchange. All of life, he says, comes in pouches, and what is a purse but a sealable pouch? Enough said: the more cluttered with precious or semi-precious stones the better. His purses remain empty, unlabeled, some of them priceless. This is the only bit of him that recalls the shoes of Imelda Marcos, who created for dictionaries the one word she wished to be remembered by: *Imeldific*, which means plutocratic impulse-buying. She had shoes, not skeletons, in her closets, she said, and Shrop had purses, or did when he tidied up and stashed them away. Has Shrop a word for himself? Actually, he has: it's *shropeux*, meaning *amnesiac purser*.

He dwells on the delights of idyll, the only ones he has to counter the horrors of the killers with. After three years he recalls vividly a woman in a wheelchair carried down the full length of one tower by two men, just, he tells himself, *because she was there*. Much else, that others recall, he has forgotten, now omits from his life; he may have lost sixty per cent of the catastrophe, but the pain has never left him, indeed has blossomed more because what provoked it has vanished.

Quent is much better at remembering, but what he brings to the occasion seems of a different temper from Shrop's: no Idlewild, no bits of movies, but an overture to the squalid, whatever your opinion of the insect world is. Of his dreamy, poignant marginal interests, Shrop is fond, as of the only stuff that makes his life worthwhile, but he can see that his own particular lotus is another man's poison. He sees the somnolent Tumulty on the rug opening her legs wide and seductively swaying them about as if offering the unshaven Cave of Ali Baba to any watcher not averse to climbing roaches and equally swift beetles. She seems lost in imminent desire, waiting for Quent to wake up or come back to life, having wholly assented in his decision to clog his apartment with creatures that usually prompt disgust. Shrop senses an era is over, and a clinic too.

What does it feel like to plod through the symbolism of pain, put there to distract us pointedly, right to the immediate cause of it? A kick in the belly, a bullet in the nape, a volley through the heartspoon behind the red target pinned on by the man with the blindfold and the last cigarette? Or, as we have witnessed, like the woman with a screed of DNA in one hand, to be handed in, and in her other a cube of ice with which she cools her abraded eyes while looking at cardboard signs that just say *Missing*? Or is it like landing on your own two feet after jumping hand in hand with your secretary from the 99th floor while a bottle of Beck's stands untoppled on the bar five floors below you? Or is it as dead-feeling as a huge twisted steel girder arriving by barge at Freshkill dump, en route to China or Indonesia? What does it *feel like* to be killed before you feel pain? Is there a momentary reprieve in that? Why have the thousands entombed not told us? What law forbids them to write their four-word autobiographies? "It doesn't hurt, Mamma." That would be enough for us, just to know that the disintegrative dunt marches faster than the nerves can burn. That might do it, tempting thousands more to leap, say, hand in hand or not. Is that the problem then: to be blotted out before anything hurts at all, reassuring those whose faith in the loving god moves mountains of steel, bunkers of poisonous grey silt, billows of noxious smoke?

This was the plaza where people sat or walked, smiling just to be there in the uneven benison of sunlight, awaiting nothing in particular except a train, closing time, or the completion of a sandwich nibbled, swallowed, slid home where it belongs. Those who know claim the plaza was supposed to bear only the weight of people on their feet or their backsides, not a force majeure of many-ton cranes with huge pincers. Well, it somehow holds, appalling eyeful that it is, having fed its horror into thousands of eyes daily: pilgrims, not calm strollers being social in the main street of some Italian town as the sun begins to think of going down.

Oh no, a congregation of isolates now, some of whom have traveled thousands of miles just to kneel at this happenstance altar, perhaps the most rueful kind of altar there can be. Quent has been to it. Shrop has been there with him. The non-Nazis from the apartment house and Hovis Tumulty have been there too. Shipshape and stunned, therefore lacking a direction, or so Shrop thinks. Everybody who comes to behold it goes away without the slightest sense of direction, garbling north, south, east and west, unable to steer, eat, or sleep. It is what has been done to the people, not what has been smashed. They may deplore the gap-tooth in the skyline, but that isn't it, it's the pell-mell, underground shit-canned pandemonium to which the many thousand were not invited. And in those beholders who think about it, something arises that is far from cricket: that both evolution and death follow the same random course, profiting (or not), succumbing (or not) from or to the same impromptu stream of variables. Life, it just so happens, protects itself, but death protects itself better, occupying a calmer niche. Must he always be on edge?

Now the crashing has stopped, there are no more inaudible cries toward which doomed firemen shove themselves merely in hope of hearing, possibly believing that the sound of a scramble coming nearer might prompt a final squeak from who knows whom. Shrop will go back, to replay his sense of what took place at Ground Zero, yet not to show his face to anyone. He does not need to abase himself before invertebrates, as that last and lowest order goes on and on. He does need, however, to try and persuade himself that what is flukey is immaculate and will give way to nothing better, no matter how long he lives, gradually losing memory until he doesn't remember doing so, while his old-time shrink makes an educated man's heroic lunges into the busy market of entomology. One has heard it said of two men that, together, they made a whole man, or that each became a catalyst to the other. Not so here: they have gone their separate ways in the same direction, after a sizeable wait, only to feel numbed differently. It will not be Shrop sitting in the wheelchair, or any chair, hearing out the disjointed shrink, or Quent listening, admitting, forensically allocuting (as villains do on his favorite cop show). The world is wider than that, perhaps demanding what each has learned from the other: the one man imposing on the other's life something borrowed, the other being gullible enough to accept it. But does Quent benefit from having misled his friend, deluding him into that other philosopher's life? Has Shrop been the gainer from the deceit? It will be forever hard to pin this down; we can only say they had this life together, this and that experience, but nothing reducible to patterns that tell you outright: One man felt ever after guilty while the other felt ever after far from swift. Bits of both, of course, but not enough to be characteristic.

Their conversations have changed as well.

Shrop: "How about the old basis, then, getting back on same?"

Quent: "One day I'll smash all these beetles with a potato-masher."

Shrop: "They're your beetles."

Quent: "No, I only rent them. They are their own."

Shrop cannot help feeling that there was something arbitrary about Quent's choice of beetles; *if* this was truly a *nostalgie de la boue*, and *nos-*

talgie was "homesickness" and *boue* was mud, what did it mean that he skulked or gambolled on the floor where, once upon a time, he had confessed to lying in the warm afternoon sun of September, which he called "spanieling"? Now spanieling might have made sense, but beetles, inviting in what the building abominated, was a silly trick, too obvious. More obvious than rolling around in the mud? He thinks so. And then to declare that he would bash them all to death, most of them anyway. That was vacuous, wasn't it? It would have made more sense to brew up a witches' broth in the kitchen, where the air was dank and feral to begin with: halfway there, he decides. How had Quent arrived at beetles? Were they just things to buy by the pint? Would they remember him? Did they image for him Ground Zero at its least amiable? Unless he had some deviant idea of preaching to them, plugged into the mud like a mandrake or a tuning fork, with god's own royal constellation of beetles foaming around beneath him in the underground floors.

23
A Cupped Elbow

THE TRAUMATIZED HAVE FICKLE MANNERS, GOING FROM ONE extreme to the other. A cupped elbow will feel a curt shove. An opened door will slam on the backside of the woman opened for. People will interrupt others' interruptions. "Yair" will replace "Hello" on the telephone. A willing lifter of a case to the baggage rack will beg off, citing his cardiologist. No one will light your cigarette anymore. The person blocking your advance will stand his ground as you say, "Bog off," and he answers, "Stinkeroo." Waiters will slam a warm plate in front of you and sniff. Cabbies will no longer hoist your bags or open the door for you. Doormen will appear to forget your arrival and look the other way, later in the year accepting your timorous Christmas gift without so much as a thankyou. Policemen will no longer indulge in that half-salute they vouchsafe to civilians, from one order of beings to an inferior one. The scooping up of dogdo becomes careless, leaving many a skidmark on the pavement or the grass. Waiters will bring you the next course while you are still devouring its predecessor and plonk it down without regret. Airport searchers will upend your purse and repack it with slovenly haste.

Only in the actual zero area will you find acts of exaggerated civility, where nobody bumps into anybody, and people standing transfixed in the immobility of grief receive maximum consideration in a mood almost holy. If this is where it all went down, it is also where a nation reared itself up and swallowed its sadness with innovative etiquette. A new standard of deference obtains here, amid this rollicking turmoil of a city, and if sandtrap bunkers run by sadists are where terrorists learn their ABZs, then this is where appalled mourners learn the delicate, fastidious protocol that is going to get them through the next year, as in Ravel's *Le Tombeau de Couperin*, that coronet of elegies for friends who died during the war, all meeting and melded at composer Couperin's tomb. Tomb manners, in other words, just as there is an etiquette for tennis, croquet and polo. Learned, it evokes C. Aubrey Smith perhaps, at any rate a fixed way of behaving. A Frenchwoman who has flown to New York just to join the grievers keeps murmuring, "I will care, I will care," and the locals make way for her and usher her forward nearer the posters and placards, the blown-up photographs, the poems and the drawings. It is for those present what Idlewild is for Shrop, or one of those quiescent long runs in a movie that gets Greer Garson staring at a competitor's rose. Nowadays, Shrop goes to Ground Zero for a crash course in the milk of human kindness, revulsed by almost everything, anxious to join hands with total strangers, secretly husbanding his own increasing loss (memory both deliberate and random), amazed that he alone in this crowd has lost himself in the disasters, knowing he no longer belongs in the fast world of street-smart scurry and wise-ass jeer. No, he decides to learn from the beginning how to say such things as *much obliged* and *by your leave*, empty as dead leaves but keys to a broken-hearted chivalry that has not afflicted the city since he does not even know when, but he makes outside comparisons with a connoisseur's ease: Warsaw, Rotterdam, Stalingrad, and for how long did *they* have to endure the bloodlust of an enemy who also arrived by air and then took root, installing a deadly infrastructure of torture cellars, execution walls, slaughterhouses furnished with guillotines, where (*Soldier of Orange*) the camp orderly injects a raving victim in the tongue to still his cries while they strap him in beneath the blade.

Of course, in his emotional fervor, he mixes things up a little and sometimes imposes images from the rape of Peking (1937) upon the events of the other day. Never mind, he is tuning in to the right wavelength, which reports that, on this unruly planet, no one is ever safe, and if part of the American Dream, along with 26 Amendments and 435 Representatives, specifies safety or idyll or peace, then it should be sobered up a little to read *Life is dangerous always, so plan accordingly.* Now he knows, and the truth makes his back and cheek twitch, his formal knowledge of politesse threatens to desert him in favor of a rough and ready camaraderie picked up from boys' books, from Huck Finn perhaps. He rejoices as best he can in the new decorum at Ground Zero, where people who have had people ripped raw from them in the middle of a cellphone conversation discover the presence on the big blue wet ball of thugs red in tooth and claw. He sees now that it's enough just to stand alongside people in the biggest graveyard in the world, having lost all will to walk forward, to breast the sound-barrier or winner's tape made wholly of flowers. Let us all come in last, he hears. We have no hope any more.

Almost annulled by this trundled elegy, he goes home to just sit and brood, wondering why he has lost his coordination, bumping into things, the power to sleep (to sleep *it off*), and the need for food. He does almost nothing, wondering at the white sludge caked on his shoes and spattered on his socks. The disaster seems to go on forever, renewing itself lest anyone forget its hellish impact, and, in moments of brief philosophical daylight, asking himself if the huge groundswell of misery has any connection at all with the mundane details of everyday life: orange juice, carpentry, a movie ticket. He thinks not, recognizing that humans are born to mourn even if they do not make a mess of things by marauding one another. Even without murder, and all that goes with it, he tells himself, there is prevailing death, without which the whole of human culture would be different. Sit and take it, he says. What if a red giant one day burns all the books we have left behind us? Whose fault will that be? Because we chose to write, a heap of blackened pages with nobody to read them. How episodic we are. In his mind's eye he arranges a few of his favorite concepts on an invisible line that reaches across the room:

Gather ye rosebuds while ye may.

Seize the day.

Happy over seventy thousand fathoms.

Something tiny to be glad about. Nothing much. Kernels of wisdom perhaps.

Idlewild.

Miles of celluloid on fire.

Purses, pouches.

These help him to go to sleep, at least to a puckered, pocked delirium in which he holds another's hand and jumps.

24
A Sea Anchor

NOT TO MAKE TOO FINE A POINT ON THIS, THE LITTLE DISMALS that affect the giant dreams affected Shrop in physical ways too. It was not all a silver skein of glumness running through his head. He began to wait two days to relieve his bowels and trained himself to be an astronaut by "holding" his water for hours until leaky agony at last ousted him and his will from the equation. Needless to say, he went without meals, even such delicacies (to him) as his breakfast of tofu Canadian bacon, eggbeaters, and coarse "healthy" bread. His nightly ration of fish, salmon or haddock, would often sit dried out in the refrigerator, though he did make the effort to go out and buy it from Joe the fish man, whose van parked close by. He stopped reading and answering his mail, let the answering machine's tape fill up and then erased without a care. In tinier matters, he no longer bothered to sharpen his pencils in the squeezi-sharpener, and persisted in using fiber-point pens right down to invisibility. General replacements such as shaving foam and toothpaste, Biotene mouthwash and Givenchy aftershave went by the board. He no longer troubled to replace a moldy toothbrush or clean a clogged comb under the hot water tap. Rent, subscriptions, TV cable bill went unpaid until a semi-polite note arrived. One day, in a bad mood, he dropped his address book in the garbage (a figure of speech; this human made little waste), then picked it out again two days later as a vestigial worry about continuity in the private life assailed him. He stopped wearing a necktie, shuffled about in slippers, and took to wearing boxer shorts all day, even going out in them sockless. He could tell he was becoming what wiseacres call a hostage to fortune, listening all day to classical music (impressionists mainly plus Sibelius, Mahler, and Schnittke) and subsisting on a coffee substitute made from cereal and beets. Painkiller pills he kept by him for headaches, and some unguent for the rash that had invaded his hands. His heels began to split and his post-nasal drip to spurt each morning for a full hour after he woke. All he did was replace batteries, stack up the newspapers as they arrived, almost a David Susskind figure assembling year after year of daily issues. He did, however, lay in a supply of candles and a gross of plastic gloves to read his non-existent mail with. He even took over Madame Fortescu's line about having his mail forwarded from Bucharest by his dog. After listening to his tiny radio full volume, he began to turn it quieter, fraction by fraction, until it became almost inaudible. He wanted to land on the exact spot that, so close to silence, leaked minimal sound, though he realized that after an eon the battery would fail and there would arrive a zone of delicious overlap in which the tiny sliver of sound was either his new skill or the old battery dying.

He stopped seeing his sea-anchor, Quent, and began ploughing through the Bible, in counterpoint to what he called, well, what *did* he call it? What did others call it? He wasn't the only person suffering from it: just a few millions more. Well, then, what? Atrophy of the will. Enfeebled sense of safety. No more drive than a mouse in a machine at Rockefeller University, cafard or *accidie*—he trotted out those old college words again, glad of their new adult status. Now they applied to an all-urban palsy, did they not? Could there be a new name for what ailed them all? How about Bunyan's Fret, for the man who dreamed up the Slough of Despond? What was a slough? Something like sludgy Ground Zero or the La Brea tarpits? You fell in and it was like a quicksand, say the one from which Lawrence of Arabia failed to rescue Daud, one of the two Arab youths with whom he crossed Sinai. A bog.

A marsh, like Idlewild. A latrine. It sucked you in and down, to repose among other sucked-in bodies—the quicksand did not want to eat you, oh no, but it had its heart set on keeping you, and there they lay, corpses from the previous century, some of them, with heads alongside feet, arms twisted back as if the owner were going to fly, faces bloated and black with sand slop, eyes roughened, tongues lolling: the place where all despond dreamers yearned to go.

Sometimes he felt as if he were playing with the afterlife, fidgeting around for something positive to negate: speaking and greeting, washing one's hair, *doing* the dishes rather than throwing them down the dumbwaiter. There seemed no limit to the number of tiny occupations a human could aspire to, as if each one split up into sundry other chores: the shoes, for instance, hewn up into polish, the knot, the in-shoes sole cut to the required size, the repair in which the old sole, heel, are ripped off and you start from scratch. All that, gone by the board, into Samuel Beckett's nosebag. Unable to do or want, his people just gaped at the human comedy. Shrop has done his fair share of reading, not all of it philosophy by any means, nor all forgotten either. He wavers in and out of his favorite books, as in and out of his favorite films, knowing the work was created specifically for him to sidle through. Now, he whispers, at what point does this hermit become a pariah? Am I old enough? Am I downcast enough? Have I wholly lost all belief in the inviolable nature of an American life? Will I ever recover? Not until they install me in the hanging gardens of Babylon, and leave me alone by plashing water and green trees. I want to have nothing, but I want that want witnessed.

Now is the time I need my Quent most.

I need to be reintroduced to him, stumps, medals, wheelchair and all, even the doughty Tumulty whose beaver shot resembles a Zulu shield.

"Well, Shrop, how are you?"

"Worse than ever."

"Tell me all, dear man."

"The Slough of Despond has me by the short and curlies."

"Mixed metaphors," Quent barks, "not allowed in here."

"Then I'll take my business elsewhere."

"I misled you, Shrop. My fault alone."

"Oh? There is historical trauma and cosmic trauma, Quent. The first is what you did to me in your sickeningly manipulative way. The second is what God does to us all. I sense I am somewhere in between. Lord help me."

"Lord will not, he's into self-help these days."

"Then what? It's all sliding away from me, and it won't come back. I am socially bereft because I no longer feel safe."

"Would we, you and I, have gone through a window hand in hand to certain death, impelled by flame and smoke? Would we have been content to do so? Or would we have jumped separately, as ever?" The old Quent has disappeared behind a black-brown paste of squashed beetles that has now hardened into a mask of sorts, to be tapped against with a pencil and painted white by a clown.

The blight of imaginary conversations is that imagination fails; instead of talking turkey you end up talking hummingbird. In the long run, even the most ordinary interlocutor outweighs the best imagined speech, even when you set about imagining, between yourselves, a suitable fate for the smug, smiling sadist you have seen on a video tape, or in effigy poisoning schoolchildren's milk. Setting aside the electric chair, the garotte, the noose, the gurney as the tools of some medieval barber who might have doubled as a surgeon, you recommend an oxy-acetylene flame applied to the lips and teeth, between yourselves of course, then lower down, manna to anyone who rejoices at the smell of burning hair. It comes better when vouchsafed between allies, say. Of course, the entire process of disposal, after certain finis-es already having taken place, works better in imagination than at the hands of military tribunals or civilian courts always predisposed to enclose the villain in a cage on wheels. Facetious to send him back to the country he came from, merely to enjoy the reformed status of women once he has been castrated.

All very well, but Quent is no longer talkable to, dithering in something between faint and coma, perhaps the result of licking mashed beetles or even chewing them as they ascend him. Who can help him now, whom he hasn't tried before? Tumulty the apparent disciple no longer cleans or offers argument in her boisterous Irish manner. Shrop stays away like someone who has graduated and now seeks to ply his trade in the disheveled world. So we talk to ourselves or imagine talking to each other in the old days. The trouble is, that mode of living no longer holds good, not the one in which, to fulfill some clause of evolution, you behaved sensibly, tying your shoelaces, brushing your teeth, opening a window. There he lies, presumably, in the huge fiefdom of invertebrates while I repose (fancy word for fancy stance) in the realm of the ne'er-do-well, the bum, the solipsistic pariah, where nothing makes sense, not even to those who break through the cordon and try to make sensible chat with you:

"How are you then?"

"We do not answer."

"Have you heard the news?"

"For us, there is no news. Goodbye."

"Not even the news from Somalia and Norway?"

End of conversation as not imaginary enough. And indeed, for those of us who have mentally ventured out beyond the norms and the copybook maxims, there is nothing worth reporting. We have seen the flame and doused it.

What I want to do is sweep them all into my awkward embrace, including those few spare, unlucky ones who inhaled and miserably died because whoever mailed the anthrax had found some way of beating the electrostatic charge that kept the spores in place, allowing them to soar and be puffed. While millions survived. One day, some minia-

115

turist poet will draft the sonnet of their horror, akin to flu but deadly after a delay. One pictures the mad chemist slinking to the mailbox in Trenton, NJ to slip the little packet of doom into the clanging box among all those harmful/harmless letters of deprivation, longing, greed, all to be delivered like babes. How can anyone leading so cautious and known a life (library, hairdresser, market, florist) have succumbed to so vile a trick, out front like an advance guard in front of a horde of wailing mailmen? Don't go to Boca, we heard. Or New Jersey. Avoid Washington, D.C. and Connecticut. Don't go anywhere, and handle your mail with kid gloves. We live in a time in which no one can find out anything at all, and if they do it's too late. Nobody says "going postal" anymore to signify the madness of mailmen, who stood to suffer most. We have not seen it all yet. Milkmen, barmen, nurses and doctors beware. The corral of my open arms is nowhere wide enough for this embrace, but it is the hug of a man whose philosophy vanished in a puff of spores.

25
Doris

"THE TROUBLE IS," SHROP TELLS QUENT IN YET ANOTHER effort to make contact, even to get the relationship kick-started, "the situation is so bad, you end up wanting to breathe the air, lousy as it is. Now where's the sense in that? It's as if you have to breathe the history of the air along with the air. That kind of mess."

If Quent is attending, he cannot tell, but the man has at least washed up and now sits calmly in his wheelchair awaiting the passage of some quiet, sedate time. He makes no answer, but clasps the chair's arms as if otherwise he might take flight. Still no response. Shrop tries again, rattling off his doxology about benzene, dioxin, asbestos, PCBs, fiber-glass and lead: a cocktail for demons and deadheads. "That's what we're breathing," he says, "and arguing about."

Stirred, Quent says, "So that's the breathin' zone?"

"No, the opposite. There are wash stations too, as you know. But the energy lavished on washing increases the amount of air breathed in, surely." There was a time when Shrop longed to have a place with a view of the harbor, the Statue of Liberty serving as a nitelite for his bedroom; but no longer. Union Square is good enough for him, and will go on being so. Over the past few years, the thought had some-times come to him that they, the Ground Zero group, were breathing the air of an alien planet, transported there by accident but by and large getting by, swapping innocence for experience, the usual for the out-landish, and yes, the benign for the poisonous. Well, whatever epic or adventurous quality that life had had has gone, especially for zero breathers such as Quent: a whole generation learning not to open win-dows, always to wear a mask, and keep a cylinder of oxygen handy. If life in this Manhattan neighborhood had ever been cozy, it had changed into something not rich and strange, but fiery and toxic. Who was to say how their lungs would look after ten years of it, the com-plex team of gases inhaled in gentle increments by obstinate people? Is this what had wrought such sudden and unlikely changes in Quent, the shrink and former pilot? Shrop had no idea. From ugly gases to bee-tles and roaches? The shift was remarkable and skewed. In the old days,

Quent had been the epitome of patient listening and unforceful suggestion, a man less to be relied upon than staked out with one's personal flag as a new colony, to be ever celebrated yet never granted eventual independence. Now he had become part of some weird terrorist insect play in which the insects that had not died in the catastrophe had multiplied. Or so Shrop thinks, unable to adjust to the new landscape Quent arranged around himself, completely redoing the redoubtable Tumulty, another Doris toweled from the bath, enlisting her into a cleansing regime unlike the olden one.

So, Shrop broods, he has a hold on her I had never imagined. She's a camp follower, in tune with his twists and twitches, never to be reborn a second time. She said she had two children, but neither Shrop nor Quent has ever seen them, concluding that they belong to some permanent crèche of the night, troughing on sarnies as she calls them (bacon and sardine sandwiches). Such elementary fare consorts well with her shape, and Shrop wondered why she never showed up with a sarnie in her fist, a chip off the old block, either to munch on while cleaning or to use as a mop on the shiny parts of the floor. She, who Shrop thought incapable of change, from blockish unsuasible presence to monstrous odalisque. Surely Quent had merely become a different kind of magician from the kind he used to be.

Shrop tries again, but Quent rations out his answers. His medals are back in their tissue-lined boxes, his chest has healed, the creepie-crawlies have (mostly) departed, though Shrop crushed a few on the way in today. What next? Frogs or grass parakeets? Was there a text for his radical revisions of the universe, or was he just an amateur doodling with the available equipment, casting around for unprecedented sensations, not in the most original manner possible, but disturbingly enough. Now you had to watch where you were going. Was he someone to whom the intended audience felt superior? *Comedy.* Or someone to whom the audience felt inferior? *Tragedy.* In his travels, Shrop (instead of working at Cambridge with Rosselli, as Quent had persuaded him he did), had sat at the feet of Lionel Trilling and Jacques Barzun, who ran a joint seminar whose title Shrop forgets, except that Trilling once lauded him for a small speech on Walter Bagehot and the British constitution while Barzun with a flinty 2-H pencil tattooed one of Shrop's essays. Where had tragedy and comedy come from then? From someone else in the same seminar at Columbia, the university that fulsomely celebrated its faculty past and present while ignoring its own graduates, that miscellaneous cash-cow distributed hither and yon, the horns in New Jersey, the tail in Pennsylvania, the udder in New York, and so on. Was Quent, with all his vagaries, tragic or comic? Neither, he was forever fresh, adaptable, sly, as Shrop never could be, being an amnesiac.

Now and then Shrop gets glimpses of the domain he used to inhabit *qua* philosopher, in particular the spider's web of related concepts. For example, under the stimulus of some TV news broadcast, he recovers words he once related to one another in unique ways: evil, cruel, brutal, sadistic, devilish, and so forth. But he cannot figure out anymore their bearing on one another, or ferret out the overarching concept, say a word like sin, that irrevocably bound them all together. He does not doubt that he once upon a time had such an idea, but it has deserted him, so now he wallows around, assembling a kit whose plan is missing and whose parts remain incomplete. Nor did he publish, so that avenue of recovery is closed. Best to start again, he thinks, but the old impulse has quit him, and the mental topography has changed, very much post-existentialist, but he knows that he once knew. He knows something else too, though fuzzily:

"I *am not* Wittgenstein," he cries to Quent. "I never was."

Quent knows and makes no sign. Perhaps he could even be prosecuted for thus betraying a patient. And struck off.

It is not enough to be not Wittgenstein, and he knows it. He is not Plato either, or Kant. Would either be more fun? His only way, he concludes, warmly pressing Tumulty's huge ham of a hand in some aimless gesture of self-reassurance, is to see what the words say when they come to mind. Is this the clue?

26
A Good Angle

NOW HE IS A BOXER SLOWLY BEING ANNIHILATED IN THE NEXT-to-last round, feeling not only the thud-thud against his jaw, but the caramba crash in his solar plexus. He is being pounded by a man with three arms. All very well to wipe the persp away, grace him with Vaseline, ram outsize Q-tips up his nose to absorb the blood, press the Endswell against his split eyebrow, pour cold water down his shorts to shock his privates, tell him to take deeper than deep breaths, then hold them, let them out slowly. *They* have not been hit, neither Coalsack Pete nor One-Eye. Raunchville veterans as they are. I am never going to eat again, he says, I am going to let the other guy slam one side of my intestine hard against the other, with nothing in there but gas. Nothing to vent in either direction, nothing to nauseate me. Nothing to throw up, nothing to dump, and then they'll find out how light I'll be, cornering and skipping, not even water in my gut to please them. That's the way to manage it, get the crowd roaring, oh yes, can't you see that guy's transparent, you can see right through his gut, and every punch just goes through him, out the other side, and then withdraws just like from saran wrap. That is how it's going to be, a hollow man with elastic innards. Then the eye won't matter, the crushed nose, the missing teeth, the nearly amputated tongue, all of them imaginary to the guy who loses his fist in the cellophane gut of the former champion, whose wits have deserted him even as he staggers across the ring to have the big gaudy belt arranged around his middle. Who am I, folks? You're the champ, you have nobody else left to beat, son. You're on top and can carry yourself lightly on the balls of your feet, a man awesomely gentle in the streets, don't run from him, he's the champ, defender of the faith, protector of the realm, as it says on the huge shell of the centerpiece.

Can he take it then? Sure, he's tough as old flint, old boots. He doesn't wince or whinge. He ripples his back and flexes his bicepses. No need to rehearse anything in the dressing room, or grope after the referee's instructions. He knows what to do, even while the ref is clearing seconds from the ring. He coils himself up, sets the starter leg behind him, and is halfway into his run as the bell sounds. The first blow is what happens next, quite crushing Sponson's nose, who has not even raised his hands yet, but is neatly posed to give the crowd a good angle on a great man. Wow, I never saw anyone move that fast or with glove held so far back it must have travelled four feet to catch up with his shoulder, and then forward, with all the extra speed of the run. He's as good as dead already, this Sponson, poleaxed, the beads of sweat from his face swatted somehow forward on their way to the Pleiades. It's over in the first minute, like something else we know about, so fast it almost dizzies the eye as it arrives, turns and burrows into what will not resist it.

So what is this belly-ache of yours? Where did it come from? Higher up. Did you eat some hollow food? Is it the space left by some crashing airplane, flown through and left behind? Will it never heal again? Will there be pictures of it in the medical encyclopedias? This patient has a gravestone in his gut, dragging him down, making him want to crawl, bite the carpet, rummage around in his tripes to ease the fit of his hollow men. Nothing left to digest with? No, I am not the man whose belly had a window cut in it so you could see the process of digestion from without. You had to shine a light of course. Why does such a crash, a duet, make you never want to eat again, turn you against food as against the whole technique of sustaining life by calorie intake? Not even a jam of beetles will pass muster, I do not need it. I'll be like Gandhi then, spinning away with not even a swig. Thus to show common cause, instead of weeping over spilled milk. What I'll do is ram both my boxing gloves into the space in my stomach, to keep the membranes from rubbing together. It's as if the jet had flown right into my belly and out the other side. Is there not nuclear radiation in the jet fuel itself, just to add to the mess, just as there is hydrochloric acid in the stomach of all of us? Wash, feel the scald of that.

Can I help you? Bandages.

Tourniquet then.

Triage?

Are you moaning, Quent?

Shrop, what made this gaping hole in you?

There is no end to these conversations. Tumulty is not a nurse; if she espies blood she rams the side of her gigantic butt against the wound and presses down. She has been known to loll on an open wound and keep it closed. Keep her by all means then. Let her perform with her heart in it. Let her come clean as if lying among fresh-pointed speargrass in average springtime, awaiting her lover with a sprig of hawthorn between her teeth and a daisy in her hair.

"Have you two been messing around again?"

She has this blunt way of talking.

"Getting into something nasty?"

"Who? Us?"

She does not answer, but slaps us hard with a box of kotex she has brought with her today to use as swabs or bandages. She never arrives without something absorbent.

I ask her about Quent, but at first she gets evasive, blinking heavily and dragging at the backside of her jeans. "Where is he then?" Apparently he took a cab uptown to his tailor's, no doubt to have something fitted. But what?

"Oh," she answers laboriously, "one of those university outfits you get for being clever. Some kind of fancy dress."

"Oh those," I say, ironically remembering. "What good would those be to a man without legs? Unless he gets a special fit."

"That must be it," she says eagerly.

"Then who helped him in and out, with the wheelchair?"

"The yellow proletariat," she says. "For a big tip and waiting time." But he is nowhere to be seen, perhaps steering himself back in the electric chair, a phrase he loves.

We await him; he does not arrive, but could have gone to dinner at a time when restaurant staff are more than willing to help you in and out, wheelchair or parachute.

An odd smell of teak (sawn) and custard is coming off her.

Or is it a milky acid, a keen reaching smell with a streak of baby caca in it? Beetles, I deduce.

She spruces the place up, finally making headway with the creepie-crawlies, about which she says nothing whatever, though I with my renowned imagination am dreaming up locusts.

"Them," she says, "they wasn't worth cookin'."

27
Voices Off

SHROP HAS BEGUN WONDERING IF TRYING NOT TO BE EDGY MAKES you more irritable than ever. What is it, he wonders, that irritates him so, and he dismisses the usual answers such as nerves, sexual frustration, fever, disappointment, and settles for the feeling that his body is going to come apart, one piece falling off here, another one there, because of a high poisonous wind from Ground Zero, detaching his feet and hands, his ears, his eyes, his head, and so on. That same wind demolishes them all, not necessarily sending them as far as a Brooklyn landfill, but deadly because an entire population has been damned.

So is damnation *it*?

No, it is the lack of safety in all things, the rough underbelly of the American Dream turning out to have steel needles embedded in it, pointing outward for any fool who cares to stroke it. Just think of all the pieces, ferried off to Brooklyn and a mass grave: lopped heads, feet, hands, the lot, awaiting the newest Dr. Frankenstein who vows he will one day construct a human being perfect in all ways, and never irritable.

Or is it the loss of smugness about that Dream, the knowing that you can go on living in a fool's paradise like the middle-aged professor Rath in *The Blue Angel*, only to find it biting you in the kishkes after a few nights of bliss? But who ever guaranteed the dream, said the country was inviolable, promised that there would be no cryptoterrorists (so-called) in the flood of immigrants, here not to prosper but to destroy? He drops things. He bites his tongue and his inside cheeks. His eyes prickle and water. His ears make a wobbly sound. His groin develops a gamey-smelling crotch rot. His legs fail him: claudication, named after the Emperor Claudius, as if that somehow ennobled the limp. His balls twinge with something more than the habitual stone ache. His nose blocks. Out of his mouth from his throat come little pastilles of brown mucus, texture of coffee-grounds. His fresh-washed hair itches him to death as if thistledown powder has fallen from the sky. His fourth finger on the left hand resumes its downward droop, clearly an arthritis of some kind. His liver pains him. He walks into things. He is fast losing his depth perception. His heart flutters. His bladder is ever full. He goes constipated for days on end. His voice, usually a brisk bass-baritone, becomes blurred and rheumy as if he has been eating cream. His ears fill with wax. He shaves but it itches at once, even when he cauterizes it with the strongest pomade. He coughs uncontrollably and swallows wrong, persuaded a hummingbird flies just behind his head.

So it is all this then? No, it is as if his universe is leaking away, dribbling down between his knees. Hoping for he knows not what, he begins making sorties up and down the halls of Quent's building, making a start with the woman who claims her dog forwards her mail from Bucharest. "Oh, he was well trained," she explains. "He reads Cyrillic, of course, and always pays extra at the post office. He has a long tongue for stamps, trots to the post office with the mail in a basket below his chin, and new-stamps the next address with a postmark surgically set into his paw. It's easy once you know how." So much for Madame Fortescu whose name, if she were English, would end in an *e*. Wisely, the dog never sends on magazines or boxes but stacks them up in his kennel against her return.

It bothers and alienates him that this lady makes no sense and is therefore just as irritated as he. Clearly, she is plaguing him, taking him for all he's worth, but not leveling. Just a spoof. So he asks Madame Heinkel of the private jet and the two permanent pilots, but she tells him to get lost and, with strange idiom for a Heinkel, accuses him of too much hat and not enough cattle. Bangs the door. So this is it: he's irritated because Quent's neighbors either make fun of him or shut him out. And where is Quent anyway? Tumulty says no, a haircut, then when he returns she will bathe him like the lamb he is.

So he decides to cheer up, trying to dream his own lyrical version of Idlewild, the moment in *Revenge* when José Ferrer's innocent pal Ignacio, who never says much in a year, vents his admiration for Kevin Costner, who is seeking inamorata Madeleine Stowe in the brothels of darkest Mexico: I tell you, this is a great man who could cross all the oceans to find her, with one noble horse and a bloody knife, and even if I were dead I would want to aid him and go with him over all the mountains to find her, so great is this hero with the big hands and the gallant face. I would even—

Shrop interrupts himself. That's not what young Ignacio said, it was much milder and shorter. Why am I romancing, then? Is ordinary life not enough for me? Will I find Miss Stowe, her cheek slashed by her husband Anthony Quinn and drag her away from all those brutes unbuttoning their flies with pristine lasciviousness? Still the irritation, or the irritation theme, persists. What is bugging him, he thinks, is the inadequacy of the idyllic world to soothe the inhabitant of the real one. There is no comfort, muchachos. Well, when was there ever? Was not the world always a mixmaster, plying you with both evil and good, daring you to try, or to give up? Isn't that it? Is America the broken what angers me? Who ever said that America was unique and would not be like all other countries, subject to the tyrant's sword, the devil's plots? Why, life was uneven and dangerous, what with plagues and roaring boys, even in the time of Chaucer and Shakespeare, Byrd and Dowland. Yet they contrived to live among the torsion, the non-stop twisting of the human soul.

He tells himself not to accept irritation, as being too simple a response to a complex world. Things have moved on. Some outfit called Hugo Neu Schitzer East is picking up the massive debris of the American Dream that had sat through a siege of almost two thousand degrees, and here he was mourning it still because two Platonic forms had been ruined by kismet kamikazes. Quite simply, he was irritated because *nobody* should have done it, because human achievement on the planet suddenly seemed to him useless, a mere candied invitation to the crazies to destroy. When he was a boy, he had been a member of a gang that trapped other boys and twisted their arm skin in opposite directions until they squealed, and then twisted it again, even harder, proof having been sought that torture worked. That was "The Snake," he told himself. You had to be tough to withstand it. But even tougher to apply it.

Unable to discern in everyday life things that had gone wrong or awry, Shrop began to pick on bizarre reports that told him, as well as many others, they were indeed living in an unusual, even unprecedented time. It was not that almost everyone reported a headache, but that a certain Beast of Cricklewood, in fact a lynx, had stalked the streets of Purchase, NY, unidentified, for months, while in New Delhi a Monkey Man—short, human body, with a monkey's head and metal claws—had committed numerous nighttime attacks. In the Pacific area, a gigantic stick insect had been identified as a "walking sausage." Crocodiles had been found in Vienna. A minor tornado had deluged a Wiltshire golf course with goldfish and koi carp. Frogs had poured, and were pouring, from the Italian skies. Sand from the Sahara (ah, *this* he understood and saw as normal) was landing on the cars of Europe. It was clear to him, however, that the world was twisting about, trying to be different. Evolution, he persuaded himself, was scratching itself and trying to be flashy. Had the two topless towers not been attacked, he wondered, would all this have seemed in the least strange? One injection of the weird was enough to draw attention to all the weird stuff that had lain doggo for years, unsaluted and unappraised. It was like (he tried in his befuddled way to regain his Shakespeare) the night in *Macbeth* when the horses go mad in the stable and start to eat one another, just because other unnatural things are happening in the human domain (Duncan is being murdered). All things go together, he told himself: first one, then all the rest, in wholesale perversion.

And there is no stopping it, he told himself. The chaos goes on and on, and soon you find yourself in a world whose creatures you do not recognize, among chemical processes hitherto unknown. The dune-fondler comes to the fore, a new species from the Algerian desert, and the Libyan swont, a creature with rounded teeth. Photoanalysis replaces photosynthesis; the plant in the room sucks up the oxygen. On another planet, he decided, such things might be commonplace, and one would soon get used to them, but on Earth the hopping feco-pod, for instance, would always be a noxious novelty. A turd was not expected to sprout feet with which to hop around, to the disgust of humans at any rate. But, he decided, one could really get into the frame of mind that accepted such abnormalities without having to deal with them in the flesh. The idea of them would not be so hard to deal with and might even engender original thought of one kind or another. Ever on the qui vive for the outrageous, he would keep a weather eye open for new species originating themselves in commonplace circumstances, whether that included Quent or left him out.

So imagine him, then, no longer murmuring Oh what a chubby vulva or watching a plundered couple wheel their market cart along the avenue to their sardines-and-bagel hovel, but someone suffering from dispersed personality, not even craving the open-air cage and concrete floor of the captured terrorist, or the cellars of the SS, but addicted for reasons unknown to a disconsolate yearning for a *place* unknown, wondering what equipment he will need to survive there. Language, that ferocious mirror, will not help him, nor will a sign language spoken by the elbow, whose face is speckled like that of Big Ben. Whenever if ever he gets there, he tells himself, "I shall re-ignite like a bird." Fat chance. He will become a carcass-cutter, at whom the other embalmers will throw stones after he has made the taboo slit in the abdomen through which to draw the innards out. He will empty out the brains through the nostrils and allow no more than thirty-five days in natron (baking soda and salt as found plentifully in the desert), so as to cross the arms before rigor sets in. He will refresh himself throughout the process by swigging five different types of beer, each gauged carefully for bitterness, mildness, froth, and aroma. He will secrete amulets within the wraps, reminding himself that there are 132 rooms in the White House, but in the white house of the body more than a thousand, all eager not to die. Ah, he sighs, knowing there is always another life even after death of parents and spouse, removal of breast or testicle, final certification into a rubber room, stem cell invasion of the rotting pancreas.

But where and how?

He does not know, but reassures himself he will, once the day arrives. He has noticed how, especially at Quent's, when the phone is put down during a ring, the bell emits an odd double sound, half uplift jingle saying come get me, the other half a downfall jangle. It is as if the phone has been throttled, he says. Never do it. Always wait out the full campanology of the ring, even when it amounts to no more than a barbarous whirr or bark.

He returns to the places he imagines he is going to end up. Good, bad, or ugly. He knows it is Egypt, but refuses to name it, preferring to nickname it Blefuscu or Cockaigne, content that at least it isn't *here*. He will revivify his sex life with lettuce-seed oil, squeezed out from the seeds in a superhuman press, perfect his voice by chanting in a stepped pyramid along with other tourists, who also believe in sharpening razors; drifting over Giza in a hot-air balloon, almost a fighter pilot above an ancient war, surviving to wear the honorific bull's tail, worshipping the Sphinx as a barbaric simian ogre from fifteen thousand B.C., developing an immunity to the electric catfish of the Nile, tolerant even of careless embalmers who chop off toes that do not fit the casket, ever cognizant that a pyramid is the upside-down version of the declining sun's leaky fan, determined to build a pyramid or *mastaba* of his own using the iron oxide that makes things red, ruling by candlelight like Mycerinus the chubby good-natured king with the smallest of the three Giza pyramids.

Wild barley with Nile bread.

Pharaoh means great house, from the Persian.

Or was it the Hebrew?

Crook and flail in his arms.

Mahat will mean Order.

Who will be beheaded, heads set between their drawn-up legs?

He is getting ready for a life of white linen sails.

You can't just sit around waiting. You have to show willing, "pleasing and powerful" enough to have been a king.

Copper and turquoise then.

He will always be looking east, for whatever.

Will he become a capturer of cows and Nubians, like the Sneferu of old?

Figs and ducks then.

Sailing around on the Nile with girls got up in nothing but fishnet, to stir his aching pubes. A king's life. Using camel dung for baldness, bridging his defunct teeth with golden arches.

After all this, the present has no bite at all, no matter what cleverness Quent has rigged. Shrop will waft away, his lost philosophy dangling behind him like a canceled flag, like all those European currencies gobbled up by the abstract-sounding euro. He is not going to give in, no fear, he is going to achieve an acme of resigned accomplishment, certain that the more casually he drifts from this world the easier it will be to enter the other one. He is fast becoming a resurrectionist, even gathering up his snapshots of "a previous life" and mounting them in fresh-minted albums whose tacky see-throughs clutch at his fingers as if yearning to roll over them and meld them into the photogravures beneath.

What had become of that damned philosophy of his, crippled and vacated by an act of terroristic atrocity or merely by some perversion of friendship, an abdication from care? Orally at least, he dimly recalled, it had been entitled The External Riviera of the Actual World, but that was not it exactly, and he wondered if, in mentally shuffling through its various thwarted incarnations, he had not hit on the correct title and passed it by, unrecognizing and going blank. It was almost like blowing one's nose into a tissue you then tried to fling from you into the waste, but it refused to go, attached by the merest mote of moisture. In this case, though, not enough had stuck fast for him to get his ancient wits together. The blank blah of the blank world, he murmured, one day it would come clear and he would *know*, wondering why he had ever had trouble with the mere name of the thing. Well then, he mused, what about The Eternal Riviera of the blank blank? Useless. Or The Useless Riviera of the— He quit in despair, reminding himself of a childhood saw that said the more you try to think of something the less it will come.

Instead, no doubt because he had connections, he took on a new job (anything to fasten body and soul together): doing voiceover for a history program, in fact voicing English translations of voices in some instances long gone, but resurrected at the channel's pleasure. So, for a short while (who knew how long these series would last?), he became an island full of voices: a Luftwaffe fighter pilot, Günther Rall; Ribbentrop, Hitler's champagne salesman disguised as a foreign minister; survivor of a Russian firing squad; Count Ciano, executed by shots in the back while he hunched in a chair, and many more, all conjured up from within his historical locker, tempting him to disappear into borrowed throats. Indeed, reading his scripts with average emphasis and Germanic, Slavic, or Italian mannerisms, he toyed with the idea of disappearing altogether, of not speaking to anyone except when "being" someone's voice, some historical personage bitten in the rear by history. A sedulous listener, that forgotten breed, would actually hear Shrop's unique voice on several quite separate occasions, so that Ciano, for instance, sounded like Günther Rall, because the timbre and glottal phonics remained identical. What a fascinating idea, he thought, akin to the transmigration of souls of which the ancients spoke. His voice over time would always evoke the image of the super multinational hero or victim, summoned up by the History Channel for Columbia professors to prate about during the intervals. The trouble was that, after he had begun to listen to himself broadcast after broadcast, always noting the sameness of his vocal manner and so bringing together in one epic mask a host of historic figures, he began to weary of the whole idea. Having committed himself to the frail permanence of tape, he suddenly quit, the man of a thousand voices (only one really) echoing whom? Was it Lon Chaney's father, the man with a thousand faces? The money helped, though, without in the least restoring his memory. Yes, he would tell himself now and then, I am like an old cutlery drawer consecrated to forks, needled to death at one end where the tines dig in each time the drawer's slammed shut. I wonder who arranges the forks so that the tines all point in the same direction. Now *that's* memory, isn't it? The drawer remembers and no doubt winces at the thought of the next onslaught. It's better, anyway, than the can-you-sink-lower of the sidekick effects man to the Aussie croc-odilist, for whom, each time a snake or croc flails tail at him, the side-kick makes the swishing sound of a cane. Whoosh-whoosh. Wowee, that was close. So what was it that held him back from the last most shameful thing?

Perhaps the multitude of his historical impersonations helped. Something at any rate guided him back to the idea of Quent's other clients. Were there any? All invented? Or did they come to see the priest instead? Were they scared off or did they show up by night? Or did Quent see them elsewhere? Shrop was firmly committed by now to the notion that they were all ex-Nazis, come to make their peace about hanging children in the cloakroom of their own school, from the very clothes pegs assigned to them. No other horror would serve. Because of one horror, he mopped up all others, and then presumed himself guilty of all. No doubt the visiting priest, the Quent-quietener, was a fake, just another escaped Nazi biding his time in a different armband until the grand resurgence came about, the Fourth Reich hard on the heels of the Terror years.

As it turned out, these people did seek further audience with Quent, but on quite different grounds, as we shall see. To Shrop a dripping wall was truly an impetigo of the skull. Somehow, these Nazi fugitives had also been on the radio and TV with him, their voices disguised of course in his own classic tones, which made them feel closer to him. As for Hovis Tumulty, he had already dispossessed her of her own name and refound her as Ilse Koch, foul dominatrix of a certain exter-mination camp, where she paraded with bull whip, and crêpe de chine knickers carefully hidden. Poor Hovis, heir to the afflicted, the curator of shattered souls, now made to do duty for Frau Koch, the beast-mistress of that notorious hell, a woman whose voice he was forever denied access to, for obvious reasons.

Poor Shrop too, limping from imposture to imposture until some-thing better turned up, something compatible with Idlewild or that Austrian lake, if only he could remember it as the millrace of lost mem-ory coursed past him and his mental capstans.

28
Cunard

HIS MIND, FORCED IN UPON ITSELF, HAS BEGUN TO ROAM FAR and wide, never quite becoming irrelevant, but retrieving (if ever he had them) glimpses of long-forgotten civilizations in which, of course, worse things had always happened, so that, as day ended and predictable dreams began and then spent themselves, he could never quite tell himself this is how the world ends. The world, presumably, began worse and gradually got better. Of course. If you believed that, then you were a meliorist, not entitled to count on dismal endings or to brood too precisely on Ground Zero, low-ranking in the scale of human abomination: brief and desultory unless you happened to be in the midst of it, but for Londoners and Berliners a mere mite of the awful. Why, those Romans, he muses, for all their hygiene and domestic correctness, kept huge pits just beyond the city gates, in which the usual offal and debris lay cheek by jowl with aborted babies, defunct admirals, and rotting politicians, as if depravity were the lower end of propriety. Beyond a certain point, decorum *(pro patria* and all such junk) vanished and the world became a midden, an eyesore to survey and a chiding wen to optimists. Is New York like that, he wonders, dumping its sundered steel hither and yon in the rest of the world? Are we that short-sighted, murmuring in our temporally bewildered way, *Leave me alone already,* as if the future that was to be has already come about, but we cling to the adverb anyway, making it predict the past? In such conundrums he finds the gist of the present, the benign alongside the despicable, and no one able to do anything about it, the long finger of Manhattan extended out into the future, a patsy waiting for the next thing to happen. Paralysis, the word he has been veering toward, lands in his brain and stays put, found at last and treasured, as if he were some poor wretch with a cleft palate, unable to say certain things until he undergoes something called intervelar veloplasty (which he dare not utter). That sort of handicap. So he murmurs *paralysis,* as if to banish the word or embed it, he isn't quite sure, his mind still pursuing the schizophrenic Romans and their muddled ways.

Would it be more palatable, he wonders, if instead of a dump there were some kind of heap, something inching up to the skies with the debris of every day? Would not such a structure have vestigial dignity, more a law unto itself than any rubbish heap? Another topless tower to fell? He shudders at the thought, knowing that all these matters have already been settled, by accident and indolence fused, and history has been written, stamped with the tiny seal that says *Funereal* or *Done For*, himself included in it without even having tried to join or escape. Their plane has already crashed and the vast, dimensionless ocean has poured into the wrecked fuselage, sweeping all before it, passive as a cigar tube tossed into the briny. Go, hurtless souls, he whispers, trying to amass the dead and gone, who did not want to die, not ever. Go bloat the canon of carrion. He is not quite sure where such expressions have come from, but he knows they were well intended, not his own certainly, but perhaps murmured in some forgotten movie made newly relevant, such as *On The Beach,* paltry visual echo of Nevil Shute's novel, with an image of a certain actor's sportscar rough-riding over all. When death takes the initiative out of your hands, where you never wished it anyway, then you have succumbed to what Henry James called the insolence of accident, the something else of chance. Now, what was that other Jamesian word? Dream on, he tells himself, you will never remember, old coot, you will have to survive without it, destined for the demi-paradise of incomplete quotations, half straddling the fence, half slithering down the other side. Oh to be firm forever, banning air raids with a wink, annulling bombs with a quote from Eric von Stroheim. Back, he commands Ann Baxter, the soubrette, swatting his fly-whisk at her: "Two steps back," even while Dino Galvani chants opera in the shower.

Willy-nilly an inhaler of powdered glass, he should be able to gather it up, a handful per month, say, certainly enough over the past three years, to confront Quent with a thimbleful. An eyedropperful. But no, it has to be breathed into the lungs, where it takes root like a generation of pernicious atoms, fonder of the pinkest lungs, those of children. He smiles at one recollection from his badly remembered Egyptian lore: well-to-do men wore gold dust in their eyes to imply divinity, about which quality they never had any doubt. Inhaling as we do, he thinks, we may be a little godlike ourselves instead of behaving as if we have been invited to chew cactus. These things have been sent to us; it is as if I am Caesar, penning a sentence pegged on an opening ablative absolute: *These things having been sent us, we . . .*

Such his version of bedlam, with his mind unable to calm itself, unable as it were to stick itself in an up-to-date version of the old Tranquillizing Chair that rammed a box on your head and strapped you in, preferably in a vat of bone-chilling water. His mind lolls in this mess, lamenting among other things the decline of friendship, even that of enmity. Your friends just lolled back, taciturn unto eternity, knowing that to say any more would merely complicate matters further—more to be said about what was never worth saying anyway. Thus he prefigures the dearth of friendship at the same time as hoping for someone, something, fresh out of the ruck. There could be yet, he muses, a new alliance, like a fresh-minted lettuce leaf, born of trial and hardship, even if speckled with powdered glass, like greenery too near a volcano.

He sighs cogitatively: Oh, friends; friend ahoy.

It is going to take some effort, he sees that. It might even be his last twist, the Herculean endeavor of a failing man, eager for friendship even while falling from a great height, having jumped.

Among all those others on their way down wingless.

No Quent to haul him out of it, or to tell him he is mistaken: the emergency does not exist, has never happened, it is all a mirage of misery.

Catch me, Quent, he murmurs. Why so distant?

No answer, not even in sign language, a little twitch in the air where the intact legs might have been. Ha, he grunts bitterly, there is no there there, not even the old familiar nothing, the Hopi shawl over the limbo of limblessness. It's odd, he tells himself, with all the survivors going around prating about how disaster has brought them closer together, whereas it has truly tugged them even farther apart, enforcing a new isolation, each individual contemplating the smeared chimera of his or her own non-death, hardly to be even summed up because the entire thing lapses into a reverse elegy about the absence of something we know nothing about. And the dead, any more than those old Egyptians he dotes on, have not spoken up, and they never will, through either splintered steel or brute medallions.

He is negotiating with an unknown version of the unknown, hardly worth a wink of a linnet's eye, he thinks, but this shlocky brand of negotiation is all that's left for him, a mere sign of his abiding presence as his mind, what's left of it, twitches on, as if Plato were to review the spate of Platonism that came after him. Impossible, he murmurs. I never used to need help for all that, in the old days, when I was *compos mentis*; but not now, my dears, when I am a compensatory leftover, a dehydrated pickle left on the tray for the scooper-up to brush off, down into the Roman dump we have made of our city. Mercy me, do all of us persist merely in order to persist? After reading that old poem years ago, do I too rejoice at having to construct something to rejoice about?

* * *

The *Queen Elizabeth* has docked before at Pier 88 to pay homage to the dead of September 2001, and the Spirit cruise ship, anchored in the harbor, has been a kitchen for half a million donated meals. *The Princess Diana*, however, is special, built to consolidate a myth (or so Shrop thinks, subscribing as he does to the conspiracy theory that she was killed to keep the royal line free of Arab blood). He has been here before in his fumbling way, bearing a once-hot shepherd's pie for someone unchosen, but this visit is unique, and he journeys up to Pier 88 as guardian of his swarming head, heedless of snow and ice pellets, proud of the cooling pie in his hands. The stares of various watchers are Manhattan stares, incuriously sullen, and he ignores them, a man on a repeated mission at dawn to watch the *Diana*'s flag slump to half mast, the passengers (a seven-continent world cruise) and crew assemble on deck, the evergreen wreath tilt into the sea in homage to the dead. This kind of ritual has been going on for three years, by ocean liner, seaplane, skiff, and parachute, a surfeit of honor, no doubt, but impossible to terminate as if indeed it will really bring back the lost. Shrop does not believe in miracles, but an excess of tribute warms him up. Maybe, he muses, Diana will surface after all to denounce the Anglo-American plot against her and her beloved.

After the singing, ragged and frozen, of "Amazing Grace," there come five blasts from the ship of an old convoy sound, evoking wartime days. The ship's master disappears from view and the perfunctory yet devout ceremony is over. Manhattan has paid its dues once again and Shrop, among hundreds of early morning mourners, has eased his soul anew, although beginning to wonder as he walks to the subway station if it is Diana or the thousands of dead he has come to honor, and at once begins to munch his pie, mind on the blurred image of the huge ocean liner poised on the water in the slow-motion blizzard coming in from the west, adding a touch of defiance to the liner's attitude, Hawaii-bound as she is. A huge tomb has floated in and out, he thinks, and it will come again courtesy of Cunard, White Star or any other shipping line based in Southampton or Liverpool with its embalmed princess entombed below decks in Tut-like splendor, reminding her millions how she sat on the lip of the French ambulance and waited it out.

By the time he has returned home, he has eaten his pie, believing there is something Dickensian about his performance, Twistian or Copperfeldian, he cannot be sure, but he feels nineteenth-century today, requiring a gloss from the Salvation Army, the Boys' Brigade, or the Band of Hope, as if a princess has been drowned in the putrid waters off Pier 88 and will not survive to become an old reigning queen. Clearly he would like to be going on to Quent's, to rid himself of so much contorted ballast, but Quent has gone on to epic things, not seaside funerals at all, and the Shrops, if many, have to succor themselves with torpid memories or sketchy prophecy. He wilts as he undoes the lock-encrusted door, wondering why the denizens of his own building lack the glamorous sinfulness of Madame Heinkel's fugitive troupe. In the refrigerator he finds another shepherd's pie. You had to buy them in pairs, so he plans to warm it for lunch. It is only eight in the morning. He almost yields to a desire to go back to sleep, dreaming of the *Princess Diana* edging south, where things grow and prosper, only to glance out the window at all that soft white pelting fluff, ideal dream material really, and lingers in his chair, slowly succumbing to winter. Would Quent be at all interested in his morning escapade, his casual fusion of conspiracy, rumor and funeral? Surely, he thinks, the pair of them overlap in this, staging scenes from thwarted, jittery lives, just to see who's watching and caring. Later today he will pay some bills; as he dozes off along that memory-strewn lane, he wonders if he will mix them up as usual, brewing tempests in official teapots.

29
Wandervogel

DISASSEMBLED MEMORIES ARE COMING TOGETHER ONCE MORE, triggered by Princess Diana and her commemorative ocean liner. He is a graduate student again, teaching a bit, teamed up with half a dozen others for bonehead English. One of these, Wandervogel, hidden behind his lushly foreign name, has developed a bad habit of opening up other people's mail, removing such things as checks and photographs, and, in Shrop's case, helping himself to any review copies that show up (Shrop supplementing his grant with some tentative hackwork). "I wouldn't bother reviewing this piece of shit," writes Wandervogel on the title page, returning the book defaced with wild scribbles in the margin, and sometimes whole paragraphs crossed out and graded C plus. It is almost as if he is exercising divine right, conferred upon him in some old baronial vineyard in upper Saxony. That he is writing on the side some anthology-conspectus to be called *Goethe in America* is well-known; what is less known is that he helps himself to the prentice work of his contemporaries, sending out their essays under his own name, publishing one or two that meet his personal intellectual standards in semi-respectable magazines that actually ask him for more, which he never supplies, always canny. Powerless to stop him in his foolhardy presumptions, Shrop and pals resort to anger, telling him off until he charms them by denying everything, always blaming someone else, denying even his own marginal cracks.

"Let's," says one beefy, red-haired graduate named Thorpe, "beat him up with cakes of soap in pillow cases. The prick."

"Let's report him to the Dean," says Shrop, averse to violence even of the pettiest sort.

All of a sudden, Wandervogel the Depraved vanishes, withdrawn from studies and classes both, his hovel in John Jay Hall reassigned, the stench of his incessant cooking quite gone. The yarn is that he has gone into politics, joining the retinue of Huntingdon Hartford. No, he already moved on, into the French Foreign Legion, leaving his well-to-do Estonian wife behind. No, he is in the CIA, or at least the Navy version of it, rising fast, like a diver yearning for the bends. Well, they sigh, no more invasion of our mail, no more review copies detained for a month (Shrop), no more checks paid into the wrong bank. Little heard from in this interim, he once phones Shrop to announce winning the Schnitzler Drama Prize in the same year as publishing his tome on Goethe, but that is all. Shrop knows, though, that someone with Wandervogel's perverse gifts and blurred conscience will surface in ways more consequential, not exactly assassination or grand theft, but something ingenious developed in the condemned playground where espionage meets bluster, swank the most covert maneuvers known. Der Vogel, as Shrop calls him, is only practicing, tempted past terrorism to cunning stage-management while he rises up the ladder of ranks, kicking his colonelcy behind as he reaches an admiralty all his own. And then what? The firing squad, or even, as Shrop reminisces, polished off on the machine-gun ranges at one of the elite military colleges: blown to bits in a second. Or awarded the Medal of Arts, or something such, for services rendered.

When he does show up again it is because, on the Net and certain TV news shows, he has been arrested in Vienna for trying to sell details of the British-American plot against Diana and her fiancé. She was pregnant, he tells Dodi Fayed's father, who owns Harrod's in London. They tampered with the car so that it could be electronically messed with from a distance. The charge is fraud and he will be tried at an American military tribunal held in secret, never to be heard from again, a lost bird of prey soaring out of sight. Shrop cannot believe his ears.

* * *

Whenever he wanders through Tribeca, with his leer of envy on technicolor display, from Canal Street to the Twin Towers, he remembers the fact that in Tribeca a new property owner's average annual income exceeds four hundred thousand dollars. Surely they could put up with a bit of calamity? He wonders if they paint Red Swastikas on their roofs, as one would in an emergency. Has anyone knocked on Quent's door offering outlandish largesse: "Yes, you lost your legs in the previous war, but that must have made it hard to get about during ours." Shrop feels left out of all this bounty, would almost be willing to crash something: into Tribeca just to raise their sense of damage. Jesus, he says, just like a terrorist. He abandons the idea, even in retrospect, as unworthy of a survivor, especially a hobo of the streets such as himself. No, we are humbly waiting to be bombed out, becoming better adjusted with each blitz, so much so that we peer skyward and laugh. To hell with them. We're as tough as any; we have been through *our* wars already

He shakes loose from this pipe-dream or idyll, relegating it back to boyhood and babyhood, beyond even that. Was there ever once a Wandervogel, manipulating other people's lives and habits, or was he just an extension of Richard Strauss's Till Eulenspiegel, all merry pranks and nothing serious except those final squeaks as the prankster hangs? With deliberate mental force, he shifts his mind to a belated question: wandering around the neighborhoods, he has noticed new signs in the store windows, signs more befitting the sleek self-congratulation of Palm Beach than the battered hardball of Manhattan:

Here we are again, just when you were thinking we were gone for good. Never forget, we have you in mind, with attitude.

Or:

Do we need you? We sure do. Here we are again, to meet all your needs in this time of trial. We will never desert you knowingly.

Or this:

Back in business. God bless the good old USA. Some of us were goners, some not. Hi, and welcome back.

After *three years*, he murmurs! They still haven't gotten over it, whereas the rest of the world is used to it. It has to happen many more times before you adjust. He waits for his ship to come in, for the imbecile sadist's next move after the Eiffel Tower, Big Ben, the QE 2, and Grand Central.

He remembers an early exchange with Wandervogel, at some party or other, when the man candidly put his point of view, explaining (if that was not too servile a word) that he believed in asserting himself in response to the overpowering élan, as he put it, of his nature. Come what may in retaliation, he said.

"So you believe in shoving people about?" Shrop had commented.

"Yes, but shoving myself as well."

Something percussive but also devious remained in Shrop's mind, their conversation's spoor; no one should have been surprised by whatever Wandervogel did next. Indeed, that category of the Next, so long as anybody had the patience to keep an eye on the man, and report him, became an unknown dimension. Always something new out of Wandervogel, which sounded as if he were a master of originality, the unheard-of and the far-out, but only a seamless polymath could have said so, able to make profound and learned comparisons. All the same, Shrop tried testing Wandervogel against Quent, as leader, schemer, alias, rival, and many other roles, only to come up short, convinced there was a patent difference between the two he could never find. These thoughts led him to devise a theory of how surprise figured in human behavior, from self-surprise to shock. Without it, no one had any glamour, but, over-endowed with it, had no integrity. It was only a half-theory, of course. With Shrop in these days, all theories are half-theories because he tends to forget the half he began with and, sometimes in panic at having cooked up a theory, has thrown away. Clearly, thoughts of Wandervogel have stirred him up, proffering an image of the initiative-ridden man who recklessly shoves aside all the confetti of the rest of life and chases a flawless name, like Horatio Nelson, say, or André Malraux, always getting it right, whether saying at the perfect moment "Kiss me, Hardy," or, like Malraux, stealing Cambodian statuary before anyone heeded it. Shrop would love to become some pharaoh of timing and savvy, but he feels doomed to be a retainer, a follower, forced to wear a dominant style or to make so consummate a job of disguising his role as a man of parts that everyone thinks him a paragon, to be emulated, like a man who has read all of Stendhal and knows it by heart. Was it really true that all he had ever been was derivative? A copycat freak? Some evil shudder in daily life had jerked him loose from his admittedly insufficient moorings: the disaster pronounced unique, but far from so, more a loss of a nation's virginity than a cosmic singularity. He knew this and was unable to fix it, any more than thousands of other Manhattanites, some of whom had applied for money for trauma, nerves, and consultation fees, though some he knew were still, even now, just waiting it out, hoping for the twitch, the jitters, the constant *crise de cafard* to stop. It was a matter of overriding circumstances, was it not? Whatever came your way, you had to master it, not be its slave. Why, even Quent had seemed to come off the rails under the impact of the carnage, and who could have predicted *that* of the amputee shrink?

So, Shrop muses, am I trying to develop some new version of heroism? Not so much assertive as agile, limber, adapting to events, something short of outright defiance or denial. At its crudest, the trauma or whatever had to do with the shakes, with being bounced about, but at its subtlest it had to do with the inappropriate, the unseemly. All you need do, he thinks, is buy the premise that life is full of contraries, and there you are: you were always right, on the side of the discerning angels, which meant of course that the American Dream and its dreamers had simply underrated the element of discord. You were supposed, even obligated, to go through life shaking and quaking, prey to good *and* *bad* dreams, like the people of Shakespeare's time, and Thomas Jefferson's, and the Dalai Lama's. No exceptions. No cloud-cuckoo land. No lost horizons. If you couldn't rise to this, you just put up with stress and appealed to the Red Cross.

He has become reluctantly aware of how much he muses, now that Quent has gone his own way, and now he wonders if, talking to him all this time, he has only been talking to himself without his usual edge, with all the courtesies due himself in their seemly places. Talking to Quent, did he put too glad or gracious a face on things, come off as too sure of himself, awaiting the shrink to cut him down to size? Surely that was not what shrinks do? The shrink is a sounding board, he tells himself, not a censor; but Quent was a friend as well, and one before whom to cut a not altogether unworthy figure.

Thus begins one of the most troubling emotional passages in Shrop's life. He can only imagine, now, how it would have been to go to another shrink to discuss his friendship with Quent, or how Quent would have been after regularly discussing their friendship with someone else. Why, they could have gone together to the same shrink, a discerning savant who might have saved them from this crisis. Too late, he murmurs or muses, aware that people who talk to themselves are more than a mere convenience for novelists or dramatists; a trap, even. No, they embody that swooshing interiority without which the human is nobody at all, just a Pavlovian puppy. At least he could take a pride in that. No, he corrected himself, he could take a pride in that at least. What was the right way of saying it? He finds himself increasingly concerned with perfection; as a boy going out to ride his bike, he would hear his mother, Annabel Pugh, call after him the somewhat meaningless phrase, "And come back at the first sign of rain!" Once you were wet, returning, he thinks, could you get wetter? Perhaps her counsel had to do with short rides only, from which you might return only partly wet; but if you were five miles out and already drenched, why not press on as far as Rangoon to achieve some kind of monsoon godhead?

His computer has begun to malfunction, the faster he types garbling the message more and more, omitting whole words or printing them back to front or omitting one or two letters: *backo fotor ih a lete or to,* and so on, reducing him to a new kind of gibberish unintended by the designer, surely, unless for such malefactions he was now roosting in a penal colony on the moon. So now the e-mail is scrambled and has already provoked several flawless complaints from friends in the movie-reviewing business or other philosophers who too have lost their train of thought (or the stations to be called at have been repositioned away from the tracks). His friends have a deciduous quality, elfin and sleek, from half-committed Nazi-hunters to suicidal philatelists, communicating mainly by e-mail because it seems sent sooner than written.

He hears the crash, corresponding to a certain metrical foot he salvages from his freshman class for the nightclub on the corner, daily dumping the night's empties into a huge hopper full of broken glass. Who will want them anyway, except a Venetian eager for melting down? He braces himself for the first crash, which often doesn't come when he expects it (glass-dumpers take their own time), followed by a clashing, chiming slither, capped by a second crash as the rest of the empties pour down. Perhaps it takes the form of *dit-dah-dit,* not iambic, not spondee, not even amphibrach, but *what* then? Has the educational system, that finger-sucking whore, failed completely, thus ill-equipping him for a life among real men? Or fake poets? Then he should go back, certainly for the recalled freshman year, taught by Schnauzer or Bisson in their prentice phase.

Crash goes another load of glass, matching the crash in his PC. The outside world is regrouping itself. Drinking habits are back to normal after the atrocity three years ago. It was a *spondee,* he delightedly exclaims: one crash after another, nothing in between.

But that is all. There ensues an agony of waiting. Will there be more of what he now calls *crashendo?* Has the nightclub, 231, a numerologist's midden, failed? He hopes not. It's company, to say the least.

30
Bolthole

H E LIKES HIS LITTLE PLACE, HIS BOLTHOLE, IN CERTAIN MOODS
wondering if he will ever go on to his true destiny of con-
trolling the drawbridge over some river, squatting in his little
caboose-cabin as the warning signs go up and the two-way traffic glides
to a halt every quarter of an hour. There he might even sleep, some
nights, locked in safely with an apple and *The New Republic*, outside on
his mini-platform a comfy chair to which he has affixed a clip-on para-
sol, enterprisingly packing the hollow underside of the plastic arm with
bits of plywood to stop it from wobbling. Here, in between withdrawn
bridges, he can snooze or read. Any of New York's waterways would
do, he thinks, provided he applied in time; the jobs went so fast with a
whole population of Manhattan Steppenwolves to draw on. Thanks to
notable manual dexterity he would be a formidable candidate, plus his
sturdy patient bladder, his tested eyes, his way of thriving foodless on
the phenomenology of yachts cruising through the V opened by a
bridge's twin halves. He would *do*, he knows, just so long as within his
bridgeman's cab he had a few supplies: Elmer's glue, chips of plywood,
a hacksaw blade, a blob of bubblegum, tea and sugar, the usual hot-
plate. He inhabits a small world, would like it even smaller, he thinks,
until it fits him like a bullet-proof jacket. No room for Quent, or even
his marauding black beetles. He would call it the stethoscope room,
where he could listen to his chest and yet keep the results private. Some
vague hint of his supposed Austro-Hungarian idyll stirs him, but he
soon forgets it, half-revelling in memories of yachts; bound for the
briny with ogling girls and pipe-puffing young salts, one of whom he
might have been back in his salad days. Yes, he recalls, a meerschaum
pipe such as yachtsmen smoked you made from sea-spume, foam,
though it took a bit of nautical experience to get it right the first time
as one pipe segue'ed into the next, and you realized only much later
that you had made a series of foamy white pipes out of a series of mer-
maid's tails.

An apartment house was an ocean liner really, just another ship of
fools with a greasy super in the basement kicking the dumbwaiter to
make it behave. So, when he looks out at the disheveled city, he sees

only the ocean with a few scattered ships ready to pass in the night, no U-boats lurking, no nuclear subs grinding through the darkest depths. At heart he's a lover of sail, addicted to inland waterways and wide, flat estuaries. Yet he has never lost his love of surprise, as when he used to say to Quent, "What do *you* have in mind?" and Quent embarked on some exotic take-off of a familiar tale, with Shrop playing Robinson Crusoe and himself playing Man Friday, embellishing the story of one profane man, Alexander Selkirk, who survived fictionally only because of someone else there on the island: servant-slave, interlocutor, friend. Just so. Well, no more of that music, evidently. Now Shrop feels really marooned with no bridge to raise and lower, no makeshift philosopher to become instead of himself, but only the deadly air of Ground Zero to inhale during his evening walks, always aimed at the twin towers but always deflected. Oh, he could get through, if he really tried, to the viewing parapet, but something sheepish makes him turn away and study the environs instead, with twitching knees and stinging eyes. Is he looking for, hoping for, Quent, thinking the island is really an island, full of ungracious noises?

Home, he rearranges his purses.

Sets an ice cube in the middle of hot soup.

Tries to recall what exactly the Something Riviera of the Something Else World was.

Resists calling Quent, to whom a phone has become a deadly weapon.

Wonders about Hovis Tumulty in her Ilse Koch version and asks himself Is he really aboard a troop carrier containing Nazi prisoners of war, all being treated demurely as required by the Geneva Convention?

For months now, it may even be seasons or years, Shrop has busied himself with the dim intuition that, as he grows and matures, he is edging into the shadow of some fabled figure of local gossip, even history or literature. As if he had heard of Odysseus, say, which of course he has, he senses the wanderer in himself as well as the renowned homesickness of that worthy man, more alluded to than read about. As if, beginning to learn the privileges and delights of skulking underground out of sight, he senses he is becoming an Underground Man, respected yet scorned. As if, having some knowledge of the Japanese soldier who stayed on his island long after the cease-fire, suspicious and righteous, he emerged only after sustained cajolements by friends and veterans—a national hero or a war criminal. This, Shrop decides,

143

is the thematic part of life, in which whatever legend gathers about him begins to make its presence felt. His store of heroes is not large, but he takes them seriously, wondering nonetheless if they somehow blend together: Odysseus into Underground Man into the Japanese soldier. He thinks not, but finds himself haunted by another figure, about whom he has heard, transplanted from another culture: the enigmatic Rat Man of Paris, whom he has heard described as having a not very certain relationship with civilization, toward which he feints without putting his heart into it. The murderous assault on the twin towers may have bounced Shrop into pretty much the same predicament, or so he thinks, debating if there can truly be influence or merely derivation in these matters. Perhaps, he tells himself, I am only one among thousands, each wondering if he might be unique.

Lawrence of Arabia? No.

Charlie Chaplin? Hardly.

The Elephant Man? Nice try, but no.

He never plays this game for long, immodestly assuming he might indeed be unique even when he goes out in what he likes to think of as mufti: shiny black garbage bags stapled together to compose a suit of sables in which he might pass muster among the de rigueur black of Manhattan. As it is, he goes out busily reflecting the sun, in part a tantalizing see-through as passers-by watch him and try to peer within. Is he naked in there or not? Crudely cut eyeholes, the work of nail scissors, reveal his blue eyes, but no one is looking at them. He ends up wetting himself on occasion (out for too long) or losing several pounds like the man sheathed in vinyl at a sex party. That he is following in the wake of some predecessor he never doubts, but he has trouble creating the right mental set for his see-through walks among people who figure him for some elegiac promenader designed to remind them of earlier woes, lest the catastrophes in between distract them.

Yes, he needs the book of the character, he decides, even a cheap paperback encrusted with rotting fruit and hosed down with sheep dip, borrowed, bought, or stolen, with or without the author's portrait, whoever he be that remarkable he who has passed into history along with his stolen creation. After all, there was once upon a time a real Rat Man who harassed boulevardiers with the rat ill-hidden inside his coat. Thus, he says complacently, the purloined figure enters myth only to go back into history sea-changed by immersion in the human mind. I could be part of that too. He vows to try, not having much to go on, but willing if need be to haunt the park, act on stage, get arrested, give interviews about topical scandals. Anything, just to get himself noticed and fulfilled. No more shrinkage, he says, cursing Quent and all like him. He intends to become one of the walking wounded bandaged to within an inch of his life. How's that for what he has come to call, in fake Brooklynese, A Pocklyptic situation? Only the dead know Brooklyn, and they are out of date.

Now more than ever, he fancies keeping a low profile, reducing his memberships, subscriptions, pledges, gifts, all in accord with his circumstances. The twin lights over his kitchenette do not work, thanks to a broken switch unmended. Rain comes in at the ill-fitting western window. In the refrigerator, the freezer unit thaws. The couch is lumpy and unsupporting; the cushions roll around onto the floor, but do nothing to ease the sit of his body. A drawer pull in the bedroom has failed, making it impossible to tug the drawer out, and he vows to fix it either by winding dental floss around the shaft of the pin, then gluing it in place in the widened hole, or buying a pretty knob at the drug store. There is too much to do, given the extraordinary stresses of his daily life, the lateness and hazard of the mail (he still dreads anthrax), the frying crackle that has plagued his phone ever since September 11, 2001, the lack of hot water during the devastating nights. How did he ever find time to tend his purses, write movie reviews, do voice-over for the Factual channel, or answer mail? He feels overcome by trivia, yet when he gropes around for the big vital thing he would otherwise be doing he cannot think of it. Like his philosophy, and the title it languishes under, it has vanished. The one huge thing in his life is lamenting the absence of people, and for this he blames the aerial attack on the towers.

Yet, he chides himself, it's the same worldwide, isn't it? If the woman above you is constantly rolling her furniture about, just for the hell of it and not in order to clean (who cleans a dozen times a day?), would she not also be there in Semipalatinsk, Kyoto, or Rio? The mad took over civilization long ago, not with a view to doing anything in particular about it, but just for kicks, to ram their bad behavior down everybody's throats. In the midst of all this sociological carnage, overlaid by terror bombings and such, there are just a few reliable certainties, such as (he cozily exemplifies) his box of calorie-free meringues: when you bite one in half, the break comes in two even faces, a clean flat cut proving that the cells of the meringue—no sugar—have been correctly aligned and all repose in the same direction. No jagged edges. This pleases him so much that, once launched, he can devour an entire boxful, mostly of egg whites and air, while watching on the TV Nigella, the latest Brit sensation, whose useful, ungroomed hands belie her clever brain. Her fans watch to see Nigella, not her bytes.

Where otherwise, he yearns, have those crumb-caked greasy paws been lurking? She is almost too competent to be true, and glamorous to boot. She's a glamour-puss all right. Now, when did *that* useful expression bite the dust?

In the bathroom he pauses to admire the little card mounted above his stack of fresh towels, the text discreetly small beneath a huge pale blue drop of water teardrop shape:

Do you feel you need Fresh Towels?
If you would like your towels replaced, please leave your used towels on the floor, which is the place for used towels.

"Assholes," he mutters. "Assholes all."

Towels left hanging on the towel rack tell us
that you wish to reuse them.

"Behold the talking towel," he whispers.

Using towels more than once saves hundreds of pounds of detergent and thousands of gallons of water each year.

To re-order, call National Hotel Register Co. at _____

Out in the elevator in disgust, he notes a sign from The Management, forbidding the wheeling into the lobby of carts from the nearby Quikshop, an old habit of long-term denizens who have roosted here from Long before Nigella. Her chic consists in her being the daughter of a former Cabinet minister, so clearly she hails from the ranks of the well-fed and the privileged, and conducts herself with a sort of throwaway delicacy that at the same time stomachs nothing fanciful. She eats like a prisoner of war, and at Sunday breakfast, as staged for TV, she affects a wolfhound gourmandise. Shrop prizes her as he would the ghost of Christmas past, as did, presumably many of the English ministerial class: a well-to-do no-nonsense woman among the Blimps.

What worries Shrop is the way he has of seeing himself as comical, indeed as a creature of absurdist disrepute, when in fact he genuinely believes his ailments and cockeyed obsessions have been caused by bombardment. He has been shaken up (shook up in the vernacular) and shaken into what he regards as errant maladaptation or silly tricks, like a dog gone to seed or an eccentric polar bear. He cannot quite work out the whys and wherefores, but he remains convinced that, if Quent has become weird, he (Shrop) has become so in a more organic, predictable way. They have both gone their separate ways into the pantomime of poignancy. All that was required was their parting from each other, from the nexus in which Shrop's gullibility played into the hands of Quent's tendency to domineer. So Shrop, now the lucky legatee of a long-distance system so cheap it must be heaven-sent, is obliged to dial an 800 number, followed by a secret code that admits him to yet another code, whose digits added up free him to dial the number he actually wants. This laborious system costs him peanuts, but he has to be careful, he warns himself, not to construe its arrival in his mental landscape as something funny, oh no, but as a legitimate sequel to the disaster of years ago, when the core of things got so badly Blitzed that nothing simple was ever feasible again, but edged into being, frayed and fevered from commotion in the matrix, like a baby born of a mother with too much cortisol flowing through her. Agitated is the word he craves but declines to utter. We have been agitated, then re-agitated by the memory of it, and so forth. In Florida he has driven through suburbs that confront the speedster with signs that proclaim this is an area of *Calmed Traffic*, which means there are speed bumps. Well, he would dearly like to be self-conducting through an area of calmed traffic, speed bumps or no. Manhattan is not it, but, oddly enough, he dare not leave.

Dimly recollecting his days as a pool cleaner, Shrop realizes that these were his most pensive, when he leaned forward into the depths while trying to erase a shadow: a cloud passing over, or even his own head. At such junctures, he fancied he had plumbed the depths of human being and was dealing, more than ever Dante and Virgil did, with the core of carnality. He did not call it that, though, because it seemed a pretentious term, and eventually cooked up what seemed less bombastic: *levity retrofire*, which meant the way the most awful events seemed somehow comic when viewed against certain standards, the sun or the Pacific Ocean. The awkwardness of the phrase, indeed its semi-military overtone, eluded him altogether, but we should not forget that he was a philosopher, or at least an ex-philosopher. With his recall of his own system has gone his sensitivity to jargon. He is glad of any language that, like money, finds its way into his hands or mouth. Nonetheless, he is much bemused by this retrofire of his because, hitherto, until the bombardment or Blitz, he had always thought the comic and the tragic stayed in their own boxes, never suspecting that the tragic became comic and vice versa. The tragic, so much of it, is too much to endure. The comic, so much of it, is also too much to endure. You die laughing. Both wear you out.

31
A Shave

THE DESIRE TO STARVE HIMSELF TO DEATH HAS NOT LEFT SHROP. It would solve so many problems and blot out Ground Zero forever, as well as the compensatory idylls of Idlewild and movies seen but ill-remembered, as well as the brain phantom of his lost philosophy. Even when fasting, though, Gandhi sipped a little orange juice, presumably to maintain contact with the already rotting British Empire, or with salt and his family. For Shrop, no juice: he wants to maintain as little contact as possible with the Rialto, fancy nameplate for what's going on. His stomach has few cravings. He has been, over three years since the massacre, sickened by events, yet this is only what millions of others have undergone all over the planet. He feels special. He feels special about events. But he isn't special at all, not even his quirks and cranks qualifying him for that. He's just another eccentric, pushed this way and that by circumstance and genes, virtually unable to cope with a fairly standard situation. Having more or less lost a friend and shrink hardly qualifies him as special; he knows that, but cannot shed the delusion that what happened happened in a special way. He has not yet reached the view that America is right in the mainstream of disaster, much envied and therefore much despised. Americans, he is only now just beginning to suspect, tend to feel pleased with themselves because they live in a society adjusted to their feeling so. Yes, he says, when we watch the obligatory commercials, no matter how much we resent them, there is always this vestigial covetousness that says I can *have* all this if I want it, and one commercial haunts him: for his birthday, husband receives a model car, a Jaguar of some sort, in a celluloid see-through box, an ideal gift for a boy or girl, but not quite the toy of his dreams, and his disappointment shows—until he notices a Polaroid picture between his wife's exposed toes, and it's a picture of a full-size Jaguar sitting outside beribboned. Now this is more like American present-giving, and Shrop, not remembering any too well, wonders if such a scene could happen in French advertising, or German, not to mention in actual life. He doubts it. It's uniquely American, and possibly true to life, certainly good for Jaguars, and the evil thought crosses his mind that a dozen of those, crammed to the gills with explosives, could wreak havoc if driven against certain prominent American targets: a school, a hotel, an embassy or two, thus gratifying a wealthy assassin on two levels. Once again he has caught himself groaning about fate in the world of one well-to-do country, whose poor seem to attract no attention: they will be killed along with the plutocrats for what they do not even have and never dream about. The vision of a down-at-heel depression America tortures him; who on earth would want to butcher that? Yet, as he knows, remembering something oblique, people tend to live on past the phenomena with which their history has become involved. The temptation to live in the present, no matter how squalid, not even as Cioran says to keep abreast of the incurable, appeals to no one. People, he tells himself, find an idyll and never live apart from it. Even though a state of mind is obsolete, its lovers fondle it because it has their respect and has met their needs.

What then of long-lost Quent with his elaborate, worked-at name and his fabulous war record, his civilian handicap? Is there any way of construing him, overloaded as he seems with hangovers from history? If Shrop can find no way out or through, what hope for Quent, who has already yielded to Ground Zero in an almost theatrical way? Am I qualified to second-guess him from a distance? Shrop wonders, deciding that you have to have befriended someone to know how distance can destroy, once its damp, barbaric hand has intervened. Friendship, he imagines, cannot survive power, no matter who has it, or increasing age, because in each case the powerful or aging party belongs more to power or age than to the friend.

Well, he says, I'm glad I don't have to think that fucker through again. Insult to injury is what it is. He feels incompetent for modern life, a fell example of modern technocratic man marooned in the Kalahari, where the only residents, the bushmen, who own nothing, never sleep with their heads down—too many crawlers ready to invade the ear. Instead, they prop themselves up on one elbow cushioned in soft sand, and rest their heads on their palms. Why, even Laurence van der Post managed to do it. This is how inept Shrop feels for life so long after the massacre, with the fires beneath still going, the crushed dead still entombed, the grievers still on station as if there really were a local cross. He will never get that elbow into the sand or rest his head, to sleep, on his palm. Too late in life to change his spots, he will let the centipedes prance on his eardrums, and make the best of it, with gazelles and hyenas wandering up to and beyond him, at home in god's own country, at least until the sun dries up the ground, abolishes the shallow lakes, and greets the baby pelicans with an unending parched plateau. That's me, he says, complaining again; but notice, the bushmen have nothing and will never be assaulted by terrorists. Imagine living there and, all of your life, propping your head on your hand while lying down, almost a parody of lazy Romans dining while the city burns.

For long enough he has had the jitters, all the way from first losing the first inkling of his philosophy, then some pieces of his beloved Idlewild, followed by the professional roster of the film critic. Now he has the double jitters, about what comes next: an even more massive massacre, as if World War Two's six million Jews were all to perish in the same few seconds. Could such a thing come to pass and what might it be called? But of course he can't go on looking behind him, both left and right, creeping up to the door at night and crouching beside the triple locks wondering what godawful creature lurked the other side with teeth in its eyes, red-hot globules balanced in the palms of its hands. It is no use handling each day's mail with an adapted pantograph made from several erector sets, keeping the envelope and letter at a distance and slitting the envelope with dun steel rods, only then exposing the letter and its envelope to an illuminated magnifying glass run by an electric motor. When the mail arrives, he feels quite mechanized and trusts this contraption more than he trusts his ears, his nose, his eyes. Who knows how many times he has saved himself already, from anthrax or worse? Shrop also wonders if the water in his radiators could be made toxic, but decides against anything so foolhardy, whereas those lucky ones (Quent) with air have little to be grateful for. He ends the thought, thanking the gods that his very electricity is safe.

Some possibly benign force has again drawn Shrop back to Ground Zero, not so much to find anything (the site hardly changes, owned by fire, gravity, and death) as to subscribe to its tainted atmosphere, maybe even in one of the later stages of self-abasement. A cool breeze has mustered from out of nowhere, making him yearn for an old swing number: *You came along, from out of nowhere.* Basie or Goodman? It too is gone from him. He walks with a grudging push. He needs the air, he tells himself, decreasingly bad air, combining morgue and midden, plus that overheated charcoal smell of New York, a stink of hops on braziers. The trot does him good, not so much feeding his lungs as stretching them. There is always, from whatever compass point, a gaggle of tourists just obliged to come and see, even three years later, but exactly what he cannot tell. He walks with his hands clasped behind

common sense? Shrop has trouble linking the massacre of three years ago (and of other massacres since then) to any rational system at all, so, for him, only an insane planet would deign to meddle with humans at their most lethal and sadistic. He does not care about suave aspirant freshmen at posh Pakistani schools who avow their hatred of the big, smug, bullying US of A at the same time as coveting places at the country's finest colleges. He believes in all narrative's advancing through paradox (Anthony Quinn's army of Howitat helpers is his son; Lawrence executes the man he saved in the desert—so "it was not written after all"). Those boys, full of contraries, will gain their places in the freshman class, but in the end be struck down by syphilis, prejudice, and poor grades. Something like that. He shrugs. Why is the US so hospitable to foreign students anyway, half-suspecting they will never leave and so provide a new elite class of well-to-do immigrants?

Dismal meditations of this kind yield to a keen whiff of gasoline, not the oil so common in that place. At no one's bidding, Quent is dousing himself with liquid from a can, still sitting there in the offing, his striped robe catching the sun in drab blurts of light. No haste, like someone taking a sit-down bath, just making sure that every place be soaked. Quent pauses, still not having noticed Shrop behind him, and then quietly, no fuss, flicks the lighter and applies it to himself, his final untrammeled thought being standard: a solitary man is nobody. There follows an explosive gust and then a blur of fire climbing and widening to cover a bigger figure than that of an isolated man toward whom several in uniform run until they check themselves, realizing there is no point. A beginning wail of horrified lamentation rises from the skimpy crowd on the fringe of Ground Zero. Do people actually do this to themselves without so much as a word, a gesture, a cough? Acrid smoke clouds this zone of abiding smoke. The wheelchair itself appears engulfed as the crackling begins to subside. There is no distinguishing the robe from the forlorn bulk of the man. The robe's hue is not that of the flames into which it has melted, burning up. Not a sound from the terrible, quiet image even as Shrop tries to move toward it only to be held back. Some kind of a statement has been made, he is sure of that, but what it was he has no idea, having been unable to predict Quent's next move. Does he smell burning flesh? He thinks so, appalled by the serenity of the preamble, unnerved by the continuing thought of Quent taxiing to his end, robe in place, gas can in his lap, no word to Shrop certainly, or to anyone there, as if to say, "Enough. Watch me." Shrop decides to walk away, choked and sickened, to find Tumulty and ask if there was any message. Quentin Montefiore del Patugina has gone up in smoke, which surely was enough, considering where he did it. O Lord, thou pluckest out burning.

A gaggle of putative ex-Nazis, inflamed because Shrop has been seen tinkering with their doors in the apartment building, has now come after Shrop, chasing him away from the scene of Quent's immolation, of which he has only an emergency memory. He quite misinterprets their motives, assigning them to the failed Third Reich rather than to successfully locked doors. They catch up with him, force him to the ground, and, drily barbering him, create a Mohawk haircut then and there, heedless of his cries and struggles. Parts of his scalp have bled, and it feels abominably cool. He has not noticed, but Hovis Tumulty is among his barbers, no doubt avenging some quasi-domestic slight of months ago. For this group, the main offense has been dealt with, and surely Shrop will not repeat it, pottering around at people's doors, plotting burglar's ingress and planning his list of booty. Little do they know him, or his spasmodic obsessions.

What has happened to him in the course of barbering is something new, but not in type: a new, unanticipated and not even pertinent idea, quite ousting his mostly forgotten philosophy of old, and having nothing to do with the humiliation he was going through. What he needed to do, he discovered, was attend to some kind of proto-phonics that established why the Ancient Greeks hit on such a word and sound as *faex*, for turd, the Japanese on *ahodori* for albatross, the Indo-Europeans on *meldh* for speaking to the deity. It would take years, provided no one had already written a definitive book on the subject. How indeed did a word get born from within a noise different from other glottal noises? Who sat in authority over such matters? Who made it law? Already his head hurts less, perhaps stimulated into uncanny activity by its ordeal.

Tumulty strides slowly forward from the scene of this triumph, slithering her thighs together as if the hair shield between were some crucial emblem, akin to that of the true Nazi Ilse Koch, whose slow murderous saunter, bullwhip in hand, opened cut-throat razor in the other, is not so much a whimsical motion as an instrument of history. By the time Shrop has come to accept his enforced haircut (a parody of "short back and sides"), it is too late for him and Quent. The fire sermon has been spoken, and they have heeded it.

32
Hoboken Cut

MAY HEAVEN SPARE HIM: SHROP FEELS DISSED. NOT ONLY HAS Quent removed himself from the zone, he has as the poet says transformed himself into something rich and strange. Now Shrop, his defenses down and ragged, remembers the body of Shelley blazing away in the Italian night after drowning, stoked by Byron and one other, and something nearly vampiric takes him over. He wants at least to have gone up in smoke with the old master: opened, made patent, exposed to the elements and certain corrosive forces such as fuel and fire, air and mercy and heroism, to none of which he can aspire, bewitched as he is with the tiny impedimenta of daily living, which now seem part of an ignoble sequel, merely "what he did afterward," an inessential postscript to Quent's rise to glory, and he a Catholic at that. Before the burning, Shrop had not felt too bad about his own last ineradicable twitch three years after the onslaught: a poor thing, but his own. Now, though, he drifts into the minor league of communicants, either to have to start again or live with it as it has been, the driftwood of his obsession. Surely the man might have waited, offering a partnership even if only to be rejected at the last, Shrop deciding to soldier on, not merely one of the walking wounded (bandaged almost to death et cetera), but by the skin of his teeth a survivor, indeed so little a survivor he might be supposed one of the walking dead, awakened to a new life only through mechanical means, sufficient to enable him to blather about his portion of cake or bury the rotted portion of his face into the nearest human beauty he can find. How, now, will he be able to manage that hitherto ill-balanced relationship, in the last of which he became merely a pendant, derivative at best, dissed (as he decides) at worst, a jaundice to the other's clear-cut heroic vault?

Bits and pieces of relationships famous and near mythic have begun to torment him. After all, after seeing to the burning of Shelley on that forlorn stretch of Italian coast, Byron went on to die of fever in the war of independence: not a bad segue, Shrop thinks, beginning to have trouble with tenses. Is he a dead man living in the past, presiding at the preterite of his own self, or is he a newborn neophyte looking forward to the life to come, open-ended and incomplete and therefore glistening pure, any aftermath of the bombing out of sight and gone, a lousy dream easily conquered by a thousand nights of semi-sleep.

Quent, as they say, has gone before, at his own prompting, to be sure. No one urged him to do it; from within the soiled ferment of a dream, he has done it as if it were some geometrical proof, with all corresponding angles tagged and equivalent shortest distances between points labeled AB and CD, nothing left out all the way to YZ. How perfect, Shrop thinks. Is there any superior way of doing it? Do messages come through, saying how? Do dead relatives (not who or which!) impose themselves on your daydreams and explain the simplest way, provided you are on a planet that has air? It comes from within, this decision, with apologies to no one, the deed its own apology to itself: I am doing this and am sorry only not to know how to do it, execute it, better (like Byron's Polidori, Shrop remembers from some faintly echoing lecture based on a survey course in ancient literatures, when the Romantics got half an hour).

Quent's disappearance, of course, requires some kind of response just when he is fresh out of responses, thinking he need do no more to alibi himself than amass his tatters and press on, one of the sundered, harping on the difference between a man with a shattered life and a man with a newly shattered life, a man in tatters already and a man blown to bits although left feebly standing at a street corner with his trousers down around his ankles, his tie his belt, his head a turnip, his hands ceaselessly clenching and unclenching as if something were out of his grasp but he yearned for it.

How smart, he thinks, of Quent to fuse himself in that way with all that was not him, leaving nothing behind for mourners to squabble over. He has not gone near the charred remains, not out of aversion, but out of conviction that Quent had handed himself over completely to that other domain. He still hears in that seething conflagration the scouring whine of jets passing overhead: something utterly inhuman called upon to make the deed final and impersonal. The only subsequent talking with old Quent would be with oneself, the talking that remains open-ended and, unless you are most ingenious, goes nowhere at all. Such is a fate little known to shrinks; how many, how few, can there have ever been to think and act on those lines? The grimace of disgust is partly for himself as well; the human become his/her own crematorium is not something he would care to dwell on, although of late his tendency to lugubrious thoughts has plagued him daily. To

Shrop it is a hurdle never to be cleared, implying an almost intolerable amount of self-absorption. Thank goodness, he thinks, it has not yet become the way of the world, an implanted folkway never to be changed, so much taken for granted that families keep an immolation book, with photographs and souvenirs of the grotesque event.

Chacun à son . . . he murmurs, unable to complete the tag with such horrors in mind, realizing now that Quent has drawn a line beyond which he, Shrop, did not go, not even in imagination on days of maximum disappointment. Oh no, it was not one of the possible fates. Or was it? Were there no circumstances that would propel him into it, on a whim or in a fit of appalling need? If so, was there not some metaphorical equivalent that St. Peter would accept at the gate at the last moment as the trump sounded? Shrop was nothing if not a seeker of equivalence, one who matched one body of things with another, hoping to find lasting matches. A similist, as he liked to call himself, he was still responding to a tendency he had first discovered when in the first flush of philosophy-writing, which was to say philosophy on the run, while doing something else, in other words philosophy as a reflection on the mere, dastardly process of being taken alive, witness Shrop's steady answer to piddling critics of movies and books: "Why, he's just trying to tell us how it feels to be alive, that's all. Isn't that enough?" Well, old Quent had told them, and the problem with that was the assimilation of it, a lesson too stark to be endured, compared for some reason with Shelley's drowning, or others' jump. Shrop can see he is in for months of anguished pondering that is going to lead nowhere, at least not on the level of ideas, with always behind it the lurking problem of what to do about it all, how to translate stoic niceties or doomed mind into a flagrant act. It might even be no use writing about it beforehand, as in some "suicide letter," but rather something to be called A Preamble to Burning. He jokes about this, of course, if only to set his mind free of the actual event, but it is no joke to him, and it would always remain so, even in the happiest of times: a friend gone, in flames, a leader and confidant turned to charcoal on the spot, to Shrop one of the more hideous transformations as distinct, he supposes, from bacterial cadaver or the sweet, swollen face of drowning. He has been put to school in the harshest manner possible, harsher than he has ever imagined, and words are not going to help him, not even the most heart-rending poetry—Gottfried Benn, say, or Dylan Thomas read with full intensity. He is on his mental own now, unless some substitute for Quent should come along, and how likely is that? The splintered, shattered, absentee mind is going to fend for itself in some travesty of the wounded, blinded, amputated warrior flailing around on the battlefield in a frenzy of insufficiency, doing his worst while others watch with aghast compassion, wondering who will put him out of his misery? And all this, he reckons, because of a momentary Blitz, making worse the aggravations of a normal day, pushing them too far, giving them teeth.

On a whim deciding it is time to move, and to hell with all the forwarding and tax complications it will bring, he tries it out with those special no-lease, rent up front hide-outs that all have the same tired-looking lamp next to a derelict armchair and the same roachy garlic smell in the kitchenette (or, as some say, *kitchenne*, for the tiniest niche). First, he tries a place with bathroom at its north-east corner, but finds it too bleak, then one with bathroom at its north-west corner (too soothing), then one with bathroom to the south, which almost pleases him, except that is what he is leaving, so he settles for a place two doors away on his old street, with bathroom squarely confronting painter's north, just to see if it bleakens his soul. He has already seen too much, from bathroom vents that do not work if the light is on, chests of drawers that spill all their drawers out if you so much as pull one, and, in such commodious premises, too little of the top sheet on the bed turned down, so it tickles his heartspoon in the night. Things have to be just so. Too many light switches, he grumbles, dangling from their sockets like carrion in the beak of a predator, a mare's nest of bare wires and broken finials. The only constant remains the dust-caked screen of the TV, behind which, he presumes, Nigella is awaiting him.

Strange indeed to find the Quent business making everything more severe. Obliged to mail a packet of clippings to Paris, he goes to the post office only to have the clerk tell him that air mail to Europe is now taking two weeks instead of mere days, and all he can murmur in response is a lame, "I imagine so." He can usually improve on that, especially after witnessing some female philatelist picking and choosing stamps for a good twenty minutes with a postal clerk intent mainly on her cleavage, in which an entire collection of erstwhile French colonials could be hidden. He is not in the best of moods, on any occasion, for anything. His ideal retort, the sort the French refer to as *l'esprit de l'escalier*, meaning the smart line you dream up too late (on the staircase, leaving) should have been, "Oh, you mean instead of the camel train I usually use for such mail." But too late. He goes to buy milk and rolls, glad to be able to do anything so mundane in the high world of the apocalypse, de-Quented, although there is no shortage of other shrinks. The only shortage or lack is of candidates for burning, who have taken the three-year-old Blitz too much to heart. Quent left little behind in written form, although you could never tell what might surface later, or from whose hands.

The upshot of all this strenuous, expensive activity is that, for a month or so, he is the proud proprietor of five boltholes, in only one of which he has his few possessions, including a big album that contains letters from various newspapers to which he has sent copy only to have it returned to him in the stamped addressed envelope together with a brief letter inviting him to take their correspondence course in how to write, only five hundred dollars a throw. One in particular irks him: the longer course introducing the Beverly Hills School of Writing, that teaches you how to discover the philosophy of life implicit in any book under review, even if there appears to be no such thing in the entire text. He wonders what to do with all this paid-for property, thinking that he should spend one fifth of each day in each or favor the ones in which he got the best sleeps, nightly anyway. He does nothing, of course, although dreaming of offering the rooms to some derelict of the back streets. He stays on Hoboken Cut, an almost obsolete name for something postally known as Eighth or Ninth, he is never sure. In effect, he has not moved at all but spread his imperial longings far and wide over at least three streets, realizing that no bomb could change him much, whereas this Blitz has changed him for the worse, making him even more hesitant, jittery, gauche.

What horrifies him in the wake of Quent's death is the impromptu, ragged protocol at the airlines' check-in counters, not that he goes anywhere near them. He sees the fiasco on the TV news: the removal and inspection of shoes, the dropping of trousers, the close and almost covetous inspection of the groin area of by the main lustmaster on duty (especially of untidy-looking men). Being not without funds, though he never tells, he devises his own way of evading these inspections, ignoring the commercial carriers altogether and, in his poshest accent, ordering a private jet to take him from Teterboro to JFK and back (thoughts of long-lost Idlewild hovering) at the cost of several years' rent. And off he goes, to encounter red carpet unrolled at the fizzing mouth of the Hawker 800's fuselage, the parade of tea and scones, proper use of the lavatory. It will not take long apart from the ground delays, which far exceed any time in the air, but the whole time he exults because he is cheating the entire system of high-flown point-less rigmarole, going and coming just like someone boarding a covered wagon in the old West.

"Ready for take-off, sir?"

"Spool 'em up, Lindy," he answers. Off he goes, a man in mufti rid-ing silver wings for the joy of it, standing in no line, baring no groin, sloughing no shoe.

To friends as far-flung as New Zealand and Lion-sur-Mer, Oslo and Newfoundland, he has communicated the wretched news about Quent, soft-pedaling the inferno of course ("None of their never-mind," Shrop claims). Addressing his envelope to France, he stops at the street address—*Impasse des Jonquilles*—wondering about the French convention of lower-case letters where everyone else has capitals, but arrested mainly by a thought: Does this mean a street blocked by daf-fodils, Wordsworthian style (Keep off the daffodils, property of Gaffer Wordsworth) or is it a street on which daffodils are not allowed? They fight them off and erect barriers of barbed wire. Either way, it's an impasse. They shall not pass, he hears, *ils ne passeront pas*, and he won-ders where in hell he first heard that. How like him to have his friends abroad, at a safe distance to safeguard intimacy in either direction or to insulate them from his tactless outbursts about Nazis and others. He is full of tricks, though, carefully setting the airmail sticker to France at a careless angle, simulating the feckless thumb of a post office clerk, hid-ing the obsessive parallel-to-the-horizon placing of the man with a pat-tern complex marred by bombing. He gives the game away, however, by carefully aligning yet another sticker, with a B-24 on it, that came in a free set in the mail. Or, if it was not free, he did not notice the price.

How, Shrop has to figure out, does the fate of Quent square with such brute facts as digging through a mound of mangled steel with pick and shovel, from time to time calling out as if to address the heap, will-ing someone to be there awaiting discovery? Not something personal and subjective, Shrop thinks, but something like that, stark beyond question, as one picking through the mass with an abstracted, spent, tortured, bony look—the adjectives pile up while each teaspoonful of the unrewarding gets put aside, a failure, because beneath the dig there are some sixty feet to go until the pooled water down at the bedrock. The situation is that hard. To engage in this, with gulls, grackles and sparrows clustering around you, is more than poignant, Shrop says, it is enough to explain the behavior of a Quent, who knows the firefighter's fire-retardant gear gives him a better chance of being found than just about anyone else. It preserves the bones. Then there is the difference between someone looking for anyone and someone looking for a special someone with haunted, clenched face, a look that announces membership in the most intimate club of all. That is what drove Quent to it, not some idle quirk of cafard waltzing into the open.

Shrop would dearly like to abandon this train of thought, but it will not abandon him, drawing his mind to the awesome gulf between pondering it and actually doing something about it for personal reasons, as if discovery of the departed dead were a boon within the family even as the energy to dig peters out and the Herculean demand becomes mental only, virtually pleading with the morass to hand up a living, breathing soul or just a known cadaver newly lost. The horrors of such application have nothing to do with daily life but evoke a Jeremiah, alone at the slab, talking to it and whoever still lies buried in it, recently enough to still carry a name, whatever the disintegration down beneath. The spectacle of diggers talking to the mass they investigate with teaspoon delicatesse matches the shock of being involved in the conflagration and collapse, those layers upon layers of impacted floors with their cars, as if the trim and nobility of the body could survive so ghastly a compression. We just want anything recognizable, they say when they recover breath, which is not often, and their doing this lasts for years long after they have quit and gone home for the last time, their job abandoned to the gulls and sparrows, whose peck into the debris is eternal.

This is the basalt conundrum that wounds Shrop, asking him why he too did not go up in smoke with his old friend.

It is not Quent he sees in battered fireman's helmet and workman's blues, marching around with his familiar pre-paraplegic rueful bounce, it is himself bungling his pill intake for the day and allowing the instantly caustic blue Inderal to catch in the back of his throat, at once creating the flow that burns (God alone knows what it does to the heart when it gets there). The pains of life are legion; he has taught himself that, somewhat like unearthing the stark upward-pointing needle that grows from the heart of palm trees, too sharp for birds to land on. He knows, but the forlorn scene at Zero is beyond comparisons and must be left in its own dumb language, unique and inhuman.

It was clear that Quent, in his final days, felt he was doing good of some kind, but that must have been the same feeling as led to his self-immolation: out on his own with no reference points, the unique following the unique, the creation of his own universe, an act having nothing to do with such honored categories as comedy and tragedy, help or indifference. Shrop feels the inward stab that excludes him from Quent's ultimate doom. Is it then the same doom as being buried under all that ruined steel and called out by relatives as if you were the genius loci refusing to show a face?

Two things occupy him almost to the brink of opportunist tedium. Why did it take Quent three years to arrive at his decision? And what is it about Ground Zero that so enrages everyone? To the first of these, he answers that Quent had to wake out of a useful dream, a dream of being useful to others as a kind of rehabilitation that in the end went for naught. The other question, dazzling in its completeness, he finds much more difficult, but in some way he thinks the two problems are connected, as if it took Quent three years to be dazzled by an event that had no meaning beyond the everyday clutter about motives and outcomes. After three years, Quent had discovered that something had happened that was nothing—not a symbol or an emblem, but an experience having nothing to do with life or even death, what Shrop ages ago had with some reluctance called an anti-biotic, an anti-life thing. This means of course that he has no way of domesticating it into the grids called air-raids, nihilism, or sadism, all of which may pertain, but only peripherally. What was this nothing, then, that had driven his shrink and friend to an extreme measure whose impact had best be called circumstantial, Quent having left no record behind him? He had just gone and not come back, much as the atrocity had done its atrocious thing and ended. Could it be, Shrop wondered, that giving up his shattered life was Quent's way of forging an emotional response to the nullity of Ground Zero?

Shrop has spent time in the sub-tropics, where nothing delights him more than a deluge that, an hour after it ends, has disappeared and the world of concrete shows no sign of its ever having been. The speed of that rejoices him, who readily sees the rain soaking into the earth to do its usual thing, but he really enjoys the stark contrast of the rain gone and the hot concrete basking bonily all over again in the tropic sun. A whole climate with the world in its control gets better results, he thinks, than a man trying to spit into a plate full of crumbs. In a high wind, yes.

He enjoys the idea of a thing and all that is not that thing. Those straight lines gratify him, the "double-cutting" involved in the dichotomy.

So what of Quent, then? Did he really arrive at a nothing that matched the nothingness of a criminal event? What simplism, Shrop thinks, but what else have we to go on? No rationalization left behind. Did he just one day measure the full extent of his grief? Had he, after many days at the Zero, at last tired of the misery and the gross absence of beloved bodies? Was it all a build-up nobody knew about? Did he run out of responses to the gratuitous nature of the event? Was his word-hoard of anti-Islam curses at last empty? Having been a soldier himself, had he with grievous apprehension reached his snapping point, at which officers burst into tears and bury their faces in the mud?

33
Painter's North

ORE OR LESS TO HONOR THE MEMORY OF HIS DEAD FRIEND, although staidly aware that one does not usually wait years before doing so, he begins to make lists of people, even those in reserve or cold storage, put away like life-rafts or life preservers against another evil day. The last time he invited them out was when they assembled, most of them, at a downtown restaurant and ate cold shrimp in memory of what only days ago had been intact. Now he retrieved the image of himself not exactly as a social butterfly, but at least an energetic moth, recognizing that the very process (old envelopes as well as the battered, out of date Rolodex) evoked treading on a lattice of water lilies while toeing the silt for anaconda or trout, or in the wrong country (not Thailand) hoping to come upon an elephant in the main thoroughfare with a red traffic light tied to its tail. Not everyone accepts his invitation, some even saying he lived like a well-heeled pariah, but he was willing to let rot what had already festered, and there were certainly enough live pals to build a quorum of what he called the old contemptibles, as if they had survived a foreign war together. All this, an upheaval among coevals, to memorialize a man who had set fire to himself in a public street. If there was something untoward and queasy in the implied proceeding, it eluded Shrop, whose festive side was bursting out all over, long suppressed in the interests of giving up or surrendering the ghost, as they say because there is nothing else to give, not after those named Butler, Ielpi, Lee, O'Berg and Vigiano packed it in stunned by the spectacle of men singing to a slab with claw hammer in hand. Not among them, Shrop has joined them ages ago, but to what purpose? The stack of ID cards found amid the rubble of the north tower is not his, nor any one of them his to look for, ferreting, unearthing, going sixty feet down for. He is not one of those men earning six figures at a desk job who gave it up to work for thirty dollars an hour at Ground Zero, having been denied a leave of absence. The dead are talking to the bereaved in that special sign language of the gone, inaudible to others, but couched in the idiom of the close-knit family that takes for granted canceled retirements and vacations, honor guards with flags at crucial junctures, intimacy with a

steaming midden that no longer belongs to anybody but them. Shrop
does not know their tribal language, but catches the tremor and timbre
of it within the quaking of his mind that examines a new dump for the
exact flavor of Quent, the man on wheels who said, simply, if anyone is
to fathom him, *I have had enough*. Was that it? What did he say at the very
last? A cough, yes, Goodbye to Park Slope, which just about covers it
for everyone involved. Shrop is trying to bury the horror deep within
his recoiling mind, but it lives on and burns away.

So, what? Recovery of a lost philosophy? Mourning for said friend
carried to inordinate lengths because, let's face it, said friend was a war
hero condemned to live legless in a wheelchair, of which quietened and
calmed mode of life (as those Florida road signs had it of traffic in the
suburbs) he had wearied, mentally denouncing the slow drive, the
speed bumps of an over-civil procession. The other reasons had to do
with weather, employment, and personal eccentricity; usually, someone
who lived in the city was in fact an urban animal and included among
his fetishes the need to socialize, indeed to befriend, but Shrop was different, quite without others' knowledge allowing their personalities and
their last appearances to pool in his mind ox-bow fashion, delighting
and enlivening him as, in the solitude of his book alcove, he went over
and over again the antics and dicta of the Last Party, as if he were some
museum proprietor or the ringleader of a disbanded circus.

Anyway, the invitations went out, by e-mail in most cases, and the
word followed it: Shrop had come to life again, and a murmur began
among people who not merely liked him but thought he had had something serious to say, even *propounding* it, which had then left him as one
of the golden *ahodoris* of Japan are apt to do. You had to reckon with
the albatross's naughtier side, the clingy death-hug that Coleridge
among other nautical poets had limned so well. Shrop was not exactly
dicing with death, but he wasn't ruling it out either, and the savviest of
the invitees wondered if he himself intended or fancied something
such: the lopsided possibility of at least one overdue mourner's biting
the dust in the very throes of lament. Those familiar with Shrop's mercurial side (that had whisked him into and out of the History Channel
as a fill-in impersonator with a German accent, and as a movie critic
with a penchant for getting plots wrong) knew that, far from poisoning his guests, he was not above talking them into some twin of
apoplexy or planting the seed of a slow-functioning despair not unlike
his own. You never knew. You never know. Yet, contrary to what he

165

thought about himself, they relished his rare presence, spotting him as one of their own who had gone beyond in a spirit of questing noesis: to see what was on the other side of the barbed wire or where the dictionary in its lazy fashion said *etymology unknown*. Well, by Jonah, Shrop would find out in his fashion of a lethargic Orson Welles and throw a party to tell. His small quarters imposed a limit on the crowd, but not in Shrop's imagination; he half-believed in rubber rooms, so, having invited a dozen more than his rooms would comfortably hold, he invited a dozen more to shove the walls outward, into (he often hoped) the *Lebensraum* of the escaped Nazis who populated most apartment houses in the city.

They were not to know, although the best of them had their suspicions (*le soupçon du balcon*) that, outside on the so-called balcony too narrow to accommodate him other than sideways, he went out barefoot with an angled sandpaper board to file down the calluses on his heels. He walked like someone freed of earthly constraint, and this they attributed to the build-up, rectified, from his permanent yet intermittent diabetes. He filed his heels somewhere, if not into the toilet or the bath, then out there where the dust blew away and infected the rest of the city with his lost philosophy. With rough heels, he loved to walk down the ramp in the foyer, sliding recklessly in new shoes, bringing the smooth into the roughy, as New Zealanders say.

Why does he try? They asked, but no one was quite sure. Because, some said, he does not believe in the impossible. It is never too late to mourn anyone, just as it is never too late to die. He would have agreed, though often duty-bound to curb the hectic, playful side of his being in the interests of a severer polity befitting his status as a philosopher of the old school.

Thierry-Molyneux, the French aviator-painter, is the first to arrive, with Amaranth his novelist wife, now busy on a new book about Brillat-Savarin. He flies loops and circuits, then paints his track on silkscreen while she hovers on the ground within her chosen century, which is not ours. Close behind them comes Tarquin Andreyev, an expert on Russian literature also writing a novel about Rumania and its erstwhile dictator. His wife, an omnivorous editor, bears someone else's proofs in her fist, no doubt hoping for a quiet moment in which to work on them, like someone on a train or a plane. If their conversation is anything like whist, no one notices as the radio astronomer A. Lark Sang arrives with his usual retinue of cooks, *valets de chambre*, and sexual surrogates, he insisting on showing off his ancient address-book, bulging and broken, if a black book of sorts then long since given over to charcoal. Rubber bands hold it together, but, truth told, as Shrop knows, Lark Sang has memorized the entire contents and brought the tattered *aide-memoire* only as a showpiece, a bit of upside-down snobbery that goes with his two neckties worn simultaneously to denote an even club life. The wife of the moment has dressed like a boy and bears with her the *A. Lark Sang Halloween Box* (it is not the season), hoping to flog it to people with less sense of time than of fleeting fame.

Those arriving together although not socially compatible include the literary editor Manthanas Despues, the man with two beards, one on either side of his chin, a notorious fugu chef with a reputation for treating enemies to dinner, and Lomar Antecedent, the most handsome man in the Naked City, once reputed to have applied for newsreading work with two dozen networks, all of which jobs he got; he had gone to Andorra, however, and wed Juanita del Rio after, it was claimed, a series of agonizing corridas and bull-related afflictions, to satisfy her parents. She was an elegant dancer, with an engaging manner of singing under her breath while performing the most elaborate contortions of her solo. These people, Shrop muses, are they bizarre because he happens to know them? Is it his fault, or would they be like that with anyone? Surely they know other people. It was worth pondering, though: friends, or rather defensively fended off acquaintances kept at an improper distance could easily develop bad habits, or uncouth humors, when left to their own devices, when insufficiently befriended, which is how Shrop tends to treat even his closest and dearest, his main motive to preserve his fond impression of their last meeting, reluctant to add the last drop that spills the cup over. Now here they all are, eager for him, and with their oddities saved up. He will have to exercise himself nobly today to cater to all their most exquisite leanings. But once a year, that's all. To hell with it, he muses, I can cope with that, for Quent. It has actually been years, time for accumulated grief to turn into something else, rich, strange, and unknown in the textbooks. Despues is telling some tale about Bali, where his career must by now be notorious, specifying how in the surfing hotels they charge you extra if you have had a tattoo done upon you and left as it were skid-marks on the sheets, which they send someone to check between breakfast and check-out, always charging extra for the duplicate imprint. No one cares, Bali is as remote as Duluth, and

Lomar has had his face redone, not that it needed it, thus achieving what Shrop thinks an impossible degree of pulchritude, best seen from any angle, a process he facilitates, constantly repositioning his head by angling his neck, wanting no one to miss anything. Juanita watches all this with a keen sense of ownership: all of him is on loan to her, she thinks, courtesy of her parents, the devisers of appalling wedding tests even after marriage, on their infrequent visits to Manhattan setting up wall bars in their apartment just to make sure he still qualifies for their agile daughter. Shrop thanks God for his own semi-misanthropic stance, with nobody to test him save, alas, Quent, the bosom tyrant, to whom he drinks right off in a swordswallower's gulp, an imperfect gin tainted with a sprig of mint.

The party is warming up, he can tell that, and his addition of music by Charles Ives adds, he hopes, the right lugubrious touch, not an insistent mourning note, but flakes of discordant elegy calculated to denote the passage of many years. Here comes Irving Skalkottas, years after his divorce unable to change his joint checking account to a single one and, at restaurants, always having food brought to a carefully maintained second place at table, of which he takes no gastric advantage. He has only just preceded the novelist-teacher, Jack Immelmans, constant squire to a rather elderly judge, nicknamed Pony Aberystwith, whom he tends to be seen around with although no one knows if they combine carnally in private. A Type-Two diabetic, he works wonders with a diet of gin and vodka without, he claims, any pancreas at all: thin, gaunt, yet debonairly fetching, as if sheer see-through were the next stop in his charmed approach to zerophagy. She is a prodigious reader, although not of his rompish novels, having not yet reached the twentieth century in any of her literary binges, rather as if rehearsing for C-SPAN. Shrop adores these people and wonders that he manages to live without them.

In his fretsome way, Shrop wonders if he is getting it right, as unaccustomed to throwing parties as at attending funerals. Quent the beloved was cremated twice, once at his own hand, the second time by last will and testament, so Shrop wonders if it was worth it, unable to shake from his tousled head the notion that all human activity was ridiculous, devised not so much by people as by some malign chamberlain anxious to watch his creatures go through preposterous tricks. Was human life in fact more serious, more solemn, than Shrop knew? Had he all his life suffered from an inability to take the misfortunes of others with the same seriousness he applied to himself? Was that a vice? Well, hardly a party vice, and he dismissed the thought although vestigially wondering if he suffered from what he called carnage euphoria, having reared himself on A. Lark Sang's constant reminder that he was a *TV* radio astronomer, this addressed to people who might otherwise have gotten it wrong, supposing him to be a *radio* TV astronomer or something such. Or had some winsome TV smirk set it off?, reminding him that the portmanteau of life was innately irreverent and the most appalling things that happened were festive to the eye of the overseeing tyrant, whose play-TV it all was, Blitz and *auto-da-fé* notwithstanding, even the holiest most devout moments in human life were a mere fatuous recurrence.

Shrop can scarcely believe his ears. The whole room seems to be lying or getting things wrong. Or is it merely an echo effect from the bumpy ceiling? Voices (and minds) merge, grievously disorchestrated. Yes, one is saying, it's an attempt to return the world to the anagram, no not a unit of weight. Are you foolish? Another voice is continuing: As in von Wilhelm's *The Phalarope Condescending,* see? He would receive his patients with organ at the ready, unzipped, just a bead of sweat or lava at the tip, a sort of doglike stance, and things would go from there. It cannot be, darling, he claims his PC just delivers up gibberish whenever he writes something out, so he spends his days trying to figure out what he's just thought, which in his case, with *his* history of things forgotten, is disastrous. No, it was Schweinbaum, the red-haired sensualist. No, you fool, it was Woidswuth, the man with a handshake full of dead fingers. You ought to know your Romantics better. They say he pays more in tax than Spain has for its army. Well, let him pay it and then belt up. I am told on reliable authority that his first wife, the dental hygienist, was strangled in the chair by a visiting dentist. He pulled her through, then. Oh, kind of, you might say, but she'd been up to unhygienic things. They always are, on a diet of red meat.

The next voice, if succession is possible, is authoritative as a train announcement and loud: Quite simple, really, if you take ordure, then it's *or-*, for gold, and *dure*, which implies permanence or the lasting. *Hard.* Hard gold, my bonnies, and hard to come by, take my word for it. Oh, I thought it meant something else. Well, it doesn't, take it from me. The Voice moves on to the next problem, overtaken by someone intent on a little door into his stomach, with hinges, and through which they were able to observe his digestion. No, that's lower down, after—

we know, we know, there is no need to be vulgar, Creamie. I'm not Creamie, I'm Brie. Such lovely skin. That's what the midwife said, shoving her hand through the blood and stuff. The meconium, you mean. Whatever. You can't get too technical in a lay group such as this. Why, he used to train ferrets to steal from mailboxes, whereas in India, in the post offices at the railway stations if you so much as put your hand inside to retrieve your letters a waiting rat would bite it. Well, just look at India. Wasn't Mountbatten a German? Well, it goes to show then. They had a hand in everything long before 1914. Who was this Lebensraum then, a poet or what? Painter's north, I'd say. Dauber's dumbshow, love, that's more like it. Now it's bloody elephants, what they used to call a trunk call. "Trunks," the operator used to shrill at you. "*Caller*, do you wish *trunks?*"

Well, I at least have a conscience, Shrop tells himself in the midst of the hubbub as the standard cocktail party jabber assumes sway over them and pushes them all to extravagant extremes. He applied for a job by hiring a skywriting plane? Did he get the job? No, the plane crashed, and lawsuits followed. Whatever mess you get into, don't hire Zootwasser, he has a bad name. If there's one thing I hate in things, it's cream. Oh, *I* am quite otherwise. I suppose it all depends on what you were breastfed, if you were. When mother's milk clots, you are in trouble. Or paradise, darling, it all depends. And then he raped her with a nailfile. How, oh, I suppose the nailfiles have it, especially on nailfile day. There are limits to algebra of course, as Lady Hester Stanhope, that old coot of an Arabian horsewoman, discovered from her seat in the saddle. Oh, not when he asked for two lemonades in the officers' club in Cairo after crossing Sinai. *We've crossed Sinai*, he said, *we bloody have*. Not the bloody bit. How would *you* know? Have you seen it lately? Well, then, don't boast, darling. Do they even remember him after three years, it made the papers, yes, but you know how public inattention wolfs things down, one human life in extremis, nay three thousand, is only a flash in the panmixis of all that happens in one day, in a split second of a given day. I am truly appalled, I really am.

*   *   *

This party, Shrop is telling himself with almost pedagogical heaviness, is a triumph of life. We just can't sustain the right degree of what is it? Gravitas? It's beyond us. We have to make light of what's lousy because we don't know what on earth to do with it otherwise. Life is full of wrong impressions. Is this why, after someone's killed at an airshow, they have a rip-roaring booze-up to drown their sorrows? Have I discovered the wake, after all this time? Well, it's for Quent, not Finnegan. I am not so glad I caused all this gaggle to come into being. Something crass and childish about it, like letting kids loose in a graveyard. Clearly, Quent is still real to him, not semi-indecipherable as a postmark, but clear as the lines on his own hand. I feel like Erich von Stroheim insisting, as he did, that extras in costume dramas be fitted out with historically correct underwear, silk of course. Like him, I am asking for my masterpiece, *Greed,* to be released in an eight-hour version. There are no masterpieces of grief, are there, unless the one for Diana, in which I played no part. I should have done the whole thing alone. Maybe I did, for the past three years. How come we find it so hard to keep a straight face once we have reached a suitable distance from the funeral? Is there no one in charge of homogeneous response? A few tears, and then raucous laughter sets in as another cosmic joke bites the slate.

Now people are arriving in streams as if from some other party, in exhilarated mood and not expecting to be met at the door but smoothly adjusting the instant they walk in, hailing and halloing, grabbing a drink as if it were the most natural act in the world. Elspeth Snow, London-loving poetess, is reciting the long list of those whose work she fancies, from Tod Smirnoff to Janet Kleist, highly un-English names to Shrop, who stopped at Dickens. With Elspeth comes her squire, a flaccid-looking young man in butcher's striped apron, no doubt looking for the next carcass to cut up. Tommaso Glint, Fellow of the Royal Society, is already talking about his favorite insect, the bombardier beetle, to an enthralled crowd who seem to hear only snatches of what he says, though his wife Marta fills in the gaps for him. How, Shrop wonders, can anyone be heard? How can anyone be narrating or reminiscing amid the racket? He assumes lip-reading skills he never knew about before, and wonders when Tommaso will break into his set-piece about the Stauffenberg plotters, relatives of whom he knew, including the one who said it took twenty minutes to die at the end of a hempen rope. It will take only slightly longer, Shrop thinks, among the decibels of the evening; he finds himself helpless among the surges as the whole of Manhattan arrives to celebrate the break-up of his three-year famine. He is trying to tell Rita Tournier, the opera singer, how he once saved a girl friend from humiliation in a Tucson department store when they decided to cut her credit card in two with a huge scissors. "I am this lady's attorney," Shrop says he said, "and you have committed *wrongful dishonor* on her. Desist at once." They did, and she bought a whole drawerful of underwear as they reeled away to look up the phrase. Does he really tell it, or is the voice of his imagination so loud? Peggy Detmarin overhears him, though, and starts to laugh; she has heard him before, she who conducts a yearly seminar on dreams, which in the distant past he has attended, loaded with wonted nightmares in which certain friends, such as the Blazes, Micah and Minnie, have appeared, also throwing a party, but abandoning their guests early on and retreating to a private room to have dinner naked while guests said good night to one another and assumed the worst about their hosts. What can you expect, he used to say, from professional philosophers who both wore make-up in which to receive their unwanted guests? He sees a buoyant pianist sidle in, gloved hands at the ready, fingers pronged into a paradise of talcum powder, searching for the piano, which Shrop long ago sold. It would have been Liszt anyway, Shrop decides, and hardly audible among the throng. A tall, bald, insipid-looking pharaoh of a glass technologist is inspecting the flutes, holding them up to the lights and writing them off. He will not drink from these. Rita Tournier, mezzo-soprano, brushes past, helpless in the grip of the ronde's billows and surges, smiling defeat. In a fit of quixotic impetuosity he planks the palm of his hand against her dress lower down and exclaims almost in the forgotten manner of Peter the Great (who got under tables and felt at *his* guests as they sat, crying *foramen habet!*). She is wearing no underwear, which as he knew somehow liberates her voice, and her thatch is open to all who venture to accost her. The expression on her face does not change; she is habituated to the grab. Now he finds himself opposite Mort Ampersand, the critic of romanticism who shows blue movies in the caboose abandoned in his tiny herbal garden, always the same movies as if the constant lewd were the only one, especially to invited friends. The ronde sweeps them in opposite directions away from each other, Mort toward the uppity-looking glass technologist (stout, pink, and sweaty), Shrop in the direction of Mortimer T., the man with three doctorates, on Twain, Camus, and Pavese, all three of whom a fourth will connect in plausible complitspeak. Does he, Shrop asks himself, collect three salaries as well, with a fourth in the offing? He will not be able to ask this evening thanks to the swirl of people, a fool's *grande foule*, as he cleverly thinks.

But he can wonder about them all, which one of them is having gas problems (beets and celery mingled), which five are smoking grass, and who will be first in the queue for the solitary toilet. Yet another goes in search of the piano, the constantly jogging mother whose daughter plays, mostly when no one wants her to. There they go, questing, musicless, but eager to parade their wares.

The sudden apparition of Hovis Tumulty, thinned down and radiant, stops him in his tracks. Now she has become the alias of herself, with an anonymous young cross-dresser in tow, the Hovis of tomorrow, clearly having survived the in-between years, shedding, he guesses, fifty pounds per year.

"Hi-ya," he says.

"Gotcha," she answers.

"Well, look at you."

"Why doncha?" she blurts.

He smiles a hostly smile and moves on, aghast at mutability and no longer able to remember the huge Hovis of old. Now she is thin and keen, no doubt a boy. He wonders if the crypto-Nazis are here too, no doubt in uniform, but not a single SS is in sight, though several guests are standing swastika-legged in the toilet queue, awaiting their turn at the oasis and quietly cursing their host for serving so much beer. Now he gets it: all the levity that was missing from his philosophical life has shown up tonight. He may not remember it, but something will stick, and the ready benison of humor and wit will abide, or so he hopes. It is as if his serious philosophical ideas have come back to him but flicked into a higher register where ordinary people live, smiling because they have been trained to do so by incessant commercials, in other words showing their teeth in the American way. The visage of the American philosophe now haunts him, the very type of the wholly enclosed solipsistic monad he had become. Or so he decides, wondering how many parties he has to give in order to have light-hearted epiphanies at which—he groans at the vast inundation of chattering people who will have trampled his lares and penates to dust, yapped about Yul Brynner, the abominated artiste Edie Sedgwick superstar, and the latest Rumanian to copy Cioran, on whom he dotes.

The names are fake, he now knows it. They come out of the night to deceive him with their latest masks, just a species of human lava midway between popcorn and excelsior, best tipped out into the coolish evening, for this is only one of their many incarnations and he would be better off with a solitary guest, say, Lon Chaney's father crawling in on hands and knees with a boxer's gumshield in his mouth. His old yearning for solitude is coming back, he can tell, and he begins in the midst of all that howling to brood on the purity of absence, the need to feel around him the hug of unused air.

* * *

Something has gone desperately wrong. The whole island is pouring into and through his compact quarters. Guests appear to be walking on people, maybe in search of their host, more probably the one toilet; they have arrived with full bladders only to discover a way-station jammed to the hilt. It is no longer his party, but theirs, prey to dusty-looking middle-aged women he did not invite, and one man he may have once known who, with his sons, went in for the manufacture of telescopes: an amateur dealer and manufacturer, who now seeks a tele-scope barrel to pee into. Here and there he recognizes those less than friendly, from Dabenstein, a man with only one tic: addressing every-one he talks to, i.e. imposes his bony presence upon, using the same phrase: "You're confused, buddy." New York must have heard this vol-untary a million times, both the successive mayors and the bums, all of them failures in whatever they practiced. If it is not Dabenstein, it is the more amiable image of Jack McManion, tennis player with a niacin flush, his past clouded by alcohol and his early training too, nonethe-less able in the afternoons to batter the ball about with startling proficiency. Yet he, like the rare-book dealer Humidor, uninvited, is a fidget, always bearing with him a dozen volumes culled at random, with which he pesters those he runs into, whether snorting Chlazz, a furtive little accountant suffering from reticulitis, or Harris the dean of eco-nomics at Staten Island Academy, a man with an appalling habit of banging his skull against the cinder blocks that form his office (or any other blocks conveniently placed nearby). It was said he had success-fully over the years flattened one side of his head with the battery, so it was time, for symmetry's sake, to flatten the other, but he never did, which gave his face an ablated, custom-made look.

These, Shrop told himself, were the uninvited. They *are*, having heard of his first party in years and willing to parley a mere acquaintance into an invitation, somehow converting silence into piled-up fervor. Were they, Shrop hopes, just passing through, here to exhibit their unchanged tics and mannerisms, as if to reassure the hoi polloi before sauntering out again appeased, but hungry for more conviviality. Among them, only Desiréee Phlum, voluptuous and fragrant, entices Shrop with her venereal allure, a call girl uncalled, so to speak, too beautiful to be dealt with by an entire generation of insecure lechers. She has not been propositioned in years, but continues to thrive in more or less intact radiance, a trollop in waiting now given to reading while at rest. If only Shrop were younger, he thinks, she would be worth the try, but even as host he fears rebuff and so passes her by with a carefully manufactured nod and a slight trailing motion of his right hand to denote delicacy. Some other time, Desiréee Phlum, he whispers as he bypasses her golden aura, in renewed search for Hovis Tumulty, former cleaning lady thinned out into something butch and mangy. Shrop is on the prowl at his own party for those in whom life has installed fatal mutations; he wants to get to them, and at them, before they surrender to evolution at its punctuated worst. Does he know only creeps, after all this time, or is he deceiving himself, having reared himself on, say, little professors who know nothing but maintain their ignorance within a sagely chosen rhetoric of the calcified ignoramus, never completing a sentence or a quotation, laughing devoutly if in doubt until the crisis has passed, and actually cultivating the demeanor of the *petit maître* petomane, ever ready to mask *dunno* with a smell. Shrop has met them all, on subway trains, in men's rooms, and in the green rooms of failing TV channels, experts on Experience, always willing to begin a sentence with "When it comes right down to it, in the best of possible worlds, the popular sentiment tends to go with . . ." They last within their own fumes, almost getting away with fraud.

34
A Certain Ghost

T THIS POINT, AS SHROP KNOWS WELL, HE TENDS TO HALLUCI-
nate, unable to bear the onslaught of curious, hostile eyes,
today inflicting on himself the portly, tweeded build of a certain ghost who has appeared before, in French Foreign Legion uniform, kepi and all, or the blue serge of the CIA man, a colonel in mufti,
going about his clandestine business in several languages, including
Arabic (which makes him rare). It is this same Wandervogel, as he is
known to intimates, who has appeared to him before, retailing tales of
Princess Diana, the born survivor loathed by Princess Margaret and
the other royals, and put out to grass in a speeding Mercedes. Tonight,
however, Der Vogel tells a tale about a certain chateau in France,
Chenonceau, not mythical at all, home to Catherine de Médicis, the
wounded from the trenches of World War One, and then the Nazis of
the next war. The uncanny thing about the chateau is that the Nazis
occupied one end of it whereas the other end of the long gallery span-
ning the Cher River was in unoccupied Vichy France. And its troubled,
double nature continues, actually changing your emotions as you walk
from one end to the other.

"Is this," Shrop asks, "a good way out of this party then? Can I board
the gallery in Nazi country and escape to Vichy at the other end?"

Wandervogel's ghost never answers questions as direct as this, certainly not those with a practical, topical implication. "Go see," he says
and disappears. Such is tonight's hallucination. The chateau vanishes,
the party reappears, minus Desiréee Phlum, that plum for picking, and
all the other uninviteds. Perhaps Shrop has been exaggerating after all,
cooking up monsters from an after-dinner sleep when in fact they are
haunting other soirées, with better drinks and solider food. Wordlessly,
Shrop goes from group to group, shaking hands in the sign language
that pronounces party over, but they misinterpret the handshake as
more conviviality, an incentive to stay on and regale the night with even
more elaborate lies while Shrop, to anger them, goes to sit on the toilet, locking the door behind him.

This is the festivity he has successfully dammed up forever, lapping
at his barricades without quite getting through to him, and he wonders

what bearing, if any, these uncorrected folkways have on the events of this or that year. Does nothing affect them? Is this laughter, this back-slapping, permanent as the *Kaiser Permanente* say? Does it outlast every-thing, a safety valve from God? As if he were some helpless survivor from the first World War, Shrop decides to opt for the *Kaiser Permanente* in the teeth of incessant mishap, knowing he has only to walk the full extent of the Chenonceau gallery to save himself from all of them.

Along the dun, dank, dark Chenonceau gallery he treads, ears primed for ancient voices, knowing the far end is the pagan grail, as if he has read the whole of French medieval literature. He will discover something unusual out there, he knows, perhaps an anti-social thing to befit his gathering mood. At least, he muses, I have done my duty for the next ten years. If I go back, I can party out on the strength of it all; even a handshake is enough to get you invited back. But over there in Vichy, the observances will be different: an uninfected France, to be sure, minus jackboots and red, white and black insignia. No barbed wire. No executions in courtyards. We will be able to get on with our scruffy little lives. He breathes in deeply the gradually increasing smell of garlic with its smothered sunlight and Neapolitan swank. It does not feel different, not yet. Can it be miles? No, he is just walking slowly, wondering if at the far end he will debouch into a gorgeous courtyard where someone is playing a viol, or an illustrious chamber laden with Balzacian pieces all polished to death and shel-tered with dropcloths. It is going to be blissful, he can tell. Thank Zeus for Vichy and its water.

No guards. No frontier. No sneaky cameras to record him for pos-terity as one who has broken through the sound barrier of history. Will he go back? Not for years.

He badly needs this reprieve, and never mind what spiked helmet guards it. No one at all. He minces into an open room in which some-thing huge and round, covered by a subdued-looking rug, sits on an elaborate hand-carved pedestal that bears the word *Columbus* on its dusty nameplate. Clearly, whatever this relic is, it has few visitors, marooned in what looks like a catalog room with maps on its walls. Ah, he sighs, this is where you have to come to get directions. It is the way-station, the information booth for all comers. The oak stand has been brutalized, he can see that, and he imagines a posse of Nazis kicking it around as protocol compels them to go back to the other side to reoc-cupy la belle France.

Off comes the dust-laden rug to reveal a four-foot globe of the world, in fact one of four, the others being kept at the German Embassy in London, up at Hitler's Obersalzberg mountain retreat in Bavaria, and the other in the Reich Chancellery in Berlin. This, though, is the globe the Führer fancied, the original one in fact, and now the only one to survive. A gift from Reich architect Gerdy Troost, it was prized because it used to be kept at party HQ in Munich, the home of the Nazi government, unshyly housed beneath the full blare of a search-light, and once revealed to Neville Chamberlain in 1938, when to Munich he groveled to plead with Herr Hitler, which was when James Joyce (an Irishman and out of it) complained "Why don't they leave Czechoslovakia alone and read *Finnegans Wake?*" Neither potentate did any such thing. There, in 1938, Hitler showing off the searchlit globe was like some huckster offering a condemned peach: *Suck on that, Neville, old son, you'll die of it.* He did, unable to put teeth into his infamous *peace-in-our-time* brag on his return. He had literally been shown Hitler's sphere of influence, the devil's backside mounted in a bracket. It is said that Hitler stared at his globe for hours, at least until the advancing hordes of Russians and others began to close in on Germany. Not long after, American GIs damaged the oak bracket, but otherwise left the globe intact, after which it sat in the entrance to the card index room in the Munich library, an antique guarding an antic system.

"They have overrun Europe," some newspaper whined.

"They overran me," whined Chamberlain.

You would have thought that Hitler, fixated on his globe, would have had the overrun portions painted black as countries fell one after another, or at least smeared with Führer dung to match his fecal obsessions. But no, nothing so histrionic, done by someone with a rubber hand or a slave with naked palm.

Musing on Hitler and his retinue, Shrop thinks back to the lost or abandoned multitude of his party, then recalls how readers of *The Times* wrote in to suggest suitable destinations for the Elephant Man: a light-house, a school for the blind, and Dartmoor, among them. Was he headed for anything such? He could walk that long hallway in a reversed baseball cap, only faintly aware of how, seen thus as he approached, the cap evoked the one fitted to the condemned's head before electrocution. Nothing that fierce either. All he has had to do is resign himself to the awfulness of life, and let it go at that. Creative people, one of whom he thinks himself, joining a vast legion, are those who constantly need to comment on life, and the act of commentary keeps them creative. *A thought for walking to the tune of* is how he thinks of this, recognizing that almost any thought will do for walking with, most of all when someone such as he advances along that perhaps endless corridor, brushing against the ghosts of Mars, but fending them off, nodding at a whole host of new strangers.

What am I doing?

I am doing the *Chenonceau*, which means a nervous sarabande executed in a distinct mood of world-weariness, ever hoping for something better, but doubting its power to break through the crust of mundanity.

Ah, then, the longer you walk in here, the longer the walk seems. It is no doubt circular, designed thus to circumvent the real globe and keep the aspirant going, whatever his chosen dance. It is a way, he concludes while energizing his walk, in which you surrender your life without actually doing so, as with (he thanks Zeus for his enduring even if smudgy education) the Latin tag that prefaces *The Waste Land*, actually faltering or soaring into Greek twice, at the last blurting ἀποθανεῖν θέλω, which sentiment he in his educated way breaks down as he walks, separating *apo* (from) from *thanein* (to die), graced with *thelo*, which means I want. It's easy really, he says. Ask a sibyl for the truth and the old bitch lays it on you straight. I only wish that man's poems didn't merge, with all the best-known bits seeming to come from all the poems, so that, for me, his poems make up one big poem of contortionist's lament: a heartrending flux you are obliged to recite as best you can while Chenonceau-ing your way through. The best way to say goodbye to the world is to form a microcosm of it and then say goodbye to that, knowing you will be forgiven for saying *au revoir* to the model. As at a party, thrown even as you slit your wrists and take a final pee into warm water already pinking.

So, he thinks, as he prepares to say farewell to the world of punished phenomena, what's the inhibition against taking credit for having loved the books? Why, on the one hand, are you cajoled to get an education, but on the other forbidden to parade its contents, as if the nation wanted to seem dumber than it is? Ah, the dumbing down, he decides, that's what gets you in the long run. Never quote your specimens lest you offend somebody less versed. Well, I am heading for the last allusion-fest, where everybody sighs, as at puns. Puns abolish time, do they not? That's what I always used to think. It doesn't matter now. The same with

ideas: not only are you not supposed to behave as if you've been educated (ἀποθανεῖν θέλο and all that), but you're supposed never to
acknowledge the presence of thinking in human life—thinking the flaw,
the weakness, the flop. Pretty bad. Was it Rat Man, or some other, who
in the not so distant past narrated his own execution, erect in front
of an oak tree, and, as soon as it was finished, dispensing with the
services of Captain Jünger, the firing squad guru rumored to be a hundred and fifty years old, who re-narrated the whole event more to his
liking? Did that not show his educated nature, the Rat Man's or someone else's? Actually showing off *in extremis*. Such volte-faces appeal to
him, but remember you mustn't use all those fancy French phrases generated in the minds of self-confessed weaklings.

We are watching a funeral procession of one undertaken in a
wretched mood, but bound to culminate in a triumph of sorts. How will
he ever stop pondering the miscellaneous booty of a lifetime's reading,
or of an adulthood's moviegoing? Who would ever want to waste all
that? Or all the overtures designed but never made, dragged back out of
ineptitude or tact? He is honest. He makes love to his flops. Shrop's
flops. It could almost be a circus act, he thinks, the real final thing, as
when a cigar-fancier tells you before lighting up to dip your Havana in
Armagnac, not Cognac. It's called life experience, a phrase both halves
of which are redundant. 'Twould be better, he knows, pronounced as
_____ _____, leaving lipreaders to guess. For years the world of
good-humor men rack their brains for a phrase that fits, coming up with
"vile computers," which nearly fits or "snotty telltales," which neither
fits nor observes the pause between words. He wants to leave the cliché
world behind while extracting those parts of it he found unique (not
much), so as to—well, what? Not tell his grandchildren, or himself, but
to parade in the aether along with all the poised, crouching e-mails of
no consequence but vast urgency some of his moments in and out of
time: the banners of his own waste land, he says.

Spectrum-lovers tend to have a blurred sense of color, gladder of
light's existence than of hyperfine shadings that figure in the grosser
declension of orange into yellow and yellow-green into greeny blue.
Being something of an amateur synesthetist (word of his own devising), Shrop the incipient intellectual likens this blur of the senses to the
vision of someone just released from hospital after at least a month,
from arsenical greens and mellow grays into a technicolor world worthy of Todd AO. You go in ravished by color. You come out blurred

only to re-encounter the clash of close hues, and you are glad, at least if you are Shrop who, in his TV movie-watching career has seen only three or four movies of bewitching color, at least two by Bertolucci, whose master cameraman Vince Storaro leads the field, and one other, mistitled *Air Rage* by some glitch in the cable feed, but revealing (in every sense) the fate of a recent widow whose bankrupt husband has just walked out of the wrong door in a high-flying jet, in search of the toilet. Her life, as she tries to start a huge marijuana crop in a small English hamlet, embodies the pained sense she has of how everything seems different, suddenly, untenderly, final. Shrop's review, far too long, they dubbed wordy and told him to cut, *cut the cackle, buddy, and attend* to what unpretentious viewers would get from the plot. *Less atmosphere,* Shrop, please. This he thinks akin to the notorious Beverly Hills doctrine of don't review what's wrong with the book, ferret out the author's philarsaphy arv life even if he doesn't have one. *Affirm.*

Anyhow, Shrop refused to tamper, and his review, mangled, appeared late, late in his career as movie-critic, revamped by a viral apprentice who likened the film to *Whisky Galore,* filched from a heave-ho romp by Compton Mackenzie. End of grieving grassy widow. Shrop believes that, having trodden his way along the Chenonceau maze, he has at last come out into a supreme form of daylight akin to that in the misnamed movie, whose crisp finitudes were an education for the eye, color as God must have dreamed it up for his palette on the first day. Color such as that could unhinge your soul, persuading you that you had never seen the world before but been fobbed off with a replica, as at some mediocre midway. How was he ever going to tell or write about so ineffable a development, vouchsafed almost no one else, unless it had been old Newton staring at the sun too much (he who knew better), and obliged to sit in darkness in his Trinity College rooms for three weeks afterward? Photophilic, Shrop told himself, that's me. Reborn with kaleidoscopic keenness. Now a word, *vouchsafe,* nibbled at him. How wonderful. What in hell was a vouch? Suddenly his world was like listening to Franz Krommer after hearing Bach.

Kindertotenlieder

For some time he has been aware of a scheme to equip certain natives with an Amigo, pop-tech name for a brain implant derived from the word *amygdala,* no doubt intended to convert the Masai into supermen and titans of testosterone. He has heard of such schemes before and does not believe in them; they are most often a cover for something else much less complex. But here in Africa he has seen operatives in their brand-new khaki shorts and big game-hunter shirts all epaulettes and military pockets cabaling with selected natives while the sound of jets disturbs the plains and all on them. It is, he decides, an illusion of light, with the dust misleading the eye. There are really lions here after all. The days pass. One operative, at once replaced, is helicoptered out with a gangrenous leg. In the distance, tents go up as extra jets arrive, never thundering overhead but seeming to spiral slowly down to land, shrill and vertical, in one of which, he will discover, his friend-to-be, Quent, is at the controls, the youngest major of them all, his mind crammed with mission, promotion, and exotic sabotage. Shrop is not part of this, but he remains fiercely aware, romantically inhaling that oh so old African dust of horn, dung, and beefy heat. No rains yet, and not much guidance.

With a humanist's skepticism about military and scientific affairs, he reviews the rumors about selected pastoral Masai who will (a) go into space as part of a new program sponsored by a famous anthropology department; (b) go to Harvard for accelerated Ph.D.s; (c) become guards at a new military prison camp in Kisumu; (d) become group leaders in the latest anti-poaching campaign; and (e) become trainees and officers in a crack new squadron of remotely operated reconnaissance jets; the joke, if that, being that these jets will in fact have "pilots of peace" while retaining their stealth-remote designation. Shrop favors a new TV version of *Othello* instead, having had some experience of disinformation; but he has seen a film displaying the implanting of Amigos in the shaven head, and the cocoon of blood applied after the gadget has been lodged. What is his role here? A careless eye to watch the military at their most devious. He has heard of plots involving tennis balls loaded with explosives, and radioactive globes of the world for political erotomaniacs to crouch over, but the top line here is fool's fodder, a charade for hired fops, and he is already preparing savage lines for the piece he is going to write on his return as he wonders where they will send him next to bamboozle and fluff.

Now that salient, initial conversation with Quent comes back to him in all its offhand glory. The man had managed to wind a medium-length python around his arm, and Shrop, on a rubberneck quizzical mission of his own, bureaucratized as an SNP/666, had just dismounted from his Land Rover, camera in hand, rifle slung over shoulder.

The usual question, to which Quent answered, "I am trying to work out what he thinks about. What he's thinking about. The old snake-and horse-brain puzzle, yknow."

"Allowing for translation and the usual problems of putting problems into snakes' brains, I suppose?"

"All taken care of. Who are *you*?"

They gabbed, joked, and grew less defensive, adjourning after lunch in the usual African manner, to wait out the heat of the day. They and the python made three. Quent told him about being vetted and trained overseas at the RAF's officer training unit, Romney on the Isle of Wight, which Shrop and he found amusing since *wight* was the old word for human being, but used no longer. It was like being stationed on the Isle of Man.

"That was the old days," Quent sighed, "of trying to pass muster. They had also taken on several Arab nations, their budding officers, I mean, already qualified pilots, but not qualified officers."

"Klar." Whoever thought of him as a "war correspondent"?

"One of my supervisors was a young officer, a novelist he said, looking for raw material. I guess he found it. As you might expect, most of the entry class passed the course, but more than I'd expected. They were pretty lax. The politics of the day required it."

"Yeah," Shrop told him, "even I read about the time some of them retracted their landing gear, loaded for bear as they were, right there on the runway, so as not to have to bomb Israelis. Them was the days, indeed. The politics have changed."

"When you look at them," Quent said, "all clean shaven and erect in their bearing, they looked like sword-of-honor candidates, proud possessors of the required OQs, I mean Officer Qualities. It was an illusion, of course. There were not that many Americans in the intake that year. Just a few, to act as spies. I'm joking of course."

"Oh, joke away. I'm with you. Until I kick."

Chatting away over fresh-caught game, tough but fragrant meat, they rapidly established a camaraderie that owed much to their skeptical mental backgrounds, Shrop the jack of all trades, Quent the pilot and who knew what else besides. They shared prejudices and nostalgias, fleeting or abiding vignettes of war and skirmish, half-baked notions of what was foreign or alien, empty knee-jerk reactions to the role of women in their lives. And of animals too. Bored by their reminiscences, the python uncoiled and slid away in search of more crushable meat, leaving them with a final tootle of its tapered tail, turning not its back but its tip. "There's always another," Quent observed. "You can always hope to find one that's more talkative, like you."

"Oh," Shrop told him, "out in the veldt I am at my most reptilian. I am merely an observer, but mostly I keep my thoughts to myself, like the cautionary old or young bastard I'm supposed to be. Just cruising around looking for trouble." Quent then told him, as if sensing the need for a story, an anecdote, about the day when their new VTOL jets would be junked by Britain's Royal Navy as costing too much in maintenance, which is when subsidiary nations would pick them up for a song, and the day not far away. "They're super for now," he said, "but every dog has his day. The brass are always thinking ahead. We buy this stuff from them in its prime, then we sell to nations we should never trust, which means they will for years have a second-rate air force to bluster around with, even while pieces are dropping off the planes and the glass cockpits are going wrong. It's the brass's way. For now, though, these jump jets are the bee's knees. You won't find *these* in any but the best bazaars, and I'm one of the few to get to fly them."

Then Shrop, faintly aware of having been too complacent an accomplice in this afternoon of African delight, trapped between Pliny's *Always something new* and *The Flame Trees of Thika*, began to quiz him more aggressively, about the Masai and the amigos, their future, the earthly sublunary point of setting up an air force or at least a wing of first-strike fighter-bombers in the middle of nowhere, and he got nothing but evasion. Fronts, Quent told him, all fronts. Like Patton being sent hither and yon to fool the Nazis about the coming invasion, and the plywood army with carpenter's ordnance warping and faltering all over a field. It was clear to Shrop that whatever was going on was Top Secret, an enigma wrapped in a mystery clad in a no trespassing bundle. Something about the Masai as robot pilots nagged at him, though, and so he asked, only to hear, "Not yet, not yet, it's preliminary, a fact-finding mission with fake hardware. The amigos? Any competent Zulu" (*sic*) "will have that out of his hair by morning. He prefers blood to the aether. We make a big noise with our jets and they marvel at that, but it's all really a combo of propaganda and publicity stunt. Somewhere that's nowhere enabling us to show off our goods. It's hardly the May Day Parade out here, is it?"

As a memory, was it getting cobwebby around the edges? Not a bit, it had gained right-angle starkness, reminding Shrop how, out there, he had thought how useless he was, he the only correspondent who could identify the obtuse thudding of Prokofiev's piano music, the same who had refused one newspaper's invitation to head for South America, all expenses paid (funeral included) to look for a certain GruppenFührer Rolf Stundt, who had figured in a friend's anti-Nazi novel. Truth was, Stundt was one a few entirely imaginary characters in the novel. Well, he mused, in my berserk, tweedy fashion, I have lived, thrown parties and abandoned them, sidled along echoing galleries between hell and heaven to, what does Dante call it? In order to be *sullen in the sweet air.* Well, not all the time. Yet who will follow me? That memory of the aspirant Quent, fresh from training in a raw climate, his mind full of Brit phrases and mannerisms, learning the ropes out in darkest Africa for some imaginary purpose. The evil thing about this life may be that, for better or for worse, it is *all* imaginary. In the America I just came from, they are digging up graves with backhoes, smashing casks and vaults, and spreading the remains of actual people in wooded areas behind the cemeteries, hitherto the domain of wild hogs, all for money.

So, too, was it the bright and beautiful stanza of life it should be, now his vision had unclouded to reveal Earth in all its chromatic glory? Almost, he thought. But I no longer deal in almosts, I plump for the grand slam. I allow no B plusses. If, as I have deduced, the world is a mêlée of anti-lifers and *anti*-anti-lifers, with few in-between, both raising hell (like an evil child) for different reasons, where do I stand? Aloof arbiter? Consummate chef? Villain of the piece? Savior? Hardly. No, I remain the inconspicuous consumer I always was, but pulled away from the power source, like someone mumbling the little poem the Elephant Man composed before his premature end. I may be among the grotesques, but I have not yet lost my hair, my teeth, or my pre-lunch resonance of voice, of which I am proud. Catch me then, you opera lovers salivating to the thump of the guillotine in the Poulenc and the actual scream of Lulu in the Berg, and you have not just Shrop the Rat Man, but Shrop the Baritone Rat, resonant for your pleasure, sagging slowly down to his reward amid the ghosts of Mars, the Julia Bugles and the Melpomene Hunters.

Under a glowering sky with the wind down like something felled, Quent was actually flying his jet, taking off at speed as if following the lines of some invisible Great Dipper, then turning, returning to the exact spot he had started from, with an appalling scream of down-pointed Pegasus engines as he lowered the jet to one hundred, fifty, twenty feet and remained there, hovering firmer than any chopper, with around him a miasmic mirage matching the one in the distance that interfered with the horizon and foreshortened the veldt. Veldtschmerz indeed. At a respectful, safe distance a ring of the Masai had formed, with spears and other trophies such as shields and bits and bobs from another civilization (sunglasses, tiny coil-bound notebooks). A lump of something at Ground Zero caught my attention, and I filmed it before I realized what it was: a male lion pawing at a trio of dead cubs, which clearly it had killed not long ago. It was going to eat them, I guessed, perish the thought. How inert that loafing lion was. How had it come there? Who had unloaded it or tempted it in? Heedless of the ripped-steel racket of the jets above him, he roared, but the roar was lost, and now the Harrier began descending, lower and lower, until the full force of its downblast, over twenty thousand pounds of it, burned into the transfixed lion, it yielding to an even louder roar that went beyond the roar into an absolute realm of incinerating dominance the lion could not of course comprehend. The veldt filled with that acrid, lascivious, caca stench of singed meat as the lion breathed its last amid the scene of carnage, the remains of some other lion's cubs blasted far away toward the stupefied onlooking Masai. The stench reminded Shrop of a doctor's office encounter when he asked some young Turk of an MD if the taste of mucus from the ripest, greenest interval of a cold did not, for its tainted, almost decorative sweetness, evoke glycerin. All answer he got for his enterprising pains was no. Ever since, he had joined the notion of glycerin to that of a cold, out of spite. After all, as the Autolycus of the scribbler's trade, the picker up of unconsidered items, he was the one who had ferreted out from several textbooks why phlegm was so stringy and elastic; it was similar to a chainlink fence and rarely broke or gave way, an indestructible doyley. Such information Shrop kept to himself against a sniffly day followed by a chain-link cough. Here, viewing the cooked and molten lion, he began to heave as if something vile and dark had to come up, and come it did, not so much to honor the lion (or Quent) as to free him of green bilge, in its gross midst a hard brown blob of gruesome aspect, one of the satanic peas of creation.

For that lion, contrary to the Bible, out of the strong came forth no sweetness, or even a neutral vapor, just a stinging blight of nature unnaturally combusted, with the faintest whiff of turpentine. In the Bible, though, bees had cached their gold in the lion's belly, hence the time-honored sweetness that burst or jutted forth. Naught here but char, a protein indistinguishable from antelope or ostrich. Whatever they had witnessed, Shrop thought as Quent maneuvered away to land, just outside the circle of jabbering Masai, torn between panic and admiration, it was not one of the miracles of nature, any more than the obliteration of Hiroshima and Nagasaki had been. Somehow, even though the constituent explosives came from within the same natural larder, there was something unethical about Quent's deafening demolition of the lion. Shrop could hardly define it, but it made his blood run cold as he envisioned a future of lion-hunters scouring the veldt in their howling jets for something to incinerate for the hell of doing it faster than any barbecue. If the Masai, Amigos and all, were disgusted, they who used to tackle lions with only a spear to win their manhood, it was only right, but Quent came from abundant, insuperable power, and took his strength from those powers. It is one thing, Shrop thought, to use a spear and perhaps get it wrong and be mauled, even killed. It is another to roast a lion with mighty roiling torrents of scalding oil-rich air on fire just because the lion has a glorious pelt or mane, just as the precarious ungainly chap known as H.G. Wells, prolific diabetic, had to run uphill far behind his Rebecca on twinkle-toes, such tiny feet for so chubby a man. Why set fire to either, the lion or the man, for his very quiddity? Shrop knew what the standard wisdom said: All bombed-out towns look alike, no matter how much angel-dust is scattered on them. The human mind looks for sameness long before it looks for difference. Sameness soothes, difference unnerves. H.G. Wells was lucky all his life for never having to stand beneath a pouring, ruining jetstream.

This was why, Shrop thought, nothing came tumbling from the sky—firestorm, tornado, ball lightning—in retaliation. He remembered what a fancy Asian restaurant and a cheap Italian toilet had in common: they made you pay extra for both rice and paper. It would have been just, he thought, no matter how much you had begun to enjoy the ripostes and spiky point of view of Quent, the test-pilot adventurer having sold soul to the grand muftis of murky technology, to see him enveloped in a cloud of unknowing, just for his own mind's sake, not knowing warship from worship, but intent on kudos through kibosh. Shrop rather liked that, always on the hunt for catchy phrases to lard his columns with. Quent survived to bring about the melt-down of more marauding lions, with Shrop to watch after him.

There, thinks the soul-twisted though sympathetic observer, go all of us but for chance and accident. There they stand, two late recruits to the bemusing madhouse upriver, privy to the indelicate dismemberment of the African sanctus, bonded together in fire and curiosity like two old-style alchemists long after the Renaissance is over, pushing even farther the power of steel over meat and fur. Caught up in some ancient folkway, they are a parody of the Masai, energized by that dark satanic mill up north, where slaves and sadists inflame each other, prisoners of their saliva.

The Masai do not quite know what to make of Quent, the lion-dispatcher. Lions have devoured their cattle and have always been the enemy, mauling and raiding, ever available to the next young warrior as part of the unnecessary, Mother Nature's dangerous gift. They might admire the hotshot pilot with the latest machine, but something holds them back; he is not doing it for the cattle, is he? They are not sure, but have to respect a hero, no matter how disproportionate the odds have been. Shrop watches Quent make a gentle feeler of a landing, clamber out of the quelled jet, and walk untidily toward them with a brash-complacent smile. It is not every day you pulverize a lion, and he expects something in reward, hardly a medal, but *something*, which they speedily choose and bestow, having so little. They wrap him around in a dark red checkercloth much the same as the one they all wear, robe of honor but also a sweatsmock of the veldt, no more and no less what the typical young lion-killer received, but of course to Quent it is all robes of honor rolled into one, even a little bit greasy and unwashed from its former owners, diffusing about him a taint of younger winners who all lacked his own private bouquet of turpentine and hot painted metal. He is the newest warrior, a stranger out there, but a promise of contraptions to come, an odd echo of Masai robot pilots in the air force of the future: gratuitously installed where no pilot need be, just to gratify the whim of some globe-trotting politician.

So this is where that final robe came from, washed of course and maybe disinfected, but one and the same, the tunic of prowess, worth perhaps a dollar or two, it being no more than a cheap bolt of cloth from some kaffir bazaar, but ponderously esteemed. No need for epaulets, medals, hash-marks, little red collar tabs, red stripes along the trousers, Blue Maxes at the throat; none of that came near the cloth, the clout, at least not as Shrop saw it, he having witnessed the spiral of smoke rise from Quent's fling. Wrapped in the same way, tight up to the jawbone as if to keep out the African sun, tucked in around the amputated thighs to honor a mutilation Quent had never dreamed of in that early escapade, though Harriers had bitten and killed careless, debonair pilots making (they thought) the easy transition from trainer jets to this preposterous hybrid. It would always be a matter of switching fast and confidently from horizontal to vertical flight, and sometimes uneasy pilots blended the two and achieved a diagonal, unable to swap either for the other. To Quent, the virtuoso, the plane was magic, and he was earmarked to become a flying instructor, unless he made a fuss about missing out on the action, in which case they would send him where he ached to be.

"Always a first time," Shrop remembered having said, or something such. The silence with the Harrier's jets shut down was the veldt's again, to pit with its own stark harmony of creature calls, indifferent all to plane or lion. Life shrugged on.

"My first lion," came the reply. "It could become a habit."

"Better not."

"Oh?"

"Leave it to the Masai, I mean. Go after the real big game."

Quent had stared at him, apparently silenced or deciding against further prattle with a mere observer. The ring of Masai had broken up after the token, bass-voiced words of congratulation during the (as Shrop thought of it) winding ceremony, with the man twizzled inside the shortening length of cloth, no Masai, but persona grata for that afternoon. It was as if Quent had come and stolen the golden apples of the sun, neither trespassing nor poaching, but helping himself with undreamed-of means, though, to be bureaucratic about it, how he had arranged to be out on the veldt with the latest attack jet, for his own amusement as if playing cards or hunting flamingo, Shrop had no idea. Rank hath its privileges, he murmured, and Quent was already over-promoted. A law unto himself, or soon to be so. For some reason he had taken to the Harrier, maybe because it appealed to something devious in his own nature, to what went at a slant when it should have been straight, evoking no doubt the image of the cheat, the con man, descending upon you in deadly marksmanship when you expected the damned thing to fly over you and then come back. Oh glory, Shrop thought, this is the wave of the future: burn a lion, burn a man.

Perhaps now, Shrop remembers thinking, the Masai would insist on lions' death by jet, no more of that oldfangled spear and shield routine, with a gamble on courage and the luck of the draw with a paw. This would complicate their lives no end, of course, with entire air forces being drafted in to keep down the lion count. Or would it? Maybe the Quentian theory was that one Harrier did for all; you just had to keep it in the neighborhood, ready for action. And the price would soar, with the Masai, those virtuosi of grassland agility, reduced below the poverty level. There might even be an absence of body wraps. This was the future, though, and Quent was today the victor with no spoils to show for it; why, what earthly use was the blasted body of the lion where once there had been a palatable carcass of lion steaks to come? Or did they eat meat at all? Lion's meat? The blood of the lion usually went to waste anyway, whether by jet or spear. Surely, however, the spectacular sight of a young boy pricking a lion as it lunged at him would be lost forever, no longer a target for itchy cameramen, the lithe body against the tawny one as the thunderclouds gathered, and the boy's yelps and the lion's mumbled roar. The appearance of the Harrier was not an improvement; Shrop knew this, but his new friend was looking to him for admiration. Was there even the faintest chance of the lion's bringing down the jet? It might be done with a flailing paw, he supposed, with the plane at its lowest reach, or even through an uncharacteristic leap by a lioness, at any rate. He imagined the headline: Lion fells jump-jet, pilot burned. If this was the old world bring low the new. He was half in favor of it. Maybe even a Roman game might be fudged from such an event, with prizes and thumbs jutted down. To be that anachronistic appealed to him, given as he was to time-sliding and defying the pedants who worked out the dates of everything and insisted on a strict progression from Lascaux to Leonardo.

In his favorite book of the mind's eye, though, he wanted the lion and the jump-jet kept apart, handed back to older dispensations. The Masai deserved to be left alone with their threadbare, nimble adjustments, to blood and sleep in the crook of the arm, while the jet deserved its own era for its ascendancy over mute, stubborn land, its cleverness at avoiding fog, its ability to land on the spot. Shrop, now and then a passionate mixer of species and strategies, sometimes wanted bread separate from butter until the magic moment of the smear. He could not explain this, least of all to Quent, whose view of so-called progress was impetuous.

35
Old Vichy

AND THAT WAS ALL SO LONG AGO, IN ANOTHER LIFE, THE EXTENT of time being so vast without including the days of knowing Quent. So long ago it predated him. At least that is how it feels. Yet he had to have known him to have any memory of him. Now at least, he knows why he wrapped himself in fabric before taking off; he knows what the fabric was, as well as its mythic charge. Having done the Chenonceau to his satisfaction, Shrop feels he is alive in an afterlife both selective and voluptuous; the going-away party had put him in the clear, ridding him, much as his old malfunctioning memory had done, of so much clutter. Was there not about his post-life something angelic, pure, redeemed, or was he still fooling himself? One look at the colors around him should have persuaded him: had there ever been in his life a hue such as the aubergine confronting him in trees and grass? What was this purified color that seemed to have been the primal artist's first attempt at it, coming out so irresistible he had omitted to complete the color, thus gifting the world, for some, with a green more fragile and diaphanous than ever seen? Had this happened with all the other colors? What was this washed, rinsed, purged aspect to the spectrum, almost as if colors had become media through which to see other colors? It was as if some huge yearning soul had transformed colors with its sheer intensity, operating in a reborn world. It was not a matter of beauty, though that came into the reckoning; it was a matter of seeing without illusion and of, so he reasoned, managing to perceive his world without going to the trouble of wondering what any given thing *was*. Don't ask if the sky's the sky, just respond to all that Rayleigh scattering deployed above. He knew something of how light particles bounced about, but the pristine colors about him seemed somehow *breathed* through, that was it.

Perhaps there were other bonuses to come in this realm he had so facilely named Vichy (=unoccupied by the vile enemy), but so far the excitement had been all visual. Memories of Quent nagged at him, especially of that fatal day when all the constituent motives of the man's life had seemed to come together to propel him elsewhere in— what had it been? A joyless caper? An *auto-da-fé?* It was hard for Shrop to figure out the nature of the event, apart from its extreme outlines. Quent's bravado had never died, but was it fair to associate the lion and the Harrier with the dreadful public burning? He did not know, but assumed a man had a right to go off at angles whenever he chose.

If his old quarters had been cramped and decrepit, his new ones were worse, although exquisitely tinted. Now he lived in an old clapped-out car, a Mercedes, one that in its time must have gone flashing along the little streets of Palm Beach braying with its horn, in that horn-rich town, Look at me, aren't I cute? I have been bought with wealth. Now, though, nothing worked except the radio and a scratchy cell-phone abandoned on the dashboard like a lost voice. Tiny beetles ran all over the car, no doubt picking up moss and mites. He slept in the back, with his legs arranged to go between the two front seats as if horizontally treading into an unknown region alive only in the dark. He has settled in here without demur, somehow knowing it had been prepared for him, not so much one of the homeless as one of the mindless (which is not to say that, should he ever recover his wits and recoup his old forgotten philosophy of life, his life would improve and his living conditions at once mutate into something plush). Oh no, he felt he had arrived at some juncture where it was important only to wait and remain quite passive. Something has been arranged for me, he tells himself, just the way I transitioned into the Chenonceau. Go with the flow, and something miraculous will become clear.

Why should he be so sure, only to be hauled out, rotten and stinky, in a year's time after merely waiting for nothing? Had not some character in a Hawthorne story done a similar thing? Was this part of an American folkway then, not original at all? He knows he has not been trying to be original, but only to shed the load, to keep from being perpetually on edge. To be fished out as an unidentifiable bum is not a prospect he relishes, but he is going to go through with it, certain that some force is writing him, settling him well clear of outrage and pain, as if he has to wait here while the world returns to its senses. So, as he says in conversation, he's hanging. Hanging out. Hoping. Hushing the inner man who keeps arguing about the life to come. Scales have fallen from his eyes, and maybe that is enough to be going on with; later will come his reconciliation with the absurd and a new only semi-querulous delight in the incomprehensible acts of other people. He likes to think of this period of his life, if indeed he is still alive, as the Tropopause, a term filched from astronomy and vaguely applied, the stress being on *pause*, the *tropo* being the merest hint at something tropical and fabulous. If Shrop is going to take it on the chin, he will spend the time in between arranging his chin at the most propitious angle, like a pugilist in paradise. Until he tanks.

Can it really be true, he wonders, that he has also developed a new attitude to language? He seems to be using words he has never used before, from aubergine to tropopause, and it occurs to him that certain vocabularies go with certain occupations; the right words come to mind automatically and do not have to be learned. Deep in his mind the old craving to have his philosophy back occupies him whenever he wakes or drifts off, a pipe-dream not yet abandoned. How, he wonders, can a man evolve the scheme that makes sense of his life and then lose it, like a pair of sunglasses? How can this be possible? Shrop finds himself torn with desire for the old scheme and eagerness to build a new one, but he will not build anew until he's certain the old one is gone forever. It used to be oh so good and useful, and the terrorist outrage of years ago tilted the slippery slope down which it raced to extinction.

How, Shrop moans, can I undo history?

By sheer force of anachronism?

By changing my vocabulary?

Getting a new job, dubbing old Nazi warriors for some new, derivative series?

Here in old Vichy, he misses his venerable family doctor, Dr. Drummond who, bent on retiring, referred him to a certain young Turk by means of a letter, which the new doctor, Foenitz, read aloud to him, thus enumerating his most cantankerous qualities, his notion that the doctor served the convenience of the patient, and so forth. In short, an introductory character assassination based on the old premise that the patient was the doctor's fodder, anathema to Shrop, who has always insisted on interrogating bedside boors, especially those from not-so-fashionable universities. Foenitz, after reading this putrid tract aloud to get them on a friendly footing, then proceeded to ridicule every treatment Shrop had ever had, even down to the medications, fancifully warning him of a Nuremberg hernia, a halved-egg shape gathered up on his stomach, a warning he later rescinded; it had only been for effect. "I'll love to get my hands on you in the lab," he says, indicating a future of milk and honey, in which the amiable going-on into which Shrop has persuaded a series of three sawboneses over the years is bound to spoil a series of brutal impositions all designed to up the bill. This is not Shrop's way at all, and he experiences momentary delight when another doctor, in the same building, sees him not finding his way, sets an arm around his shoulders and affably guides him. Now *this* is the way to do it, Shrop decides, smarting at the lack of geniality in this particular practice. This man, with the graying curls, suffers from unique affability and promises a future. Dr. Palazzo in short, resonantly named, neatly garbed in white with his name embroidered in scarlet on his breast.

Shrop is relieved. He has a mentor after all, with whom to discuss movies and the non-fiction channels. Foenitz he writes off as yet another Nazi, obtuse and bumptious, hardly eligible for the profession, but merely a variation on the theme of medical students known and found wanting in the diploma mill up the road. What exasperates Shrop about nearly all the doctors he has known, and writhed under, is their determination to find something wrong with him, even when he is, as he fancies, in perfect health. They hammer and prod until they think they have found something, and sketch out a regimen that will cure him. The air of professional disappointment he discerns when an annual is over and done with ("You have the smallest prostate in the world") infuriates him; the prospectors for gold have found no ore, and that irks them in the halo of their five-year overture. What he wants from them is a genial accommodation to his bizarre ways, an understanding that he is not like other men, but special and extraordinary, indeed one whose life has been shattered by terrorist outrage, so that he is no longer the happy-go-lucky Shrop of old, but nervous Nellie in Vichy, where remaining Nazis might lurk. He wants his doctors to reassure him that all will be well, that now in a complete retirement resembling numb abeyance, he is going to survive and thrive. Give me a few pills, he says, and let me go about my business, which he no longer can do.

He longs to stab Foenitz in the back, for rudeness, incompetence (he counsels the consumption of butter and cheese, anathema to Shrop), and generally patronizes the rest of his profession, proffering no white coat but grimy shirtsleeves rolled up, a swaying candle-drip of coryza mucus dangling from one nostril, and on his beefy hands the meat shreds you expect of a butcher. Pumped-up Brooklyn is how Shrop dubs him, into and out of med school by accident, then let loose with a treadmill and a fire-extinguisher full of lidocaine. But why refer anyone to him? Drummond's last twist of the knife, just to reveal how low an opinion he has always had of Shrop, while taking his money? Shrop barely knows, reckoning himself lucky to have survived first the one, then the other. Instead of this guerre, he engages Dr. Palazzo, with the lapis-lazuli name and the rinsied curls.

There is an important point to be made here about our twitching Shrop. He is not looking to be made well, but to recruit allies in the ongoing pursuit of calm, which means what he doesn't complain about won't be looked at, whereas most doctors love to go ferreting after things, hardly realizing that they have missed their true vocation in being helpmeets, incurious enablers. Shrop would be his own best doctor of course, and has considered the shift, in the end deciding against it because he will not be able to prescribe the pills he needs, not even the placebos. What he adores to do is lie back, freely exhibiting (or presenting) his signs, happy in the certainty that nothing will ever be done about them. This precious passivity, in the teeth of some putative rough going-over by a Foenitz, is something he has tried to safeguard all his life, believing it a godsend. The corrective view eludes him and his bouts of pain he sees as something to be endured in the interests of poise. He is willing to put up with a great deal in the interests of his equanimity, the supreme medical condition that used to be, before the terrorists moved. Even now, in his never-never land, he hopes to attain some kind of serenity, even if it entails giving up reading or watching movies. He has heard somewhere that humans are made in such a way that emotional involvement of any kind—tragic or delectable—works against them. They are better left alone in the eternal quietus of indifference. To grieve, to rejoice, does them ill, and that is what he aims for, realistically seeing he has little chance of any such withdrawal, with or without doctors. The main chore, as he does it, is never to respond, to ape the dumb ox of Hemingway or absurdly living man of Raymond Queneau (he is an intellectual after all, entitled to glean a modicum from his reading). What did Queneau the mathematician say? How does one live in an absurd world? *Absurdly.* And that is how, Shrop thinks, he is living now, closer to his old ambition than before, thanks to the horrors and the ensuing dither. Will he go to see Dr. Palazzo? Probably not, but he will keep the good doctor's image close to his heart, safeguard and talisman, toady and yea-sayer. So long as the doctor's image hangs fire up there, all will be well, and all that happens will be seen to have happened on his watch, even inspired by him, with his name on it and the correct entry made in the bulging book of records.

In his weird way, Shrop tends to regard doctors as the authors of their diseases, no longer allowed traffic with their book, not for the most minor alteration. Disease, he knows, is an art form in which nature carves according to intransigent will, on the bodies of fatalists the world over.

Damn the wheel and forever be unable to drive. Curse the sawbones, and be forever sick. Such lumpish thoughts afflict Shrop daily as he peers skyward wondering where the next onslaught will come from. He has the notion that any sick man can easily become a completely sick man, adding miseries until his composure is gone forever. One hint from a newspaper that the most recent neo-Nazis have affiliated themselves with the Real Madrid soccer team convinced him that the true terrorists in this day and age are really Nazis after all, with behavior to match. Little has changed, whether the Nazis are Nazis or have renamed themselves Youths of Canillejas. Nowadays, he grumbles, there is a Nazi Internet and all follows from that. On it goes, the seizing of knuckledusters, machetes, slingshots and swastika flags. Firm ground he calls it. He has not been the same since Dr. Palazzo shoved a long steel tube down his throat in quest of, of course, phlegm that obstructed his breathing and guaranteed his cough. He has not thought so well of Palazzo since, sensing an ogre where he had divined an angel. Now his throat is sore for a different reason, and he soothes it, or tries to, with molasses and Swiss lozenges supposedly used by blowers of long Alpine trumpets. Is he really going downhill in readiness for the real onset of serious affliction? Is this the consequence of living in a new world, at least metaphorically tasting the waters of Vichy, or would he have gone downhill anywhere?

He tries to make a list of what ails him, convinced that lists have magical powers and dominate the situation more than any discursive account. So he starts, with the hollow in his skull present from birth, the calipers having pressed too hard. It was that or remain forever in Mother. So he came out laterally squashed, with a dent just where he parted his hair, and he wonders if it could have been filled in, with plasticine even. Was this why he tended to walk lopsided? Perhaps from the same cause, there grows at the back of his neck a chunk of superfluous skull that feels like a misplaced rib and indicates a strength in that region absent on the other side. A brain brace, he calls it, and this is only the beginning. Lower down, a deviated septum, source of blood and sneezing, completes the set, never attended to in spite of its constant scabbing. He regards it as one of his trials. A wisdom tooth has shoved some of his teeth out of whack, alas, but not out of place although they ride a little higher than usual thanks to the wisdom tooth reposing horizontal beneath. Tooth wobble is the predictable result, but he visits no dentist unless in agony, preferring to floss and swoosh an antibacterial liquid around the gaps between his teeth, catching bacteria just in time, but aware that the sour taste of morning is the bouquet of bacterial ordure. Sometimes the mouthwash he uses bites the back of his throat, precluding, as he sees things, the need to brush his tongue. He and the bacteria fight nonstop, either on the very brink of winning provided the duel goes on. His throat, and what's in it, puzzles him: he wakes with a resonant, deep voice that lasts a few hours, but then smoothes out into a less imposing register that, by dinner, has declined into a soft jabber. To do him justice on the airwaves, or in the tape machine, the studios have to catch him before lunch, when he is in the best voice of his day, somehow letting voice speak for him in its own right, reckless and profound. He loves to do this, but shrinks from the rest of the day when his voice loses its edge. Phlegm, he mutters, I am always at the mercy of phlegm, with its chain-link fences. Having had pneumonia in his teens, before antibiotics ruled the roost, he has a lasting tender spot between his shoulder blades that always excites X-ray technicians, who misread it as something serious and devilish. It never is, says Shrop. I am invulnerable. His liver is tender enough to qualify him for liverish, and has remained so even into his non-drinking days, so maybe his gall bladder is malfunctioning after all. He adds a broken arm from football to his twisted knee and his tacky rear end, where a fistula has lain quietly in wait for a serious revolt. His waste exits sideways. He shrinks from the very thought of "roofing," as they call it, as from even the fairy touch of Dr. Hansen, who spends his life peering into the darkness of other beings. The droopy fourth left finger completes his set of woes, to which he adds the atrial fibrillation that has advanced from mere irregularity to regular irregularity to an irregular irregularity, an emblem of sheer chaos, against which, to quieten and slow, he takes the same propranolol that has barred the gate to the migraines of his childhood, causing him to think of himself in the old days as the lightning-rod man. His heels plague him with their tenderness, their rough scales, but he files them down with midlife vigor and rubs fragrant cream into the pores, then wears thick woolen socks to bed, to save the sheets. All in all, he has a weighty list, worthy of acceptance at any of the major hospitals, and with further plights in prospect. Oh yes, psoriasis, he reminds himself, I'm always forgetting that, for which they prescribe the most expensive ointment in the world.

Such is his list, but he can never quite bring himself to the point of organizing it, say from the most serious ailments to the least, or alphabetically, or according to the number of letters in the name, thus making at least moderate sense of the bill of his particulars. No, he tends to splurge as the miscellaneous clutch of life re-exerts its old hold and he begins to write the ills on separate cards, thus making him surrender to what he would never have thought other than a jumble. How can he tidy up when coarse phenomena keep distracting him from a neatness he would otherwise attain? Some ancient philosophical distinction hovers behind this dilemma, say the Many and the One. With all his nagging heart, he remains certain that the One would be easier to manage, like a huge oversized hot-water bottle, whereas the Many—it speaks for itself, it dismays like confetti and refuses to stay put. Yet he cannot discipline phenomena as he would like, not even with the help of rigidly compartmented reference books and indexes that are a model of regimentation. One day, he thinks, because the body is habituated to the Many, the body will succumb entirely, requiring the same uniform spray of formaldehyde. Oddly, he does not quite believe in death, believing in a few select beings to whom it will not happen, believers in the Many, which is to say not letting the left hand know what ails the right until long after Doomsday. Will I plunge in, he wonders, with a half double gainer, or will I be allowed to seep into it, cell by cell, in a mortal takeover bid? As is my wont.

As ever, Shrop is trying to figure out if he is performing no worse than the muddled Shrop of old, or if the events of the last few years have gradually eroded his savvy along with his well-being, so much so that he no longer has enough *nous* to gauge his doings. Certainly he has suffered the usual lapses in memory and tenderness, more than many, he thinks, having lost his philosophy of life as well. The questions elude him: can he even formulate it as he would have done in earlier days? Is he just losing his presence of mind in the normal course of things—deteriorating?—or has something special intervened to rid him of his old skill in fielding difficult questions? How can the loser appraise his loss? Half the time he is aware of having passed beyond, into some blithe condition he once anticipated as the Something Riviera of the External or Eternal World, a margin full of orchids, while the other half he spends fidgeting and maundering, aware of his presence in no region at all save the familiar one of hopes denied, ambitions wasted, friendships and loves smashed. If he has to choose, beyond the Chenonceau, it will of course be the more blissful of the two, and possibly the more deceitful.

He wishes his mind well, but would love to go back in history to subtract the atrocity that deprived him of so much and sent his mind packing.

May there not be, he wonders, an onslaught especially designed to ruin minds, not so much mangle bodies wholesale (which he takes for granted) as plague minds with viruses, scrambling logic and blurring connections? It is this kind of horror that puzzles and occupies him, he being an exponent of things mental. He has seen the effect in others: too much blinking, an uncertain walk, the tremor in handshakes that used to be firm, the eye that refuses to focus, the embrace that founders in a brusque clip approximating a search for the shoulder holster. People's ways have become wobbly, he decides, and of course it is on their ways that whole social codes have based themselves. Still, if you have a thousand people all behaving much as they used to, but with a tiny variant in each performance, it will add up to something sundered, lost, mutated, ruined. You have to be observant to notice these slight changes in deportment, but they are there, amounting to only one step backward in social amenity, but a distinct loss that a Margaret Mead would have been among the first to spot in the ways of those coming of age in Samoa: a reluctance ever, any more, to catch a thrown ball, or refusing to hold a stare for longer than seconds. He knows how things are and condemns himself for having backslid a social tad. No, more than that; his flaws are multiplying, and he will soon become a second-rate human being.

If all this quasi-reasoning sounds simple, it is, yet not to him, who in the grossest physical sense feels chunks missing from his brain, neutralized or cut away, leaving him with malformed suet. He would love to rid himself of the suspicion that a neanderthal, that maligned forebear, stumps through his present, belying the parchments dangling lopsided from his wall ever since the day of the explosions; he has never had the heart to straighten them, convinced no doubt that they have some zany talismanic power over him and must not be tilted.

What shall he put into his brain, out of his mind as he is? Or into those frames? Can it be bought at the five and ten? He hypothesizes: a

199

man walking on air, blind, with no idea who is walking toward or alongside him. People stare at him in unusual ways, as if a fencing slash on his cheek has suddenly arrived from Junker Germany, or a tooth has begun inching down below his upper lip, destined to become a sabre. He makes random guesses at his oddness, wishing some artist would fix his face, his carriage, forever, no longer leaving their appearance to whim or fad. Not quite afraid to go out, even in Vichy, he feels the temptation to become a shut-in, a sloth of timetables and schedules, all his food in cans, his debris vacuumed up, all his leavings flushed away.

Despite all kinds of mishandlings, sloppy forwardings, myopic readings by machines that ought to know better, a letter has found its way to him, a feat comparable to the Angel Gabriel's having refereed a soccer match out in the Meadowlands. Shrop doesn't quite understand it since it refers to such things as neighbors and neighbors' homes, these being houses. If it had referred to cars parked next to him, he would have been wiser, especially if the car had been derelict. Clearly he is not the intended recipient, but he delights in the vision proffered of high-bourgeois living as written about by genteel ladies in the SUNY suburbs.

Just so you know what you escaped (he reads) there was the potential buyer with 3 large dogs who wanted to build a six-foot fence (not the dogs but the owner); he never came through with an offer because the thought of 3 large dogs in *our house*, as was, was not pleasant. Then we had an offer from a man who is moving from Atlanta who seemed to think we should be impressed with his job at the university as Economic Development *Ergotrator* (we were impressed that he would be the only person in his office). He made a low, almost underhanded offer. Anyway, we sold the house to a biotech man married to a woman Doctor. They have two small boys. Rose said the kids looked like happy kids.

Now, for the first time, the idea of placebo nags at him. Strange that it never has before, given his lost philosophical bent and his command of awkward circumstances. It is not a technical version he has, but a rough, approximate one, positing some kind of a do-er for the universe who hits you with the real thing or lulls you with an ineffectual fake. The real thing he knows all about, having endured and repelled it for years, marveling at the universe's involuntary misbehavior. The fake or imitation he finds fascinating, wondering if there is any real difference between the two, then deciding that, of course, there is: the do-er wants to train you, see how you get on with something that is mostly in the mind. The numberless things that dog and ruin him may be all placebo, best interpreted by the ever-ready mind, indeed a mind that, upon seeing placebo among the non-placebo, readily makes the wrong assumption and responds as if to the real thing.

Is this, then, how he has been behaving for years? This is bad, or good, stuff, says his universe: respond as you will, and off he has gone, construing neutral inoffensive paste as the real thing, thus proving how circular the mind can be, relaxing with a pseudo-tranquillizer. He suspects wrongly that his old, lost philosophy went along these lines, revealing the mind to the mind as the gullible genius it really is. In fact, he has never ventured into this most speculative of waters, though now, he feels, he should, eager to know how much of the world's orneriness is real, how much a child's plasticine model. In the long run, he decides, a whole world of placebo will be a happy place in which to live. You will not have to trek the length of the Chenonceau, for example, and you will not have to go off the deep end like Quent, that imitation Masai. The trick has to be how to tell the placebo from the other, thus discovering how much of the real world is the mind's fleecy fabrication. This makes us better, Shrop, he hears. He takes it, this pellet of flour and water, and it cures him. Now, how apply that trick to affairs of state or mortality? Here is your death, Shrop, he hears, take it and die. It is a fake, but he dies anyway. Surely then, the placebo has its limits, when a dose of real cyanide will finish you off, no holds barred, whatever your mind decides.

The never-never land between the fatal and the imaginable haunts him, fudged up by a joker as it surely is. How did it come into being, courtesy of whose mind or strategy? He is trying, of course, to harness placebo in total, the world being nothing else but propaganda, and all he has learned about Vichy France, say, being mere rumor. He pauses on the lip of the putative and wishes he had more command of what changes lives forever, even those of mere onlookers or distant rubbernecks, headline scanners. Something in the country's thesaurus of beliefs breaks and remains broken ever after. The rot begins. America the broken.

You can see he is headed toward some last round-up of the imagination, wondering at the extent of its power and gradually admitting himself mystified by the mechanism that enables people to fool themselves into accepting fake effects as real, and proving the shift by the action of a substance or a myth on their very pulses. If this is a philosophical dilemma, he is no longer trained for it, unable at the crucial point to know why the mind fools itself with some things, but not with others. He is willing to deal with placebo, but only if its effect controls everything, which it clearly does not. Mind over matter, he whispers, but only for shitting purposes. Perhaps, he wonders, there is a certain twitch the mind can attempt, moving from a rather helpless position to one more powerful, but how to get to it when surrounded by the evidence of what's unthinkable? Is there no way of moving oddly behaving people back to their norms? He knows about shell-shock, of course, and much prefers its bluntness to toxic shock syndrome, or whatever, and he shudders at the old way of correcting it, more brutal than vulnerable. The placebos will please him, as they should, but he would like the real thing, so-called, to please him too, no longer having its querulous, diabolical way as he struggles to grapple with illness, death, misery, the entire ball of wax. How wonderful to discover that your friends and siblings died only in their minds, and maybe lived on in the malign supposition that they were dead. He would know and treat the difference with purposeful amiability.

You would think that so philosophical a man, whether an intellectual or not, would have grounded his school of thought in something such, filching perhaps from Plato and Platonism; but no, he inclines more to Leibnizian monads, something he has now left behind him. He worries about such abstruse stuff because he wants 9.11 not to have happened, or, if it had to happen, being something genial and palatable. The mind examines this reputed horror and says, Oh well, if you must, I know the whole thing is a mere scenario, best-case, existing only as a mirage exists. Then, he supposes, all those people unhinged by the event and its implication for the American Dream would go about their normal business again, and the Red Cross, for instance, could squander all its ill-gotten gain on an endless vacation for the entire staff, in Hawaii say. The trouble is, in a world that knows and creates placebo, there is the wolverine Other that genuinely ruins and adores the circumstances which provoked it. Aldous Huxley would have invented a remedial pill, of course, but Huxley had long ago vanished into the realm beyond the door of perception, a lost leader without much faith in anything. Then why think of him? Shrop once doted on *Brave New World*, a book that for him implied a spineless opposite. If one could only up the range of abomination humans could stomach, so that whatever Pearl Harbor or 9.11 came along it would merely smooth itself into the senseless flow of phenomena, neither malign nor friendly. If only. He doubts the power even of the placebic mind to cause any such change. Why, people just did not remember, and perhaps oblivion was the only cure remaining, though he recalls the strenuous attempt a few years ago to hymn the dead by installing huge searchlights that bored into the deep sky, apparently reminding no one at all that such towers of light, so called, had their origin in Albert Speer's minutely orchestrated Nuremberg rallies and the cathedral of light in which Nazis clicked heels and bellowed slogans. Then, he thought, the sooner an amnesia drug disguised as a placebo came along, the better.

Shrop tries to count up his losses, which he feels are gigantic, against his gains, which total zero. Such an experience of total loss, about which he dare not think in terms of noses, minds, bloodlines, and voices, unfits him for the remainder of the century. Or so he thinks, wondering how on earth he will get by. He must still reckon with what he has hidden away.

Peers tenderly at his face in the rearview mirror, finds it as mushroom pale as that of an English soccer manager, drained to bleach by the drizzle of the English Midlands, big ring under each eye, the whole unappetizing and drear: a face of Manhattan, whose acid rain whitens faces while the coats, trews, and footgear get blacker. Such a face comes of worry, that much is certain, but of a specialized kind: not just someone's being missing or dead, but trying to cope with the person's loss while resisting the temptation to think of them in any detail, which is to say contending with loss in the abstract, fighting doom with *oblivion*, even to the point of pretending you yourself are nobody either. The French, when they were here, recording and filming, actually picked up the thump of bodies landing after jumping, akin he supposes to the rhythmic thump of the guillotine blade in Poulenc's operatic version of Georges Bernanos's novel about Catholic nuns going to their fate. Shrop thanks the powers that be for the insolent, fruitless way his culture shows up, distracting him to another world not yet extinct, boldly suggesting there is, amid the grief and the sense of sheer amputation, something else to live for, in no matter how far-fetched and drab a form. Shrop sometimes thinks he will settle, has already done so, for anything that did not begin with a life, could he but find it. And decides to go back to live in his hovel. No more car.

An old problem in mind control asks you not to think of a three-legged pink elephant or some such impromptu freak, and of course you can't. Shrop's version of this problem has long been worse, but over the years he has become better at it, keeping out an adored face of damp porcelain, somewhat Irish in texture, although without the cheekbone blush favored by some colleens. Equally, the perfect teeth he has found difficult, and the mellow brown eyes in perfect proportion to the width of the brow. If you start young in this, as he did not, you can probably get somewhere, forever trapping the visual memory before it gets started, but it takes a painful time and may most profitably be tried by people of abstract bent, like himself, or as he used to be, who can sweep the unique delights of the face away into some holding tank of the mind. Having already begun to lose his philosophy before disaster struck, he should have been better at losing, or avidly omitting, other things, but he was not, and so the first year of it was hell.

He kept trying nonetheless, even if all he ended up with, an artifact of purest misery, were the cement slab of a human crushed to a depth of only a few inches, a grosser trouvaille than most brains can stand. All the same, he tried, and after a couple of years it began to work, as if the very mind retained some glimmering of once in a very distant incarnation being no more than an unshaped bolus of promising matter. Or so he tells himself when the pressure to memoriously forget becomes too much. Training the mind while in all other ways giving it free, even excessive rein has been an exceptional chore, but he has given it what freshmen call the college try. As a result, he keeps in some disadvantaged corner of his mind an empty shape rather like a tall, narrow triangular slice of cake, in which the maltreated memory lives, far from any deformed elephant, and silkily importunate. The test, as always, has been to fend off or sever the face and the physique not in full flight but like a sinister midwife intent on abortion. He would never have thought his mind could rise to such a challenge: damping out the very creature he needed to retain if he was to grieve at all, but he had a stab at it in every waking second, and so more-or-less enabled himself to go on living. But the need has made him ache with longing, even if, at his most rigorous, the need has remained an abstract beautiful shape, popped there in the mind like a core of fluffy marble.

Others have helped him in this, of course, but without actually being able to interfere with his brain, managing at best to provide an overture to stoicism, by no means his strong suit. His thankyou he has said a thousand times, even while resisting the natural desire to take it out in talk at least with friends. He has remained virtually alone in this, unable to banish memory or quite to withstand its conversion into a drilled fetish, evocative but strangely bleak—all his own perverse work of course, even to the point of blotting out her name by an old route sometimes tried in college days, of writing down a word many times until it loses idiosyncratic vigor and can no longer be recognized. It has almost worked, somewhat like tampering with never uttering the true name of God, but getting it across as Yahweh. Well, he has no Yahweh of his own, in either sense, and so has to make do with such an impalpable cipher as "the space from which I have just removed x^2." Not much of a technique, of course, as he readily admits, but capable of being spelled out among friends as "getting there very slowly, Quent," or "beginning to haunt me with the absence of certain other things, not the actual name, oh no, but, for instance, *daffodil, hernia, telescope*." A beginning, at the far end of which he foresees being surrounded by a language of unfamiliar words, or rather of defamiliarized ones. He dreads this, but not as much as the prospect of losing her name altogether, or even facets of her personality such as her delightful way of always buying presents for her friends against the actual day, birthdays or holidays, nothing much but a thoughtful anticipation of the event, so much so that one of her closets was neatly arranged, her gifts tidily wrapped with affectionate card affixed, maybe a year ahead. She rarely got this far ahead of herself, of course, and managed to keep the little pink cupboard tidy, almost as if it were a porch in her mind, loaded but never crammed. Remembering thus, of course, he recognizes he has already broken his rules, allowing one seed of memory to spread itself out like a flake of potassium permanganate tinting a glass of water. He has not had much experience of permanganate in glasses, or even in beakers, but he drives on in this tender alchemy of his, knowing that to try is something, never to try is never to try. The ideal position, he knows, is to ask in the most distant way imaginable *Where is she?*, genuinely having misplaced her amid the shoals and reefs of recollection, where for all he knows she may be anonymously lurking, a butter hamlet of deft prowess likely to do a fast swim past his receptors, enough to provoke a frisson and draw him after it into a dangerous memory hunt. He has been there too often already, almost always in a losing posture.

36
Memes

S O ALL HE HAS TO DO IS BANISH MEMORY, LIKE A RENEGADE
Proust, as he once joked to himself. Get it out of there. Evict the
beloved face. Change history, which would be easier, but this
dour effort is part of history too and indeed would not exist had not
history gone a certain way, with towers toppling and physiognomy
ruined. Writing things down helps not a jot, nor chanting near-gibber-
ish rhymes from *The Mikado*, in the bathroom or not. The one and only
destructive technique, he has found, is to neutralize the face while
somehow numbing the name: a clumsy, compound exercise he hates,
but there is nothing else save, he wryly laments, trepanning or electro-
shock, to neither of which he has gone. Hence, to all who have known
him, that face of his own, oddly contorted in the act of trying to be less
than human, actually abnegating a piece of what separates us from the
camel or the death watch beetle (if indeed that is true). To some it may
seem the onset of a smile, or the terminus of a scowl, but it remains virtually unknown among the verifiable tics, converting him into a pioneer,
who will probably never lose the vile trick once he has it pure. He is
aiming at eternity of course. There will be no return match unless (the
mind boggles) in some shape *she* will start forgetting him.

Weary of the derelict car, perhaps even wearier of the battered
rearview mirror in which his occasional life conducts itself, he heads
back to his apartment, noting how the maids, tiny gabbling Bahamians,
vacuum around the table but never under it, no doubt afraid of never
getting back into the external world. Standing, then crossing the room
in which toothsome Nigella has pranced, he notices something bizarre:
as he walks parallel to the huge wall mirror, then traverses the brief gap
before the next mirror picks up the visual refrain, he gets thinner. After
a little cogitation he realizes that the effect of the half-inch gap is
somehow to narrow his physique, perhaps a matter of two missing
slices. If he stands opposite the gap, he thins doubly because, he reckons, the one side of the first mirror lacks the half inch while the next
side of the second mirror also lacks a half. If he walks past them fast
he loses only half an inch in width, but if he stands still in a certain
place he loses a whole inch and determines to stand there forever,

attenuated by magic the average fifth-grader could condescendingly explain. Since, however, he has been living on capital, whether this be Vichy France or New York, NY, he will have to return to employment (to put it as prettily as one can), with all his qualifications in hand.

Half-remembering the poem about a not impossible she, he half-remembers, as almost everything, his notion of a truly impossible she: banished, blanked, left out. It is never going to be easy; it abolishes a goodly fraction of his earlier life, and maybe almost all of his life to come, if he gets through the next few years even with the scapegrace uncertainty with which he has negotiated the last three. It will not be a matter of replacement, there being no person to replace. This ought to cheer him up, but it does not because the emotions she had plugged into would not exist any more, he is sure of that and feels subtracted, amputated, beheaded. He has heard of some scientist's theory that certain mystical entities, the guardians of a generation's culture, pass unblemished from one period to the next, heedless and flawless, never mind what messes the nation has gotten itself into. These he remembers, again vaguely, as *memes*, four-dimensional epitomes that never die. Perhaps a certain she has become one of them as a kind of super-Nigella, an archangel of the mind, best lofted to that spiritual plane as the safest place to be. He does not think he has been destined for this end. Life is more random than that, but it may come to seem his portion, dished out by an only randomly caring evolution that wants nothing to go wholly to waste.

He should not, of course, have allowed even the principle of compression to invade his thoughts, because presence breeds analogy and analogy sets the mind racing to vindicate detail and single out inconsistencies. The devastating image that now leaks through, after so much straining to keep out anything of the kind, is that of a concertina on its end, with the keys massed vertically on top of one another: layers of repose, he now sees, and feels his mind heave at the thought of layers only inches high and his beloved fearsomely squashed within, never to be allowed out. Gone, now, all his effort to spare his mind the outcome, the hopelessness of things terminal; he will never be able to shut this image out of his mind, as with the elephant. It is not a matter of rolling the image back up and putting it away in some abandoned corner of the brain; it now has wolfish freedom to invade all discernment, polluting and ruining it, so much so that he would love some reason not to think at all, and this is not it. For once without laboring he has hit on the image that will savage him lifelong, an approximate analogy to be sure, but accurate enough to swamp his mind when he is least expecting it, all because of a slip, a fidget, a moment of unguarded groping, yielding up for him and who knew who else the concertina of cadavers, a homely thought to be getting on with. And he, who has spent so much time in fending off the devil's sugar must now cope with it, almost befriend it, because the truth admitted is the truth enthroned. He no longer has the resources to argue against it, preposterous and unthinkable as it is, even without her face and body to flesh out the awful general image. It is an experience akin to something he remembers from childhood, prized booty of his parents: a black-bound picture book, *The Horrors of War,* purchased on who knew what masochistic impulse, with a bright red sticker sealing the last thirty pages or so as "too frightful for persons of delicate sensibility to view." Of course, the seal was broken before he got to it, and the way to the horrors lay open, even if he did not qualify as a person of such-and-such a sensibility. He might have been ten, and he has never forgotten the grotesque rearrangements of human anatomy therein placed on view by eager cameramen. He might have learned better, but his visual virginity was lost, and now he feels it disappear all over again for lack of being gatekeeper to his own eyes.

Now he longs for empty-headedness, that old insult proffered to doodling children, who do not care if their heads rattle or not. If empty, how can heads rattle anyway? These childhood objections have a role for him, gravid as he feels with torture surpassing anything in that forbidden book. No counter-image prevails, no laser-like red line of logic sears through, burning away irrelevant dross along with central image. It is too late to do again what he has spent much of three years shutting out. The image, he knows, is now as much part of him as his spine, his brain stem. So why did he not arm himself against its even hovering near him, a shadow of nothing specific, say, just some looming chunk of apparatus with a belt on its back and a thousand tunes to regale you with? He no longer has the wherewithal to guard against it, to annul its future as a permanent resident of his brainpan, and so issues himself a deadly membership card that spells out his dismal future unless he can somehow shake that piece of memory loose, its damage done. How do that?

Would the Quents have ever enabled him to do so? Quite probably, since Quent kept it at bay through some adroit technique of mental censorship for three years. Amazing how Quent, God love him, kept others' demons at bay while numbing his own, without ever vouchsafing a glimpse of his technique, and he a Johnny-come-lately shrink at that. Oh for Quent, he moans, to sort him out and put him right, aborting demons before they even check in or, in a more workaday mode, clock on. If Quent ever had his concertinas to cope with, and an ex-fighter-pilot must, he never said, never gave that ravished wince of the overpowered. Useless therefore to comb back through experience, hoping to glean how Quent had done it in his extremest days. Quent the do-er had long been fortified against his own rebellious mind, and his secret had gone with him.

Shrop sighs for all that's lost, willing some renewal to take place, polishing the vapid mind to a bright chromium finish, merely to be able to get on with things. It does not come, he knows. You have to use the old equipment to the end, and then presumably, if it gets reissued, it must start from scratch. No used car of the mind, not even one of those understated pre-owned models. Shrop now longs to go home, across another Chenonceau, to a place unknown, where he can turn in his used mind for a dutiful blank, a tabula rasa he has always identified as a mind shaved clean of its pelting weather. Why, if some far from budding actress can use Ground Zero as part of her umpteenth wedding, then surely that would be the right place for Shropian self-renewal. 192 songs, he's told, have already come into being to commemorate the horrors of that day, he is unsure why, and if they have actually been sung in situ, amid the wristwatches, handguns, and bits of human physique that occupy the place. Once upon a time, he knows, in France, someone was appointed to rebury the 1914-18 war dead, surely the most gruesome of work, and he wonders if it was ever completed, this funereal chore. Is any such thing ever completed? There is always the mind spoor, he tells himself, that no person of delicate sensibility can efface. So why try? Does he have to live on with a used, protected set? Having soldiered through the last three years, in a mostly anesthetized state, he finds the future hugely dreadful, with the image of the full truth laid out before him like the ruin of a Crusader castle. Talking to the dead, whose truth you now consent to know, may be one way of re-establishing communion, but at this he's a tyro, not only lacking etiquette but also unaccustomed to the limits of monomania, the absence of a cherished voice. Will that be the way? Did Quent talk in this fashion to colleagues who had been shot down and slaughtered?

From whom to learn it? At least, he tells himself, backing away from the prospect of being the solitary voice in the echo chamber of death, he will be spared the horrors of worrying about her after his own demise, she having gone before, and he not in the least worried about himself, already death's pawn.

It has never much appealed to him to seek sympathy from others, which he finds harrowing, almost a double whammy: there is your grief, and then there is others' interference with it. So he wanders off, ever alert for a new spot to park the almost useless bolthole of a car, its engine just about equal to the chore of relocation, but not more. His habitual mode of walking he has filched from Chaucer, or so it looks: he stares down as if hunting wild life, or using his feet as diviners, seeking water or gold in the sidewalks—a plunging, side-spilling gait which he manages to transfer to the car as well in the short distances he has to drive. Once Monad Two gets towed away for the last time by a police force antagonized even by mourning, he will let it go, weirdly echoing what he used to say about his mind: once he has begun to lose it, it will not be to regain it, an echo he finds savagely amusing for its importation of putative power into a turn of phrase that holds none. On one of his retrieval walks, perhaps his most social act apart from sea-bass buying, he runs into a much thinned-out Hovis Tumulty, who as ever finds him suitably fashioned for grief, but enormously pent-up, even to the point of plosion.

"How's it going, Shrop?"

"It's gone."

"Have you seen anybody?"

"Why, are there still people left?"

"Look at me, then." She says it with mock indignation.

"You have that Palm Beach skinny look."

"I'm working at it," she says uncomfortably.

"Then do less of it."

"Puerto Rican boyfriend. An administrator."

"Don't they eat in Puerto Rico? I could offer you some frozen sea-bass, honey. All you do is open the microwave, defrost it, stick it on a paper plate with a piece of kitchen towel over it with your name on it just to make sure, especially if you are sharing a microwave, and four minutes, then two, you have a tenderly cooked fillet. Come to dinner!"

This invitation has cost him, but he manages to utter it in the conventional way, with an uplift intonation on the last word as if he has said something quite different—assegai or coral isle, say. "Come to assegai! Come to coral isle!" Enough of that. He has made his gesture.

She no's him, pleads something simmering already, but does not reciprocate the invitation, having no desire for an impromptu cleaning of his apartment. Suddenly she is gone, tugged away in the general press of people all hastening home with their stiff sea bass and the money they have saved by buying it.

For some reason, almost as if he has retraced his steps from Vichy, along the Chenonceau, he keeps bumping into people from his party so long ago: a producer, who jocularly calls him the voice of Nazi Germany and invites him to a new siege of voice-over ("aviators and inventors, Shrop!"); Dromgoole has never been so effusive as this, shouting offers in the street. Peggy Detmarin and Rita Tournier, a shrink and an opera singer complete the set, managing to extort from him something he must have said before: "Still no underwear, honey?" and "Any rancid dreams for sale?" But they know him, astonished to see him out and about as if he has escaped from a zoo, although one for mourners. They know about his grief and how he has for so long managed or mismanaged it, like someone obsessed with an invisible religion, his mind tugged by main force to the planet Astra Zemblya, no time for the living, owing himself to the dead. They more than tolerate him, who has been driven mad and then some by loss, a man obliged to base a new eccentricity upon the one he has always been famous for. He has always collected purses, for instance. All the same, whenever these guests make sane overtures to him out of compassion, he feels spavined, as if the most notable thing about him has gone unnoticed, and he no longer knows how to depict it to them apart from, like Hamlet, bearing about him always a cameo of the departed, a kind of honorable badge exempting him from too many words. They are supposed to sense the vast *tsunami* within him and make allowances while just a few of them think he's making a meal of it. His own version, from a few years ago, he takes from the Concorde which, at "Eefrra" (Heathrow), taxiing at only thirty miles an hour down the runway, had its afterburners suddenly switch on, at which point the pilot shut them down again. That jolt out of nowhere, capable of driving the plane to screaming maximum, reminds him of himself, plodding along but hugely hefted from behind, with in front of him nothing but the unprejudiced aether. What a farce we are, he thinks, we men without women, even if only temporarily so. We go through hell, but everyone thinks we are laudable masters of our fate so long as we don't pester them with it. In truth, while he looks almost normal with just a touch of permanent flush, he feels his head is going to burst from water pressure, nay steam, and high blood pressure as well. What did that bullying doctor say to him after they took his blood for tests? "Who *told* you you'd had a stroke?"

"A *TIA*," Shrop says. "Who told me? *Doctors.*"

"Ah, doctors," says the contemptuous other. "Ah, *doctors.*"

The prospect of returning to the studios for more voice-over (not for a second does he think Dromgoole was jesting) does not please Shrop, who deep down has little desire to work again at anything productive. Only poverty, that ever-looming specter, will goad him to it, with, of course, a new shirt, a fresh tie (Bermuda colors), and newly polished shoes. Spic and span, he thinks, a sort of army spit and polish, though, he dilatorily thinks, assuming the vocal cords of other men, mostly dead and gone, will give him an out, send him packing to their advantage. Well, who then? He knows of Goddard the rocket pioneer and Sir George Cayley, the aviator, but he might have to bone up on these fellows, and as usual fudge their accents, their vocal pace and their breathing habits. He'll do it then. No, he won't. Only hours of cogitation will bring it about, just as irksome as figuring out why the cleaning women vacuum his floor only after spilling onto it his pens and pencils, which they then vacuum among, bending and snapping them as if the secret police have entered during the night, determined to stop him from writing.

37
Cells

T ALKING TO THE DEAD IN THE LANGUAGE OF BOTH THE DEAD and the living, he begins, and it is as if he is the first to invent language, expecting no response but actually finding heart, ever greater and greater heart, in that non-response. He omits the concertina image as much as possible, dreading what might be an answering squeak. He vaguely remembers how the ancient Greeks used certain particles to lead the listener into answering yes or no, as it were to keep the conversation on track, and he is tempted to improvise something such calculated to tip off the listener not to answer back, thus smothering reciprocity before it arises. Each day, he says, not moving his mouth, I take out the cells of your beautiful body one by one, carefully setting them aside, and I polish them one by one, bestowing a kiss on each before reverentially sliding it back into place, beginning with your head of course, and working down through the shoulders to the rest. The slightest dross merits an extra kiss, the kiss in itself leaving no mark because formed to barely make contact, as in Europe, where a gentleman stops his lips short of the target, the hand, bowing thoroughly, but fractionally at the last instant holding back. Thus. How then, I can hear you asking, do you make the cleanser's contact, if you do not touch? Does the very look purify? It sounds like a problem. Ah, he sighs, how well I know you. Yes, the swain's attentive gaze purifies like light, a special gift vouchsafed those of us on edge. So this process can go on for days. The cleansing of cells may occupy something like a month, most of all when the special allure of a cell in the lip or nose bridge merits a longer look, which is when the artificer peers and glows at the workmanship displayed. So fine, it sings. Replacing it makes the whole body glow too, there is such rejoicing to have it back in the goodly naked company. The question arises, of course, about how to pluck the cell from its niche, which I do by sheer will, wanting in the extreme, and it attends my guidance as I lavish upon it adoration tinged with envy, having no such illustrious cells myself, being something of a rough-cut ordinary. Never mind, I get there, if a slowcoach. It amazes me how one can feel for an individual cell among so many (otherwise, how would one even begin?), and yet, when the moment comes to reinstall it, pop it goes into place only to be instantly unrecognizable among its peers. The odd thing is first spotting it, then as it were losing it again among such splendor. They do not address me, except with their glow, but they know they are being tended and relished, millions of them, and of course over time one develops a technique, which is a kind of prophetic dabble, as in water divining, say. Only among the devoutest devotees, I think, does the art of this rise to the highest level, there being no book about it. No, it all depends on the swain's gaze, which may or may not be practiced enough not to involve him in all manner of beginner's preparation, extending the skill acquired from peering into the lady's eyes, say, or into her cleavage. Not that such early work goes to waste, it merely sets up the scheme in readiness for the days of mature ministration. After a while, you learn the scale of glossiness, reflection, ability to roll among other cells in accordance with the owner's wishes, which I have come to call fair game or fair travel, and I often imagine my own body, vastly shrunken, permitted to roam among the most active of the cells, weary of the barren world, eager for perfection's company. The placing of cells is unique, but no human could come up with it, of course. It falls into design as it falls into place, as if briefed on the physics of landing on one's feet, though in this case the motion is more of a curbed roll. The temptation, I suppose, is to hold on to one or more cells for company, as an ingot of perfection, inspiring and consoling, but I never do it, fearing some harmony will become disrupted and fail to come to final glory. So I leave well alone, guiding each and every cell with a courtier's deference, oh yes. I may linger, but I do not poach. Whether or not you sense my movements I cannot tell, but there must be the tiniest response as I brush over, in some sequence, aluminum, mica, beryllium, sand, each with its own resonance in the vital symphony of your well-being. A sedulous performer such as I am not would bone up on the periodic table, of course, noting the numbers and quiddities, but I tend to take them in the round, applying an equal homage to each, and hoping the body will forgive me, among so many to be forgiven. One might pray during this, but not I, my conviction being that you do not pray to the very miracle you are handling; handling it is the prayer, and the fervent mind-wish, if that be prayer, is to put her back together again after so much hullabaloo.

How amazing to witness the gradual coordination come back as patient reassembly goes on. I am rather like the diligent craftsman who, in some lonely hangar favored by sparrows and gulls, tries to reassemble pieces of blighted airliner, all the shreds quiet and distraught, needing a careful eye to unbend and adjust them. He, she, alas, has the constant puzzle of where each fragment fits, whereas I tend to know the basic shape and have only cells to deal with, which all looking alike flop out and away, but not too far. Both the plane-swain and I talk to ourselves as we work, of course, vastly regretting the tendency of the world's things to break apart after so much gorgeous building. For all the world, when I do this I may be in some hangar, but I doubt it; I am in some other, straitened place I do not care to raise my eyes to see. The colors ravish me, forming a language of their own, the reds coming toward me, the blues receding, the blues also scattering according to one Rayleigh. Why the other colors do not have a patron saint I do not know, but I am all for energetic red that seeks me out amid the average beige of the universe itself. Still, there is no retouching the tint, you leave it as it always was, with just a hint of dilapidation to come as the lapis wilts. This is a kind of preliminary to the ultimate caress, after much has been restored, and you know again even with the pursed lips stopping short the tongue's glide along, say, the doeskin neck or the cherished ear lobe. Can this be as far as you get when hoping for more? It is more than you should hope for amid the spoils. Part of the lovely re-encounter stays in the mind of the swain, of course, where it came from, but just a flake or two of rekindled desire may come off the cell as your pious rosebud lips skim the terrain, remembering the old days when life was a fulfilled promise, and you whispered word games to entice each other, wondering if the two favorite American expressions were "All set" and the word "schedule." We overheard agitated agents muttering schedule, schedule, and various versions from soprano to bass of voices chiming in to warble all set, all set, as if to hear such words at all was to mimic them in sheer joy at having them to say. Yes, we were all set, on schedule, as they say. We were. And now we are not. Or is it were, we having come so far beyond catastrophe that continues to leak into the fiercest wild dream. Even those with no English learn to say "all set" while learning, and nobody can tell the difference, especially if they keep on saying "schedule, schedule" as if it were "baa, baa, black sheep."

Her presence thus, these days, is not like a string of pearls, though that might be a suitable beginning image, but more a constellation of pearls scattered across light years of sky. Polishing them and keeping

38
Razorwire

"**D**EAREST BEING," HE BEGINS AGAIN, ONLY TOO AWARE OF having slid from addressing her as you, she whom in his day he had variously addressed as Creature, Entity, Perfection, Lady, Sweets, Honey, X², Giant, Eleganz, Trout, and Rabbit, and mentally narrows his text so as to seem to be writing to her (one way of not shying away from the imperative you):

Canto

Are you all right in there? Will it do? So long as I can reach you there, thus, and make the best of a bad job. All I ever asked for was to live forever and with you. Not a hell of a lot, don't you think? You are not abandoned, oh no, but ferociously missed. I realize I am not addressing the customary form of you, the creature of delight I always went on about, knowing how uxorious I came to be, and never minding it, happy enough to feed on you and to keep counting the years since we (old expression) plighted our troth. Do folk still do that, or has the phrase died out in favor of the one-night stanza? Forgive me the levity, I have to ease myself somehow when I recognize the gulf between now and how you used to be. One has to keep trying, eh non? I would always keep trying, even if there were less of you to dote on than there is. We have to make allowances, even to fate. I would much rather cuddle up and plant kisses in between your shoulder blades, which you always acknowledged with a shrug, not of indifference, no, but of dorsal delight! *Hausser les épaules* and all that. I will never forget how you sailed through Paris one time, short of French but graciously inspired, keen enough to explain *Je suis une américaine tragique, je suis perdue.* After they had stopped laughing, they showed you how and where to go, they who have the reputation of being so judgmental. Not so, never so. You seem to be forever where I cannot find you, which makes of *me* an *américain tragique*, more than you will ever know, me with my

odd little vocal jobs and my absent-minded reviewing, behind me
somewhere like a schoolbag full of octopuses, an entire philosophy of life, just vanished down the tubes for reasons unknown.
Maybe because, finding you, I did not need it any more. Isn't that
old Occam's theory, reducing all you need to the minimum? I no
longer keep these things rolled up in mental tissue paper, which
my sister pronounces not as in a sneeze, but tiss-you. Amazing
even to say it and know your sneeze-count is closed for keeps. I
find closing up shop a chore of the fiercest hardness, as if I am
preparing for a suicide, like the old Jews in those movies, sending the kid off to America before pulling the chain on the gas
and lying down in one another's arms to await the gritty end.
That sort of penultissimo feeling, as with the Koestlers.
Remember *them? Darkness at Noon* and at every other fucking
time as well. No more fucking time, I mean, no more fucking-
time, that's what I mean. It is like being amputated in all your
glory, the private act embodied in the same phrase as conveys the
dark backward abyss called time. I am wandering already, but
surely this mode of address, the left-over addressing himself to
the remnant, the mereness of it all, that's how it has to be: two
américains tragiques. I have to look away from this putative text a
moment to clear my aching vision. Sorry. Back in ten. Gone to
lunch, as people say.

Shrop wipes both eyes, wishing it were with carbolic soap or alcohol, anything to make the tears even bigger.

What a crock. Poor joke. That's me, acting the fool on the great
occasion, drumming up a smart remark, the truth being that for
going on years now I have been unable to confront, evoke,
mention you without feeling a ton of razorwire slicing through
my gut. The old cafard, you know. I don't know of any seemly
way of coping with unmentionable sorrow. The English of
Americans is not it, nor what the Brits call the Queen's either.
There should be some old runic tongue for blurting out the full
texture of the horrors dumped on us, we who have little to be
blamed for. Then some gross scratch will meet our needs, as if a
neanderthal had tried to scrape this itch. Damn the poor bloody
neanderthals, they too must have felt wiped out and left precious

little indignation behind them. *Infra dig.* Remember how we used to say that, along with various other tags, *de gustibus* over a forbidden pernod in Paris on a mellow carmine-streaked evening, or that old favorite *anima Rabelaisii habitans in sicco,* which yours truly freely rendered, for your ears only in a bread and butter kiosk in Bombay, as the balls of Rabelais drying out in a desiccator. What a life, peppered with Latin tags as our own chosen language. Now, how in Latin would one say I am a tragic American? Never. They had no words for much of that. By God, we *are* tragic Americans now, fer shure. That, my endless love, was the vowels of sheer bitterness, when horror shuts your mouth for years as you try to put Humpty Dumpty back together again. Him, yes. I henceforth promise to converse with you nightly, after I have walked the non-existent dog. I feel I should walk a Siberian tiger instead, gambling on the fact that he will not eat me among the evening traffic, but secretly hoping he will. Be a good Siberian and take me by the nape of the neck, old son. So we can flirt together again as in the aulden tyme.

He mops his brow, searching for thorns, then takes a deep breath as, mentally, he turns the overdue page, and tries to address her in a shout, for which upper-case letters have to do. He is ploughing an ancient field. He raises his mental voice, to blast through that heap of debris, but just as soon abandons the shift.

PLEASE GIVE ME A SIGN—

He breaks off, stupefied.

And resumes his more temperate approach, committed once more to the diligent mental feeler he has so far managed to come up with, successful or not.

Vouchsafe—I will look the word up later—any kind of a gesture. My mind creaks and stalls. There must be another way of doing this, more politic, more devout. Your face, yes, ever present, it does not go away, urges me on, still scintillant. I could talk for the sake of talking, as so often in previous life. Good will devouring its own tail, so to speak. I reach an impasse, I halt, I go around it, but are you still there? Perhaps we should be using the language of birds, or snails, squirrels or beetles, anything to get through for an exchange. Yet there is no exchange: you end up with what you brought to the occasion, no more, no less. Surely something must have changed hands, with so much to try for, so much never said in all those years, postponed for a rainy day, when sentences could afford to be longer, clauses ampler. Isn't this how we used to talk to one another, one on one, with no holds barred, the candid and tender always explicit? I may be doing this all wrong, myself having no stony fortress to speak from, saying things too easily while you may still be striving to get out the first hampered word. I can well imagine it is so within the dump. Yet there is no address, no wavelength to stretch myself out for. I cannot come knocking, apart from this, my eternal one, and your voice is the only one I do not hear. I heave and shove against what resists me, but it is too massive, it looms vast in the mind's eye, and, who knows, perhaps you have been lugged away already, unidentified, all of you that is left behind flimsy as a wishbone. Surely you are still somewhere, not finally dispersed as with the dust of cremations. Can it be that you are only present wherever I myself am? Matching my steps, my mistakes? Is there anyone to consult, some expert of the airwaves, of the trained aether? I should have taken smart advice before embarking on this, a procedure I suppose you would call it, a clumsy way of getting through. Or, worse, the one way of not managing to do it. Is there somewhere any kind of guidance for those of us maundering around in informal language, the talk of the bed, the couch, the midnight phone? I come to you most unrehearsed, spasming my words out, a kind of sky-writing I suppose, yet humiliated by so much space, weeping between bouts of impulsive chatter. This was not the way to go, it was not, but, short of slipping a love-letter into the wailing wall, and hoping, hoping, what other method can there be? All questions, I know, but sometimes the mind folds up, knowing it knows nothing and stands naked, convulsed, open to suggestion but closed to the merest intimate syllable.

He tells her he is waiting, will always wait, but does not go so far as to say he will never dry up, but assail (right word?) the mass of leftovers until it yields and furnishes a way in, through, so that nothing he says is quite lost, even if noted down by some amanuensis of stone and steel, biding his-her-its time before passing the words on. Is there, he wonders, any difference between this and talking to oneself? Is it aimless, is it like calling along the full length of the Chenonceau and expecting the words to carry all the way to Vichy? He would gladly suppress all his conjured-up metaphor for one bald exchange, with her saying how it was to be like Lucy in those baleful poems of Wordsworth, taught him as an early teen and never allowed to go to waste, almost a portent, he suspects, a pointer indicating eventual home.

Are you there, sweet one, my ineffable? Venture just a word, a simple one, and I will be ever grateful, asking nothing more. Do they not permit you even a word, *pour encourager les autres?* I could speak the language backwards and it would still make no sense, would it? *Ti dluow, esnes on*—that kind of gibberish just begging to be deciphered. Who was it said life is like a cryptogram waiting to be deciphered? It is worse than that, much worse, my intellectual giant. I must be using the wrong vocabulary, not as good at this as you were with French, making your way through Rabelaisian thickets to the right restaurant or the shop for diary refills. *Ti dluow, esnes on*—you see, I continue to try, sensing that speaking backwards I might make my way through, an American tragique taken pity on by the lords of masonry. You see, it doesn't work, not even if I switch things around a bit and try *It dluow, sense on*. Almost, I guess, not not the right combination. There must be thousands. If only I had taken the trouble, after three years of silence and aversion, to work them all through until hitting on the right one. It would have taken longer than three years, I bet, so perhaps I am being previous and should go back to my ponderings. The right idiom will come up like a flash one rainy day and from then on everything will be all set. I'll be through. So: *On esnes, dluow ti*. Which does not work either, certainly not the language of Wordsworth, who himself had some theory about the language of men, simple and unaffected enough to get through. I should have come to you better read, because the problem is with the language, isn't it? It's always with what you say that the trouble begins. One always needs more advice, more experience, more practice. It is no use going up against the huge forces that beset us with only the merest idea of what to say and how to say it. No use at all. A whimper serves just as well, a whine, a bleat, a groan. Such the true language of deprivation, never meant to be more explicit than that, in other words a retreat from clearness. I remember Admiral Canaria, the head of German counterintelligence, alone in his cell at Flossenburg camp, managing to tap out messages to the Dane next door by using a simple grid for words. Great Dane indeed. They had actual conversations until the guards hauled out the Admiral one chilly morning, to the tune of dogs barking, as they always did when something was afoot. At least he managed to talk through the wall, as in some play of Shakespeare's. Was it not Bottom who made a chink in the wall with his fingers, a horizontal V-sign, through which the lovers could talk? If only I were better read then, a better rememberer, remembering the ways and means but unable to achieve it when paralyzed by anonymous stone. Do I hear you, clearing your throat, reaching out a battered hand? Did something just stir in the depths of the rubble, coming to light as slowly as an atom climbs through the body of the sun to the outside? How many years would that be? Hundreds at least and maybe more. I have information of sorts, but, as it were, do not know how to repair a clock. Do I desist and try again later, as if the operator has intervened, interpreting for me a busy signal I can just as well interpret for myself? Is there a raincheck for this, my perfect? Dare you hand out such a thing? Surely I need not take a number, as at the deli, nor stand in line with eager hands, correct money in hand. A hint will do. A wink, *un clin d'oeil* as we used to say in our boulevardier French. All I need is guidance, from sunrise to sunset, the right bus, the right train, the right café at the appointed hour, the reservation made. Then what a huge backlog of love and chat! Really, a conversation that, once begun, does not end, the reservation goes on for life, the map of how to get there engraved on our minds. Come home, please.

His blood pressure has soared, his head aches, sweat coats his skin, his legs feel jittery even as he unpeels his nose from the window pane, the cool of the glass long ago dispersed, his eyes red and sore, his entire body creaking from the sullen effort of it all, peering out at what he cannot see, fine-tuning his punished ears for the message that never comes. Was this why he threw that bash and walked away from it into what he thought was Vichy France? Has it all been too much to bear, with Quent going his own way after so much lively talk? Is he just starved for conversation? No, he is just starved for life; conversation he finds easy, as he should after so poised a career on TV.

Starts again, mustering his best words before some wall falls on *him*. One day, he murmurs, when the USA has become a minor power and nobody even remembers what close harmony was (the Andrews Sisters gone into oblivion along with the Ink Spots, never mind the Big Bands, and people refer to one another generically—Miss Thing, say), he will get the hang of it, she having nobly waited him out. He recalls that pellucid green, bright as the color of the vine snake with only enough venom to kill a bird or a mouse, the yellow blaze around the local park as daffodils exploded one April, and wishes again for Vichy or Idlewild: a haven, a kennel, a golden sanctuary. How about Mauritius?

So, my exquisita, we are stymied once again, having all the right motives but lured off track by mineral mysteries beyond our comprehension. A shower of kisses might work the trick, though feeling harsh as lips graze the dingy stone. In old Egypt, you know, they wrapped the pharaohs in best linen, tucking little sets of steps into the folds, up which he would mount in the afterlife, and a neck rest so that pharaoh's head shall never seem asleep. They call that resurrection, meaning the old boy will serve the new king. Well, you would think such a thing might be available to us, but I have stepped outside and faced the wall, planting kisses like someone demented, and come away with only a whiff of concrete, a taste of brownstone bad enough to see me through to my own demise. If I had been wrapped in amulets, say a hundred and fifty of them, as with the pharaohs, I might have prevailed, but not so, no hope. It is an object lesson to all lovers: do your kissing while you are alive. There is no way through to the wounded world. Look at Admiral Canaria, hanged before breakfast, with several Nazis holding on to him to speed things up, tripling the natty little sailor's weight, you see, and within the hour flakes from his burning were floating into the cell of the Dane he'd spoken with through the wall. The human life has precious little staying power when confronted with a zealous murderer. Only graffito remains. I can daub messages of utmost love on any leftover rubble, hoping some prodigy of sight will help you to see them. Perhaps, my silkiest angel, you are no longer among us, but transported, elevated, pilot of some pilotless vehicle that cruises over us speechless at a mere hundred miles an hour and not very high either. Surely, from such, rather than a deathwatch U-2 or a Blackbird, you might manage some trainspotting or high-rise camera-work, saying Look, there he is, a misery, a slowcoach slough of despond fugitive, aching to be deader than he is, not knowing where to apply for a visa to heaven. Pity him, then, the homeless hobo trashed by a boiling sleep, abandoned in full spate, gifted with a useless language, destined for a faint, trivial life working on some silver beach, moving from guest to guest with a silken cloth with which to polish their sunglasses. With mouth stopped, he craves a butt-plug for the brain, shaped accordingly, and feels like the first of expendable men.

Now his cravings evaporate, and turn miserably sour as he shunts from walnuts to heroin.

39
We Drown

I T IS REALLY A MATTER OF HOW MUCH STAMINA SHROP CAN MUSTER, voicing into the void, with any chance of an answer depending on the bizarre alchemy of simulated presence. Examples have been few and far between of only the deluded's being able to transform a one-way song into a double act. Even the most imaginative of partners loses heart, and Shrop has gone from a shut-out, no matter how sensitive and revulsed an example, to a gladsome self-supply, either way a short route into pain. What other way to go? It is a problem, of thousands, a complex trick involving ventriloquism and hyperactive memory, plus an almost complete denial of the obvious. Akin perhaps to calling on God and getting answer, this process of brave address has something in common with the allocution required in courts of law, but it has an almost hysterical component few can manage. Shrop has not been doing too badly, given the circumstances and his previous three years of turning away from the very idea. If he has come full circle, it has been with a jolt, a gathering sequel of frustrated righteousness for which no human event has prepared him. It would be one thing to have achieved communion from scratch, having beforehand eliminated short cuts and obvious ploys. The mental waste land he starts from does not cooperate with him, indeed lolls there to taunt and block him, he whose one mission has been, after years of refusal, to establish the merest of contact, even one built on delusion. The words, which came readily enough on some occasions, have begun to fail him, dropping away like shot rabbits. He goes on trying, just for its own sake, but cruelly aware of the concertina structure untouched because everything in it is too far gone for retrieval. He would like to switch modes of address, from verbal to gesture, from that to hyperventilated song, but this would only amount to fooling oneself yet again. The heart-ache, the jitters, the sense of floating, do not go away, and now he berates himself for even trying. Has he never read those medieval tales in which the lovers, pent-up in separate prison towers, scream daylong to each other, demanding union, but not even within earshot of one another? He has read them, but like so much of his acquired intellectual fodder, it has fallen away, a casualty of war, a victim of accumulated stress, like his beloved philosophy. Here is a man who, as the saying has it, is perilously close to losing his mind, expression that suggests one of his aircraft is missing, as they used to say in news bulletins about aircraft in the Second War.

One of his philosophies is missing, then. Perhaps he had several and they jostled one another into a kind of extinction. The impossible, about which other thinkers have worried, has become his bread and butter, and no Tertullian he. The result now, although he does not see this, is the beginning of a gradual decline from buoyant intervention: sure of himself after so long a lay-off, he leaps into the breach, not quite a bridegroom but certainly a hopeful monster. This was how it was at first, almost as if some bunch of acolytes were cheering him on, knowing the impetus had all to come from him, rejoicing because he had to invent something to rejoice about. And now his most outright verbal acts, some of them oral indeed, such as calling her Cuddleskin and using off-color words such as *skanky*, desert him. It is not that he becomes less articulate than usual, but that his trust in language dims, requiring an extra effort to break the shell of silence and poke out into the shocking world. Now he says I love you more than before, and adjusts his rhetoric into versions of the kiss, none of this stuff he hasn't tried already, but more so, as if reduced to bananas after nonstop caviar. This is the lover *in extremis*, then, and fast running out of even the most elementary vows and endearments, all of it bouncing back at him who, in the beginning, would not have credited any such thing, so extreme his fervor had been after turning away from the rubble for so long and contriving a life savagely emptied.

I will always love you, he whispers, I will always be there to fondle and touch. I have had the high jinks removed from me, believe it, and so have only the most elementary tributes left for you, you miracle of women. I am reduced, as they say, to a shadow of my former self, invisible if I turn sideways. You have to see me front on, then, as even my shadow shrinks and whoever measures me finds a dwindling man. I will have to brush up if I am to go on, forever repeating myself in dismal solo. One bit of a word would rev me up again, but I am running on empty and out of breath as well. How easily the mind empties out when the devil intervenes. I am much the same creature as before, but dumber in all senses. I would belittle myself even further, but do not have the heart to do that as memory begins to sink into the ooze. We did this or that, but less often, always in the same words. I am a man upset. It hurts. I look away, at nothing. You are not there. Even your ghost is missing. We are always apart and always will be. It is cruel. I do not like it. Or wish it on anybody else. I may back down. My face is a nobody's face. Are you a nobody too? Have you been dissed? I still have kisses, but can't get them through. I would gladly pay. Do not even know where to aim. Nobody helps. They will soon be laughing at me. It doesn't pay. To be fobbed off like this. It isn't fair, by Jove it's not. They suck you up and you're gone. A goner. I am a goner too. Used to be better. Once could talk backwards. No hope of that now. It is rough enough talking the right way around. When arriving, say goodbye. When leaving say hi. Ta ta, the Brits say on leaving. Do they say anything when they show up? There must be a method, but not for me. Just a cussword or two. Can you see me? Do you even need me? I now say To Go at the end of all I say. I have kind words To Go. They'll not come back. I fuck up, therefore I am. I'll say anything for spit. Come on, let's try you, I say, but she never comes out of hiding. Who put her there? All of whom are dead. Which grants me little scope for revenge. Unless. A dish best eaten cold by a well-versed executioner. Could take long, but be worth it. Some ingenious finale with oxyacetylene blow torch just for effect. Do they advertise? In *Professional Soldier*, say? On the Internet too. I could get a small, dismayed gang together against the real Nazis. A room with chains and a hoist. A dungeon preferably. Impaling's good. Remember Vlad? Then the forest fire among the privates. All in an evening's work. I could manage it. So could a friend or two. Then try to tell her how the day has gone. Come back, make a comeback, dearest one. The invisible, unfindable, unreachable, untraceable, unidentifiable, invulnerable. Surely there are some other bad boys left for me to talk to. Razor in hand, oh yes. Come to me, darling, for the penalty of a thousand cuts. Yonder beloved smile, a mild purr from the arsenal of delight.

Shrop knows he has approached, then gone beyond some limit, only to come back empty-handed, and he feels worse for his excursion having left no initials on her walls (Kilroy or someone) and no opportunis-

tic kiss on the twelve-barred gate. Returned to face his own powerless-
ness, he tries to summon up all the great occasions of his life, so as to
gather up the energy within them, and with that to make a final run at
the blockade where her voice and face lie hidden. It does not work, as he
says, and all over the world the grievers are congregating, unable to
plunge to where they would rather be. It is not as if some grand trunk
road led them homeward, to the sentenced Other, silently marooned
amid the gods of the copybook headings. Reaching the soul of Mussolini
through the 44 volumes of his *Opera Omnia* would be easier, were that
find of any merit. There has to be room for us on the other side, Shrop
murmurs to all his confrères. They can't just leave us in the lurch like this:
no warning, no last letter, no ultimate kiss. This is the land of wasted
love, now owned by self-righteous killers. We drown.

Instead of saying it alone, I ask others to join in, especially those
who have lost someone. On we go, pleading and praising. To no
answer. Why are we so unattractive? Will no one leap off the airwaves to make us merry? We are special people, of course, the
bereaved just as much as the lost. Grieving is bereaving, and
bereaving is a way of being lost. All of our useless cries—Are you
there? Will you come out and see us? Is there no allowance for
the shattered soul?—fall on deaf ears and exploded minds. You
are chanting to rock, to impossibly shrunken layers, for whom it
is no good throwing any kind of bash. We have no future, have
not had much of a past. The hammer blow comes next, impersonal as a year's weather, and all our minds need succoring, to be
taken out, aired and polished, then replaced with a watchmaker's
precision. If it works at all and, whoever you are, you get a glim-
mer, a squeak, from the other side, a cuticle moon.

40
Sakhakot

I MPROMPTU BAGELS WITH HOVIS TUMULTY HELPED SETTLE HIS LIFE somewhat, the encounter restoring him to an earlier stability when Hovis looked heavier and, presumably, did heavier work. Now, she said, looking even more emaciated than ever, she was married but still cleaning houses. No, he said, thanking her, he was thinking of moving away, once he'd settled down in his own mind. She smelled of peppermint and Lysol, almost a winning combination that tempted him to hire her. Her husband, it turned out, owned a gunshop in the suburbs, mention of which enlivened him no end. Invited to make a visit, he accepted in a dream, having little idea of guns, gunshops or their owners, but anticipating a fat proprietor (name Enrique or "Rique"). When would he go? Tomorrow, he suggested, eager for something novel and American. "It will take me out of myself and remind me of my semi-military days, long wound up in cobwebs. I really would enjoy it, thanks." With that settled, they embarked on second bagels (a brunch really) and had their coffee replenished. It seemed Hovis and Shrop were back in business after all. She explained the trains and drew a rough map on a napkin, saying how pleased Riq was going to be, and much more amicably than in recent months. Not a word about Quent, or Shrop's buried inamorata.

Back home, Shrop began thinking about destinations, and tugged out some folders and a couple of airline guides, these hoarded since his Idlewild days and much out of date, but he wanted only to get a rough idea of where to go—as he thought wryly, the schedules and even the carriers may change, but they never move cities although they do build the Brasilias. He spent a soothing hour looking at these old treasures, supposing that the air fares and the motel prices had jumped out of sight. His savings from reviewing movies and providing voice over for WNYY were still adequate. How haggard she was, although pleasantly ruddy, no doubt from so much work on her knees, scouring floors for beetles and such. She was a freshair girl though thin, no doubt from a new abstention, bread or potatoes.

Now, murmuring his new-found mantra, "I'll never leave you, I'll never budge," he riffles through the Yellow Pages to find gunshops and is amazed by how many brandish the Stars and Stripes. It is a wonderland, ranging from "Concealed Weapon Certification" (a pun?) and Adult Airguns to Muzzle Loading Headquarters and All Major Brands (Beretta, Glock, Benelli, Weatherby, and Ruger), from Fly Fishing Supplies to Leica and Leupold, Swanrovski and Zeiss Optics, "Fully Automatic Machine Guns" and MicroTec and Benchmade Automatic Knives to Collectibles and Factory Reloads.

This was Enrique's paradise of armaments. He also offered an NRA Concealed Weapons Course and Eye and Ear Protection. Ignoring archery supplies, bowling pins and fishing licenses, Shrop began to envision a new kind of day, though casting an envious eye at Pattons (Your Special Order Headquarters). He could become a walkabout arsenal, with everything concealed, though he noticed in every ad an absence of dynamite sticks and plastique, which they no doubt kept under the counter with the de rigueur bourbon. Sandwiched between Guitars and Gutters, this was a poem in cold steel such as he had never dreamed of invading, although he had several times pored over the delicately licentious descriptions purveyed in the same Yellow Pages under Escort Services. He made a mental note to spend more time flicking through them in search, maybe, of The Something Riviera of the External World. He may have been a greenhorn in some things, but persistent he always was. He wanted something that made him dangerous to know, excluding *Mein Kampf* from the list, of course. This is to say he wanted A Reputation such as he had never quite had, though renowned for introversion, loyalty, and wit.

In no time Riq has signed him on for the full course, preparatory to unleashing him on the miscreant world as a small disguised army destined for Mecca or Pakistan (he favors the latter as a kind of dry run for the big occasion). After Riq, he journeys home, marveling at the silence of the shooting range (through the earphones that abolish noise he hears the reports only as a distant tap-tap created by goblins or gnomes, not even drumlike). From Cricinfo's ads on the Internet, he begins to order cricket supplies: a bat, some knee pads, mitts for the hands with hard rubber knuckle protection, even a shiny red ball, and of course a cable-knit sweater, cream trews, buckskin boots and a natty blazer with a fake crest over the pocket. This costs him almost as much as the Glock and just about maxes out his solitary credit card. He adores the thought of arriving at the Pakistani border as a cricket fanatic, in a country that worships the game almost as much as India and even allows free admission to all cricket grounds to children. He will be like Jesus with portable cross, arriving to play on the dried-out lawns of Islam.

Sifting through his pamphlets and videos, he does not take long to discover that, in all of Pakistan there is one town that manufactures guns. Here, where men carry guns as women wear flowers, it is customary to spy on one's neighbor and take occasional potshots at him from your tower. Sakhakot is a market town of towers and forges, expert weapon-smiths copying just about any model brought in from the outside world. Shrop at once decides to go there, leaving his newly acquired weapon behind; it will be easy to obtain a light, fast-firing Heckler and Koch machine pistol, and to rent one of those tower rooms.

With a few words of the native tongue, plus his overwhelming load of English, he arrives at the entry point in cricket togs, looking for all the world like a middle-aged English schoolboy, or even a Pakistani one returning from a few years at Eton. To be sure, he is a little tubbier, and surer of himself, but he causes much merriment with his cricket sweater and buckskin boots, not least because he is American, and the Pakis are too ignorant to know how many Americans play the game. They whisk him through as a "sports tourist" who seems not to know that the Pakistani national team, world-famed, is currently playing Test matches in Africa; the real action is on TV, and he soon gets the point.

We leave him there in his ersatz shooting gallery, vaguely aware that the phut-phut of caps being busted answers his pleas to the layer cake at Ground Zero. He is confident that fate will bring fugitive terrorists to the village in pursuit of guns or rounds, and then his moment will strike, most probably his last. In the meantime, as if the front of his mind required some allegro to the rest, he rejoices in life's endless fund of trivia: bristles from an old toothbrush coming loose and drifting around his mouth as he brushes, like stiff seeds; one of those un-air conditioned Pakistani groceries in the high mountain wind, with buff plastic bags blowing around the alleyways like outsize condoms. While he waits he renews his appeals to her to answer him direct from wherever, with all of her transmuting skill: Sonia Judith Goldblatt, translator.